He had just gotten out of the shower, his dark hair in wet slicks across his head.... When he saw her he stood very still, but didn't say a word. She told herself to turn away, but she could do little more than take in his chiseled form.... With both hands, he raked his hair back from his forehead, his chest and stomach muscles rippling. Still Grace couldn't move. Her breath caught when he took a step toward her.

"What are you doing?" she asked.

"I'm not sure."

Grace tried to scoff. "Then let me enlighten you. You're walking."

"That I know."

"Toward me."

"I know that, too."

He didn't stop until they were only inches apart. She could hardly breathe, and she had to force her hands to stay at her sides.

"Why are you walking toward me when I clearly drive you crazy, not to mention the fact that you have an entire list of women as exhibited by the slew of phone messages you got today?"

"Were you jealous?" One corner of his lips tilted in a half smile.

"Absolutely not."

"I don't believe you."

By Linda Francis Lee
Published by Ivy Books:

DOVE'S WAY
SWAN'S GRACE
NIGHTINGALE'S GATE
THE WAYS OF GRACE

THE
WAYS OF
GRACE

Linda Francis Lee

IVY BOOKS • NEW YORK

An Ivy Book
Published by The Ballantine Publishing Group
Copyright © 2002 by Linda Francis Lee
Excerpt from *Looking for Lacey* copyright © 2002 by Linda Francis Lee

This book contains an excerpt from the forthcoming paperback edition of *Looking for Lacey* by Linda Francis Lee. This excerpt has been set for this edition only and may not reflect the final content of the forthcoming edition.

www.ballantinebooks.com

ISBN 0-8041-1995-3

Manufactured in the United States of America

First Edition: September 2002

10 9 8 7 6 5 4 3 2 1

As always,
for Michael

Chapter
One

Jack Berenger slipped out of bed and strode naked across the room. Despite the frigid, late-February cold, he was hot. He felt restless, caged. It was nearly one in the morning, the New York City streets quiet, but he couldn't sleep.

He pulled on a pair of faded denim, button-fly jeans that hung low on his hips, the top button undone, and walked to the desk by the window of his Upper West Side brownstone. He had brought home a stack of patient files from the hospital, difficult cases that he wanted to review. But before he could switch on the lamp, his hand froze when he glanced outside and saw her.

In spite of the hour, a woman sat on a wooden bench in front of the small church across the narrow street. She wore a shimmering white wedding gown that flowed in disarray around her ankles, then spilled over the snow-covered ground. He had never seen her before, but a certain stillness, an ease to the restlessness that he had felt, sliced through him, sensation running down his spine, settling low.

His eyes narrowed as he straightened away from the desk and moved closer to the window, his broad hand bracing against the wooden frame.

In the glow of the overarching streetlamps that lined the

way, he could tell her hair was brown, almost black, wild curls pulled away from her face. She sat leaning forward with her elbows on her knees, her delicate hands clutching a bouquet of white roses. Slowly, carefully, she pulled petal after petal from a single bud.

He loves me, he loves me not.

Jack could almost hear the chant, though if she was sitting in the dark, alone, in that dress, he guessed she probably already knew the answer.

Hours ago he had just finished his shift at St. Luke's Hospital emergency room when the medics had wheeled in yet another accident victim. The day had been busy, too busy. The reality of another victim that was so close to dying had hit Jack hard.

St. Luke's was just south of Harlem, and as the only Level One trauma unit covering some of the most dangerous parts of Manhattan, St. Luke's saw the worst of the dying. A first-year resident had just come on duty, and the shift nurse told Jack to keep heading out the door. He needed the rest; they would see to it. But he had tossed his bag aside and pulled on surgical gear as adrenaline rushed through him.

It was always the same. The driving need to pull someone back from death, like an ongoing battle he fought that never seemed to end. That day he saved the patient. But when they were done, Jack hadn't said a word in response to the chorus of congratulations as he tugged off his surgical gear, then washed up with raw intensity. He wanted away, needed to feel the bite of winter wind against his skin.

With his body aching from fatigue and his mind numb, he headed out, the automatic hospital doors opening with a *whoosh*, expelling him into the streets like a tired breath to stare at the towering heights of the Cathedral Church of

Saint John the Divine that stood next door, both haunting and hopeful. But he didn't have the energy to consider who had truly won the round that day.

He headed for his old rented studio nearby, before he remembered he had moved. Slinging his black canvas carry-all over his shoulder, he had shoved his hands into shearling pockets and headed south down Amsterdam Avenue. He didn't take the subway, or hail a cab. He had walked the long blocks from the hospital, the streets crowded with cars, the sidewalks overflowing with people from all walks of life, growing more homogenous as he came closer to his new apartment on West Sixty-ninth Street. But neither the walk nor the cold had helped.

He had considered calling one of the many women who tried to maintain his attention. But just then he'd had no interest in the endless ways they tried to please him. Instead, he had turned on a CD, Bach flaring through his two-story, high-ceilinged apartment, but still the restlessness hadn't eased. So he drove. He slid into the seat of his black BMW, windows tinted as if they could shut out the world, and merged impatiently with traffic, finally making it onto the West Side Highway, where he concentrated on the car, the lane, the speed.

But driving hadn't helped.

Now, hours later, he stood in front of the window, the curtains hanging open, the golden lights of the always glowing city spilling inside. His body was numb. But the sight of the woman sitting down below seared through his mind, demanding his attention in a way that had nothing to do with emergency rooms or battles to keep patients alive.

She must have sensed he was there, because her fingers stilled on the petals. She glanced up, and he knew she saw him in the darkened window.

She studied him, her head tilting in thought. She didn't

seem worried or embarrassed, and after a second she went back to tugging the petals.

He wasn't sure why he did it, but he turned away and pulled on heavy boots and a sheepskin jacket, not taking the time to find a shirt. Just as he headed out the door, he grabbed an extra coat. But by the time he had taken the stairs to the ground floor and pushed out the front door into the crystal-clear night, she was gone.

The street was empty, with no sign that anyone had been there. The only proof that he hadn't been dreaming was a handful of white rose petals swirling in a gust of wind, the imprint of her white satin gown marking the snow.

Jack stood on the sidewalk, his heart beating in a hard, driving rhythm, the coat held forgotten in his hand. He drew a harsh, deep breath and hardly understood what he felt. The ironclad control he always kept close around him had slipped. At least that's what he told himself. He ignored the thought that it was more than that.

The wind buffeted against him, and for the first time he noticed the stinging bite of cold. Cursing whatever idiocy had driven him outside, he told himself he wanted nothing to do with a woman who would sit out in the middle of the night pulling at petals in some archaic lover's game. But when he turned back to the doorway, his mind went still.

She was there, standing on the sidewalk, no more than a half-dozen steps away.

"Were you looking for me?" she asked, the words quiet, barely heard, swept off with the breeze.

She was beautiful in a china doll sort of way, with full red lips, and blue eyes, wide and intense. There was still no question that he didn't know her, had never seen her before. She was a stranger. Late twenties, he would guess, though with a vulnerability about her that made her seem younger.

Cold wrapped around them, but something about her sent heat carving through his body. For reasons he couldn't explain, he felt the need to touch her, to taste her. He wanted to lose himself inside her.

Without thinking about what he was doing, he took the steps that separated them. The top of her head barely came to his chin. Up close he could see the slight chatter of her teeth and the pale translucence of her skin. But more than that, he could see that she had been crying.

He knew he should find a cab, wrap her in his coat, and send her home. Instead, he slowly reached up and traced the delicate line of her jaw. Her lips parted in a silent, startled gasp. Concern flared in her eyes, as if suddenly she wondered what she was doing there on this street with him. But then it was gone, replaced by something else, something world-wise and weary. Then she was in his arms.

As long as he lived he would never be able to explain why it happened, or even how. As a doctor, he knew better than anyone the dangers of such an act. But his mouth came down on hers in a demand that felt primal and all consuming. She clung to him, her lips as hungry as his, neither able to get enough. Her breath came in ragged little gasps. Her damp cheeks brushed against his, and on some level he understood that she was crying again. But when he started to pull away, she whimpered and held tight.

In the deep, oily blackness surrounding the etched rectangle of glass in the front door, for half a second he caught sight of their murky reflection, both strangers to him now. But that didn't stop him.

Never letting go of her, their mouths still slanting together in demand, he fumbled with the key and got them inside, landing with a crash against the metal mailboxes in the tiny foyer of the brownstone. Locks and hinges ground into his back as he ran his hands down her body, the coat dropping to the floor as he cupped her hips, then lifted her up and wrapped her legs around his waist, the long white train tangling around his heavy black boots.

"This is crazy," he whispered.

But then she slipped her hands inside his jacket, and the cold of her flesh touching his bare skin sank bone deep. He opened the suede leather and sheepskin sides farther, and her satin-clad body melted against his. Icy to hot, searing them both.

Their lips were ravenous, exploring, never parting, as they managed to lurch and stumble their way up the single narrow flight of stairs to his unlocked apartment. He didn't even consider the second flight inside which ascended to his bedroom. Dim golden light from the streetlamps drifted in through the windows as he ripped off his coat and backed her against the wall, capturing her hands above her head. He felt the intensity, and the madness.

Raising his head, he looked into her eyes, and saw a mirror of his own bewilderment at what was happening. But he also saw the need, and the wariness of that emotion.

"Who are you?" he asked, desire tangling in his gut like a hard knot.

He could tell that she debated her answer. Her hair had come loose, and her lips were swollen from his kiss. She pulled her hands away from his, then touched her mouth, barely, gently. Then she took his fingers and looked at his palm for an eternity.

"Holly," she said.

When she looked back into his eyes, he had no idea if she was lying or not. But she didn't ask his name in return. Instead, she smiled in a way that seemed at once achingly sad and resigned, before adding, "I know you."

This took Jack by surprise, and his shoulders braced. "You know me? From where?"

"I don't mean it like that. I just mean that we are two of a kind. I recognize the look in your eyes."

Two of a kind.

Tension flashed through him as he thought of what *kind* of a woman she was to be sitting on the steps in the cold, dressed in a wedding gown, or that she was in his apartment at all.

"I've insulted you," she whispered, half amused, half exasperated. "I just mean that most people go a lifetime without ever meeting their same sort."

His eyes narrowed, but he could only look at her, take in her lips and blue eyes, combined with hair dark and wild. And her skin, white and pure, the gentle curve of her breasts beneath the satin. An innocent temptress. A curious mix of defiance and vulnerability. But most of all, whoever she was, she had stilled the restlessness in his mind.

When she started to release his hand, her nose wrinkling with regret, Jack groaned helplessly, his fingers curling around hers. Then she was back in his arms.

They started out gently this time, tasting, teasing, then rapidly grew heated. They kissed and sought each other in a sexual dance across the room before Jack's hip jarred against the edge of the massive dining table. With a primitive groan, he leaned back and pulled her between his thighs. Her breath caught when he pressed her lower body against his hardness, her fingers and nails curling into his chest, then trailing low.

But soon, whatever patience they had managed wore thin. Their breaths mixed together in a ragged pant, and they tore at each other's clothes. Her fingers worked at his jeans. But the long line of satin-covered buttons that ran down her back weren't as easy.

"Damn the buttons," she whispered raggedly.

In one swift motion, he pulled at the shoulders, and the

bodice ripped free. Her skin had warmed, the alabaster curves taking on the heat of his body. He kissed and nipped, not talking. His lips burned down her jaw to her throat, then lower, taking one turgid peak into his mouth. She gasped, her fingers tangling in his hair.

When her head fell back, he held her securely with one arm, then ran the other across the table, sending books and cutlery to the floor with a crash.

He laid her back on the mahogany table, then gathered the hem of her gown, his palm sliding up her stockinged thigh. She wore a garter and sheer silk finery that gave way with little more than a sharp tug. He kicked off his boots and jeans, then came over her, his weight supported on his forearms.

For one long second they looked at each other. But the time for sanity, that place where they could have stopped, was passed by, like a missed turnaround on a dark road at night. In that second, everything changed and nothing else mattered. As nothing else had, she made him forget, a palliative for the restlessness.

When she reached up and traced a line over his heart, he could do little more than whisper her name, whether real or not, then sink his hard flesh inside of her.

She was tight, and she cried out. He couldn't imagine that she was a virgin, but he felt certain she hadn't been with a man for a very long time. His heart thundered, and his body throbbed with the need to pound hard and deep. But he understood the greater need to be gentle.

He started to pull away, so he could ease their bodies together more slowly. Misunderstanding, she only held on tighter. "Don't leave me," she whispered. But he didn't have the chance to respond. She brushed against him, and words were lost as he groaned and began to move within her, slowly, steadily. And he forgot.

Their bodies came together with spiraling intensity. It seemed she tried to melt into him, seeking and wanting, needing something far greater than what he could provide in a not-so-simple joining between two strangers.

They held each other, sensation shivering through them, as he thrust inside her, his back arching, her hands clutching his strong arms. He couldn't look away from her, their gazes locked until her eyes fluttered closed, her lips parting, and he could feel her body shatter. Then, only then, did he bury his face in her hair and find his release.

Afterward, they lay together without saying a word as their breaths eased, the only sounds coming from a lone car or truck drifting through the deserted streets. They remained that way for long minutes, then Jack lifted up on his elbow.

He didn't say a word, just looked at her, and she grew uncomfortable. For the first time, she seemed to become aware of their surroundings, the hard table beneath them, his naked thigh entwined with hers.

"This isn't like me. Really." She worried her lip. "I should go."

But just when he started to speak, to ask her all the things he should have asked in the first place, his pager went off.

"Damn."

Only the hospital staff had the number, and they only used it in an emergency.

"I'll be back in a minute," he said, then rolled off the table, not bothering with his jeans.

He used the kitchen phone to call in, and didn't talk for long. He gave instructions to the resident who was concerned about the accident victim from earlier. Then Jack returned.

But by then she was gone.

He stood in a long beam of drifting city light, his hands braced on his hips. This time there were no rose petals or imprints in the snow to prove she had been there, only the crash of books and cutlery, mixed with a disarray of satin buttons scattered across the floor. Staring at the mess, Jack Berenger wondered what the hell he had just done.

Chapter
Two

Grace Colebrook woke slowly to the warm touch of sunshine streaming in through the uncovered windows. She had been dreaming again, of heat. Warmth. The gentle kiss of sun and sand against bare skin on a wide stretch of glistening white beach in a place far away from the cold and gray winter streets.

Drifting half in, half out of sleep, she burrowed deep into comforter and blankets, not wanting to wake. But the murky state between dreams and reality shattered when a bellowing truck horn blared outside, and she sat up in bed with a start. She blinked, then blinked again, her breath catching in her chest as she realized she wasn't on a beach . . . and last night hadn't been a dream.

She squeezed her eyes shut, her dark brown hair unpinned and unruly around her face as she prayed she was mistaken. But reality surged unkindly, coming to light when she opened her eyes and saw her white satin wedding gown lying in a tangled heap on the hardwood floor.

Grace fell over, face first, into her pillow. "Ugh," she groaned into the stuffing. "What have I done? What was I thinking?"

Of course, the truth was, she hadn't been thinking when she had walked into the arms of a stranger last night. Her one-night stand.

Little did the man know they were neighbors.

Her groan grew louder as she rolled over onto her back, her arms flung out on either side of her. A week ago, Mrs. Neimark in 1A had filled her in on details relating to the man who had purchased apartment 2A in the building. Jack Berenger.

He was a doctor, and successful. Mrs. Neimark had guessed he was well into his thirties, though with no wife or family to be seen, she had sniffed indignantly.

Now, after having actually been in the man's two-floor apartment directly below hers, Grace could guess the rest. He was a man of money and breeding, though not necessarily the kind of breeding produced by old money. If Grace had to guess, she'd say he was from a family full of an exacting kind of love that came with strict demands. His world was ordered and controlled. He was a man who existed with bands of icy reserve around his emotions, and he had hated the control he had lost last night when they had come together. Grace had seen it in his eyes.

Thankfully, while she knew who he was, she was sure that he didn't have a clue about her identity. In the short week he had lived in the building, their paths had never crossed.

Perhaps she could move—that, or she'd have to start using the fire escape to get in and out of the building so she wouldn't have to pass by his door.

With a miserable grimace, she wondered again what she had done.

But of course she knew. She'd had a completely unforgivable sexual encounter with a virtual stranger, lied about her name, then sneaked out of his apartment without so much as a word of explanation or good-bye. She had fallen lower than low, had become a woman of dubious morals, a tramp, one step away from a guest-starring role on *Sex and the City*.

Her eyes flashed open at the thought. *Sex and the City,* a woman of the new millennium, in charge of her own destiny. There was that, she reasoned, a small flicker of completely and utterly inappropriate pride swelling inside her. And sure, sex with a stranger was light-years away from a white-picket-fence world in the suburbs she had worked a lifetime for, but then again, she was nearly thirty, and her chances of getting a white-picket anything were getting slimmer by the week. Besides, the fact of the matter was the sex had been incredible.

It was easier to think about that than to remember how he had looked at her, his eyes filled with a darkness that was all too familiar. No, it was easier to focus on the sex.

If she had only known what she was missing, she might have tried a little harder to have some sooner. Not that she hadn't tried. She had, but since her one, single, uninspired mistake in college, she realized now she hadn't really put her heart into getting the deed done. Let people say what they would about her—mostly that she was smart, sensible, and would never compare with her stunningly beautiful older sister, Suzanne—but Grace Colebrook had known deep down that she had never been cheap. At least she hadn't been until last night.

Her grimace turning to another groan, Grace wished she could take it all back, forget every single thing that had happened in the past twenty-four hours. But thoughts of her neighbor circled relentlessly through her mind.

How to explain what had happened out on the street, standing there with such a strikingly sensual man looking at her with such hungry intensity? How to explain the fire that had raced through her body, the need that had filled her, making reality recede into the murky shadows of the night. Then the sensation of his strong hands drifting over her bare skin. For one amazingly incredible space in time, she had been someone else. Someone free. Nothing else had mattered, not the cold, not the wedding . . .

The wedding. Ugh. Grace covered her head with her arms and prayed it was all a bad dream. Of course it wasn't, and no matter how she tried to keep the thoughts at bay, she had to face the facts sooner or later. She had walked out of her wedding, slipping away through the hallowed doors of Saint Thomas Church.

Though what else was she supposed to do but call the wedding off?

Wanting a moment of peace and quiet before she walked up the aisle, she had gone to the south gallery of the massive stone and stained-glass church, and walked in on the sight of her fiancé's bare backside clamped between the gartered thighs of one of Suzanne's closest friends. Not the best way to start a marriage that was supposed to last a lifetime.

In a moment of uncharacteristic defiance, her mind numb to her mother's protests and her sister's frantic reasoning, she had dashed out the thick wood-and-glass doors, down the granite steps to Fifth Avenue, with her wedding gown trailing behind her in a spill of flowing white. Wanting nothing more than to escape, she had surprised the waiting livery driver when she slammed into the limousine without a groom and told him to drive. And he had. He drove Grace from one end of Manhattan to the other, only saying, "It's your money," when she asked if he would drive her out to Coney Island.

But the amusement park had been cold and barren, the rides and games looking dismal and lonely without their garish display of multicolored lights. At nearly one in the morning, the driver had dropped her off at her apartment, and mindless of the cold, she had walked across the street to the little church that was so different from the one on Fifth Avenue.

Her heart had pounded, and tears had burned in her throat, choking her. Then she had looked up and seen the man in the window. Even in the dark she could see the hard, chiseled strength of him, the way he filled the window when he braced his hand against the frame and leaned forward. Stepping into his arms had seemed as natural as breathing when he came outside.

Dropping her arms away from her head, Grace punched the mattress. It had been idiotic, dim-witted, and irresponsible, to say the least.

Swearing she would never be so irresponsible again, Grace whipped her legs over the side of the bed. She might have experienced a night of inexcusable behavior, but she would seal it over with hard cement and return to the life of perfect decorum that she had lived for the last twenty-nine years.

She sat quietly for a moment, waiting, testing. Good. Her guilt was beginning to fade.

She wore long underwear, the top covered in tiny blue flowers, the bottoms decorated with miniature green wreaths and red bows. When she had raced into her apartment earlier, the sky still dark, she had ripped off the wedding gown that she'd held on precariously as she made her mad dash upstairs, then had grabbed whatever was at hand. Coordinating nightwear hadn't been a top priority. Leaping into the safe confines of her bed and pulling the covers firmly over her head had been.

Searching with her feet, she found the only pair of shoes that were handy. Low-heeled mules with ostrich feathers. Never in her life had she worn anything so flamboyant. She was more the sensible tweed and fuzzy slipper sort. But when she had seen the mules in the window at Bergdorf Goodman, she had felt a moment of excitement at the thought that they would go perfectly with her wedding night trousseau. Surely if there was ever a time when a woman could afford a little outrageousness, it was on her wedding night.

The glimmering mix of optimism and repentance she had managed to rustle up tried to fade at the thought. But that wouldn't do. She would not let this get to her.

She clicked across the room and gathered up the wedding gown. She would have liked to stuff it into the garbage can. But while her mother might never get over her younger daughter breaking off her engagement after the processional music had already begun, she would have an apoplectic fit if Grace threw away a hugely expensive Vera Wang gown. Instead, Grace shoved the jumble of satin into the dark recesses of her closet, then slammed the door shut.

The sun streamed through the windows, brightening her already bright apartment. The walls were painted a pale yellow, with white trim, and hardwood floors were covered here and there with hook rugs of yellow and blue flowers. The furniture was an eclectic mix; lots of Country French made interesting with an assortment of treasures Grace had picked up over the years. Hand-thrown pots from Bolivia, wood-carved boxes from Santa Fe, and an assortment of glass and mirrors that had caught her attention along the way.

The apartment was in perfect order except for the stacks of boxes, small and large, some half opened, others still closed and wrapped. Wedding gifts, hundreds of them, and Grace knew she would have to start the arduous task of returning each one.

Unfortunately, or perhaps fortunately, Grace was more

upset about having become a cliché than she was about losing Walter. She had known him for three years, and during that time they had talked of life and life's issues, and children—most of all children, the one thing she wanted in life more than any other.

She closed her eyes against the sting of unshed tears that threatened. Turning away, she looked out the window without seeing.

Her mother and sister had insisted he was an ideal match for her, and somehow Grace had started to believe they were right. His blond sunniness and frequent smile made it easy to believe he would be the perfect husband and father. She had gotten so caught up in the whirlwind of wedding plans and hopes for the future that she had stamped out any of the hints of concern that whispered through her head. Hadn't she and Walter shared the same sense of humor? Hadn't they shared the same opinions on movies and meals? Hadn't they both loved the name Louisa for their first little girl?

Too bad they hadn't shared the same bed before marrying. But Walter had wanted to wait for their wedding night. The fact was, had they not waited, she might have seen him for the flat-cheeked, pasty white, pimply butt louse that he was a whole lot sooner.

The thought made her smile wryly. Better that than give in to the futile tears that had been burning since the moment, sixteen hours, twenty-three minutes, and nineteen seconds ago, when she had fatefully taken that last step into the church's gallery. Clearly God had a plan.

Of course now, sitting alone in her apartment, doing her best to forget the wedding gifts and her one-night stand, she wasn't at all certain what that plan could be. The fact was she was on the verge of turning thirty, had a mother and sister who drove her to distraction, a father who had a predilection for infidelity, and now had no prospects for a family of her own.

But regardless of that, Grace wasn't about to go through with a marriage that would no doubt end in disaster, even if she hadn't realized it until the last second.

Having dealt with the wedding gown, Grace started clicking back across the room, then suddenly stopped dead in her tracks. Belatedly she thought about how clicking footsteps from low-heeled mules on a hardwood floor would cause an echoing racket in the apartment below. Furtively, she kicked off the shoes and tiptoed the rest of the way. No need to stir anyone up, namely her new neighbor, and drive him upstairs to complain about the noise.

If he did, wouldn't he be in for a surprise.

Would he pound up the stairs, barely awake, those soft jeans thrown on, hanging low on his hips, no shirt to be seen? What would he do when he realized who she was? Her heart started a slow, hard beat.

Stop. No more thoughts of the man. She was going to avoid her neighbor like the plague, even if it meant never wearing her fabulous low-heeled mules again.

Grace tugged her hair into a ponytail holder, pulled a thick robe tight around her long underwear, then went to the kitchen. Of all the rooms in her apartment, she loved the kitchen best. She had painted the walls the same pale yellow, then added a hand-stenciled floral border around the window and doorway. White cabinets melted into a white tile backsplash, with an occasional flowered tile mixed in. The window looked out over a redbrick courtyard four floors below that was lined with snow-covered gardens and wooden chairs. She loved to bake, if not cook, and found a reassuring calm in mixing flour and sugar, sweet pungent vanilla with cinnamon and nutmeg.

The telephone rang. Already the readout on her answering machine showed twenty-three messages, no doubt left by her mother and sister. What was one more? But after a moment's hesitation, she padded back into the living room to answer it.

"Hello."

"There you are! Mother and I have been worried sick! I've been calling all night. Where have you been?"

A guilty burn surged into Grace's cheeks at the sound of her older sister's voice. Suzanne. Tall, beautiful, the picture of elegance and good manners, with an innate sense of underlying drama that only their mother could top.

Grace had never quite fit in with her family, rejecting the theatrics, refusing to give in to the shuddering burn of intensity that shimmered around the Colebrooks like moths circling a flame. For years she had been determined to avoid that precarious edge her mother and father flirted with like they didn't know any other way to exist. To Grace, normalcy was infinitely exotic, desired.

She wasn't sure she could take her sister just then, so she held the phone away from her mouth and thought Third World. "Ah, miss, I know not who it is you are looking for."

"Don't try to use that fake Pakistani voice with me, Grace."

She tried the Chinese Herbalist. "So sorry. Wrong numba." Then she hung up. One way or the other, it worked.

Ignoring the phone when it started ringing again, Grace made a cup of Earl Grey breakfast tea mixed with milk and sugar, then went to the window seat at the front of the building. She curled up on the cushion and pressed her forehead against the cool glass pane. It was this as much as the kitchen that had sold her on the place three months ago, when she and Walter had decided they should buy instead of rent. It wasn't the house in the suburbs she had dreamed of, but he had promised that would come soon enough. She had believed him. So much for trusting her gut.

Thankfully, the apartment was hers. As a wedding gift, her father had given her the down payment, though he had made her promise to put the paperwork in her name alone. Clearly men recognized their own type.

The intercom buzzed, announcing someone was at the door downstairs. Instantly Grace thought it might be her sister. But it was Saturday, and Saturday lunch with friends was a must for Suzanne. She might have taken the time to call, but she wouldn't have taken the time to come clear across Central Park to talk some sense into her. She'd do that on a Monday morning or a Tuesday afternoon. Off days.

For half a second, Grace's heart skipped at the thought that it might be Jack Berenger. But the fact was it couldn't be him. Truly he had no idea where she lived, and surely she hadn't made that much noise. Besides, she reasoned, biting her lip, someone who lived in the building wouldn't go outside and press the buzzer; he would simply come to her door.

Tentatively, Grace pressed the button and leaned forward. "Who is it?"

"Walter."

Grace leaped back as if burned. *Walter?*

Her mind raced. Was he there to apologize?

She felt a surge of elation. Walter! He'd come to grovel, to get down on his hands and knees and beg her forgiveness. She could hardly wait. She would sit back, let him go on, put her finger to her chin in consideration. Then she'd tell him to go stuff himself.

She buzzed him in, then dashed to the bathroom to run a brush through her hair. At the sight of her reflection, she gasped. As quickly as she could, she splashed water on her face, used Vaseline to wipe off smears of mascara, then doused powder down her shoulders. Racing to her bedroom, she ripped off her robe, threw on a cable-knit sweater, and hopped around on one foot as she pulled on a pair of jeans. Socks came next, followed by canvas tennis shoes. She careened out into the living room just as Walter knocked for a second time.

When she opened the door, she found him leaning back against the wall, his hands braced on his thighs. He was out of breath after taking the three flights of stairs. That was the only downside to a fourth-floor walk-up, all the stairs. But the block between Columbus and Broadway was picture-perfect. Besides, it was on the opposite side of Central Park from her family.

"Hello, Walter."

He wore a Polo button-down, navy blue V-neck sweater, and khakis beneath a tan leather coat. Her favorite. When he straightened, pushing away from the wall, he gave her a sheepish grin. *The grin*—the reason she had let her mother and sister talk her into how perfect he was in the first place.

He tilted his head in that way he had about him, a lick of sandy blond hair falling forward on his forehead, and she felt her upset start to melt away. Maybe she should consider his apology.

"I forgot what a climb that is."

"It's good exercise." She had told herself it would be good for her butt and thighs. After the show in the church, she realized it would have been good for his butt and thighs. Suddenly his lick of sandy blond hair didn't look so endearing.

He shoved his hands in his pockets and rocked on his heels. "Yeah, well . . ."

The man was writhing with discomfort. Good. The apology should cost him, she thought, indignation surging back. She would make him grovel, then send him packing. Empowerment filled her.

"I need the ring back."

A minute ticked by, or maybe it was four, Grace didn't know. She could hardly assimilate the words that sounded distinctly different from an apology. "What?"

"The ring." He shrugged. "I need it back."

"That's why you're here?"

"It's not like I'm asking for the apartment."

"Are you out of your mind? It's *my* apartment."

"You've said a hundred times it's *our* apartment." He walked inside, and went over to the stack of wedding gifts. An iridescent clock lay faceup in a bed of white tissue paper. "Who sent this?"

With a disbelieving shake of her head, she focused. "Dr. and Mrs. Herbert Blackwell. I think."

"It's great. Can I keep it?"

Grace blinked. "No, you cannot keep it. It has to be returned. All the gifts have to be returned."

"Bummer."

Bummer?

"I doubt they'd miss it," he said. "The Blackwells are loaded. But I'm not going to split hairs on the apartment or the gifts. The ring's a different story. There's no question I paid for that."

"You paid for *half* the ring. You told me we should be equal partners in this relationship, and that I should pay for half, remember?"

A wry smile pulled at one edge of his mouth, and his head tilted to the side. He looked chagrined, but not defeated. "Fine, but I can't afford to kiss off fifteen hundred dollars."

Dropping her hands to her sides, Grace's shoulders

came back. "Fifteen hundred? You told me the ring cost four thousand! I gave you two!"

His chagrin grew, but still he didn't back down. He worked deals day in, day out on Wall Street. When coworkers called him a barracuda, he preened. When competitors called him a shark, he said thank you. He closed deals no matter what the circumstances, always coming out on top. She realized now that he had worked her as well.

"Hey, fifteen hundred, two thousand," he said smoothly. "Whatever. Just give me fifteen hundred and I'm out of your hair."

She stared at him. No apology, no remorse. No groveling. Only more betrayal. How could she have been so naive?

The slow burn she had felt earlier grew and intensified inside her, and it took a moment before she recognized it as anger. She, who never got angry. Not after a lifetime with a father who went through women like he went through the *Daily News*. Not after dealing with an older sister who did everything first, not to mention with flair, or a mother who was more child than adult. No, Grace Colebrook never got mad. But suddenly, standing amid the wreckage of half-opened gifts and honeymoon clothes, she felt a lifetime of fury rise up inside her and spill over like a rush of lava.

"Get out."

"Now, Grace—"

"Get out, Walter, before I call the police."

His stance grew belligerent. "I want the dough, Grace. You owe me fifteen hundred dollars."

With that, she snapped. She pulled a sterling silver candleholder out of its tissue paper wrapping and threw it. The silver flew within inches of his head, crashed into the opposite wall, then tumbled to the hardwood floor with a thud. Walter stared at the wedding gift in wide-eyed astonishment.

"You could have killed me."

"I was trying!"

"You're crazy. Crazy as that fruity mother of yours! I knew it, but I told myself it didn't matter. Your family has bucks." He leaned forward. "But even all your family's money isn't worth being married to a cold fish who doesn't know the first thing about a man."

"What are you talking about? You were the one who said you wanted to wait until we were married."

He raked his hand through his hair, his expression disdainful. "Hell, I would have been happy to wait forever, Grace. You can't kiss worth a damn, and a twelve-year-old boy has a better figure."

Her head came back like he had slapped her, and it was all she could do to hold herself together.

"Please leave," she barely managed.

"Fine. I'm outta here. But don't think I'm going to forget my money."

She fell against the door as it slammed shut behind him. When she finally heard the outer door bang closed four floors below, the glass inset rattling from the force, she took a deep breath. *A cold fish who couldn't kiss.* Mortification sliced through her. Instantly she thought of the man downstairs. Had he thought the same thing? Could she have imagined the heat she was sure he felt?

Grace drew a deep breath, refusing to think about it another second. She wouldn't let Walter get to her. He was angry and venting because she had left him at the altar. He was just saying things to justify his poor behavior. How many times had she seen her father do the very same thing? Get in trouble, then find a way to blame others. No, it wasn't her fault. Everything was going to be fine, she told herself, stuffing her concern and anger down deep, much like she had stuffed the wedding dress in the closet.

With measured steps, she walked to the kitchen. Out of habit, she took out bowls and utensils, and without thinking she got to work. What she wanted was a thick square of Desperately Decadent Double Fudge Delight. But her famous fudge was reserved for only the most dire of situations. She might have lost a fiancé and had sex with a stranger, she might have turned overnight into a person she hardly recognized, but she was not desperate. She was made of sterner stuff than that.

Instead, she pulled out flour and sugar, eggs that thankfully she had forgotten to throw out before the honeymoon trip, cream of tartar, an assortment of miniature cake tins, and before the morning was done, she had a counter lined with tiny little petit fours, made from her favorite angel food cake recipe. She's No Angel Cake. Somehow, it seemed fitting.

When she was done sprinkling crushed peppermint over the still warm, lacy white icing, she stared at her creation. Optimism slid through her veins. She was going to be fine. She just needed to figure out a way to avoid her neighbor for the next ten or so years.

Her optimism tried to wane. Perhaps, she reasoned, she should move.

Chapter
Three

Jack woke hard and aching, his body pulsing with white-hot desire. He cursed as he thought of the woman. Inhaling slowly, he remembered her name. Holly.

A breath hissed through his teeth, and his eyes narrowed. It staggered his mind that he'd had sex with a stranger . . . or that he had ever gone out to the street to find her in the first place.

He tried to rationalize that he was a doctor, and a woman sitting alone in the freezing night had needed help. But he knew it wasn't that simple. He had felt stirrings when he saw her, and those stirrings had turned to fire when he had gone outside, then found her only a few feet away. He had wanted her in a way he had never wanted any woman. As long as he lived, he knew he would never forget the way she had stepped into his arms, passion threatening to burn them up.

Hell, he couldn't even say what it was about her that attracted him. He had dated several women in the last months, all with the kind of classic beauty that turned men's heads. Holly, if that was her name, didn't come close to that kind of beauty. Her hair was dark and curly, her skin was pale, her lips full, her eyes wide and blue, coming together in a way that made him think of the girl next door—though one with a barely suppressed wildness just below the surface.

Was that the attraction? The taste of wild vulnerability?

Jack swore an oath and rolled out of bed. Whatever it was, what happened last night never should have happened. He was a doctor, he knew better, and he was certain she knew better as he remembered how she had snuck away like a common criminal.

He had been ticked as hell when he'd returned to find her gone. At least that's how he explained away the hard knot that had tightened in his chest. She had left him with more questions than answers, and a slow burn of heat sliding low at the thought of how tight and hot she was around him when he had pushed deep inside her.

"Hell," he muttered, yanking on the cold dial of his shower, stepping into the freezing water, telling himself he was glad she was gone, glad he'd never have to see her again.

An hour later, he grabbed three golf clubs out of his bag, having decided to head down to the driving range at Chelsea Piers to clear his mind.

It was Sunday, and he wasn't on duty again until Wednesday. The shift hours for an emergency room physician were both the blessing and the curse of the job. He might be on duty two or three days straight, but then he would be off for three or four days at a stretch. There were times when his schedule was regular, five days of eight-hour shifts. But ER work was anything but regular. You couldn't approach it that way. A doctor had to work with adrenaline, then step away and replenish. Working the ER day after day depleted the staff until they had little to give, and that's when mistakes were made.

On his way out, he ran into Mrs. Neimark in the entryway of the brownstone, wearing a bathrobe and carpet slippers as she swept the small square of tiles outside her door.

"Hello, Dr. Berenger," she gushed. "How nice it is to see you. Timmy is still wearing the plastic stethoscope you gave him last week. He's telling everyone he is going to be a doctor just like you."

He listened to her with a kind patience as she rambled on. But when finally she paused long enough to take a breath, he surprised himself when he cut her off midstory. "Mrs. Neimark. Do you know anyone around here named Holly?"

"Holly?" she asked, as confused by the name as the abrupt change in her subject. "Well, no, can't say that I do. Maybe if you tell me a little more about her, I can put a name with a face."

He chided himself for asking. The woman was gone, and good riddance.

"No need. I was just curious."

After a quick farewell, he caught a cab at the corner, and after a short ten-minute, careening no-traffic ride, the taxi dropped him off in front of the largest indoor sports complex in an urban area. Chelsea Piers had been written up in several national magazines for the sheer ambition of the plan, and then again for the success of the endeavor that was built on a series of old piers that jutted into the Hudson River. An equestrian ring and stable stood to the side of the circular drive, and hunt seat riders were taking their mounts over a series of jumps.

Jack walked down a long, wide-open corridor that took him past a gymnasium, a basketball court, a hockey rink, pleasure cruise boat docks, restaurants, a bakery, then finally the golf center. Chelsea Piers had a four-story driving range that faced the river, with huge nets that kept the balls from launching out into the water.

The place was packed, but Jack managed to get a slot soon after he arrived. He started with a round of fifty balls, working his way through his nine iron, five iron, then driver, his body extending itself like a professional with each swing.

"Hey, buddy, let me show you how it should be done."

Jack froze, the club in the air, his concentration shot, and looked back to see who the hell had interrupted him. Frustration turned to a grumbling joy when he found his brother standing behind him, a wide, devilish smile cracked on his face.

"You little shit, what are you doing here?" he demanded.

Despite his harsh words, both men smiled as Jack set his club aside and pulled his younger brother into a bone-crushing hug.

Hugh stood nearly as tall as Jack's six-foot-two frame, with the same dark hair and eyes. Despite the ten-year age difference, anyone who saw the men together would know they were brothers. But where Jack's eyes were fathomless, Hugh's shone with good humor, and his crooked smile drew people to his side. Jack's glacial stare was known to intimidate, and had sent more than one person running in the opposite direction.

"Let me have that club," Hugh Berenger stated, stepping away and taking up Jack's driver. "Stand back and weep, my friend. Let me show you a thing or two about the game of golf."

Hugh didn't bother to warm up, and his first swing sent the little white ball soaring through the air, arcing forward in a straight line, dropping down just around the two-hundred-yard marker. He turned back and raised a brow in challenge.

Not to be outdone, Jack took the driver, set up, then launched the next ball with a velocity that sent it sailing like a rocket so far that it smashed into the back net. Jack turned back, smiled, and extended the club with a negligent two-fingered grip.

Hugh grumbled, made an unkind comment about dubious parentage, grabbed the driver, and fired off a series of balls, ending with one that pummeled the back net. He turned back and smiled smugly.

They alternated shots through a new set of fifty balls, uttering little more than incoherent grunts and grumbling insults the rest of the time. When finally the round was complete and the electronic ball discharger slipped back inside the bright green AstroTurf for good, the brothers sat down on a low slatted bench in companionable silence.

"You still keep me on my toes," Jack said after a moment.

"You still make me work my ass off to keep up with you," Hugh replied.

Jack slapped Hugh's leg. "Come on, I'll buy you a beer."

They pushed up and made their way to the New York Brewery, which stood at the end of the complex. They ordered a round of dark beer with some of the best burgers and fries in the city.

"How'd you find me?" Jack asked when the burgers arrived.

"It wasn't hard. You weren't at home, or at the hospital, and I knew that you've been seeing Stacy Middleton. So when I called her and she hadn't seen you—by the way, she's not too happy about that—I figured you'd be down here smacking the hell out of some little white balls."

They leaned back in their chairs and looked out through the wide expanse of window overlooking the river. A towering white cruise ship with waving passengers standing along the side glided through the water toward New York

Harbor, its deep, rumbling horn filling the skies as it made its way out to sea.

"What's up that you needed to track me down?" Jack asked. "Is something wrong?"

Hugh glanced over at his big brother, and his expression was suddenly grim. "No, buddy, nothing's wrong."

Jack cursed himself for asking the question.

Raised poor in a run-down part of Brooklyn, the boys had been forced to grow up fast. You didn't survive the rough neighborhoods without knowing how to manage the streets. Their parents had loved them. But their mother had been the strong one in the family, and had forced Jack and Hugh to do something with their lives. If they didn't do their homework, she took a belt to them. Jack had always known it had hurt her more than it hurt them. But how else to make young boys toe the line when neighborhood kids were dropping out and doing drugs. From an early age Jack had been forced to step into the role of caretaker for his little brother.

"I'm here with good news," Hugh added. "I'm getting married."

Jack stiffened. "Married? To who?"

"You know who," Hugh chastised. "Nadine."

"Ah, Hugh, she's using you."

A palpable tension sliced between them, the edges sharp and cutting.

"Don't do this, Jack," Hugh warned.

"You hardly know her."

"I know her well enough to know that she's the one."

Jack tossed his napkin on the table.

"Damn it, Jack, I love Nadine, and I'm going to marry her. Whether you approve or not."

Jack looked at his brother, and realized in a startling flash of insight how unfair he was being. The realization was a surprise, a surprise because he had spent a lifetime taking care of his little brother. It never occurred to him to do anything less. But Hugh was an adult now, more than capable of taking care of himself.

"Hey, I'm sorry," he said, meaning it. "She's a damn lucky woman."

Hugh nodded, his smile returning with ease. "You've only met her once, and the two of you got off on the wrong foot. If you spend more time together, you'll love her. Let me bring her around."

Jack doubted he was right, and he had little interest in seeing her again. The woman was shallow and money hungry, caring only about what kind of a car he drove and where he lived. But who was he to judge?

He lifted his mug. "A toast. My greatest hope for you and your future."

But before Hugh drank, he added, "To us. I'd say we both deserve a bit of peace and happiness. I've found Nadine. I only wish you'd find someone, too."

Jack had little choice but to drink, though he doubted peace was in the offing. The nightmares of his past wouldn't allow it.

When they were done, Jack paid the bill, then they walked out to the taxi stand together.

"I'm glad you came down and found me," Jack said. "We don't see each other often enough anymore. And if Nadine is the woman who does it for you, then congratulations," he added, meaning it.

Hugh slipped into the first cab. When the second car pulled up, Jack let the people behind him go ahead. He wanted to walk.

He crossed over to Seventh Avenue, then headed north. His little brother was getting married. A reluctant smile skimmed over his lips. But the smile didn't last long when inevitable thoughts of the woman from last night surged in his mind.

Those eyes. That passion. Like fire unleashed.

Who was she? he wondered.

Walking beneath the early afternoon winter sun, Jack wasn't certain which would be worse. Seeing her again, or not.

Chapter
Four

Well after two in the afternoon on Monday, Grace cracked open her apartment door and listened.

Technically, she didn't have to be back at work for two weeks. Yesterday she had kept herself busy by going through the overflowing stack of industry magazines that had piled up during the last month, before taking a long bath, the water filled with mint oil and chamomile, then making a healthy meal of chicken salad served over half of an imported avocado, surrounded by fresh fruits and vegetables she'd had delivered from the corner market. Anything to keep from having to leave her apartment and walk past Jack Berenger's door.

But finally on Monday, she forced herself to face the fact that she couldn't stay inside forever. She packed up the remaining iced cakes in a foil-lined box and decided to go into the office. She pulled on her black wool coat and scarf over her tweed suit and low-heeled shoes.

When she walked out into the hallway, all was quiet. Taking the few steps to the banister, she leaned over, glanced down the zigzagging staircase that led to the ground floor, and saw no one. More important, she didn't see Jack Berenger.

When Grace had stepped into his arms that crazy night, she had truly given no thought to the fact that she would have to pass by his door every time she wanted to leave the building. While the fire escape could get her outside, it probably couldn't do it without plummeting her to the frozen ground below in a heap of sensible wool and smashed She's No Angel Cakes.

But there was no going back, and Grace knew instinctually—albeit a tad too late—that she should avoid a man like Jack Berenger on principle. Like her father, he was a doctor, and according to Mrs. Neimark—the nosy Mrs. Kravitz of West Sixty-ninth Street—he'd had more than one overtly affectionate woman over to his apartment in the short week he had lived there. Not that Grace was surprised. Of her father's medical colleagues, she couldn't think of a single one who was still married to his first wife. A plethora of obliging nurses and adoring patients proved temptations that very few doctors seemed able to resist.

Grabbing her handbag and the box of cakes, Grace clicked the door shut as quietly as she could, turned the keys in the locks, then carefully made her way down the first two flights of stairs. She held her breath as she tiptoed past the very door through which she had fled, and had just reached the ground floor, exhaling in a rush, when her luck ran dry.

He stood on the front steps, holding the door open, talking to Mrs. Neimark's little boy, Timmy, and his best friend, Marvin, from next door. For a second Grace couldn't move.

She heard his voice, just barely, deep and clear, and she could all but feel the way his words had rumbled against her bare skin when he had trailed his lips down her spine. A shiver raced through her, and her breath grew shallow.

He was as extraordinary in the light of day as he had been in the glowing darkness of the dimly lit night. Tall and elegant, his massive shoulders narrowed to a hard-muscled waist. Black hair swept back from his forehead, then down to brush the collar of his white button-down shirt. His eyes, dark and unfathomable, were just then glimmering with a quiet mirth as he listened to some entertaining tale the boys told him.

He wore the same thick leather coat lined with shearling that he had worn two nights before, with faded denim jeans and black work boots. He looked ruggedly masculine and handsome. Just the kind of man who, under normal circumstances, wouldn't give a woman like her a second glance. She felt embarrassment creep into her cheeks at the thought of his reaction when he saw her without the professionally applied makeup and beautifully styled hair.

The realization gave her a start of surprise—and hope. Maybe he wouldn't even recognize her.

Jack said something that made the boys laugh, and at the same time he casually glanced inside the building. Just when she thought he hadn't seen her, whatever he was saying cut off.

Slowly, he straightened and turned to face her. When he did, their eyes met. The amusement in his expression shifted with surprise, then quickly hardened to something different, something at once accusatory and heated.

So much for the hope that he wouldn't recognize her.

Grace sucked in her breath, and after one paralyzed moment, she took three unconscious steps backward.

Without a word to Timmy or Marvin, Jack pushed the rest of the way through the front door. At that, Grace turned and ran, taking the steps as fast as she could in heels.

"Holly?"

In the second it took to realize he was calling out to *her,* she felt the prick of embarrassed guilt. But what was a little white lie when considered against the bigger picture of sexual promiscuity, she reasoned. Did he really think she'd give him her real name?

"Holly!"

She kept going.

"Who are you calling, Dr. Berenger?" Timmy inquired. "That's Grace."

"Grace!" both boys called out, her name echoing against the mahogany wainscoted walls and hardwood steps.

Drat.

Grace stopped at the top of the first flight and hung her head. Ignoring her new neighbor was one thing, ignoring the boys was another. Cracking her lips in what she hoped would pass for a smile, she leaned over the banister.

The boys had come into the first level of the building, their heads craning back as they peered up the stairs. Timmy, with his mop of dark brown curls. Marvin, with his wiry red hair and face full of freckles. And Jack Berenger. He stood at the bottom of the steps and looked up at her as if finding it hard to believe she was standing there at all.

"Hey there, Timmy," she offered, her smile straining on her lips. "Hi, Marvin."

"Dr. Berenger thinks your name is Holly," Timmy stated with the scoffing, disbelieving humor of a six-year-old.

The man in question, however, didn't appear to see the humor in the situation. Whatever remnant heat had been in his eyes, evaporated. He looked murderous, though Grace couldn't have said why.

Because she had lied about her name?

Because they lived in the same building?

Because she had slipped away without a word?

Reluctantly, she retraced her steps until she stood no more than a few feet from him, the box of cakes resting on her hip. She hoped she looked cool and unconcerned.

Timmy and Marvin's humor congealed into delight at the sight of the box.

"What did you cook today?" Marvin inquired with a hopeful grin. "Can we have some?"

"Only if you are very, very sweet." She loved these boys, loved all the kids on the block, and they loved her.

Timmy and Marvin raced up to her, their smiles so dear, and Grace felt her heart melt. "All right. One apiece." She flipped up the top.

"Petal fours." They groaned in disappointment.

Jack's gaze had never wavered, but at this he glanced into the box.

"That's what they call petit fours," she explained. "As you can see, it's not their favorite."

"Do you got any brownies in there?" Marvin asked, rising up on his toes to get a better look.

"Nope. Sorry. It's this or nothing, kiddos."

They shrugged, then each took a cake. Despite their lack of enthusiasm, the boys made quick work of the confections.

Jack stood back, his thick sheepskin gloves held taut between his hands as he scanned the length of her. "You said your name was Holly," he stated, his voice as cold as the blustery winter chill outside, his expression saying as clearly as words that he thought her not only loose, but a liar, to boot.

Cheek-burning mortification did battle with deep-seated guilt, but what was there to say? She had learned long ago that the best way to deal with precarious and uncomfortable situations was to act like she didn't care.

She attempted a nonchalant shrug as she balanced the box with one hand, then used the other to whip her woolen scarf around her shoulders with a panache she had practiced in front of the mirror. "I was going for literary allusion. Holly Golightly."

His eyes narrowed, though she wasn't sure if he was confused or simply angrier.

"You know, from the book."

No response.

"Truman Capote," she prompted. "Holly Golightly from *Breakfast at Tiffany's*. Audrey Hepburn was in the movie."

"Oh, yeah," he replied grimly, "the call girl who lived above the writer in the brownstone in Manhattan."

She almost smiled her delight that he got the reference, but on second thought, she wasn't all that keen about being compared with a call girl. She had been thinking more along the lines of comparing herself with Audrey Hepburn.

"For your information," she stated primly, "she was an escort."

"Is there a difference?"

Probably not, she thought glumly, wishing she had come up with a more wholesome character for her allusion. But she didn't have any experience coming up with fake names at the drop of a hat.

"Well, now we've met," she said, pasting on a smile. "No time to linger. I've got to get to work."

He glanced at his watch, and she cringed knowing that it was nearly three in the afternoon. No telling what kind of a job he thought she had. But she wasn't about to explain that it didn't matter if she went in at three or eight-thirty, because she wasn't expected for the next two weeks. Let him think what he wanted.

"Ciao!"

"Ciao, Grace!" the boys called in unison. "Thanks for the cake."

"You're welcome."

She made it out the front door, down the steps, and scanned the street unsuccessfully for a cab. The air was frigid, taking her breath, but the sky was bright and almost painfully blue. As fast as she could without looking like she was running, she pulled on sunglasses and headed for Broadway. But she didn't get more than half a town house away when Jack came up beside her.

"We need to talk," he said.

"Do we? I can't see why." *Please, please, let a cab appear.*

"In case you've forgotten, we slept together."

Clearly he wasn't going to do the gentlemanly thing and let the matter go.

"I always assumed sleeping with someone involved a bed. Unless I'm mistaken, I'd say we simply had sex."

Oh my God, her mind shrieked. What was she saying? But her mouth was working without the benefit of her brain, much as it had that night.

"After that," he continued undeterred, his jaw growing tight, "you left my apartment without a word."

He had her there.

"What did you expect?" she managed. "A handwritten thank-you note on engraved stationery propped up on your entry hall table? If it means so much to you, I'll send one in the morning."

She was sure he cursed.

He walked beside her easily while she struggled to appear mature and sophisticated despite the cracks and uneven pavement, not to mention the sand and cinders that had been tossed down for the snow.

"I'm not looking for a thank-you note," he ground out, catching her arm with ease when she slipped. "I simply expected . . ."

His words trailed off, and she glanced over at him, her skin tingling beneath the coat where he held her. She pulled her arm away without ever stopping. "What did you expect?"

He dragged his hand through his hair. "I don't know. But I didn't expect you to sneak out."

Something in his voice tugged at her. She was being emotional and wishful, and perhaps even hopeful their joining had meant something—if only that he didn't think she was a cold fish. She shook the thought away. It was absurd to care. "Is that in a book somewhere? Emily Post's *Perfect Guide to One-night Stands*. Perhaps I should order a copy."

"Are you always this flip?"

"I try." Which she did. It was easier that way, no need to have real and deep conversations about things that meant so much they hurt. She had showed that side of herself to Walter, reluctantly, carefully, and he had tossed it back in her face. Verbal quips and retorts were better. Safer.

"You slept with a stranger," he ground out. "How can you be flip about that?"

"Actually," she mused, refusing to flinch, "*you* slept with a stranger. *I* knew who you were."

She could all but feel the tension that snaked through him.

"How do you know me?" he demanded.

"Mrs. Neimark told me all about you, who you are, what you do, where you work. A person would be hard-pressed to get a better recommendation than a co-op apartment application summary from the president of the co-op board. You, on the other hand, had no idea who I was. So technically you should feel worse about this than I do."

He shoved his hands in his pockets and stopped in his tracks. Grace kept walking.

"Don't I deserve any kind of an explanation about what happened that night?"

Grace sighed, then after three more precarious steps

through cinders and slicks of ice, she stopped. Knowing she would live to regret it, she turned back. At the sight of him standing there, so tall and massive, she felt a strange twist in her heart. Just looking at Jack Berenger with his dark hair and even darker eyes, the chiseled jaw and shoulders, it was hard to imagine that he cared one whit about what had happened between them. But then she noticed the same darkness she had seen in his eyes that night.

"What do you want to know?" she asked quietly.

"Your full name would help. Your full *real* name. You obviously already know mine."

She felt a crooked smile pull across her lips. "Colebrook. Grace Colebrook. And if it will make you feel better, I am twenty-nine years old, am a picture of perfect health, and I moved into the building three months ago, though let me tell you, my apartment was considerably less expensive than yours. Of course, I'm in a fourth-floor walk-up, with only one bedroom, unless you count the hideaway attic the realtor swore could make a second floor, while you're in an expensively renovated two-floor apartment with who knows how many bedrooms and baths."

That was the trouble with her, when she got nervous, she talked a mile a minute. But it didn't look as if he was really listening to the last part of what she said. He stepped closer.

"All right, Grace Colebrook, of perfectly good health, why were you sitting outside in a wedding dress to begin with? Were you getting married?" His eyes narrowed, and he glanced at her fingers. "Hell, are you married? Or was the gown a costume, and you're some actress from an off-Broadway show?"

Her smile disappeared, and her heart pounded with every step he took closer. A harsh bite of laughter burst out of her. "Actress? No. It just seemed like a bad play. But the truth is, I really was supposed to get married."

He considered her words. "Why didn't you?"

"I changed my mind." She didn't expand. She knew she still sounded flip, but her throat felt too tight, making it difficult to say anything.

"That's it?"

"Do the specifics matter? I doubt it. But, if you must know, I found my fiancé in a precarious position."

"Precarious financial position?"

"Not unless he paid my sister's friend so he could slip between her thighs for a last-minute fling before he promised to love and cherish me *until death do us part.*"

Jack's darkly narrowed eyes darkened even more. "You're kidding."

"Nope."

At the word, he took the last step that separated them. In that second, she felt a protective surge of anger in him, and she would have sworn that had Walter been anywhere near, this man would have pummeled him. The thought was as foreign as it was disconcerting.

But Walter wasn't there. Instead, Jack surprised her when he reached out and gently pulled her sunglasses off the bridge of her nose. A light breeze caught in her hair, tugging a long curl from the twist at the back of her head, tossing it about her face. He folded the glasses, then gently tucked the errant strand of hair behind her ear.

Standing so close, he seemed even taller, his chest even broader. She could feel the heat of him, in spite of the cold.

Words mixed with sensation, stumbling around in her mind as she tried to remember what she was talking about. "I decided right there in the church," she hurried on, "that the promise *for better or for worse* didn't count if the vows hadn't already been spoken. I walked out. It's as simple as that."

"I'm sorry."

"No need to be. Life goes on."

He took in the length of her, her mouth, her breasts, as if remembering, his gaze running over her in a way that made her heart hammer and her bones fuse, heat like warm molasses sliding low. When he returned his gaze to hers, the hard, exacting lines of his face had softened. She had the distinct premonition that it would be easier to avoid this man in the future if he stayed cold and demanding.

"Are you all right, Grace?" he asked quietly.

His voice was deep and rumbling, making the simple question seem intimate and sexual, and she had the urge to fall headfirst into the heat of him. But while she could forgive herself one night of idiocy, she couldn't forgive two.

Abruptly, she turned away and headed for the heavily taxied length of Broadway. Jack caught up and walked beside her.

The smile he offered flashed even, white teeth. "All right, if you don't want to talk about that night, then tell me something else. Are you from New York? Where do you work? Or tell me about your family. Surely you have one."

She, however, was not as easily won over as Timmy and Marvin by his devastatingly handsome smile. With her lips pressed tight, she thought of her sister's and mother's demands that she go through with the ceremony even after Roberta Caldwell Colebrook came up behind her just in time to see Walter fumbling with his pants and Suzanne's friend stumbling away. "Nope, no family for me."

"Come on, everyone has a family."

"I'm an orphan."

"Obviously a rich orphan to be able to afford this neighborhood," he said, his smile widening, "even if your apartment was less expensive than mine."

Was he toying with her?

"I don't own. I rent." In for a penny, in for a pound. She mentally started tabulating the lies.

"The building doesn't allow renters. You must have a very good relationship with the owner to be able to stay there."

"That's it. I have a *very* good relationship. I'm a kept woman."

"Then he hasn't done a very good job of keeping you. I might not know much about you, but I do know that until you were with me, you hadn't had sex in a very long time."

The words hit her hard, and the control she had fought so hard to maintain, slipped. Suddenly, she stopped and whirled on him, the cakes sliding up against the box sides. "What do you want from me? An apology? Okay, you've got it. I'm sorry I slept with you! I'm sorry I said my name was Holly! I'm sorry we'll have to see each other ever again! Is that what you want?"

He was quiet for a long minute as he stared at her. For a second Grace thought he would reach out and trail his fingers along her jaw as he had that fateful night. Her pulse skipped and raced, and she felt her body begin to tingle. As long as she lived she would never forget the amazing intensity of his palms cupping her breasts, his tongue entwined with hers, their legs wrapped together, or the heady sensation when he had slipped his body hard and deep into hers.

Her lips parted, and her gaze drifted low. Their breaths mingled in puffs of white, condensing in the cold—making her want to give in. She wanted to feel him touch her, hold her against his heat. Better judgment be damned.

But just when she would have leaned into him, he spoke.

"All I want to know is why it happened."

The words cemented in her mind. Suddenly she couldn't hide behind quips and witty retorts any longer. Her embarrassment and regret swelled, overwhelming her until she felt she couldn't breathe. How could she have gotten herself backed into this corner? She had walked out on her wedding, her family was furious at her, and in spite of all her reasoning, she'd had sex with a man she didn't even know.

"Because I was an idiot."

She would have turned away, should have turned away, but the expression on his face struck her hard. It was as if he really wanted to know, was as stunned by what happened as she was. She felt a frustrating need to explain.

She took a deep breath and sought the words. For him. For her. No more hiding from the truth. "It happened because I was sad and alone, and when you walked out into the night, you were so beautifully handsome, so very much alive and intense."

The words seemed inadequate, didn't come close to explaining what she had experienced when she saw him. "I know this sounds crazy, I know it sounded crazy when you came out into the night, but it felt like I couldn't do anything else, like I had known you forever and had just been waiting for you to arrive. And, most of all, I needed to be held." She took a deep breath and looked at him. "Okay?"

He didn't say a word at first, the only sounds coming from the traffic on Broadway. But finally he nodded his head. "Okay."

The gods must have taken pity on her, because a cab sped up the block. Within seconds, she had the door open. But just before she slipped inside, he called out.

"Grace."

Just that, her name, the realness of the word somehow more intimate than his bare hands on her skin.

She stopped and turned back, not sure what he would say, not sure what she wanted him to say.

"Yes?"

"Your glasses."

It took a second for her to understand what he was talking about. "Oh, yes. Thank you." She took the simple black frames, his fingers brushing against hers. She stared at his hand before she pulled away and looked up. "For what it's worth," she said, "I really haven't done anything like that before. I wasn't lying about that."

Then she was in the cab, speeding away. At the end of the block she glanced back. Jack stood where she had left him, watching her, making her wish as she had wished for little else in her life that she hadn't been so foolish that night.

Chapter
Five

Grace pressed back against the cracked vinyl seat of the taxi as it darted in and out of traffic. She tried to settle down. But thoughts of Jack Berenger weren't conducive to calm. A foolish bit of pride raced through her at the thought that he had recognized her. Even though she looked nothing like the fashion model sort she was sure a man like him would be used to, he had looked at her with an unmistakable heat burning in his eyes. And Walter had called her a cold fish.

Raising her chin a notch, she looked out the taxi window at the tall buildings of concrete and metal that thrust up into the sky as the cab headed downtown, traffic coming to a near standstill, the streets like a slow-moving parking lot of yellow taxis and black livery sedans. They crawled along until traffic thinned out and Grace arrived at the corporate headquarters of Kendrick Toys.

At the thought of work, Grace grimaced. She loved her job as the senior member of the development team for the country's second-largest toy manufacturer. Her mother abhorred the idea. If Grace had to work, Roberta Caldwell Colebrook had said, why not get a job at *Vanity Fair* or *Town & Country*?

But Grace relished the challenge of creating something new. She thrived on those amazing moments when an idea hit and it felt so right that she knew she had to run with it. She had tried to explain it to her mother, to no avail. But what she hadn't explained to anyone, and rarely allowed herself to think about, was that what she loved most about her job at Kendrick Toys was the minutes or hours she spent in the Kids' Lab, sitting behind the two-way mirror, watching children test the new toys with their wide, innocent eyes.

For a few unadulterated seconds, Grace got to sit back and do nothing more than enjoy a small child's wonder, like peering through a looking glass into a world of pure and simple delight.

She always wondered if she had ever been young like that. It amazed her that she had the ability to create any toy at all given the fact that she had grown up making martinis for her father and cold compresses for her mother. Grace remembered the time she had asked her mother for an Easy-Bake oven.

Good God, Grace, don't be so common.

Her mother had always been larger than life, cultivating her world of carefully constructed affluence, more like an eccentric southern belle than a Fifth Avenue stoically sensible patron of all things liberal and the arts. Indeed, the Colebrooks had money, but it was the kind of money accumulated through long years of work and careful investing. Most people assumed they had more money than they truly had.

Her father didn't seem to care one way or the other about what people thought, but her sister, Suzanne, took up where their mother left off and did nothing to disabuse any of her society-page friends of the notion of old and genteel wealth.

Grace had grown up in a cavernously cold apartment on Fifth Avenue. For all the years she had lived there, she had rarely brought friends home. The thought of her classmates seeing any of her mother's dramatics made long afternoons of solitary reading more appealing. It was from the stacks of books she read that she learned who she wanted to be. Bits and pieces of characters that had leaped from the pages, hammered together to form the woman she had become—so different from her mother.

Pulling up to the towering office building, Grace glanced at her watch and noticed that if she hurried, she could make it to the weekly brainstorming session. A frisson of concern pricked at her mind. In the four years she had worked for Kendrick, more of her ideas had been put into production than anyone else's, including the founder, Cecil Kendrick, himself. At least that had been the case until three months ago, when J. Hastings Rodman had joined the firm.

Jay, as he was called, had a B.A. from Princeton, an M.B.A. from the Wharton School, had become the darling of Cecil Kendrick, and he wanted her job. Though in the time he had been with the company, he had failed to come up with any ideas. But truth be told, since Jay had been hired, neither had she.

Grace had always had a bone-deep confidence in her work. But as much as she hadn't wanted to face the fact, the last three months of Jay's sneering presence had rattled her. The constant wariness that he was just waiting for her to make a mistake was taking its toll. She had started making missteps that she couldn't afford, especially with an employer like Cecil Kendrick, who was as unpredictable as he was difficult, known for firing people on the spot.

She knew everyone at Kendrick Toys, from the mailroom clerk to Cecil Kendrick himself. She cared about each of them and their families. So when she stepped out of the elevator on the eleventh floor, she was instantly surrounded by people who offered their support, made unflattering remarks about Walter, and swore she'd find someone better and more deserving. She felt embarrassed by all the attention, but moved by their concern.

When she entered the conference room, the creative team sat around the long, oval mahogany table, a wall of windows looking out over Broadway and Twenty-fourth Street. Grace jerked to a halt at the sight of Jay sitting in her chair. It was a little thing, but significant. Technically, no one had their own chair, but everyone sat in the same seat. As the senior member of the team, Grace always sat at the foot of the table, with Cecil Kendrick at the head.

Grace raised a brow, but Jay didn't move. He sat like a king before his court in his Ralph Lauren pin-striped suit, the kind of blue shirt with white collar that she hated, a bow tie and suspenders. His blue eyes stared out at her through tortoiseshell frames in silent challenge.

"Grace," the group greeted at the sight of her.

Cecil looked up from a printout he was reading. "Look who's here. The girl who walked out of her wedding. Who would have believed that our levelheaded little Grace would have bolted?"

Everyone in the conference room grew uncomfortable and suddenly became interested in whatever paperwork was in front of them.

If Grace hadn't been so surprised by Cecil's words, she would have blushed. Disconcerted, she headed for an empty seat. But before she could sit down, Mark Beacher, her closest friend, spoke up.

"Hey, Jay," he quipped, "you're in Grace's chair."

Cecil looked on, but he did nothing more than sit back like he wanted to see who would win this little skirmish.

The company founder had graduated from the school of internal warfare, and seemed to believe that survival of the fittest should apply to all areas of life. It was Grace who called this gathering of people a team. Cecil pitted his employees against one another at every turn.

"I'm fine here," Grace said.

"Good heavens, I'm sorry," Jay offered grandly, pushing up and gathering his things. "Far be it from me to step on anyone's toes, especially after the escapade you've been through."

Grace was certain the whole room could hear her teeth grind.

"Thank you, Jay, and really that wasn't necessary," she said, setting the thankfully still fluffy cakes on the table. But not a single soul made a move toward the box.

"Enough nonsense," Cecil Kendrick barked, suddenly impatient. "Just sit the hell down. We have a lot to cover today, namely the fact that we aren't off to the greatest start this year. Where in Hades are the ideas, people? I want this to be the biggest and best year for Kendrick Toys ever, which means we need some damned good toys. As long as you're here, Grace, get things started."

As usual, he turned the meeting over to her and sat back to listen. Though this time Grace was certain she detected a note of reluctance in her employer.

"Yes, well, thank you, Cecil," she managed, unprepared to head the meeting today. She sought the ease she had always felt in this position. She should have been confident. But she had begun to question everything she did. It had gotten so bad that she had been afraid to toss out any idea at all.

She knew it was in her head. But out of fear, or dwindling confidence, she had stopped trusting her judgment. Every idea suddenly seemed idiotic. She questioned each concept for so long and with such intensity, rather than just

tossing it out, that in the end anything so closely scruti-
nized seemed impossibly stupid.

The fact appalled her. But the truth was, sitting there
with her palms clammy and her heart racing, she couldn't
deny that she was rattled. And that was unacceptable.

She couldn't let this man defeat her. Pulling her shoulders back, she asked, "Who would like to throw out the
first idea?"

Everyone squirmed, until Mark shrugged and began. He
described an idea for a smiling doll with a fuzzy coat that,
with a few twists and reconfigurations, turned into a fuzzy
dog. "For now, I'm calling it, Dr. Tickle and Mr. Fide."

The group stared at the man with furrowed brows.

Kendrick leaned forward. "I get the play on Dr. Jekyll
and Mr. Hyde. But what the hell does *Mr. Fide* mean?"

"Granted, it needs some work, because I couldn't quite
figure out how to incorporate the dog into the name. Something that rhymed with Hyde. The best I could come up
with was Fido, but I knew Dr. Tickle and Mr. Fido didn't
work at all."

Jay burst out laughing, and embarrassment crept into
Mark's face. Grace had never been able to sit by when
others were hurt, and today was no different. Jay Rodman
hadn't come up with a single idea of his own, but he dared
laugh at others. Without thinking, she said, "I take it you
have a better idea, Jay."

For half a second, the man's eyes went wide. Kendrick
studied him, and he grew flustered. He cleared his throat,
then settled into the coolly arrogant man they all had come
to know.

"Mr. Carrot Head."

Three simple words that made every brow in the room
furrow with confusion.

He proceeded to go on about a carrot with ears and eyes

and lips. "Mr. Potato Head is very popular. It's time Mr. Potato Head got some competition," Jay said importantly.

Cecil Kendrick steepled his fingers in thought. The team studied their boss to determine his reaction, though Jay glanced at Grace, a look of bitter challenge settling on his features.

Grace, however, didn't wait. "What else do we have?"

Surprised quiet reigned for one long second before Mark cleared his throat.

"Well, we could—"

"I don't believe we've finished discussing Mr. Carrot Head," Jay interjected.

Every member of the team plastered themselves back against their chairs as if to get out of the direct line of fire. Only she and Jay leaned forward. Cecil appeared to be enjoying himself.

"What you came up with," she began, "is a rip-off of a toy that already exists, not to mention a toy that someone else has the trademark on. I'm not a lawyer, but my guess is that the manufacturer of Mr. Potato Head would come after us faster than we could turn our own heads. Besides which, Kendrick Toys does many things, but we do not imitate. Kendrick has made its name on innovation."

His face flushed red, color seeping down beneath his too-white collar, no doubt heating his garish gold-plated tie bar. Before he could get a word out, she plunged ahead.

"As I see it, we—" The words cut off. Her thoughts faltered. Suddenly it felt like she couldn't breathe. Ten sets of eyes looked at her in anticipation, but her mind had gone blank.

"Grace?" Mark prodded.

"All right," Jay interjected, his voice suddenly low and chilling. "If you don't like that idea, how about this?"

He put his hands up in the air as if framing the thought. "I call it *Pink Cadillac*."

Grace's whole body went still. Everyone else perked up.

"Pink Cadillac?" Cecil inquired, his head tilted in that way that made it clear he was intrigued. "What's the concept?"

After that, Jay ran with it. "It's a pink plastic nineteen fifty-nine Cadillac convertible with white panels and fins. We'd make two sizes. One for Barbie dolls, and another big enough for a child to actually drive around in."

The idea was great, astounding, and Grace could tell from Cecil's expression that the company would put its full efforts behind making it the toy that every little girl between the ages of four and eight had to have.

The idea *was* inspired, and it was hers.

Grace sat at the conference room table, so stunned she couldn't speak as the development team muttered grudging approval.

Cecil Kendrick smiled and nodded his head. "Good job, Jay. It's perfect."

"Excuse me, Cecil." Her heart pounded so hard that it felt like her head would explode. "That is my idea."

The room went quiet, and Cecil's smile disappeared. He stared at her for a long time before he raised a bushy eyebrow. "Are you accusing Jay of stealing, Miss Colebrook?"

Kendrick didn't call anyone Miss anything unless he was angry.

"Stealing?" she managed. "Well, sir, what I know is that I wrote up a proposal for Pink Cadillac last week." She glanced at Jay. "On Tuesday I found Mr. Rodman sitting in my office. The next day, I couldn't find the proposal. At the time, I chalked it up to pre-wedding jitters, and assumed I had simply misplaced it. I think it is clear now that I didn't misplace anything. Jay must have stolen it."

Jay came out of his chair. "This is outrageous!"

"Do you have proof of this?" Cecil asked dangerously.

Grace became aware of the stark silence and the muted sound of a fire engine siren stuck in traffic far below. Everyone in the room stared at her, though not even her dear friend Mark offered help this time.

Her stomach clenched. All her notes had been handwritten, and those had disappeared.

When long minutes ticked by without an answer, Cecil added, "Grace, could it be that since you've been less than productive recently, you're trying to claim credit for Pink Cadillac out of desperation?"

A cold chill raced through the room. No one seemed to breathe as they waited for Grace to respond. But she didn't know what to say. She had no proof. Already strained confidence shattered.

She couldn't find words. She stood up, mumbling some inane apology, needing to escape. But just before the door swung closed behind her, Cecil snorted and said, "I don't know what the hell has gotten into that girl."

"I'd say the truth has come out," Jay offered smugly. "She's more nonsense than substance." He chuckled. "More fluff than stuff," he added, amused by his words, "like those cakes she keeps bringing in here."

More fluff than stuff. The words sliced through her. In all her life she had never been fluffy or flighty. She had lived a lifetime of determined sense and sensibility, and in three short months this man had come in and turned all she had worked for upside down with his sneering lies. But she didn't turn back. She kept going, down the long, carpeted hall that led to her office, not stopping or pasting on a smile when colleagues all but leaped to get out of her way. Closing the door behind her, she fell into her chair and dropped her head onto her desk. What was happening? Why was her life falling apart? What was she doing wrong?

But she was given no chance to find answers when a knock sounded at the door.

"I'm busy."

The door clicked open anyway.

Cecil Kendrick entered and he looked as serious as she had ever seen him. His wool plaid coat was rumpled, and his white shirt hadn't been ironed, his frame massive. In college he had been a starting linebacker at Notre Dame, and his office was filled with as many football trophies as industry awards. She had heard more than once about the injury that had sidelined him his senior year—the year scouts were out looking at recruits for the NFL. His dream. His shattered dream.

Life ain't fair, babe. The school of hard knocks. Life's a bitch, then you die. All favorite pearls of wisdom of Cecil Kendrick.

He didn't bother to sit down. "I think we both know this isn't working," he began without preamble.

The words hit her like a punch. Shocked, she could only stare at him. "Pink Cadillac really was mine. You've known me for four years. How can you believe I'd lie?"

"That's hardly the point. Face it, Grace. You've lost your edge."

"Cecil, that's not true—"

"It is, and it's only gotten worse. Hell, during the last few months you've spent more time in the Kids' Lab watching who knows what than in your office working on new ideas."

"Maybe I've had a few off weeks. What with the wedding and all the plans, I haven't been as focused as I should have been. But that certainly won't be a problem now," she added hurriedly.

"Sorry, Grace, as I said, this isn't working for me

anymore. I'm letting you go." He bowed his head, shoved his meaty hands into his pockets, and turned to the door.

He was leaving, just like that. This wasn't a bad dream, it was really happening. Shock mixed with fear.

Her mind raced with things to say, how to convince him not to fire her. But the fact was, she wouldn't beg. Suddenly a calm settled over her.

Grace pushed back from the desk, the rollers gliding with smooth efficiency. She would not let him see her weak. Too many things had happened over the last few days, and with each hour that passed, she felt more and more like a person she didn't recognize.

She crossed her legs and tapped her pencil on the desktop. If she'd had a cigarette, she would have blown smoke rings in perfect circles. "I can fight you on this. You have no cause."

"But I do, Grace. You haven't come up with a single viable idea in three months, and you've just accused one of my senior executives of lying and stealing without any proof. I'd call that cause."

He turned away, then stopped at the door. "I'll expect you to clean out your desk and be gone within the hour." When he opened the door, her heart took a hard, jarring start when she saw the security guard standing outside.

"Mr. McDougal will escort you out of the building as soon as you've packed up your belongings."

Those same biting feelings she'd had earlier tried to resurface, fear, uncertainty, painful and heated, burning her up. But she wouldn't give in, not to anger, not to tears, not to fear.

With pride and dignity, Grace gathered her belongings into a cardboard box, refusing to do anything but smile at the staff members who dashed in and out of her office as the news spread. She refused to let anyone see how shaken she was.

Through a tight throat and dry mouth, she tossed off quips to the solemn-faced guard. She offered words of encouragement to her dear friend Mark, who stood with a look of utter stupefaction. She doled out joking advice as she was paraded down the same long hallway she had entered through only an hour before.

Once outside the building, the door shut firmly behind her, she stood on the sidewalk, buffeted by the bitterly cold wind and throngs of pedestrians. But she hardly noticed. She looked at the sea of strangers, the crush of sound from traffic no longer blocked out by expensive sheets of glass windowpanes, and couldn't bring up a coherent thought. Then she began to walk.

She didn't know how exactly she made it home, but by the time she did, the sun cast long winter shadows against the building when she turned onto West Sixty-ninth Street and came to the front steps of the brownstone. In her determination to leave in grand style, she had forgotten her purse.

With her box of office belongings held in her arms, she stared at the front door, the lock, and realized she didn't have a key. Fighting back a growing panic, she pressed Mrs. Neimark's buzzer.

"Please, be home," she whispered, her head pressed against the hard stone.

But no one answered. She buzzed again and again, tears burning, her throat tight. Without warning, the door pushed open, nearly crashing into her. Grace gasped in startled surprise, then cringed when she realized it was her new neighbor.

Jack's face went from surprise to concern when he looked into her eyes. Grace didn't wait around to hear what he had to say. She mumbled her thanks, and dashed underneath his arm, careening up the stairs, praying that he wouldn't follow her. Her mortification at the office was bad enough, she didn't need to add humiliation in front of this man to the mix.

She could tell the entry door stood open for a long time. Her heart pounded at the knowledge that Jack must be standing there, deciding what to do. After long seconds, the door swung closed, with no footsteps to follow. He had left the building. Thankfully. Though somehow even that made her throat tighten all the more.

Breathing heavily, she located her spare key under the umbrella holder she kept in the hall. She fumbled with the lock. When she finally pushed into the apartment, her hip banged against the brass knob, knocking the box loose from her grasp, spilling the contents in disarray across the floor. She didn't stop to pick anything up, only stumbled inside.

By then it was nearly dark, the only brightness coming from the sudden sputtering of light provided when streetlamps flickered on. The apartment was cold, and she turned up the heat. Anything to banish the chill she felt spreading through her. Then she started to pace.

She would not cry.

The telephone started to ring, but she ignored it. She turned on a light and went to the kitchen, standing in front of the refrigerator for ages before deciding nothing looked good. The thick door sucked shut, then she tugged open the freezer. She found some double-chocolate ice cream and she started eating out of the carton. But even that didn't help. She put it away, dropping the spoon in the sink, then stared out the window, her hands braced against the sink, trying to hold on. She looked straight into the backs of brownstones one block over, could see her neighbors moving around in their kitchens, their bedrooms, snapping open newspapers in living rooms, life going on as if nothing was wrong. With a jerk, she turned away and walked out of the kitchen, only to stop in her tracks.

Jack stood in the doorway, his eyes narrowed as if he wasn't sure why he was there.

"Darn it all, do you constantly have to appear out of nowhere," she demanded, hating the intensity she felt at the sight of him.

His hair had fallen forward, and he raked it back from his forehead with one hand. With the other, he held out a plaque, broken now from the drop on the floor.

"I think this is yours," he said. "I found it in the hall."

She didn't take it, only stared at him. He wore the same thick coat from that first night and this morning, and the jeans that molded to his hard thighs.

Jack turned the plaque and read, " 'Award of Excellence. Grace Colebrook.' " He looked at her.

"See, that really is my name." She whispered the words over the lump in her throat.

"I take it something happened today." He studied the box and scatter of office supplies.

She closed her eyes and pursed her lips, pulling a deep breath in through her nose, holding it, then exhaling with a sharp sigh. Gaining control. "Nothing happened." She walked over to a small writing desk against the far wall and rummaged through the drawers until she found a pack of cigarettes left over from some party. "Would you like one?"

Jack set the plaque on the entry table, then leaned back against the wall and crossed his arms on his chest. "No, thanks, I don't smoke. You don't strike me as a smoker, either."

"I smoke now. In fact, I do a lot of things now that I've never done before." She opened her arms as if to display herself, a cigarette in one hand, a lighter in the other. "I'm the newly unemployed, newly unengaged woman who has decided to start smoking."

"Are you ever serious?"

"Ah, but I am serious," she stated, tapping the cigarette on the desktop as she had seen her mother do. "I've never been more serious. In fact, I'm so serious that I'm taking a long, hard look at my life"—her voice broke, and the cigarette snapped in her fingers—"and realizing that I need to do things a tad differently."

With that, her face crumpled like a flimsy house of cards. The tears she had fought so hard to hold back spilled over, and she tossed the cigarette and lighter aside. "How did this happen? My fiancé screws another woman at my wedding, I get fired from my job because some bastard stole my idea." Her voice rose and cracked. "And I'm nearly thirty and I've never even seen a white picket fence!"

She buried her face in her hands, her world crashing in on her as she cried. Hard, racking sobs that shuddered through her body.

"Ah, hell."

Then, once again, like a scratched record playing the same few bars over and over again, she felt his arms wrap around her. She fell into him, like falling through a dark hole and having no idea where it would lead.

"God, you make me crazy," he bit out against her skin. "I don't even know you, and what I do know tells me to keep my distance. But here I am. Unable to stay away."

"If you're trying to help, that's not the way to do it," she whispered against his mouth.

He groaned, his lips nipping her ear, then he fell back against the wall and pulled her with him. When his lips found hers again, she didn't think. All she wanted was to feel the hard, sinewy line of his body pressed against hers, as if somehow by doing so, he could fill the ache in her soul.

Chapter
Six

Jack looked into her eyes, wide and innocent, lost, and he felt his irritation fade. He had been as surprised as hell when he had seen her earlier, then furious when he realized she had lied about everything. It was as if the woman from that night and the woman in the foyer were two entirely different people.

This one was prim and proper in her sensible clothes. Had he met her under any other circumstance he probably wouldn't have given her a second glance. Though looking at her now, he conceded that wasn't entirely true. Despite the prim exterior, something heated burned beneath. Something about her made him want to touch her, hold her. He knew underneath the thick clothes was a body that was sinfully delicate with sleek curves, anything but prim and mousy.

Slowly, like he had no will of his own, he reached out and ran his thumb along her jaw. The simple touch sent sensation coursing through him, filling him with a need to do more than comfort her.

He thought of the night he had made love to her—had sex, as she had crudely corrected him—and he realized that while they had been intimate, he hadn't seen her body. Not really. They had shared a frantic need, tangling in that long swath of satin, and he had the distinct desire to see her.

Frustrated by her coat, he tugged it free, tossing it aside as she stood vulnerable. He wanted to peel the layers of her clothes away to see her breasts and hips, the whiteness of her stomach, and the sweet juncture between her thighs. He wanted to cup her softness, had dreamed of doing just that every night since they had met, and in doing so turn the sadness into heat. That he could deal with. That he understood.

He kissed her then. No embrace, only the touch of her lips. Heat was instantaneous, burning but banked, and her eyes closed when he ran his hands down her arms, his fingers grazing her own.

He lost himself to the sensation of lips gently brushing together, side to side, slowly, maddeningly, until she touched him. When she did, desire erupted and he groaned into her mouth, half cry, half demand.

She inhaled raggedly when his lips trailed back to her ear, the whisper of breath sending fire carving through him as he grazed a path to the delicate skin on her neck. He nipped and sucked, and she clutched him to her. He could feel her need building, equaling his own.

"Grace," he murmured, her name both benediction and curse.

With that, the remaining remnants of caution vanished.

She clung to him, their mouths suddenly hungry and searching. Just like that first night, their kiss became a bold demand.

With one hand, he tilted her head so he could taste her more deeply as he pressed her body closer. His shaft swelled hard against her body, and he felt her shudder. He had the fleeting thought that he was giving in to something he had held tightly inside. Like letting go in a way that he would regret.

He kissed her with infinite care, the corner of her mouth,

her cheekbone, desperately, hungrily. When her eyelids fluttered closed, he kissed her there, too. His mouth slanted across hers, his tongue tracing her lips, cajoling them to open, drawing her out.

The wind outside had picked up, buffeting against the windows. But the world beyond these walls seemed distant; the storm that brewed hardly mattered.

Grace told herself she wanted just a moment of Jack's heat—that she deserved a bit of comfort after such a horrible day. But when his hand ran down her spine, she felt breathless and a little dizzy.

She opened to him, and he tasted her, their bodies so close that she felt his shuddering breath against her. His kiss made her yearn for more, despite the fact that she knew she shouldn't. She craved the feel of his strong hands on her, his fingers finding those hidden secret places that brought her body to life.

"God, who the hell are you?" he demanded raggedly.

In answer, she could only taste him. She sucked in her breath, and it was as if she had breathed him in, into herself. She loved the feel of him, the scent of him. Rugged, masculine, spicy and clean, like wild grasses.

"You make me crazy. You make me want you." He said the words like an accusation.

"Then leave," she whispered, not letting go. "I didn't ask you to come up here."

He groaned against her, a sweet vibration of sound. "You undo me."

Then she felt the last of his resistance melt away as his hands reached up, his palms lining her jaw, his fingers trailing back into her hair. Expertly, he tilted her head so he could take more of her.

"Yes, open for me," he whispered against her.

She did, despite everything she knew to be good and true.

Their tongues intertwined, making the flames between them leap higher. A moan escaped her throat, and her arms slid around his neck with maddening ease.

Was it possible for something so wrong to feel so right? she wondered as his hands burned a path down her neck to her shoulders.

He nipped at her lips before he kissed the shell of her ear. She could feel his heart, the steady beat as her fingers slipped beneath his coat, curling into his shirtfront when his arms wrapped around her, folding her into his warmth as she had wanted. That one simple movement made her feel wanted and cherished.

His hands cupped her round bottom, pulling her up against him, then rolling his hips, his forehead pressing against hers, their lips only grazing together. Bending his knees, he pressed his erection low, then slowly rose to his full height, the sensation like sin itself.

"I want you," he whispered raggedly. "Here, right now. Again."

It was crazy. She had promised herself that such behavior was a onetime thing. But she could hear his need whispering in her head like a rush of air, causing the feelings to shift and change. Desperate need turned to willing desire, sought after like a brass ring. In that moment, she couldn't think of anything more than losing herself in his arms.

"Then love me," she answered.

He loomed over her, so tall and chiseled. The fierceness of his expression should have scared her, but somehow it didn't. Somehow she knew that this man would never touch her in anger or fury. Indeed, when he pulled her close again, his touch was gentle as he kissed her, his lips trailing low to the glimpse of skin at the neckline of her blouse.

She pushed rational thought aside when he lifted her

hem. She felt his hand trailing up her thigh, the nylon rough against his palm. When he slipped his fingers beneath the waistband, then knelt as he tugged it down, she could hardly breathe. She stepped free of her underclothes, then shivered as he pulled her down beside him on the blue and yellow flowered rug.

She went willingly, only gasping when he pulled her over him, his hand sliding low to cup the nakedness of her hips beneath her tweed skirt. But when she felt the tips of his fingers drift along the curve to graze the moist heat between her thighs, she gasped.

Sensation couldn't hold back the stronger force of shame any longer. Shame for wanting this, shame for desperately needing to feel the hardness of him slip inside her and make her forget. But she was saved from herself, or from having to force herself to push away, when the phone rang.

Jack tensed, and in that instant he seemed to realize what had happened. Again, as he had said. From the expression on his face, like reason battling with desire, she realized he could hardly believe it.

Grace cursed herself. How could she have let this happen? her mind demanded. She didn't even know this man, yet she fell into his arms and all but demanded he make love to her.

She hardly recognized her life anymore, and guilt surged up inside her. She wasn't like this. She did not have indiscriminate sex with a man she didn't even know.

But despite every ounce of sanity and seemliness that she had cultivated over a lifetime, when she saw this man she felt as if a thick velvet stage curtain was finally being pulled back on a drama she was meant to play.

Disgust filled her at the ludicrous thought, the kind of thought that lust lends to rationality for justification to emerge, and she felt her heart harden. "Please let me go," she stated, her voice cold, watching as the hardness swept back into his dark eyes.

She felt the shift in him, felt a moment of regret when his hand jerked away from her skin, leaving her with a coldness that had nothing to do with the brewing storm outside.

The trilling ring of the phone sounded again, but she made no move toward it as the sound of her voice whirled through the room as the answering machine came on.

"Grace Louise, this is your mother speaking. Pick up the phone this instant."

Jack raised a brow. "Your mother?"

Grace grimaced and scrambled up from the floor, her skirt dropping down around her thighs. Hastily, she pulled on her panties.

Her mother sighed. "Grace, really, we need to talk about this . . . this unfortunate incident."

"Unfortunate incident?" Grace muttered, refusing to pick up the receiver.

"You know what I'm talking about," her mother added to her message. "The wedding, of course. Everyone is talking, and asking questions. What do you expect me to say?"

"How about showing your undivided support of your younger daughter?"

"You know Walter's mother has become a dear friend of mine. How do you expect me to face her?" Her mother sighed again, the sound tinny coming over the machine. "You can't avoid me forever, Grace."

"I can try."

Grace watched as Jack rolled to his feet. He was stunningly beautiful, all hard, sinewy muscle, sleek and smooth, but never quite at ease with the world around him.

"Need I remind you," her mother continued, "that you're no longer a young girl fresh out of college? You know how men in New York are. Why should they marry an older woman when they can have twenty-one-year-old nymphettes panting at their feet?"

"I'd hardly call myself an older woman," she grumbled.

Jack paused as he leaned over to retrieve his coat from the floor where it had landed. An incredulous look creased his face.

"What?" she demanded, when he straightened and glanced at her.

"Do you always talk to your answering machine?"

"I just know my mother, and what she is guaranteed to say."

"Well, fine," her mother said with a long-suffering sniff, "don't answer. Just think of yourself, forget about me. Though I suppose I should take comfort in the fact that it could be worse. At least you aren't a drug addict like Margery Hartwell's daughter."

"A drug addict," Grace stated incredulously. "Her mother found over-the-counter diet pills in her purse!"

"Or a promiscuous sort like Hannah Stewart's oldest. What is her name? Nancy?" Her mother hurumphed. "Donna Randolph told me just this morning that the girl had a man sleeping over when poor Hannah came for a visit. A simple visit and what does she find, the shock of her life."

"A simple, unexpected visit, no doubt."

"Hannah goes over for tea, and there for all the world to see is a naked man! Can you imagine?" Roberta Caldwell made a shuddering noise. "At least I can depend on you not to be promiscuous."

This time Grace shuddered. Jack gave her a hard, censorious look.

"Well, I'm not," Grace snapped. "Or at least I wasn't

until you came charging out into the night like some bull after a red cape."

"Don't blame this on me."

"Oh, Grace . . ." Her mother's words trailed off, then she sighed one last time. "I love you, dear. Call me. Please."

Grace nearly picked up the phone, probably would have if Jack hadn't been standing there with some kind of a frustratingly knowing look on his all-too-handsome face.

The answering machine beeped one last time as her mother hung up. Grace loved her mother, just as she loved her sister and father. But the love they shared had nothing in common with the Kodak ads or coffee commercials filled with baking bread, flannels shirts, and old-fashioned Christmas trees surrounded by hand-wrapped gifts. It was more like the complicated and convoluted soap operas that played in between the poignant commercials.

Grace pushed the thoughts away and found Jack studying her. "What are you looking at?"

"You, of course."

"Why?"

"You said you were an orphan."

Grace grimaced and gave him a head tilt and shrug. "Yeah, well, I lied."

"You're good at that."

Guilt surged higher. "Everyone's got to be good at something."

She couldn't bear his penetrating gaze one second longer, certain that she was on the verge of falling apart completely once again.

"I'm sorry," she barely managed. "Please go."

He stared at her hard. "What kind of game are you playing here?"

"No game," she whispered, "just a mistake."

If he had been dangerous before, a slow fury burned inside him now, and she realized she had insulted him in some primal way.

His eyes narrowed, and he looked at her with his lips firmly set before he turned and left without another word.

She listened as his footsteps trod down the stairs, round and round, until he banged out the front door. She walked to the window and watched him as he walked toward Columbus Avenue with the smooth grace of an athlete. He didn't hurry, though his steps were set with purpose.

Lost in thought, she was startled when the buzzer rang. Turning, she glanced down at the front stoop and found a fancily clad blonde in a gold lamé skintight gown and mink stole waving back frantically.

"Darling!" came the muffled voice drifting up to her. "Let me in. Let me in! It's freezing down here!"

Grace raced to the intercom and pressed the buzzer, then hurriedly gathered her stockings and shoes and threw them into her bedroom, slipped into her favorite new mules, then opened the door and leaned over the banister. Seconds later, the sound of high heels clomped up the steps.

"You really need to learn how to be more ladylike in those shoes," Grace hollered down.

"Easy for you to say," came the distinctly low-timbred voice, now out of breath from the climb.

Seconds later, Mark, her closest friend from work, stood before her, his heavily muscled arms rippling in odd contrast with the tiny gold lamé straps as he leaned over and caught his breath. Anyone seeing Mark Beacher at Kendrick Toys wouldn't take him for anything less than an upwardly mobile yuppie businessman, probably with a wife and two kids at home in the suburbs. Seeing him now dispelled that notion entirely.

"How are you doing, love?" he asked once he could breathe again.

She waved the words away, then kissed him on his rough and powdered cheeks. "You know me. I'm fine." She couldn't stand the thought that anyone would pity her. It was bad enough to be fired. "I'm always fine. The fact is, I am going to find another job. A better job."

"You're really okay?" He sounded doubtful.

"Really."

"If you're sure."

"Of course I'm sure. But I'm not sure what prompted the gold lamé and blond phase." She gestured to his wig. "Are you going someplace special?"

Mark moaned, distracted from her predicament. "I am going to find out if it's true that blondes have more fun."

"Now, Mark, I'm disappointed. When did you resort to clichés?"

Grace returned inside her apartment. Mark followed, having to scoot around the box of strewn office gear because his gown was so tight around the ankles that he couldn't lift his feet that high.

"Clichés have gained appeal since Gerald dumped me for that dim-witted Marilyn Monroe imposter."

"Don't let him get to you. You're going to find someone new, Mark, someone better."

"If only I could believe that."

For years, Mark had been the wild one, determined to have fun and live life to the fullest. Now, suddenly, he wanted to settle down. After turning thirty-one and realizing time was passing him by, he had set his sights on creating the kind of fulfilling alternative lifestyle that a gay man in New York had the ability to find. For months Grace and Mark had paged through wedding magazines and shopped for china patterns as Grace prepared for her marriage and Mark longed for one of his own.

Holding the powder puff in one hand and the compact in the other, Mark turned his face to what little light glowed in the room. "Did I cover everything up?"

He might as well be powdering a beard. "You look fine. Tons better than that ratty old Gerald deserves."

He snapped the compact closed. "That's right," he stated decisively. "Let's drink to that. Do you have any scotch?"

"In the pantry, left over from your last visit."

"Can I get you one?"

"No thanks."

"Not even a glass of champagne?"

"Not tonight."

Grace went to her bedroom and made quick work of changing her clothes. When she returned, Mark was pouring a single-malt scotch into a juice glass and adding a splash of water.

"Next you'll pull out a cigar," she said as she came into the kitchen. "If you're going to dress like that, you really should drink wine."

"Not my cup of tea, sweetheart." He turned around. As soon as he saw her, he groaned. "Oh, no. I knew you weren't fine."

"What?" she demanded defensively.

"You're wearing those horrid men's pajama bottoms and ripped-up sweatshirt. A sure sign that you are not fine."

She didn't respond; she simply went to the oven and turned the setting to 350 degrees, then headed for the cupboard and started pulling out bowls and pans, utensils and ingredients.

"Damn, even worse than I feared," he groaned.

When she pulled out a substantial tin of baking cocoa,

he cursed. "Not Desperately Decadent Double Fudge Delight."

"A girl's got to have a little pleasure in her life."

Mark hiked himself up on the kitchen stool. "Kendrick should be horsewhipped. And Jay is a schmuck."

"When that schmuck first arrived on the scene, you said he was cute."

"You know me. A pretty face always turns my head. But I was wrong about him. He's a prick. As soon as I heard it, I knew Pink Cadillac had to be your idea. Everyone in that room knew it, too. I said as much to Kendrick."

Grace whirled around, measuring cup in her hand. "What did he say?"

Mark sighed dramatically. "He asked for proof. I told him I didn't need anything more than your word."

With a groan, Grace turned back to the counter. "I bet that went over well. Besides, the fact is, he wanted me gone. That was his excuse."

"I know. Though it doesn't make any sense."

"It never does. Remember Letitia Trawling? The minute she stopped coming up with ideas, she was gone. And Herb Rittman?"

"Yeah, but Jay wasn't coming up with any ideas, and he wasn't fired."

"No, but eventually Kendrick would've had to fire him. Remember how Cecil talked up Jay in *Toys 'n Review* two months ago? Said his new hire was going to bring a much needed business expertise to Kendrick Toys. Cecil couldn't afford for his wonder boy to be a dud."

Mark swirled the glass. "I suppose you're right. But stop making that chocolate nightmare. Cry or punch something. You always make me nervous when you get that glassy-eyed stare and start baking."

"There is no need for drama." She mixed together flour, salt, sugar, and baking powder.

"Of course there is! You've been fired."

"Thanks for reminding me." Adding milk, vanilla, butter, and nuts, she started to stir.

"Grace, I'm telling you, it's not healthy to suppress your feelings."

"Thank you for sharing, Dr. Freud."

"It's even worse that you self-medicate with massive doses of sugar and chocolate instead of getting mad."

"I prefer the chocolate."

After she smoothed the mixture into a rectangular pan, she combined more sugar, more cocoa, brown sugar, and some very hot water in a second bowl. When she had a rich, smooth sauce, she poured it over the mixture, letting it seep in, then slipped it into the oven.

After she set the timer, she piled the dishes in the sink and wiped her hands on a linen towel. "There. Forty minutes away from chocolate heaven."

Mark took a sip of scotch. "Have you eaten yet?"

"Nope."

"When will you?"

Grace glanced at the timer. "In about thirty-nine minutes and forty-five seconds."

She padded into the living room and headed straight for the video cabinet. Mark followed. "Oh no, not *Terms of Endearment*," he groaned. "Why not be original for a change? Try something funny. Even something stupid. *Ace Ventura, Pet Detective.* You could use a good dose of someone talking with their butt."

Grace grimaced.

"Anything," he continued, "besides that utterly depressing saga that you can no doubt recite word for word by now."

Her smile lacked humor as she shot him a look of defiance, then she popped the tape into the VCR. Taking up the remote, she plopped down on the sofa, propped up her feet that were now shod in a pair of faithful fuzzy slippers, and pressed PLAY.

Mark sighed. "This is not good. Come on, let's play cards. Gin rummy? Double solitaire? Or better yet, how about charades. You adore charades."

"No, *you* adore charades."

"True, but I hate seeing you like this. I should stay," Mark said, shooing her over on the sofa to make room.

"No way. I don't need you here kibitzing the whole movie." She waved him off.

He started to sit down anyway, but a seam made a terrible straining noise.

"Go on, right now," Grace commanded with a smile. "Go show Gerald what he's missing."

At the mention of Gerald, his lips pursed. "I really would hate to miss such a great opportunity. Hell, look at me. I look fabulous."

"Beyond fabulous."

"All right. But I'll be back. You better have snapped out of this funk by then."

"Have fun," she said.

Mark grumbled, but headed for the door.

"Mark."

"Yes, doll?"

"Thanks for caring."

He tilted his head, his green eyes and white-blond wig so disconcerting with his rugged skin. "Anytime."

As soon as he was gone, she settled in as the smell of chocolate began to filter through the apartment, and she counted the minutes until the timer went off. Yep, no men, plenty of videos, and lots of chocolate. That was the ticket. She'd do well never to see the likes of Walter, J. Hastings Rodman, or Jack Berenger ever again.

Chapter
Seven

It was a well-known fact that there were three ways to cure a bad mood. Smoking, drinking, and eating. Smoking really wasn't high on Grace's list, and drinking first thing in the morning would only make her feel worse.

Which left eating.

She rolled out of bed and slipped her feet into her fuzzy slippers. Last night she had eaten nearly every square of Desperately Decadent Double Fudge Delight. As always, at the time, it was delish. But now, seeing the plate with only a few remaining morsels left on the coffee table, Grace wasn't sure she'd eat Desperately Decadent ever again.

Padding into the kitchen, she pulled open the refrigerator, studied the contents, then poured a glass of orange juice. When she returned to the living room, she saw the box of her things from the office. Last night in between videos of her video marathon, she had gathered the files and paperweights, shoved them inside the cardboard container, then stacked it beside the wedding gifts. At the dismal sight of all those boxes, she considered sending half of them to Walter and making him help with the returns. Though he would probably keep every dinner fork and fancy clock she sent.

He had called several times since he'd appeared at her

door, but not once had he asked how she was doing. All he wanted to know was when he could expect his money. But the fact was she didn't have the money to send him. Thank goodness she had some savings put away, but she had to make that last until she found another job.

What was the saying, *When it rains it pours*?

She felt a sudden craving for a Krispy Kreme doughnut. After a late night of videos and nothing but junk food for dinner, she decided an extra sugary glazed or chocolate iced was just the ticket to make her feel better.

She went to the shower, pulled on a plastic cap decorated with pink and blue flowers, then stood in the hot, steady stream of water and felt the knots in her shoulders start to ease. Once she was done, she pulled on a pair of baggy jeans, found a favorite old cable-knit sweater, woolly socks, and a pair of Doc Martens. With her hair tugged back into a scrunchy, she glanced at herself in the mirror, held back a start of surprise, and reassured herself that she looked good enough. Besides, who would she possibly run into at 5:55 in the morning?

With wallet in hand, she stepped out into the brisk winter morning. Her breath billowed in white puffs, and she bundled deep in her heavy parka as she made her way up Columbus Avenue to Seventy-second Street. The streets were empty except for the occasional taxicab drifting through the early morning hours, some lingering at corners like bright yellow prostitutes looking for a fare.

A bleary-eyed teenager wearing a green Krispy Kreme apron and paper hat was just opening the doors, the red "Hot" light glowing at one minute after six when Grace arrived. Tall stacks of white rectangular boxes with green decoration and red highlights stood up against the walls, ready to be delivered to hotels and shops for morning customers around town.

Grace looked into the curved glass case at the rows of doughnuts and wondered how she could possibly get just one. Now that she had to watch her pennies, everyone knew it was more cost-effective to buy a dozen rather than simply one. So a dozen it was, and she ate two hot, melt-in-your-mouth glazed on the way home.

Fifteen minutes after starting out, Grace banged back into the relative warmth of the brownstone foyer, her cheeks stinging from the cold. She hadn't seen a soul. But just as she got to the first floor, her luck ran dry as Jack's door opened. She didn't have a chance to mutter about rotten misfortune or even think about how she looked, because it wasn't Jack who appeared.

Grace nearly choked on her third doughnut when she came face-to-face with a woman, a really young woman—the word *nymphette* came to mind—with full breasts that were barely covered by a dress better suited for an evening out than an early morning jaunt. It didn't take a brain surgeon to figure out that she had slept there overnight, though Grace doubted much sleeping had been involved.

Even given that, Grace noted the woman looked a zillion times better than she did. But Grace was too surprised . . . upset . . . jealous—surely not—to be embarrassed.

"Can I help you?" the woman asked tartly when Grace did little more than stare at her, the box of Krispy Kremes hanging open like a mouth agape.

"Ah, no," Grace stammered. "Excuse me."

She stepped past the woman and made for the second flight of stairs. No sooner was her foot on the first step than Jack came out the door, shrugging into an overcoat, his keys jingling in his hands. Every time she had seen him before, he had been wearing jeans. This morning he wore beautiful gray flannel slacks and a crisp white dress shirt with a burgundy tie.

He looked horribly handsome, exceedingly respectable . . . and utterly surprised when he turned around and saw Grace.

She felt a flash of embarrassment when he looked her up and down and raised a brow, a hint of a smile lurking at the corner of his full, ruggedly sensual lips. She refused to think about what those lips had been doing for the last few hours.

"Good morning," he offered.

"Um, yes, well . . . morning. I just went out for doughnuts." Disconcerted, she extended the box. "Would you like one?"

The woman appeared perplexed, and Jack chuckled as he politely declined.

"Alrighty then," she added inanely, wanting to wipe that smug look right off his too-handsome face. "Have a nice day."

She dashed up the remaining flights of stairs, her lungs screaming from lack of oxygen as she fell into her apartment, swearing she was going to learn how to use the fire escape.

"Who was that?" Stacy Middleton asked, the perfect line of her Chanel-red lips pulling into a grimace of distaste.

Jack stared at Grace's retreating back, his smile fading as he heard the door bang closed. "My neighbor."

"Your neighbor looks like a bag lady. I thought this was supposed to be a nice building. I knew you should have bought on the Upper East Side."

Whatever amusement he had felt congealed. "She's had a rough couple of days."

Though why he was defending her he couldn't imagine. A breath hissed through his teeth. Last night his body had burned to take her, only to have her push him away in disgust. Afterward, he had sought out Stacy, had brought her to his apartment as if he had been trying to force Grace from his mind. But every kiss and caress had done nothing to make him forget. Thoughts of Grace had circled. It had made him so crazy that he'd finally jerked away from Stacy, telling her to get dressed while he took a shower.

Whatever it was about Grace that drew him, there was no getting around the fact that she had used him. Twice. Used him to forget. Leaving him with more questions than answers, and a slow burn of heat sliding low at the thought of how tight and hot she was around him when he had pushed deep inside her that first night.

With more force than necessary, he twisted the key in the lock. Stacy linked her arm through his. "Don't tell me Dr. Berenger is feeling doctorly toward his new neighbor. Really Jack, I hardly think she's your type."

She leaned close and pressed her breasts against his arm. Impatience snaked down his spine, and he was never impatient with the women he dated. Bored, yes. Increasingly uninterested in many of them, true. But never impatient.

He took Stacy's arm and guided her down the stairs.

"Jack?" she said, her full lips that had so expertly caressed him only hours ago now pouting. "What's wrong?" She pulled her arm away, her fingers clutching her diaphanous scarf around her hair and neck. "You're not breaking up with me, are you? You can't. No one breaks up with me." Her voice rose with each word she spoke.

"Of course not." He walked to the street and raised his hand for a cab. "I think it's time you break up with me."

"Jack!" she protested and cried, "Don't do this. I love you."

He gently cupped her chin and looked into her eyes. "No, you don't. I've just been a novelty for you. Your phone will be ringing in no time with every single guy in New York wanting a date."

"It never stopped ringing," she stated with an indignant huff.

Jack smiled. "See, you'll never miss a beat. You're beautiful and young, with your whole life ahead of you."

"Oh, Jack—"

He cut her off by pressing a kiss to her forehead. "Don't, Stace. It's over. You know it, and I know it. I'm running late, and you have a photo shoot."

Realizing this wasn't going to turn in her direction, she pulled herself together by the time a taxi pulled to a stop in front of them. She jerked her chin in the air, but just before she slipped inside she looked back, her haughty dignity turning sad.

"If you change your mind," she said, her voice quiet and resigned, "call me."

Jack didn't respond, and as soon as the cab drove away he headed for the hospital.

St. Luke's Hospital stood boxy and utilitarian next to the gothically beautiful Saint John the Divine cathedral. A person didn't have to look far to find the power of God in this neighborhood—in the hospital, where lives were often lost, and in the church, where people offered prayers in hopes of mercy. For Jack, it was a constant battle to beat God at his own game. There were times he wondered if someone was keeping score.

As the chief of trauma, he had a private office with a small changing room and a sofa that folded down into a bed for those times when he was on duty for forty-eight hours straight. After making a quick check of his messages, he pulled on a white hospital coat, then headed for the emergency room just as an ambulance pulled under the portico. Within seconds, medics wheeled in an accident victim, an almost palpable electrically charged intensity surging through the ward as vitals were called out.

"Seventy-year-old male. Minivan rolled over on the West Side Highway. BP sixty over thirty."

He had massive internal injuries, blunt trauma to the head, and multiple lacerations over the body. He wasn't expected to live. But Jack couldn't accept that, never could.

He pulled on latex gloves with a snap. His team worked with smooth efficiency, ventilating the man, itemizing damage. But seconds later, a tech cursed when the patient went into cardiac arrest.

Nurses and techs stood back to give room for resuscitation. The man's pale body lay still, too still, streaked with blood, the spread of blue and black bruising actually halting as his heart stopped beating, blood going still in his veins.

"Paddles," Jack called out as he instantly started chest compressions, the heart monitor screaming its static line.

Fury, rage, and despair hit Jack. No, he whispered silently. No, like a mantra circling in his head.

The paddles were thrust forward. With skill and assurance, Jack took them. "Stand clear."

Forty volts.

"Nothing," a nurse called.

"Sixty!"

They ramped up the machine. No help. The team worked in ordered chaos, doing everything they could, but still nothing. For four long minutes they worked, and for four long minutes the heart monitor refused to give way. The man would die.

The team stood back, feeling the same jarring, ineffectual pain of losing someone. But Jack didn't stop. He resumed chest compressions, determined, like a man obsessed.

Cindy, his head nurse, stepped forward, her gloved hands

streaked with blood, her brow over her face mask furrowed in concern. "Dr. Berenger?"

"Ventilate, Nurse Walker," was his curt response when the anesthetist only stared at him.

The team murmured uncomfortably. Cindy tried to pull him away. "Let him go, Jack."

"No," he bit out, sweat beading on his forehead as he rhythmically compressed the chest.

Suddenly the screaming flat line blipped and beeped, and the man was back.

After that, no one questioned. They worked like the cohesive team they had always been. Over the next long, ticking minutes, they connected the man to life support and got him into an operating room where they removed his spleen, sutured his intestines, and relieved pressure from his skull. When he was stabilized, they wheeled him into intensive care while relatives were found and the orthopedic surgeon arrived to deal with the man's broken bones. He was battered and bloodied beyond recognition. But with any luck, he would survive.

The rest of the shift was much the same, only getting worse when it started to rain. Jack worked fifty-eight hours straight, coming out into the early morning brightness three days later with a bone-deep weariness, to stare at the towering cathedral.

"This time the score went to me," he whispered. Then he shoved his hands into his pockets and started to walk. His normal restlessness was erased by an utter fatigue. When he finally got home, despite the early hour, he fell into bed. But sleep eluded him.

His brain felt wired, and a constant banging coming from upstairs didn't help. He tried to ignore it, but couldn't. Thoughts of Grace raced through his mind.

He crossed his arms over his head, and wondered what he felt.

Obsessed.

He told himself that was too strong of a word. He wasn't obsessed with anything. Never had been. Then why couldn't he get her out of his head?

He didn't even like the woman. She was odd, clearly wild beneath her mousy exterior. On top of it all, she lied. But he still couldn't stop thinking about her.

He was known for his single-minded concentration. But several times during his shift he found his thoughts straying to Grace Colebrook. Those eyes. Her lips, sinfully full in a way that made his body stir to life. And her body. What he had become obsessed with was seeing her naked. He wanted to see what his hands had felt.

His head jerked slightly, and he pulled a deep breath. He wanted nothing to do with Grace Colebrook. He wanted mindless sex with the likes of Stacy Middleton or any of the other women he dated.

Heavy footsteps pounded on the floor above him, then more banging. Rolling out of bed, he muttered an oath. The hardwood beneath his feet felt cool. Stepping into a pair of jeans, he walked downstairs and turned the light on in the kitchen. He pulled open the refrigerator, the light casting golden shadows in the room. He found everything he needed to make a sandwich, piling on meat and cheese until there was nothing left in the packages. He washed it down with an ice-cold beer.

Switching on the big-screen television, he flipped through the stations as he finished the long-neck. But nothing distracted him. It was dark outside and had started to rain again. If it got any colder, it would turn to snow.

He tossed the remote aside with a grunt of disgust, then headed upstairs. He had to get some sleep. But just as he lay down, more clomping footsteps sounded above him, along with the loud flare of music.

Tension and frustration spiked. With a muttered curse about inconsiderate neighbors, he threw on some clothes, slammed out his front door, then took the stairs with grumbling impatience.

He knocked on the door, relentless aggravation sliding through him that he had bought into a building with a neighbor who was driving him insane. When he didn't get an answer, he hammered his fist against the door. This time, the stereo snapped off.

"Come in."

Sure enough, when Jack turned the knob, it was unlocked and he felt his irritation grow. Who in their right mind left their door unlocked in New York City?

The minute he stepped inside, he saw Grace lying on the sofa in a tumble of curling hair and thick blankets. But before he could assimilate the sight, the smell of chocolate hit him—rich and memory-filled, reminding him of younger days, growing up, his mother's voice and laughter filling the kitchen. Then to days not so long ago. Days in Connecticut. Days he wanted to forget.

"Well, well, well, who is this?"

Jack pushed the thoughts aside, then turned away from Grace to find the largest woman he had ever seen standing in the living room. She had bright red hair that had to be fake, and she wore a short black fluttery dress that showed off calves that would have done a fullback proud. Jack's eyes narrowed as he tried to understand.

The woman came forward, and Jack had to force back a grimace of distaste. She was the ugliest female he had ever seen, and when she reached out to shake his hand, her grip was firm and solid. No dainty miss here. But in the next second Jack noticed a distinct five-o'clock shadow. His mind tilted and jarred before it finally registered that this woman was a man.

The drag queen came up to Jack. "My, my, my, aren't you handsome."

Jack tensed, his spine straightening.

Grace scoffed. "Leave him alone, Mark. He's not your type. I don't know much about Jack Berenger, but I do know that you don't stand a chance. My guess is that he goes for the exceedingly youthful, suspiciously dim, and gushingly feminine type. You aren't young, dumb, or female."

Jack's brows slammed together. Mark tsked at Grace, then said to Jack, "I don't know where she gets it. Certainly not from me. I'm very nice and polite."

"Glad to hear it," Jack responded with a tight smile.

"Grace, on the other hand, has been anything but nice and polite for the last few days."

Grace made an exasperated sound. "Excuse me. We seem to have forgotten that I'm still here."

For the first time, Jack noticed that Grace looked awful. Her skin was too pale against the thick blankets. An assortment of half-eaten chocolate bars, Krispy Kremes, kitchen glasses, and a big sprawling book lay out on the coffee table. His thoughts finally focused, and he forgot about being tired.

"Are you all right?" he asked, his voice low with concern. "You look terrible."

"This from a man who is considered a desirable part of the dating pool," she lamented to Mark. "To think people wonder why reasonably intelligent women in New York are still single and looking to chocolate to find satisfaction."

Mark laughed and walked back from the front door into the living room. "At least he asked if you were all right. As much as I'd like to stay, I've got to get downtown by seven."

"Pierre?"

"No, Charles."

"Who is Charles?" she wanted to know.

Mark glanced at Jack as if trying to decide how much he could say. "He's a prominent Wall Street banker. Big name, big bucks, and too cute for words." Mark sighed. "I'll tell you all about him later. For now, I brought you this." He extended a white box tied with a blue ribbon and bow.

Grace perked up. "A present? For me? What is it? Chocolate? You know I adore chocolate."

At the last second, Mark seemed to reconsider the gift. He hesitated and looked at Jack. "How much do you know about Grace's recent . . . streak of misfortune?"

"Mark!"

"I know enough," Jack answered, looking at Grace, remembering how she had turned to him, how she had ended up in his arms. The feel of him slipping hard and deep inside her. Heat flared. She must have noticed and imagined what he was thinking, because a blush raced into her cheeks.

Oblivious to what was going on, Mark handed Grace the box, then looked at Jack. "You have to agree that she can't lie around feeling sorry for herself for the rest of her life. Right?"

"I am not feeling sorry for myself!"

"Whatever you say."

Jack didn't say a word, he only watched Grace.

"Open it," Mark instructed.

As soon as she did, Jack saw her eyes go wide, then something in them darkened, and every thought of sex and heat vanished. Whatever was inside that box upset her.

She pulled out a T-shirt, read the front, then looked up at Mark like a little lost child. "Why?"

"Sorry, I had to do it. It's time you snapped out of this.

You've been moping around eating junk food and watching videos for the last four days."

She dropped the shirt in her lap and Jack saw what it said. MORE FLUFF THAN STUFF.

At the sight of Grace's wide-eyed pain, Jack felt an instant need to drive his fist into this man's face for hurting her.

But if Mark noticed, he didn't care. He marched forward on too-high heels, then dropped down onto his knees in front of her, his shimmery black dress fluttering around his massive thighs. "It's time you got mad, Grace. Don't you dare let that twerp Rodman get the better of you. And if you're mad at me for reminding you, good. Getting mad at me is a start."

He pushed up and headed for the door. He stopped in front of Jack. "Maybe you'll have better luck making sure she gets up. Four days of this funk is long enough."

Mark pulled on a full-length mink that had to have been made especially for him, given the size.

"How many times do I have to tell you I'm not in a funk? I'm just rejuvenating."

Mark rolled his eyes, then left.

Jack hesitated, telling himself to get the hell out of there. Instead, he stepped around the clutter. "From now on, I want you to keep your door locked," he instructed, his voice rumbling with authority. "Anyone could walk in."

"Like drag queens and unwelcome doctors?"

"I was thinking more along the lines of thieves and murderers."

"What would they do? Rob me? Kill me? They might as well," she said with a moan. "At least that way I'd get it over with quick."

"What are you talking about?"

"I'm dying."

"What?" He strode forward.

"Non-Hodgkin's lymphoma."

Jack's head came back. "When were you diagnosed?"

"Late last night."

Had she come to the emergency room and he hadn't known? "Are you sure? What are your symptoms?"

She wrinkled her nose, snuggling deeper in the blankets. "Enlarged but painless lymph nodes, fever and chills, night sweats, fatigue, weight loss—or soon to be weight loss—and no doubt an enlarged spleen."

Automatically, he sat down on the edge of the sofa and placed his hand on her forehead. In the emergency room, actions came to him quickly, automatically. Here in this apartment, with this woman, his mind was slow to make sense of her words. "You don't feel feverish."

"Well," she said with a snort, "feel these lymph nodes."

He moved the blanket aside, having to gently tug the edges from her grip, then ran his hands expertly around her jaw, down her neck to her shoulders. He started to lift her sweater, the tips of his fingers grazing her skin.

Grace gasped, then slapped his hands away, heat burning her cheeks—though a heat born of embarrassment rather than from a fever caused by the fatal disease she felt certain she had. "What are you doing?" she demanded.

His hip pressed against hers beneath the thick blankets, making her feel weak at the knees, her heart fluttering erratically. Yet another sign that she was dying, she told herself firmly.

"I'm going to examine you, Grace."

"Examine me?" she squeaked, her eyes going wide. "Like, like . . . *examine* me?"

"Grace, that's what I do."

"Examine my neck! Go back. Feel those lymph nodes.

They're gigantic." She swallowed hard, the feel of his fingers gently circling on her skin under her jaw, making her mouth go dry. "I can hardly get another bite down my throat for how swollen they are."

He narrowed his gaze as he felt the nodes in her neck with a determined professionalism. "They feel normal." He looked at her like a stern parent. "Grace, let me check the rest of your lymph nodes."

"Under my top?" she asked, wrinkling her nose.

"I won't look—will that make you feel better?"

Resigning herself, she lay back and closed her eyes. "All right, go ahead, do what you have to do."

"This isn't an execution," he said dryly.

But she hardly heard. Her skin tingled at his nearness, every one of her senses aware. His touch was warm as his hand skimmed beneath her sweater, and too late she remembered she wasn't wearing a bra. Her breath grew shallow as he pressed the nodes at the juncture of her arm and shoulder, circling down toward her breast, the heel of his palm grazing against her nipple.

She bit her lip to keep from exhaling in a rush of pent-up breath, and thankfully if he felt the taut bud that formed, he didn't mention it.

Then the other side. The same circling motion, the same palm grazing against her breast until she forgot exactly what she had thought was wrong with her.

When he was done, he sat back and looked confused. "Who diagnosed you?"

For the first time, she felt a bit sheepish.

"You didn't go to some quack in Chinatown, did you?" he asked, his voice filled with censure. "I'm all for alternative forms of healing—as long as the healer isn't some Chinese mechanic posing as a doctor with a fake diploma hanging on his wall."

"No, I didn't go to Chinatown. Or the hospital. I didn't need to." She pointed to the book on the coffee table.

He flipped the massive tome closed on his finger to get a better glimpse at the cover. *Mayo Clinic Family Health Book.* He flipped it back open and found she'd had it turned to "Non-Hodgkin's Lymphoma: Symptoms, Diagnosis, Treatments, Cures." Understanding came clear. "You diagnosed yourself?"

"You don't have to be a genius to read."

"Good thing not everyone knows about this book, or I'd be out of a job," he said, his lips tilting in a wry smile.

"A sixth grader could have diagnosed this one. The lymph nodes," she said with a tone of *isn't it obvious.* "On top of that, I was burning up. Then the instant the covers were off, I was freezing. Add to that, I'm exhausted. Utterly spent." Her face creased in consideration. "Granted, it's hard to tell about the spleen, since I'm not exactly sure where it is, but I bet it's huge, based on how horrible I feel. I can't believe you aren't taking me seriously."

Pushing aside plates, glasses, and half-wrapped Ding Dongs, he swiveled around until he sat on the table facing her. "Grace, you have listed the symptoms for a whole host of conditions." He glanced at the mess of wrappers and junk food. "You could be suffering from many things. Talk to me about the weight loss. Have you lost significant weight in a short period of time?"

He asked the question at the same time that he reached over and wiped a chocolate smear off her cheek.

"Well," she said with a sniff, "no." Then she groaned. "But I have never felt so bad in all my life! I watched *Love Story* last night, and oh dear Lord, what a horrible way to go. But at least Ali MacGraw had Ryan O'Neal to take care of her. God, the way he swept her up in his arms and carried her to the hospital, then came out and told his schmucky dad that love meant never having to say you're sorry." She dropped her head back against the cushion. "I've never seen anything so sad as watching Jenny die of Non-Hodgkin's lymphoma."

"I thought it was leukemia."

She lay there for a second, as if absorbing this information, before her eyes popped opened. "Actually, they weren't all that specific. But we share the same symptoms. And mercy, the misery she endured. The love she lost."

"I seriously doubt you have any form of cancer. It couldn't be that you've made yourself sick on junk food and massive amounts of sugar, could it?"

"Well," she mused, "I have had a thing or two in the last couple of days." Her lips pursed as she considered, then glanced one last time at the Mayo Clinic guide. "It's true. And the flu has been going around, which could explain the nausea." She didn't seem entirely convinced.

But he gave the information little thought as something else hit him square in the chest. Tension raced through him. "When was your last menstrual cycle?"

She blinked. "Eek!" she screeched, her eyes going wide. "What kind of question is that?"

"A pertinent question. Grace, could you be pregnant?"

"Pregnant?" Her mouth fell open.

His brow furrowed. "We did have sex," he said. "Have you had your period since we had relations?"

He saw the words sink in, saw a sudden startled yearning fill her eyes.

"A child," she whispered. "A baby of my own." She pressed her eyes closed for half a second, then she snapped out of it and looked at him. "No, I started . . . I had . . . I am not pregnant. But you don't have to look so relieved."

"Of course, I'm relieved. Other than on a carnal level, as

you yourself pointed out, we hardly know each other. More-over, I'm not interested in marriage or children."

"You sound like a carefree single guy. It's really hard to take, you know. A man of your age unwilling to shoulder the commitment and responsibility of a wife and children. It's because of men like you that women like me are out there unable to marry. Pretty pathetic, if you ask me," she scoffed. "Not that I would want to be your wife, or have your kids. Or, for that matter, wish it on anyone else."

If she had been looking closer she would have noticed the storm that started to brew on his features. But she wasn't. She barreled on, mindless of his mood.

"I just don't get it," she stated, gathering up the assort-ment of junk food wrappers and dishes from the coffee table. "What is it with you men that makes commitment such a problem?"

Jack didn't respond, and Grace finally looked at him closely. Concern rushed through her. "Jack, what is it? Hey, I'm sorry. My mouth was running amok. It's not a crime if you don't want to marry. Really. Stay single and unattached for the rest of your life. In this day and age, who can blame you?"

"You're wrong. I was married."

Chapter
Eight

Boston, Massachusetts—Years Earlier

Marsha Graham strode into her small house in Brookline Village, one T stop away from Harvard Medical School. Jack looked up from his textbook and yet again marveled that he would spend the rest of his life with this woman.

They had met when Jack was a junior at Harvard University, which stood proudly across the Charles River in Cambridge. She had been a freshman. They had dated ever since, the rich daddy's girl from Connecticut and the street-smart, rough-around-the-edges scholarship kid from Brooklyn. They were a storybook couple, Marsha with her white-blond hair and green eyes, Jack with his rugged darkness.

But theirs wasn't a thwarted love. Marsha's family loved Jack, and after she graduated a year early, they bought her the house in Brookline Village and found her a job teaching elementary school so she could be closer to Jack when he started attending Harvard Medical School.

Jack closed the thick medical tome and leaned back on the flowery sofa in Marsha's house. He had his own room in a run-down triplex in Jamaica Plains that the owner had converted into apartments for students. But music blared at all hours, and when Jack wasn't in class or the library, he spent much of his time at Marsha's.

Marsha set her handbag down next to her planning schedule from her job teaching first grade.

"Hey," Jack said, tossing the book aside.

He stood and stretched, then followed her into the kitchen, where she washed her hands at the sink. He stuck his head in the refrigerator and pulled out a carton of milk and some sandwich meat.

"How'd it go today?" he asked.

He started stacking ham and cheese on bread, and he had just started to search out the mustard when he realized she hadn't said a word. When he looked up she was standing in the same spot, the water still running, with tears streaking down her cheeks.

"Hey, what's wrong?"

"Everything's wrong." She buried her face in her hands and started to cry.

Crying girls had never been Jack's strong suit. His mother had been a picture of strength, and everyone else in his family was male. While he had done his share of dating, he had never allowed himself to get close enough to anyone to ever see them cry. He had sworn long ago that he wouldn't be distracted in his quest to become a doctor. Marsha had been his first and only detour.

"How can everything be wrong?" he asked gently, coming up behind her, turning off the water, then turning her around to face him.

"Mary Hamilton is getting married."

Jack stared at her for a few long seconds as he tried to figure out what that could mean. Marsha frequently started crying more when he asked seemingly reasonable questions. He wondered if she had said something about Mary Hamilton before that he should have paid attention to.

No doubt that at times talking to Marsha was as precarious as walking through a field of land mines. Hard to know when one was going to blow up in his face.

"Is there a problem with Mary Hamilton getting married? Does that increase your class load?"

"Ahhhhgghhh!"

Wrong question.

Marsha didn't say any more. She stormed out and raced to her bedroom. Jack's inclination was to head back to the apartment house. Blaring stereos were more appealing than a crying woman. But he had dated Marsha long enough to know that to leave now would only make it worse—not to mention drag it out longer. If he left, not only would she be upset over the Mary misstep, but then she'd add the "you don't care about me" routine. He had finals coming up, and the last thing he needed was Marsha wigging out on him.

With not a little reluctance, he headed down the hall to her bedroom. The door wasn't shut all the way, which was typical. Not opened; not closed and locked as if she really wanted him to keep the hell away from her.

One time after everything had finally settled down, he had mentioned this trend to Marsha. He'd never do that again. Her crying jag had started all over again.

"Hey, do you want to talk?" he asked, coming over and sitting on the bed next to her.

"No," was her muffled reply as she cried into her pillow.

Not for the first time, Jack wished Marsha was more like his mother had been. When something bothered her, she had always spoken her mind, clearly, distinctly. No one in the Berenger household had to guess.

Meeting Marsha three years ago had been like meeting someone from a different country, just as moving from

Brooklyn to Cambridge, Massachusetts, had been a whole new world. Rarified and intriguing.

He stroked her hair. "Come on, tell me what happened."

The fact was he hated to see her upset. He cared for Marsha, felt a nice, safe, gentle love that he had never experienced growing up on the streets of New York. God, how he had loved *Saturday Night Fever*. Vinnie's fight to survive the insanity of a harsh urban life to be something more than a street punk had been his own dream.

Thick gray clouds let little light into the sky, the sound of rain dripping on the thick bushes outside filling the room. Marsha's tears started to taper off as he curled a long tendril of hair behind her ear, and she rolled over.

"Mary came into the teachers' lounge this morning and showed everyone the engagement ring Richard got her. He asked her to marry him Friday night."

The tears started to well again.

"I'm the only one left! I'm the only teacher at school who isn't either married or engaged. I'm twenty years old and I'm going to be an old maid."

He swallowed back the urge to chuckle. "Twenty is hardly old."

"Age doesn't matter!" she railed. "We've been dating since my freshman year in college, Jack. I cook for you, I help you study, my parents adore you. I love you! What are you waiting for?"

Whatever sense of humor had circled in his head seconds ago went up in smoke.

"Don't you love me, Jack?" she pressed. "Don't you want to marry me?"

"Marsha, we've been over this, and we've decided we should wait until I have at least finished med school."

"You decided! I didn't get a chance to say a word."

Pulling back, Jack stood up from the bed, raking his hands through his hair.

"There you go, pulling away from me. It's always the same. Every time I talk about my life, you pull away."

"That's not true. But the fact is, I have two and a half more years of med school, and if I don't graduate at the head of my class, I'll never get into any of the top residency programs. I have to stay focused, Marsha. I thought you understood that."

"Of course I do. But why can't you go to school and be married to me at the same time?"

"Because I can't afford a wife!" He calmed himself with effort. "Marsha, you know I have responsibilities to my brother. I don't have money to support a wife. I'd have to get a full-time job. As it is, I barely have time to sleep between studying and my night shift at the hospital."

Marsha grimaced with distaste. "I still can't believe you took a job as a janitor."

"Not everyone has the kind of money you do," he said tightly.

"I just don't get why you won't let me support us."

His jaw muscles ticked. "I will not be kept by a woman."

"Good grief, Jack. I won't be keeping you. I'll be doing what hundreds of wives have done through the centuries. I'll support us until you become a doctor." She got up and came over to him, taking his arm and leaning close. "Then, once you are the wonderfully successful doctor you are going to be, I'll become the perfect country club wife, lunching with friends, taking care of our children. It will be wonderful. It's everything both of us want."

He didn't move or say a word. Finally, Marsha sighed and moved away.

"I'm not going to wait forever, Jack. I love you, but I'm ready to get married now. Not later."

She left the room and went back to the kitchen. Jack leaned up against the windowsill and stared out into the rain-drenched yard. He did want to marry her, did want the life she had painted for him during the years they had been dating. A wife and children and a quaint Connecticut town was as foreign as it was appealing. Who better than Marsha to share it with?

Two weeks after his second year of medical school, Jack married Marsha in a small ceremony in Greenwich, Connecticut, with his brother and her family circling around. His only regret was that his own parents hadn't lived long enough to see him married.

Jack took a deep breath, almost afraid to trust in his good fortune. His dreams of a new life were coming true. He knew they were meant to be happy.

When he moved his belongings out of the run-down apartment and into Marsha's little house, he couldn't imagine anything could go wrong.

Chapter
Nine

"You were married," Grace said, stunned.

He didn't respond. He stood at the window looking out into the stormy night.

She shook herself. "I can't imagine why I'm surprised. I shouldn't be. I just never thought. I didn't think." She threw her arms in the air. "Of course you would have been married." Her spine straightened as a thought occurred to her. "You aren't still, are you?"

"No," he said, his voice clipped.

"Good." She cringed. "I mean, not good as in *that's great*, but good that I didn't have to add adultery to my list of sins. The fact is you're smart, handsome, you have a job." And while all indications were that he shared her father's predilection for a long line of women at his beck and call, even her father had been married—more than once. But she didn't add that.

What Grace found disconcerting was the reminder of how little she knew about this man. Every time she saw him she felt breathless at the thought that this powerful stranger knew her so intimately. She was more aware of every glance, every flick of his finger. Every brush of his body, whether accidental or not, made every cell of her body come alive with awareness. But she hadn't even known something as essential as the fact that he had been married.

Then there were those few seconds when she had thought of the possibility of being pregnant. The amazement that the one thing she wanted more than any other in the world could come true—only to be dashed in the next second by the reality that she'd had her period. In a short space of time she had experienced an unadulterated elation, followed cruelly by an absurd disappointment.

"How long were you married?" she asked.

He braced his hands against the casing. "Sixteen years."

"Oh, my gosh!" No six-month mistake, no seven-year itch. This was serious. She wasn't sure what she felt, or what she should feel. Not that she should feel anything, she told herself firmly. He was simply a neighbor, albeit an intimate neighbor, she groaned silently. "What happened? Are you divorced, or, oh God, is she—"

"We divorced."

She could see only his silhouette, which appeared like cold, hard stone. No emotion, no glimpse of what he was feeling about having been married to a woman for so long.

"Did you love her?" she couldn't help herself from asking.

Sharply, he turned away from the window. "I've got to get to bed. I've been up for three days straight."

"Just like that? You drop the whole marriage bomb on me, then you say you've got to go?"

He stopped midway to the door and looked at her, his countenance as stormy as the sky outside. "My past is none of your concern."

After that, he left. She stood there staring at the closed door, then called out, "That isn't fair!"

But he didn't return. Not that she expected him to.

She knew him in the intimate sense, but she knew virtually nothing about the man himself—other than the fact that she had seen enough to know that he had bad news written all over him. She might have had sex with him, but she would not turn into one of those women who dropped everything whenever he deigned to glance her way. Getting attached to that kind of man spelled nothing but heartache.

Her miserable mood turned grim, and she muttered about too many willing women in the world, then swore to herself that she would never have sex with him again. Ever. No kissing, no touching, not even any accidental brush up against him. No matter what.

The following day, after Grace had sworn off irresponsible behavior once and for all, she knew it was high time she started returning the wedding gifts. She also needed to start looking for a job. But first she needed a résumé.

With Simon and Garfunkel playing in the background, she began to list her accomplishments. Kendrick Toys' Very High Potential list every year that she had been employed. Outstanding Innovation Award three years in a row. Then there was her most prized achievement. Toy Creator of the Year. She had come up with Girlfriends' Feathered Mules, which every little girl under the age of twelve had to have.

When she sat back and looked at her list, even she was a tad impressed. But her pride turned to frustration at the memory of how utterly unfair it was that she had been fired. Frustration, however, wouldn't do any good. Only hard work and determination would. She was going to turn lemons into lemonade. She would find the silver lining. She would send out her résumé, start a health regime, and put together a budget. She'd go to Fairway Market, fill her refrigerator full of carrots and alfalfa sprouts, and join a gym. No clogged arteries or thighs ballooning to the size of California redwoods with the consistency of cottage cheese for her.

Over the next several hours, Grace dutifully made up a list of toy companies in New York, printed off a résumé for each one, wrote up cover letters, and had the entire batch mailed off before the end of the day.

But by the time she returned from the post office, her heart started a slow, steady beat of anxiety. What if none of the companies responded? What if she never got another job again, she despaired, her mind following suit in an out-of-control spiral. And when she glanced at the last slice of homemade pineapple upside-down cake with plenty of gooey brown sugar and sugared pineapples on top, she decided it would be a shame if it went to waste. The alfalfa sprouts could wait another day.

It was as she finished the last bite that she had the brilliant idea to throw a dinner party. What better way to keep her mind off her predicament than to share an evening with friends? While she was more of a baker than a cook, she couldn't imagine it could be that difficult.

Now, who to have to her party?

Jack Berenger.

The thought leaped out of her, and just as quickly she scratched it off her mental list.

Mark undoubtedly had a new love interest he would want to bring. She would include some of her old friends from her days at Columbia University. Her party would be a smash. Between the party planning and the massive dose of sugar, she felt the anxiety recede and a welcome bead of hope rise in its place.

First thing the next morning, the telephone rang. Out of habit, she almost didn't answer. But since she was moving on with her life, she really had to start picking up the phone.

"Grace! There you are."

Her mother's voice trilled across the line.

"Hello, Mother."

Roberta Colebrook was a beautiful woman, all soft curves and demure colors. Sometimes Grace wondered how she had sprung from the woman's loins. Roberta was pale-skinned and blond, just like Suzanne. They were light to Grace's dark, demure to Grace's boldness—but only when it came to exteriors. If someone scratched beneath the crystalline surface, they would find Roberta's ravenous need for attention, pursuing it like a shimmering phoenix rising from the ashes. Grace was the opposite, shuddering away from anything too intense—that is, until she had walked out on her wedding, then stepped into Jack Berenger's arms.

"It's high time you started picking up," her mother admonished. "It has been extremely annoying. A week without a word from you. For all I knew, you were lying there dead."

"If you were that worried, you have a key. You could have come over."

"Yes, well." She sniffed. "I've been frightfully busy."

"Hosting another charity luncheon?"

"Actually, no. It's your father."

Concern flared. "Is something wrong with Daddy?"

"Pshaw. Nothing out of the ordinary. He's still hard-headed and unable to resist anything in a skirt."

"Did Jeanette agree to the divorce?"

"Of course not. And poor, sweet Willow has given up on him."

"Poor, sweet Willow? Last time we talked, you called her a tree who'd had more than her share of dogs leaving their mark."

"Really, Grace. I would never use such language.

Though that newest hussy your father is seeing—Betty, I think she's called—is even worse."

"Daddy's seeing someone new?"

"Yes." Roberta sighed dramatically. "Of course she has loads of fake blond hair, and breasts that spill out of her dresses like she's a common harlot. What he sees in these women, I'll never know."

It didn't escape Grace's notice that her mother had fake—albeit very expensively done—blond hair, and no one would scoff at the size of her breasts. Clearly Calder Colebrook liked a certain kind of woman. Had it been anyone besides her adored father, she would have lamented such predictability.

"Where did you see him?" Grace asked.

"At his apartment."

"You went over there?"

"No." Roberta cleared her throated delicately. "I just happened to pass by and I saw him outside fawning over the woman like a fifteen-year-old schoolboy. You'd think he'd have the decency to go inside."

"What did he say when he saw you?"

"He didn't actually see me."

"Were you spying on him again?"

"Absolutely not. There was traffic on Fifth Avenue, so I had the driver take a detour. We got stuck just down from his building. But that isn't why I called. I heard you lost your job."

Grace fell back into the desk chair with a silent groan. "How?"

"I was at Lettie Nichols's apartment yesterday, and she had just spoken with Kathy Maynard, who is best friends with Joy Kendrick."

"Faster than a speeding bullet."

"Really, Grace. You should have told me. You can't

imagine how mortifying it is to have to hear such news about your very own daughter from the likes of Lettie Nichols."

"I'm sorry, Mother."

"As well you should be. To make it up to me, why don't you give Walter a call?"

"Walter! How can you ask that? I found him doing . . . having . . . with another woman. Good God, it was Suzanne's best friend."

"Don't blame this on Mercy, dear."

"Blame! I'm blaming Walter. You can forget it if you think for one second that I would ever lower myself to call him up and beg him to come back."

"Now, Grace," Roberta reproached. "I'm not suggesting you beg. Just a nice little invitation. Men will be men, you know. Do you really think Walter is any different from the millions of others out there who don't know the first thing about being faithful? The fact is, Walter would make a good provider. A woman can't turn her nose up at that."

"He was not a good provider! He made me pay for half of everything. I'll have you know that he made me pay for *more* than half of everything!"

"Grace, please. Calm down. If I've told you once I've told you a hundred times, a woman in New York needs at least one of three things. A husband, a job, or a trust fund."

Or generous alimony payments, Grace had to force herself not to add.

"Unless I'm mistaken," Roberta continued, "as of last week you don't have a job or a husband." Her voice lowered. "And while your father and I live well, he is only a doctor, not a Wall Street investment banker." The subject was clearly distasteful to her.

"Not to worry, I'm not going to come to you for help.

My savings account will tide me over until I find another job."

"Another job." Roberta sighed. "Would it really be so hard to call Walter?"

"Mother, maybe he is like every other man in America, but I will never forgive him for having sex with another woman at our very own wedding."

"Fine." Roberta drew a deep breath. "Have it your way. I've got to run. But first I wanted to let you know that a man named Donald Lowell, Maizie Lowell's youngest, will be calling you tonight."

"Not another setup! You didn't."

"I did. I'm your mother, and it's my duty to see you properly settled."

"You know your setups have never worked."

"How can you say that? I'm the one who fixed you up with Walter."

"My point, exactly."

"Funny. Now be a good girl and be nice to Donald when he calls. That's the least you can do for your mother."

Roberta always had a way of making Grace feel guilty, and when they hung up, she promised herself that she would be nice to the man, and even invite him to her party, no matter how awful he sounded.

For the next hour, Grace made calls and left messages regarding her little soiree. After that, she went out to run errands, tiptoeing down the stairs, hovering for half a second in front of Jack's door, then cursing herself for doing so, not really taking a deep breath until she got out-side. She wasn't sure how long she could exist like this, sneaking out the door, praying she wouldn't see the man.

Disgruntled, she walked to Tower Records and Videos. After giving the matter some thought, she decided she absolutely could not afford to spend the money to join a gym. A Jane Fonda videotape would have to do.

As soon as she left the store with not one but two videos, she headed to the grocery store. No sense in buying an exercise video and using it on the same day.

At the market she bought an assortment of things that looked good, healthy, and boring. As she was heading home, a bag in hand, her cell phone rang.

"Grace!" Mark cried. "Charles has stood me up."

"What?"

"I'm sitting in the middle of Café Luxembourg this very minute, I've taken the rest of the day off, and I've been stood up. Where are you?"

"I just left Fairway."

"Perfect. Meet me for lunch."

"But I've got groceries."

"No one cares. Just get over here. I've already ordered champagne, and I refuse to look like a fool by having to leave. It's my treat."

"Mark—"

"Please," he pleaded.

She had never been able to turn away a friend in need, and a quick lunch with Mark at the neighborhood restaurant couldn't hurt. In a matter of minutes she was stuffing her grocery bag under the table and ordered her favorite Luxemburger topped with blue cheese and served with crispy golden frites. When the waiter disappeared, Mark poured her a glass of champagne.

"I can't, Mark, really. Especially given the fact that it's barely noon. Besides, I've got a zillion things to do today."

"Just a glass. I can't drink this entire thing by myself."

"Well, maybe just one."

But as he went on about his boyfriend woes, one glass turned into two, and everything took on a rosy glow.

"I got your message about the party," Mark said some-time later. "Saturday is perfect. I'm going to find someone new to bring if it kills me. But enough about me. I have news for you. The rat Jay is having a hell of a time making anything work. He's frantic without you there to steal from. I imagine it won't be long before Cecil figures out his star is imploding."

"Really?" She leaned forward. "What's he doing?"

"Yelling. Who knew he was a screamer? He's panicking. Serves him right."

Grace had never been one to wish ill fortune on anyone. But she couldn't quite get herself to feel sorry for J. Hastings Rodman. He had stolen her idea and her job. A really lower than low part of her hoped he failed. But another part of her hated to think that her Pink Cadillac would go down in flames.

"Grace," Mark mused. "I've been thinking. Why don't you come up with another idea to have waiting in the wings? I bet the minute Jay crashes and burns, Cecil will be crawling back to you. If you have another one of your inspired ideas, you'll be able to write your own ticket. When this is all said and done, you just might be in a stronger position. Maybe even squeeze a little equity out of the old tightwad."

Maybe it was the champagne or maybe it was the crazy week she'd had, but she burst out laughing. "Oh, Mark, ever the optimist. He fired me. The last thing he'll do is turn around and grovel. We both know Cecil Kendrick would rather impale himself on a spike than admit he was wrong."

"We'll see. Listen, I've got to run, doll." The check was paid, and they gathered their things. Outside, they kissed cheeks, then headed off. "I'll see you on Saturday," Mark called back, just before his cab door slammed shut.

Grace walked home, relishing the feel of the crisp blue winter sky, every trace of the last storm gone. Her troubles seemed distant and manageable when she found Marvin and Timmy sitting outside the brownstone, huddled on the front steps wearing mittens and heavy coats made from vibrant colors.

"Hey, Grace! Got any cookies in there?" Marvin wanted to know, pushing up from the stoop.

"Not today," she chimed, tripping on the pavement. "But I've got plenty of Brussels sprouts."

"Brussels sprouts?" Timmy said, incensed. "That's disgusting."

"Yeah, disgusting," Marvin added in an exaggerated way and with great glee, after which both boys had a massive fit of laughter.

Ruffling the boys' hair, she slipped her key in the lock, then pulled open the outer door.

"Maybe you could make some cookies," Timmy suggested. "I bet Dr. Jack would like some a lot."

"He's our friend," Marvin announced proudly.

"He's a doctor, with lots of doctor tools. He lets us listen to our hearts with his thesisthope."

"Yeah, it was neat."

"Yep," Grace muttered, "all a doctor has to do is whip out his *thesisthope* and he has everyone falling all over themselves to be friendly."

"What?" they asked, their faces scrunched up in confusion.

"Nothing, nothing, just talking to myself about how good it is to be friendly," she fudged.

She, of course, wasn't swayed so easily as these boys.

She groaned. No, she was easier. She didn't even need a gift to fall all over the man—or his dining room table, or her floor.

"What are you all red for, Grace?"

"Me? Red? Never."

"Oh, really?"

She whirled around to find Jack in the foyer, his hands in his coat pockets, one dark brow raised in that devilish way he had when he wasn't being ominous.

Jack hadn't seen Grace in two days. He told himself he was glad. But seeing her there, he couldn't deny how she filled his head with contradictory thoughts. All he had to do was see her and the hard-won distance from life he had gained in the last year and a half tried to fade away. He wasn't sure what drew him more, the clear translucence of her skin, or those flashes of wild vulnerability.

It alarmed him that this little slip of a woman could touch such a nerve in him. He wanted to make love to her, but he didn't want anything deeper, with her or with anyone.

He didn't like the way Grace stirred up his thoughts, made him question. Made him feel. He didn't want anything to do with her. Though as often as he told himself that, he knew he was lying. He wanted her physically. He wanted her naked beneath him, moaning with pleasure as he gently rode her, making her wet and slick.

"How long have you been standing there?" she demanded.

He watched as a wariness filled her eyes, and her lips parted. Instantly he wanted to kiss her, cover her mouth with his own. He muttered a curse.

"Long enough to know that my stethoscope isn't going to get anywhere with you."

"Dr. Jack!" The boys clamored around, and when they didn't find any needleless plastic syringes or reflex hammers, they got distracted by a horn blaring down the street.

With little more than a forced smile, Grace tripped, then elbowed past him. She looped her purse over her shoulder, switched the grocery bag into her other hand, then slipped a brass key into the mailbox. Pulling open the tiny door, she peered inside, wrinkled her nose as she fished out a bundle, then slammed it closed. Biting her lower lip in a way that never failed to send heat scorching through his body, she went through the stack with a general air of disregard.

"Trash, trash, trash," she stated, tossing letter after letter into the garbage bin. "Keep," she added, and slipped a copy of *U.S. News & World Report* under her arm. "Trash, trash, trash," she finished with a sigh that Jack read as relief. No bills, he could almost hear her thinking.

When she was done, she headed for the stairs without another word. It was obvious that when she wasn't interested in having sex with him, she wanted to avoid him. Which set him on edge.

Foolishly.

The last thing he needed was to get wrapped up with this woman. But damn it all, her blatant dismissal didn't sit well. She had another think coming if she thought she could use him every time she needed a shoulder to cry on, then treat him like an inconsequential stranger afterward.

He had the momentary thought that he might be guilty of dismissing the women he dated. But he disregarded the thought just as quickly. He treated the women he dated with respect, he never dated more than one at a time, he showered them with gifts, and never made them feel used. He just didn't want to marry them. But he never turned any of them away in disgust when he knew it was time to move on.

Grace had to step past him again in order to get to the stairs. He could tell that she hesitated, as if debating the wisdom of getting so close. He could smell the citrus scent of her hair, a subtle perfume of oranges and lemon, making her smell like sunshine. Even that set him on edge, though the kind of edge that kicked like fire through his veins.

The boys had run off down the block, leaving them alone in the tiny foyer.

"Excuse me, you're in my way," she stated.

When he didn't move, her red lips parted. Just when he started to damn it all and touch her, she surprised him by bursting out in a fit of giggles. With the laughter came the distinct smell of alcohol on her breath. For the first time he noticed the blush on her cheeks, and when his eyes narrowed, she seemed to understand. With another giggle and a hiccup, she slapped her hand over her mouth.

"You've been drinking," he stated.

"Maybe just a teensy bit."

"It's barely two in the afternoon."

"I'm impressed, you can tell time." She thought that was really funny, and she had to grab the banister to keep from falling. "What's your point?"

What *was* his point, he wondered, other than the fact that every time he turned around this woman exhibited some new, less than stellar trait.

As if reading his thoughts, Grace's laughter cut off. She pulled herself together and shot him a sharp scowl. "There is a saying about men like you."

"Which is?" he asked ominously.

"It has to do with stuffed shirts, grim personalities," she said, then she bit her lip and fought to suppress a smile that told him he wasn't going to like what she said next, "and stiff spines like prim schoolteachers."

Jack felt a growl rumble in his chest. Grace only smiled wider before her blue eyes glowed with a mixture of amusement and contrition.

"Ahhh, you're insulted."

His shoulders tensed. "I am not."

"Yes, you are," she teased, twirling around, her grocery bag banging into his hip. "How cute. But don't feel bad," she persisted, her tone mock serious. "I know lots of guys who are stuffy. Okay, so maybe not," she amended. "You win the prize."

His jaw cemented.

"Now, now, don't get your Fruit of the Looms in a twist."

He wondered if he could get away with strangling her. If not, would prison be so bad? Hell, it couldn't be much worse than living in the same building with her.

"Okay, I'm sorry," she added. "To prove it, I hereby officially invite you to my dinner party. Saturday night, eight o'clock. Do you feel better?"

"I never felt bad."

"Whatever it takes to help you sleep at night." She slipped by, treading clumsily on his feet, then made it up the first flight of stairs with only one minor stumble and a few more giggles before she looked back. "It will be fun. A few friends, along with the latest man my mother wants me to go out with." She leaned over the banister and whispered loudly, "Roberta Colebrook is determined to marry me off yet."

Jack felt a sizzle of something snake down his spine at the thought. Disbelief, he told himself.

"If nothing else, you'll get a free meal—I do eat things besides Krispy Kremes and cookie dough. Plus, then the noise from the party won't be a problem."

She didn't wait for his answer. She pushed away and swung around the corner to the second flight of stairs, then disappeared.

Jack stood in the foyer, staring without seeing, the sound of her steps growing more distant until they ceased behind her slamming apartment door. He didn't move for a long time before he shook his head and reassured himself that there was no way in hell he'd go to a party given by Grace Colebrook.

Chapter
Ten

Jack muttered a curse when not two days later he stood at Grace's door, a box of chocolates in hand. To make matters worse, he stood there with his brother and his brother's fiancée, Nadine.

Earlier, in a determined effort to keep Grace and her banging party preparations out of his mind, he had left the apartment, telling himself to go to the hospital. But with the inevitability of the moon pulling at the tides, he had stopped and bought the candy. For Grace. Her favorite, chocolate, as if making up for the chocolate she hadn't gotten from Mark that horrible day.

Cursing himself for a fool, Jack had returned to the brownstone and took a quick shower, unable to stay away from the woman who lived above him, dancing in his dreams, her clicking footsteps holding the promise of something he told himself he didn't want.

But as soon as he pulled his door open, the buzzer rang. From the landing he looked straight down the stairs and could see his brother with his girlfriend through the glass insert in the door. He understood immediately that Hugh was there so that Jack and his fiancée could forge a friendship. Hugh had always needed his approval.

"Jack, you remember Nadine," Hugh said as soon as they were buzzed in.

"Of course, Nadine. It's good to see you. I understand congratulations are in order."

"Thank you, Jack. I promise to make your brother the best wife possible."

Jack saw the pride that flashed in Hugh's eyes. Jack loved his brother, and if this woman made him happy, who was he to say differently.

"I thought we'd see if you wanted to join us at Pomodoro for dinner." Hugh glanced at the gift box. "Were you coming or going?"

"Going. To a party upstairs." Loud music filtered down into the foyer, and all three of them looked up to the heights. "But I'd rather see you. Pomodoro's sounds great."

"Whose party?" Hugh asked.

"My neighbor's."

"From the sounds of it, I doubt your neighbor would mind an extra body or two. We'll go with you."

Jack's brow furrowed. "I can't imagine why you would want to go to a party of someone you don't even know."

"That's easy, Jackie boy," the younger brother said. "I want to see who is drawing the elusive Jack Berenger to a party."

When Hugh took Nadine's arm and started heading upstairs, Jack had little choice but to follow.

Now, standing in front of Grace's door, Jack could hear the voices that echoed inside, overloud laughter, and footsteps on hardwood. More than ever he regretted his decision to attend. Especially with Hugh and Nadine at his side.

No one heard his knock because of the noise. Hugh raised a brow and smiled. "Jack, what kind of friends are you hanging out with these days?"

"This is crazy. Let's go," Jack commanded.

He would leave, there was still time. He had never said he would go. But somehow he couldn't turn away, not even with Hugh looking at him with a speculative gleam, or Nadine's thick, simmering boredom.

Cursing his stupidity, he banged again, and when still no one answered, he turned the knob and entered.

As if sensing someone's arrival, the partygoers turned to the door.

"Well, well, well, look who we have here."

Jack recognized Grace's cross-dressing friend, and forced himself not to grimace.

"Well, well, indeed," Hugh remarked.

Nadine's boredom evaporated, and her smile grew sly and knowing as she looked Mark up and down. "No wonder you didn't want us to join you, Jack. Trying to keep your new *girlfriend* a secret, huh?"

Mark strolled forward wearing a short, silk chiffon dress that was relatively demure compared with the last outfit Jack saw him wearing.

Looking around, Jack saw an assortment of people, two who had to be cross-dressers, talking with a voluptuous woman who couldn't be a man unless she'd had surgery. There were two other women, plus one man who stood near the window looking extremely out of place among this ragtag group of flamboyant people in his argyle sweater, button-down shirt, and cuffed pants. He held a drink that looked like orange juice, with the faint shape of a cherry settled in the bottom.

"Jack, isn't it?" Mark asked.

"Yes, Jack Berenger."

"I'm Mark, remember, and this is my friend, Daniel. Dani, come meet Grace's new neighbor."

Introductions were made, before the woman came over, circling around Jack, making him feel like a trapped bear, a scowl breaking out on his face. Hugh and Nadine looked amused.

"Now this is the brother I know and love," Hugh quipped.

"Where's Grace?" Jack asked.

Mark laughed, then shooed everyone away. "She's in the kitchen cooking. I hope." He didn't look optimistic.

Hugh and Nadine waited in the living room, while Mark made them drinks.

Jack headed for the kitchen, where sure enough he found Grace. Her hair was pulled up in a twist, though strands were already escaping, and she had smudges of who knew what all over her face and apron. She bent over a cookbook, her brow furrowed in fierce concentration.

What surprised him the most was her outfit. Gone was the sensible tweed. She wore bright orange pants that molded to her hips, a red Lycra top that fit like a second skin, the scooped neck lined with slightly varying shades of red and orange tiny down feathers. She looked both outrageous and stunningly provocative all at once, and Jack felt the urge to throw a raincoat over her, or add the table mess to the mess on the floor and take her right there.

"I heard you were in here cooking," he said, not understanding the churn of emotion that hit him the minute he saw her. Desire? No, disgust. But he couldn't quite make himself believe it.

As soon as the thought sliced through his brain, his brow creased. Was it possible that his feelings toward her were changing?

Her head jerked up. For half a second, his brain registered the pleasure on her face at the sight of him.

"Jack, you came!"

She held a spoon in her hands, filled with a creamy chocolate icing. A cake stood to the side, just iced, the chocolate swirling in peaks and valleys. But it seemed the cake was the only thing in the room that was finished.

He came forward, extending the box.

"A present! For me!" She pulled off the bow and opened the top. "Chocolate!" Her eyes glowed. "Thank you, Jack."

"My brother insisted."

"That you bring a gift?" she asked, confused.

"That I come at all," he found himself saying, unwilling to admit how he hadn't been able to stay away.

"Ah, of course. I knew there had to be some extenuating circumstance that would bring you here," she said with amusement. "I'll have to meet this brother of yours." Before he could reply, she added, "Be a sport and put the box in the cabinet," then she went back to her recipe. If she felt anything besides a mild burst of pleasure at the sight of him, she kept it well hidden. "Dinner will be ready in no time."

Oddly disgruntled, Jack glanced around the kitchen. It was hard to believe that dinner would be ready anytime before next week.

He took in the pans that were everywhere, the staggering mess on the countertops, and flour on the floor. No wonder Mark hadn't looked optimistic.

A harsh edginess settled over him, and he didn't want to be there, not with Grace, not with the miscreants out in the living room. He suddenly hated that his brother was seeing all of this. He didn't belong here.

Without warning, he thought of the past in Connecticut. Of his life there. The perfect life. If only his mother had lived long enough to see that he had met her expectations. Respectable. Responsible.

Memory surged in his mind, of his parents in their third-floor walk-up in Brooklyn. The neighbors fighting upstairs. Then his father, taking his mother in his arms, dancing her around the cramped kitchen. And laughter. His mother laughing, his father nuzzling her cheek.

Then another memory. Years later.

Come on, Jack. Stop kidding around.

His wife's voice, looming in his head, startling him. Then his own laughter, taking his wife's hands, dancing her around the kitchen. Neat as a pin, even her apron pressed.

Come on, Marsha, have a little fun.

Her lips had pursed, her feelings hurt. It had always been a bone of contention between them. The veneer of perfection she needed in her life. Her refusal to let anyone know that he came from a tenement building in Brooklyn.

"Do you like it?"

Jack focused, and was momentarily startled at the sight of Grace, one downy feather sticking to the fullness of her lower lip.

His heart raced, and he felt buffeted by conflicting emotions. The desire to brush the feather away, and a startling picture of his life before that contrasted with what he had created in his head. Memories of his parents. Memories of Marsha. Guilt that he would feel anything other than love and respect for the woman he had once married.

He was tired, he told himself, and Grace consistently turned his thoughts upside down.

"Do I like what?" he asked in confusion. "The cake?"

"No, my new outfit. I got it in the Village at a place called Cool Clothes for Cheap. Mark insisted it was fabulous." She looked doubtful. "Do you think it's too much?"

He remembered wanting to take her on the flour-covered floor the minute he saw her. Followed by another thought of Marsha, memories of her despairing because her dinner was ruined, with only a cake standing ready. He had laughed, and twirled her around the room again. *Why don't you put on something wild and fun, then let them all eat cake,* he had whispered, his voice deep and rumbling against her ear.

But she had slapped him away, her tears turning to sobs. *Stop thinking about sex! We are having a dinner party, for God's sake, with twenty guests who will be here any minute. My first dinner party and it's ruined. Stop thinking of yourself.*

His thoughts grew grim, and he tried to pull his mind to safer grounds. Grace stared at him, as if staring at an exhibit in a zoo, absently reaching up and flicking the feather from her mouth. She didn't seem upset, she didn't seem worried, only curious about what he could be thinking.

He remembered her saying that she recognized him. Was this what she was talking about? This darkness that he felt, but wouldn't give in to? He hadn't given in to it. He had set it aside, leaving Connecticut, returning to New York, making a new life as a trauma physician. He didn't think, he didn't remember, he was too busy for that, and when he had time alone, his mind was too exhausted from the long hours at the hospital to do anything but crash into oblivion. It was oblivion that he wanted, oblivion that he sought.

But for reasons he didn't understand, Grace Colebrook made him remember.

He started to leave her apartment and never look back. He would not let this woman disrupt what he had fought hard to create. But he hadn't gotten farther than the kitchen door when his brother entered with Nadine at his side.

"So this is your new neighbor," Nadine said, her voice silky smooth.

Grace seemed to freeze at the tone of Nadine's voice; Hugh looked surprised. Nadine's green eyes smirked at the sight of such a mess.

Nadine strolled forward with her elegant attire and perfectly done hair. But before she could say a word, Hugh stepped in front of her and took Grace's hand. "You are a vision," he said, then as grand as any Frenchman, he kissed her knuckles. "Umm, chocolate," he added. "Delicious."

Jack was sure that he saw a flash of embarrassment in Grace's eyes, before it was gone and she laughed, wiping her hand on a towel. "It's a new recipe. I'm glad to hear that it turned out all right. Now tell me, who are you?"

"Beautiful, charming, and direct," Hugh clarified. "I am the younger and more desirable Berenger brother. No wonder Jack was trying to hide you from us."

"Hugh," Jack stated coldly.

Grace gave him a wicked look before turning to Hugh. "If he could help it, I'm sure your brother would just as soon have me move out altogether. I'm not his favorite neighbor. He told me that you insisted he come."

Hugh tsked. "Now, big brother. Shame on you. We found him on his way up here all on his own."

Raising a brow, she faced Jack. "Isn't that a surprise?"

"Yes, I'd say it is," Nadine interjected through clenched teeth. "She's so . . . different from the rest of the women you see."

"Don't mind her, Grace," Hugh said, pulling Nadine close to his side. "She's just a little put out because the only thing she knows about cooking is how to read a delivery menu and how to dial."

Nadine's lips pursed. But Hugh softened the blow by leaning close and kissing her cheek.

"As long as we're standing here," Hugh added grandly to his brother, "and the mood is so festive, we might as well announce that we've set a date for the wedding. May twenty-ninth."

Jack's features went hard.

"Hey, come on," Hugh said with a chuckle, "tell me you're happy for us."

With a little shake, Jack found a smile despite the fact that he couldn't believe his brother was actually going to marry this superficial woman. "I only want what will make you happy, Hugh," he equivocated.

"This is wonderful," Grace chimed in. "Let's open a bottle of champagne and toast."

"Save the toasts for the wedding reception," Hugh said. "Jack, I'd like you to be my best man."

Jack and Hugh looked at each other, their dark-eyed gazes locking. Nadine huffed.

"I'm happy, Jack," Hugh said in a low, soft voice. "Be happy for me."

Then Jack wrapped his little brother in a hard hug, even made himself kiss Nadine on the cheek. After congratulations were made all around, the newly engaged couple departed, saying they were headed for Pomodoro, when they no doubt meant they were starved and dinner here didn't look promising.

Grace and Jack stared at the empty doorway.

"So that's your brother," Grace said.

"Yes."

She looked up at him. "It must be nice to have such a close relationship with your sibling."

Jack considered the words. "Hugh is a hard one to get close to. He's generally quiet and keeps to himself."

"He didn't seem too quiet tonight. In fact, it was kind of like a tornado passing through," Grace mused.

"I know." His eyes narrowed as he considered. "As much as I hate to admit it, Nadine seems to make him happy."

"I take it you don't like her."

"No," he replied.

Grace touched her lip in a way that made her look innocent and provocative at the same time. "I guess the good
news is that she seemed to like you even less," she said.

"Actually, she liked me well enough until about a month
ago."

"What happened?"

Jack shrugged and leaned back against the counter, refusing to feel any guilt. "We went to dinner and I got tired
of her endless questions about my life and my financial
status, so I might have said something about her footwear."

"Said something? Like, *Wow, those are really great shoes?*
Or, *You have impeccable taste in low-heeled pumps?*"

His nonchalance grew a tad strained. "More like, *Did
you buy those off a hooker outside a Staten Island strip
club?*"

After one stunned moment, Grace laughed out loud,
throwing her head back with an utterly free abandon. It
was like they were alone in the world, and looking at
everything through her eyes, he saw the absurdity of it all.

"I can't imagine you saying something like that," she
said when she caught her breath.

"Neither can I. It just sort of came out."

"Big mistake," she offered.

"Hugh was amused," he countered.

"Even bigger mistake. Women love their shoes." She
extended her foot, a red and orange slip-on dangling from
her toes. "What do you think?"

"They're hideous."

Grace snorted. "You really have to learn to temper your
tongue if you want to get along with your brother's wife."

"I only care about getting along with my brother."

"You won't if you can't be nice to the woman he loves."

Jack grumbled, knowing she was right.

Grace walked back to the cookbook. "So what will you say for the toast?"

Jack considered. "I don't know. I can't imagine coming up with anything that rhymes with, 'tragic mistake.' "

For half a second, she could only stare. Then she laughed yet again with that free abandon that left him off balance.

"You'd better try harder than that, Dr. Berenger, if you want to keep your brother in your life."

Then she returned her attention to the recipe, running a chocolate-stained finger down the ingredients list as if she had already forgotten he was there.

He turned on his heel to leave, but his progress was halted when the guest wearing the argyle sweater entered the kitchen.

"Good heavens," the man said, stopping abruptly at the mayhem that reigned on the countertop and floor, his loafered foot slipping when he hit a patch of flour. He caught himself on the doorjamb, and Grace cringed.

"What has happened in here?" the man demanded.

His tone was disdainful, and Jack immediately felt a rise of anger.

"I thought we were eating at eight-thirty."

"Umm, David—"

"It's Donald."

"Of course, Donald." She tucked a wayward strand of hair behind her ear. "I've had a setback—"

He looked around him.

"Or two. Nothing to be alarmed about. I'll have dinner on the table in no time. Have another hors d'oeuvre."

"I've heard about you," he stated. "Leaving men at altars, getting fired from your job. I knew I shouldn't have let my mother talk me into this."

The words seemed to pierce through Grace, taking her

breath, before her shoulders came back and a defensive glint shimmered in the blue depths.

Ten minutes ago, Jack had thought virtually the very same thing, but hearing it from this little prick made Jack want to put his fist into his face.

Without thinking about what he was doing, Jack took a step closer to Donald until he stood only inches away. The man had to crane his neck to meet his eyes. "You're a guest here, sir, and if you're not careful, you'll answer to me."

Donald squirmed and grew red in the face, but he didn't say another word. He marched back to the living room.

Grace and Jack stood silently, until she said, "I don't need you to defend me."

Before Jack could respond, Mark called out, "How's it going in there?"

"Fine," Grace managed. "Dinner's almost ready." Then she lowered her voice. "Push the door closed," she hissed.

As soon as it swung shut, Grace gasped. Whatever cool gaiety she had managed to maintain in the face of her dinner disaster disappeared with the disdain that had been written on Donald's smug little face.

"What am I going to do? I have to hurry. I haven't even gotten the mango salad into the refrigerator yet!"

She dashed over to the counter to the opened can of mangoes, then poured them into a blender. Next she added a package of cream cheese. Her motions were hurried and frenetic as she slapped the rubber top on, then pressed the button. Instantly a grinding whir filled the room, but no matter what speed button she pushed, the white cream cheese remained flattened against the glass sides of the blender.

"Damn." She stopped the machine, opened it up, then used a knife to push the cream cheese around. Then on it went again. Two chugging grinds before the same useless whirring sound started again.

Then it happened. Too fast. All before Jack could think. She stuck the knife inside again, loosening the cream cheese, though this time she didn't stop the blender. A second later the knife hit the blades, then crashed back against the glass with such force that the container exploded into the room.

Glass flew everywhere, along with pureed mango and chunks of cream cheese. A lifetime seemed to pass before it was over, leaving Jack and Grace standing in shocked silence.

The look on Grace's face was one of sheer horror that made Jack worry. But in seconds, he determined that she wasn't hurt.

"What have I done?" Grace whispered, the look of horror melting into despair. "I promised myself this party would be a success. I just wanted to do one thing right."

In the next moment, footsteps came running, and Jack didn't think. He blocked the entrance.

"What happened in there?" Mark demanded when the door wouldn't budge. "Are you all right?"

Grace could only stare, her hands extended on either side of her, the knife in one hand, mango and cream cheese puree clumped in the bodice feathers, dripping from appliances.

"Nothing's wrong," Jack called out. "I dropped a pan on the floor and made a mess."

There was a vague grumble on the other side. "If you're sure," came the doubtful response.

"I'm sure."

The guests drifted away from the door, followed by one lone set of footsteps banging out the front door. Donald, Jack was sure. Just as he would have banged out if the roles had been reversed.

It didn't sit well that he was no different from a man like Donald.

"What is happening to me?" she whispered. "Why is my life falling apart? Why now? Why after nearly thirty years of holding it together?"

Jack would have bet money that she hardly realized that he was there.

"Perhaps I am more fluff than stuff," she added, choked.

Twenty minutes ago he would have agreed. Even now, part of him still wanted to. But as always when he was around her, his thoughts went to places he'd rather not go.

He wanted out of there, but he couldn't seem to leave. Not now. Later he would, when this disaster was taken care of, and he wouldn't come back. Later, after she was through this, he would make a point of never seeing her again.

"You'll go get cleaned up," he instructed. "I'll pick up Chinese."

She blinked at him, as if only then realizing he was there. Her despair shifted and changed to something that he couldn't name. Equally as dark, he knew, but mixed with relief.

"Thank you."

"Don't thank me too soon. We're not out of the woods yet. First we have to get this mess cleaned up."

Like cogs working in a machine, they began scraping and wiping, throwing the entire blender in the trash. With the two of them it didn't take long before the kitchen was back in reasonable order—though one lone glob of mango and cream cheese stuck to the ceiling. They both tilted their heads back and stared.

It was Grace who laughed first, a tiny shuddering giggle, and before too long even Jack had to chuckle. One lone clump of orange splattered on the pristine white. Their humor turned to laughter, until they had tears streaming down their faces. Jack reached over and wiped mango off Grace, carefully, slowly. Then somehow they were silent, their gazes locked, mangoes forgotten.

Jack looked at her, the overhead brightness highlighting her cheekbones. At the sight of her so close, a surge of unadulterated desire shot through him. She was everything he didn't want, didn't need, but again and again he was drawn to her with an intensity that left his body hard and aching.

Reaching out, he traced his finger down her cheek, through the sweet fruit. Her lips parted on an intake of breath, and when he grazed her breast with his palm, she gasped.

"This can't happen," she whispered, tugging away. "Not again."

His brow furrowed. "Why not?"

She shook herself and moved away without answering. She was flustered, her cheeks stained with red.

At the counter she busied herself with pots and pans. But Jack couldn't let it go. He came up behind her, taking her shoulders and turning her back to face him. When she tried to escape, he placed his hands on either side of her, effectively blocking her path.

She stared at him, her blue eyes wide, innocent.

He knew she was right, that they had no business together, but he wanted to hear her answer. "Why?" he demanded once again.

He saw the defiance rise up inside her, defiance and determination not to be cowed by him. She wanted to run, she wanted away, but she stood up to him. Her bravery impressed him, and irritated him in turn. Never in his life had he intimidated a woman intentionally. But again and again she turned him into a man he didn't recognize.

"Because despite what you think about me," she stated, "I'm not like that."

Instinctively he must have sneered.

"It's true," she hurried on. "But you do something to me, something I don't like, and whenever I'm near you, my mind turns sluggish and I can't think of anything but you touching me."

"I want to touch you now."

"Too bad," she snapped. "I refuse to be one in your long line of playthings."

"There's not a long line."

"More than one is too many, as far as I'm concerned. But one or ten, it hardly matters. You are everything I don't want in my life. The truth is, I don't even like you."

Her honesty took him aback. But if she noticed, it didn't concern her. Once she had started, she couldn't seem to stop. The words rushed out of her. "Think what you like, but at least I'm truthful with myself. You're a hypocrite, Jack Berenger. You want me, and you'll take me, but you hate yourself for it."

Then she pushed him away, and would have left if the kitchen door hadn't swung open just then.

"Good God, what are you two doing in here?"

"Discussing," she bit out.

Mark looked between them, then scoffed. "More like fighting. I could hear you all the way in there."

With Mark near her, Jack saw an ease come over her, the kind of ease that he hated to admit he felt whenever he was near her. He hated that it bothered him.

Grace sighed, then smiled. "We aren't fighting. I'm just having a bit of a problem with dinner."

Mark looked around. "That's an understatement."

"I vote we go out to eat," she added, pushing into the living room as if she had already forgotten Jack. "Who wants a home-cooked meal, anyway, when we have an entire city filled with great restaurants? Let me throw on a new top."

In seconds she returned, and the small group departed through the doorway. Grace hesitated and looked back, and for one brief moment her eyes met Jack's. But she quickly lowered her head, and followed without another word. No invitation to join them. No waiting for him to leave. Just a flare of emotion in her eyes, before she left him there to let himself out.

Jack returned to his apartment. He grabbed a bowl of cereal and combined it with a beer. Later, as he lay in bed staring at the ceiling, he could do little more than think of Grace.

Was she crazy? Was he crazy to be drawn to her? But most important, could he find a way to put her from his mind?

Chapter
Eleven

Grace woke the next morning, telling herself she would not be embarrassed about last night's dinner party. She would not.

She had been a tad overambitious in her menu planning, that's all. It could have happened to anyone. And no one could dispute that the cake had been heavenly. Mark, Daniel, and she had come back to the apartment after having an incredible meal of lobster casserole in a cream sauce with a deliciously crusty top, fresh asparagus, and twice-baked potatoes, to serve up the cake. There was no question that she knew how to bake.

Getting out of bed, she threw on a pair of work-out tights and an oversized sweatshirt left over from the eighties *Flashdance* craze, and pulled her hair back in a scrunchy. Then she got busy.

She cleaned the apartment, put away dishes, emptied ashtrays, and only cringed once when she saw the mango mix on the kitchen ceiling. Really, she would not be embarrassed—and she wouldn't think. She would keep her mind carefully blank.

As the day progressed, those simple words became a mantra, beating in her head like a drum. When the phone rang, she yanked up the receiver, thankful to have someone to talk to besides herself.

"Hello?"

"Grace! How are you?"

"Hey, Mark. I'm fine."

"Of course you are. But that's not why I called. I did an Internet search on your dreamy neighbor."

She squeezed her eyes closed and would have hung up the phone if it already wasn't too late. The piece she had relentlessly kept from her mind all day sprang to life full force. Jack Berenger.

"You didn't tell me he's a famous doctor."

She concentrated on something else. "Did you think the chocolate icing was too sweet?"

"It was perfect. I'm sending the article I found on him through e-mail now."

"Don't bother," she forced herself to say. She wanted no information on Jack, nothing that made her think about the man for another second. He did something to her, made her act in ways that made her shudder in the morning.

Mark laughed deliciously. "No bother. I already pressed send. Besides, you might think differently when I tell you that your ruggedly handsome, and seemingly Neaderthal-ish neighbor used to be a real mainstay of polite society. A neurosurgeon, it says. In Greenwich, Connecticut, no less."

"A neurosurgeon? In Connecticut?"

"Now there's the Grace Colebrook I know and love, ready to dish dirt at the drop of a hat."

"I do not dish!"

"True, but you are always up for a good story."

"Okay, okay," she said, caving in to curiosity, "so tell me."

"Actually, there's nothing else." He sounded sheepish.

"Nothing else! You get me hooked, then have nothing else to offer?"

"What did you expect? Anyway, I thought you weren't interested," he added smugly.

She had no idea what Mark could have found. Though perhaps something that could explain the darkness she saw in Jack eyes, that look that made her feel like she had known him a lifetime.

With the cordless phone in hand, she walked over to her computer and turned it on. While Mark chatted away about how boring Dani turned out to be, Grace read the article and understood that something must have happened if Jack left such a lucrative career in prestigious Greenwich to work as an emergency room doctor that served one of New York City's most dangerous neighborhoods. If someone was shot or maimed in Harlem, they were taken to St. Luke's.

But beyond that, she couldn't keep the thought away any longer that she owed the man an apology for last night.

Had she really told him she didn't like him? The truth was that she didn't like what he did to her. The way he made her head spin and her body come alive with a desire she had never experienced before. He brought out a wildness in her that she refused to give in to.

But the fact was he had offered to help, and she had run off like a spoiled child, not even bothering to see him to the door. So apologize she would. At the very least, she owed him that.

Or so she told herself as it was easier to explain away her need to see him because of some sense of neighborly necessity than to delve deeper and think about how she wanted to see him, wanted him to pick up where he had left off last night when his hand had brushed against her breast.

After hanging up with Mark, she showered, then took extra pains with her appearance. She blow-dried her hair so it lay flat in a long expanse of shiny brown, brushed on mascara, and even a tad of blush to her cheeks. Rummaging through her drawer, she found a blue cashmere sweater that matched her eyes, and combined it with a pair of black slacks and black suede loafers. Not frumpy or outrageous.

It was late in the day by the time she stood at his front door.

Knock, she told herself. But somehow she couldn't get her hand to move. What if he gave her that look of utter disdain that he did so well? She wasn't sure she could take that today. Then she kicked herself for being a coward, and ended up knocking with more force than was necessary.

The door opened an instant later.

"Jack!" she said, and she knew she sounded surprised.

He made a production of pulling his door open even wider and looking at the number. "Two A. Yep, it's my apartment. Who were you expecting?"

She shot him a sarcastic smile, which only made him raise one dark brow.

"I came down here to be nice," she stated indignantly.

"And you're going to be even if it kills you?"

She counted to ten, though she wasn't sure why she was angry. Because he looked really great in navy blue slacks and a white button-down Polo shirt? Because he looked at her with bored indifference? Because the minute he saw her he didn't swoop her into his arms and tell her he was glad to see her?

He pulled on his coat and picked up his keys.

"Where are you going?"

"Uptown."

"You are?" she asked, a tiny bit of whine in her voice. "I mean, you are! Great! I'm headed uptown, too," she added in a moment of inspiration. "I see no reason why we shouldn't go together."

Jack studied her, taking in her less-than-ready state to be heading out. No purse, no coat.

"I'll just be a second."

Without waiting for him to respond, she dashed up the stairs and was back in a flash, pulling on her coat.

"So why are we going uptown?" she asked, pulling on gloves as he held the outer door for her.

"*I* am going to the hospital to check on a patient. Why are *you* going?"

"Ah, well, you see . . . I have some errands to run. In the hospital neighborhood."

He looked at her skeptically. "On One Hundred Thirteenth Street? Our little neighborhood too calm for you?"

"Have you ever thought of quitting medicine and becoming a stand-up comedian?"

"That seems to be a recurring theme with us. Sharp, sarcastic humor."

They crossed the street at Broadway and Seventy-second to the subway terminal. Once inside the brick building, Jack swiped his MetroCard, then gestured for her to precede him through the turnstile.

"How romantic," she cooed. "Paying my fare. It's like our first date."

He only smiled and bowed, then swiped the card again and pushed through. Only a thin crowd of people waited for a train, some reading newspapers folded into neat rectangles, others beating out a silent rhythm to the headphones that played music in their ears.

When the number one train pulled into the station, Jack placed his hand at her back and guided her on. The doors rattled shut behind them, then opened, then shut again with finality before the train jerked and started to move. There was no place to sit, and Jack had to steady her when she bumped into a rough-looking man.

Grace smiled and apologized. The man grumbled something about silly white somethings that Grace thought better of having clarified. Thank goodness Jack hadn't heard. No sense in stirring up that macho protective thing she had seen in his eyes last night.

Between Seventy-second and the first stop at Seventy-ninth Street, Grace had to force herself not to stare at the amalgam of people. Some wore suits and ties, concentrating on their newspapers, some were construction workers at the end of their day, their heads pressed back against advertisements for continuing education courses. Some were mothers, so young they seemed children themselves, trying to keep control of two and three children at a time.

"I read an article about you in *Newsweek*," she said, turning her attention to Jack.

His eyes narrowed, and whatever humor had been there was lost. "Where did you find that?"

"Online, actually. It's amazing what these computers can do nowadays."

"Were you checking up on me?"

"Of course, though actually it was Mark who did the checking." Grace smiled at him, noticing the Asian woman who was pretending not to be listening but Grace suspected was paying close attention to the conversation. "I think he's sweet on you."

Immediately the woman glanced up to look Jack over. Jack glared. The woman tsked. Grace laughed out loud.

"That man is a menace," Jack grumbled.

"That man is my best friend. Besides, haven't you been checking up on me?"

"No."

Grace sighed, disappointed.

"But if I did, what would I find?" he asked quietly.

"You already know everything about me. Everything of importance, really. I'm as boring as a plain bagel and a cup of tepid tea."

"I would call you many things, but boring isn't one of them."

After a handful of stops, Jack guided her off the train, then up the steps into a strange mix of people.

"Where up here are you going?" Jack inquired, taking her arm. "I'll walk you there before I go to the hospital."

"Well, uh, I don't really have anyplace to go. The truth is, like I said earlier, I just wanted to be nice to you today. How long are you going to be? Why don't I wait while you check on your patient?"

Jack made a noise that sounded as if he had something painful stuck in his throat. "Hell. Come on." He took her hand and pulled her down the long block between Broadway and Amsterdam, walking straight toward the towering doors of St. John the Divine cathedral.

She looked up at the heights. "I always forget how beautiful it is."

Jack hesitated for half a step, staring up at the church before he lowered his head and continued on to the hospital emergency room.

He guided her through electronic doors, where he greeted the security guard. The waiting room was filled with people in varying states of distress.

"You can wait in my office," he said, leading her back through another set of doors.

But before they could get beyond this hub of emergency rooms, the relative peace of the hospital erupted. Grace had never seen anything like it. In seconds, the relative calm was shattered by ambulances and deafening sirens that jumbled together with paramedics and hospital staff.

Grace felt the minute Jack tensed. Automatically, she looked up and saw his face transform.

"What is it, Jack?"

He appeared startled that she was there. Without a word, he all but planted her in a prefabricated chair.

"Stay here," he commanded.

When nurses and medics saw him, Grace registered the relief that filtered through their whole bodies, like a wave rushing up from the sea.

Jack strode away, leaving her there, her eyes half closed as if she could close out the jarring sights and sounds that careened all around her. When medics raced by with a man on a gurney, bloody sheets grazing her shoulder, she leaped out of the chair. She couldn't sit . . . or find a way to leave. She ended up with her back against a wall, the chaos in the emergency room playing out before her like a horrible picture show.

Suddenly a radio dispatch went off, and she could hear scratchy voices coming over the wires. "We have a twentyish white male with bullet wound to the chest. Blood pressure falling rapidly. We've got two IVs running, and we're coming in fast."

She felt the mood in the room change yet again, the intensity swelling. But before she could understand the difference, the automatic doors *whooshed* open. All she saw was more blood, red staining white, and a lifeless man in a tangle of IV tubes and plastic drips held high by a medic.

Jack immediately took charge. At first she didn't recognize him. He wore medical dressing over his clothes, and a clear plastic shield over his eyes. Standing no more than a few inches from her, he didn't even notice her.

The paramedics rolled the unconscious man beneath a huge stainless steel lamp; then on the count of three, they lifted and placed him on a metal table. In seconds, they had the tubes and wires connected to larger machines in the room.

Like a switch had been flipped, the monitors blipped to life, the man's shaky vital signs reading out on computer screens.

"The heart or aorta must be hit," Jack stated, his voice intense and commanding. "We have to open him up."

Quick, efficient movements before Jack leaned over the man and made an incision between the ribs, then pried the chest open with some kind of a device. She nearly fainted when suddenly the rib cage popped apart, blood flowing everywhere. But she still couldn't look away, from the dying man or from Jack.

"We need blood, people," he called out. "Fast."

"It's on the way," a nurse stated.

"Not fast enough."

The nurse turned to another woman. "Go get it."

The woman hurried away as Jack continued to work. Grace stood mesmerized, then reeled when Jack put his hand inside the chest.

"BP down. Eighty over forty," a technician itemized.

"We're losing him."

"BP forty over twenty."

"Where's the goddamn blood?" Jack barked.

But the blood hadn't gotten there when suddenly the heart monitor screamed out a static line. Efforts were made to bring the young man back, but even Grace knew there would be little hope of resuscitating a man whose heart was exposed and whose blood was everywhere but inside him.

It was like a breath exhaled, the room deflating as the medical team absorbed the loss. But the moment of profound grief was forced aside when the words *Code Blue* sounded over the intercom.

For reasons Grace couldn't explain, she wanted to talk to Jack, needed to talk to him, but there was no chance. Too many people, too many broken lives wheeled into the emergency room.

"It's the good weather," a technician said, his voice somehow registering in her mind. "It brings people out in the streets, then crazy things start happening."

Grace backed away, trying to escape, but froze at the sound of raised voices behind her.

"Just tell me your name, please, miss."

"Up yours, buddy."

Grace peered around the corner and found a man in medical scrubs talking to a girl who couldn't have been more than sixteen or seventeen, though from the looks of her she had been around the block a time or two.

She was covered in blood, and one side of her face appeared to have been on the wrong side of a run-in with a set of dinner knives.

"Okay," the male nurse bit out, "then tell me your medical history."

"In your dreams, dick lips."

Conversations cut off, the people in the room turning to see what was going on, their brows furrowing. A police officer who was writing in his notepad stopped what he was doing and took notice. But the girl didn't care.

"Just sew me the fuck up, then I'm out of here."

An uneasiness filtered through the emergency room over such ugly hostility.

"Unfortunately, a doctor has to do that," the nurse said. "You'll have to wait your turn."

"Like hell I will! You just want me to sit here with all these piece-of-shit idiots so I can bleed to death."

The nurse's patience looked like it would snap, and he

pushed up from kneeling in front of her. The policeman started to come forward. At that very second Jack stepped into sight, his dark handsomeness seeming so at odds with this horrible place.

"Is there a problem here?" he asked.

Both the nurse and the girl glanced at him. The nurse sighed. The girl suddenly grew quiet.

The male nurse stepped forward. "I'm trying to get her medical history, but she seems to think it's"—he glanced at her—"how did you put it? *In my dreams, dick lips.*"

Grace couldn't believe it when the girl actually blushed, though it was hard to tell since most of her face was covered with blood.

"You like your privacy," Jack said, undeterred, his smile at once reassuring and calming as he took the girl's chart.

"Hey, man," she said, for the first time her voice sounding young and insecure, "I was only dicking—I mean playing with him."

"Come back with me, and we'll see what we can do with that face."

The girl turned to putty in Jack's hands, though seconds later he returned.

"What did you do?" the nurse grumbled. "Strangle her?"

Jack shook his head. "No, I gave her to Hank. He's the best we have for suturing." Like it was as simple as that.

Grace stood mesmerized by the power of this man. She saw him in a whole new light, understood his gift, understood why he was a doctor. She started to say something, but without warning, another gurney rolled in, the same count of three sounding before another man was lifted to another metal table just beyond a thin partition.

"We've got the shooter here," a paramedic explained.

"The shooter of the young guy brought in a few minutes ago."

The young man who had already died.

Had it really only been minutes? Grace wondered.

This man looked every bit as young as the one they had lost, maybe even younger. It didn't seem possible that this boy could have killed someone.

Immediately Grace felt foolish and naive. Despite her family's dramas, she had led a sheltered life, a privileged life.

"He was taken down by an old man who saw the whole thing. The old guy was an ex-cop. Damn good shot."

The medical staff shifted over to this man, this murderer, and for half a second Jack hesitated. No one else would have noticed, but Grace was watching, Grace recognized that look in his eyes. The despair mixed with a furious anger that was nearly palpable, his hands clenched at his sides. For half a second, she didn't think he would do anything to save the man's life.

But then he looked up, and his eyes met hers. He seemed puzzled that she was there, as if he had forgotten, as if his world inside these four walls were a different existence entirely.

"Dr. Berenger?" a nurse asked.

The voice snapped him out of that place he had been, and he looked away from Grace. He strode purposefully to the shooter, as if there had never been a moment's hesitation, and this time the patient was saved. Her chest tightened against the unfairness of it, the victim killed, the shooter saved.

She stood with her back plastered to the wall, invisible to the medical staff who worked with frenetic efficiency. Sound spun in on her, and only when a tear she didn't understand streamed down her cheek, the taste of salt stinging her lips, did she realize her mouth was open, and the sound was her own desperate murmuring.

How could Jack survive in this world of blood and death? How did he cope when he couldn't save the innocent or the damned?

Movement seemed impossible, forward or back. Then suddenly a medic halted in front of her, a big burly black man who couldn't have been more than twenty, his hospital scrubs announcing he belonged in this place in a way that she never would.

"Who the hell are you?" he demanded, but a kind smile curved on his face, showing straight teeth, white against the dark.

She searched for an answer, but couldn't think, couldn't string together enough words to make sense.

"Have you run off from the psych ward?" He took her arm, though he took it gently.

A nurse had to do a shuffle step to keep from running into them as they moved into the open.

"Who is this?" he asked the woman.

The nurse looked her over. "She's with Jack."

The orderly started to chuckle. "Not quite the place I would bring a pretty young thing like you, but Dr. Jack definitely has a mind of his own." He didn't let go of her arm as he guided her away from the commotion. "You don't need to be seeing any of the goings-on in here. Let's find you a chair out in the waiting room and get you some coffee."

He pointed to a bank of vinyl seats, then headed off. Grace stared at a grieving man and woman as they waited for news of a loved one. Then she saw through a glass partition when another paramedic team barreled through the doors, a medic straddling the patient, compressing the chest as the other rolled the gurney through the doors.

"Code Blue," the intercom crackled overhead.

Grace turned away, not wanting to see, only to come face-to-face with wounded people waiting in chairs, patients lying on stretchers, lined up against the wall, each of them praying their turn would come soon.

Stumbling, she didn't wait for coffee. She made it to the electronic door that gasped open, spitting her out into the darkened night. Dragging in a sharp, shuddering breath, she started to walk, fast, almost running, the side streets deserted and menacing.

She retraced her steps until she came to the subway stop at Broadway and 110th Street. She descended belowground as if she could bury her thoughts beneath the hard cement of New York.

Very few people waited on the platform going downtown. But still she didn't care. When the train pulled into the station, she stepped through the rattling doors and found herself alone in the car with a group of angry, rough-looking teenagers loaded with heavy gold chains, pants that were too big, hanging low on their hips, and black stretchy headdresses that looked like some sort of stocking caps.

They eyed her clothes and the diamond stud earrings.

"What are you looking at?" she demanded foolishly.

The boys hooted their laughter at her bravado, then stepped closer.

"Umm, mama. You are one hot bitch," the first of them said in a smooth purr of words.

"Very hot," another confirmed, his thick athletic shoes sliding lazily on the floor as he moved even closer. "I like those earrings, man."

She should have been scared, she knew it. The subway rocked and shot along through the underground darkness, the sound of metal wheels clacking over rail. And she was alone. But it was as if everything that had happened over the last few months came together in a hard, unyielding knot in that subway, and she turned on them, her eyes flaring. She felt insane. Teetering on the edge. But more than that, she felt a deep sense of not caring. She felt the moment when something inside her snapped.

"You want the earrings? You want to steal from me?" she demanded. "Fine. What do I care? You think I'm hot, well think again. I'm not. I'm a silly woman who has just seen more death and destruction than I care to see in a lifetime. Take the damned earrings. In fact, do you want more? Look"—she whipped back her coat and sweater sleeves from her wrist—"a watch. An expensive watch. Do you want that, too?"

The teens looked startled by her eruption, their eyes widening for a fraction of a second, and they shifted their weight. But before they could take the jewelry, the train brakes came on, making them all surge forward. Grace grabbed a railing. The boys opened their oversized Nike stances to regain balance. In seconds, the station leaped into sight, and the doors banged open at 103rd Street. But it wasn't Grace who got off. The boys did, and once the doors closed and the train started up again, they laughed and shook their heads, pointing at her.

"You crazy bitch," they yelled, their slouching figures moving away like a pack of animals.

The train pulled out, the car empty now, rocking, metal wheels clattering over iron tracks. When the subway finally stopped at Seventy-second Street, Grace got off. The station was nearly deserted, only the muted sound of traffic rumbling overhead. But when she came up to street level, noise leaped out at her, car horns blaring at the busy intersection. Yellow taxis and limousines surrounded her with glaring intensity; people bumped into her.

Unable to think straight, she started walking away from

the subway, away from her thoughts, not thinking about where she was going until she couldn't walk anymore. Finally she returned to the brownstone on Sixty-ninth Street. Facing the apartment, she looked up at her window. Darkened, lonely.

The restlessness that had started to grow inside her reared. There had to be more to her existence than this. She had seen firsthand how fragile life was, but she sat on the sidelines without truly living. Was that what drew her to Jack Berenger? That when she was in his arms she felt like she was alive, no matter how reckless and irresponsible such an act really was?

Unable to bring herself to go inside, she sank down onto the hard steps and pressed her cheek against her knees. Scenes circled in her head, of the man with no heartbeat, of the girl whose skin was shredded like paper, the obscenity of her face matching the vulgarity of her world-wise mouth. The shooter Jack had not wanted to save.

And Jack himself, forced into that world every day that he stepped through those hospital doors.

How did anyone live with that horror without paying the cost of himself? Was that the darkness in Jack? Could he barely survive the mutilated traumas? If that was it, then why did he stay? Based on the article Mark had found, Jack could have any job he wanted. Instead, he worked in an emergency room expending superhuman effort to piece together broken lives.

As if her thoughts made him appear, she looked up and found him standing in front of her, so tall, the moon high and bright, casting him in faint relief.

"Are you okay?" he asked quietly, simply, his tone so caring that she wanted to weep. "I worried when I realized you had gone."

Chapter
Twelve

She could tell by Jack's stance that he was weary and spent, and when she pushed up from the cement, standing on the bottom step so that she was nearly as tall as he, she could see sharp edges to his features that hadn't been there hours earlier when they had set out. It was hard to imagine that life could seem so different from one second to the next—the same yet changed, proving that the difference had been there all along, hidden beneath the surface of a welcome ignorance.

What else was there that she couldn't see?

Reaching out, she traced the creases of his face with her fingertips, and for one tiny second he gave in and closed his eyes. A taxi raced by, cutting through the side street to a busier thoroughfare, the lane so narrow that the rush of its wake rustled the dried leaves that curled around their feet.

On this little stretch of Sixty-ninth Street the world seemed controllable, containable. Safe. But today had forced her to confront the trauma that surrounded them, the trauma that had never been more than a few feet away her entire life, but that she had been able to keep safely from her mind.

There are moments in every person's life when their world shifts and changes. Grace felt the shift inside her like a cog slipping, not finding its place in the wheel. Sense seemed elusive until moments passed and the cog slid home, understanding exploding in her mind like the sun bursting through the clouds.

For nearly thirty years she had set about constructing an orderly world, seeking the balm of utter banality after a childhood of grand drama. She dreamed of suburbs and babies, white picket fences, and a husband who got home at six-thirty for meals of medium-rare roast beef and new potatoes, broccoli, and a chocolate cream pie that she would have made with great love and devotion. A world of safety and seemliness.

But that life eluded her. She had built a world as a toy creator, living vicariously by watching children through thick glass windows and reading books about true love. Now she had come even further from her dream into a world of sensuality that was as rich as it was foreign, the world she had worked so hard for crumbling beneath her like a rampart built on sand.

It was this man who strode into that hospital for a simple errand, then took people's lives into his hands without a thought, contrasting now with how he stared at her, his face weary, that made her world shift, bringing her perceptions crashing down around her. This man and his world had made her face her otherness, face the reality that she was more like her mother than she wanted to admit.

She had fought against her mother's exaggerated life. The wildness and desire, the deep sensuality that Grace had always sensed in herself, and had run from.

"No," she whispered. "I'm not okay."

He let his head fall back, looking up to the slice of heaven that shone down between the buildings as if searching for a god. His throat worked, one thick vein bulging out on the side, and she knew that he was fighting for control.

Then he looked at her, his eyes so intense. She felt uneasy, out of sorts as the same disconcerting thought raced through her brain that she knew this man—had known him a lifetime, though she had never seen him before he walked out into the night.

A world of emotion swirled in the depths of his eyes, and she understood that he wanted her, again, needed her in some elemental way. Just as she needed him. That was her undoing. When he reached out to her, despite everything she knew to be true and right, she did little more than curse herself before she stepped into his arms.

He gathered her to him with a groan that seeped down to her soul, her arms clutching his shoulders, her legs coming up to wrap around his waist. They held together in the granite and limestone canyon formed by rows of brownstones and low-rise prewar apartment buildings, hundreds of windows looking down on them like box seats to a Broadway play. But she didn't care, didn't think. She felt alone with this man in this city of millions.

Never letting her go, he carried her inside, his sheer, massive strength wrapped around her. No fumbling this time, no ravaged desperation. Only a fierce need, holding tight, like holding on to a lifeline.

She couldn't deny that when this man touched her, this man who was still a stranger in all ways that matter, the world seemed less foreign, less difficult to navigate. Was that why women succumbed to the wrong men? Was it because when they touched them, the rest of the world disappeared?

She didn't know, she only knew that regardless of how wrong he was for her—how much he was like her father—none of that mattered the minute he touched her or looked at her with those fathomless eyes.

He needed her, too. She had always understood that. But regardless of that truth, something about him wanted her to be someone different in order for him to accept the desire he felt for her. Or could he ever accept wanting her? Had he sensed the wildness in her all along, and rebelled against it?

She hated the question, hated that she didn't know the answer. Hated that she might care. But she pushed it away, losing herself to the feel of this man.

He never let her go as he made his way up to his apartment, kicking the door shut behind them, twisting the lock, tossing the keys on the entry hall table with a clatter. Not stopping at dining room tables or living room floors. By the time he carried her upstairs, she was crying in great breakable sobs against the collar of his white shirt. But when she started to pull back and speak, he pressed one finger to her lips. Gently. Softly. Then said, "Not now."

She understood that he wanted no words, only oblivion. He was weary down to his soul. Loosening his hold on her hips, he let her down, her body lining his. After a moment, he put her at arm's length, his eyes boring into hers as if questioning, and when he started removing her clothes, she didn't stop him.

Raising her arms, she let him tug her sweater free, the soft cashmere brushing over her skin in a whisper of sensation. He popped the snaps of her bra expertly. Then he undid the top button of her pants, peeling them down until he kneeled before her. He pressed his face to the soft curve of her belly, seeming to take her in, and Grace had the fleeting thought that this had more to do with breathing in life than sensuality. Proof that he needed comfort he wasn't willing to ask for.

With a tiny cry, she began to stroke his dark raven's hair. How selfish she was when it was her desperate annihilation that had been forefront in her mind. Not his. He had been losing and saving lives. She had only watched.

His fingers slipped beneath the elastic waistband of her

silken panties before they drifted down and puddled at her feet. He stood then, his broad palm gently sweeping over the tips of her breasts. Only a touch, barely a touch, but shivers of longing shot through her.

Stepping away, he undressed with ease, the slacks tossed aside. He worked each of the small white buttons of his shirt, never looking away from her, no embarrassment, before he stood before her in startling glory. His manhood hung thick and swollen, not fully erect. He was so masculine, like the room around them, rugged and fierce. As soon as they stood naked in the high-ceilinged room, instead of taking her to the bed, he stepped back and looked at her, just looked, as if drinking her in, his eyes dark with deeply suppressed emotion.

"I knew you'd be beautiful," he whispered raggedly.

Just that, but it made her feel wonderful and womanly, and any doubt she had was erased.

He took her hand, but he stopped when the phone started to ring. Reality intruded, and suddenly she felt shy and very aware of her nakedness as the mechanical whirl of his voice on the answering machine sounded through the room. Then the inevitable beep, and she felt him tense. She understood that he couldn't face the demands of the hospital just then, but long-held responsibility wouldn't let him ignore it either. Another voice came on, cold and tinny, inconsequential, not the hospital, and she felt a palpable relief wash through him.

Striding toward the side of the bed, the muscles in his back and thighs rippled, his butt carved and beautifully rounded, making him look like a Greek god.

He pressed a button and the phone went silent, the red light on the machine going dead. He wanted no interruptions, no reality. He returned to her, regaining her hand,

and she felt the cool wood as they left the rug and he led her across the room into the master bath.

This room was every inch as masculine as well, with bronze and black marble, recessed lights that glowed low and golden when he flipped the switch. Granite countertops were accented by hard brass spouts and handles, one long expanse of mirror reflecting her image. Every cell came alive with awareness, centering at the core of her being. The sight of them together, like an outsider looking in, was startling. His dark hair shone in the dim light, curling ever so slightly down his neck. He was tall and chiseled, his shoulders broad, tapering down into a hard, flat stomach. He appeared a warrior standing next to her, making her feel tiny and feminine. But she felt in no way less than he. In fact when he looked at her in the silvered glass she saw the power she had over him when the thick length of him swelled even more.

He tugged open the massive shower door and turned on the faucet. He stepped inside, then gently pulled her with him. The shock of cold water quickly turning hot hit her, the quick bite of pain followed by the sensual caress of warm pleasure, heightening her senses.

As water sluiced through her hair, he brushed it back from her face, but he didn't kiss her. He reached out to get a washcloth from a stack of towels on a shelf. The terry cloth soaked through before he took the soap and worked up a lather. Her breath caught at the intimacy when he ran the cloth along her shoulders, across her collarbone, then slowly lower, circling her breasts until her head fell back.

He didn't say a word, only stroked and washed her body with a gentle reverence as if washing away an afternoon of life being lost, all the while his massive body blocking the spray of water. He lifted her arm, and ran the small towel along the sensitive skin underneath. He caressed every part of her, taking pleasure in each inch of her skin. One by one, he soaped her fingers, circling in her palms, drifting over the pulse in her wrists.

Stepping aside, he allowed water to wash the billowing soap lather clean. Then he lowered his head and pressed his lips between her breasts, before one by one he took each taut nipple into his mouth, sucking, a groan working its way free from the deepest part of his chest. He laved each peak, his tongue slightly rough—intoxicating.

Her body yearned for more, but he only continued to savor her, stroking and exploring. He wrapped his arms around her to wash her bottom, his shaft pressing against her. He was erect and hard. She wanted to touch him, but he stood back, savoring her, the cloth drifting lower, over her abdomen, then lower still until his hand slipped between her thighs. He stroked carefully, the soap now spent, her stance widening of its own volition, the washcloth dragging ever so erotically across her hidden cleft. Sensation shot through her like a streak of madness, wild and beyond reason.

But he didn't linger, and when she groaned her frustration, he only gave her one last brush of pleasure with the cloth sliding slowly between her legs, before he continued on to the rest of her, ending at her bright pink-painted toenails.

When he stood, she found herself staring into his eyes, like molten heat, before her gaze drifted to his beautifully carved mouth. She wanted to touch his lips, to lock her arms around his neck and pull him close so that she could graze his lips with her own. But suddenly she realized he was going to wash himself quickly and be done.

"No," she whispered, her voice ragged.

She tugged the cloth away, demanding when he started to refuse. Then, boldly, amazing herself, she began her own slow descent over the hard plains of him. At first she thought he would stop her, as if he wouldn't allow himself to give in to any kind of pleasure. But when she tossed the rag aside and circled the soap in her hands, then cupped the fullness between his legs, every muscle in his body grew rigid. She stroked and soaped, amazed at his thick fullness growing rigid in her palms.

His long, carved fingers curled against the marble walls on either side of them, each muscle tense, the hard line of his jaw so taut it looked like he would break.

His breathing grew ragged, guttural, and just when she thought he would gain his release, he swore an oath and grabbed her hands. With his breath rasping and harsh, he held her away for several long seconds as his ironclad control returned.

He wouldn't take pleasure. She hated that he wouldn't give in, hated that he had to command himself so completely. But somehow he wouldn't leave it at that. Once he had regained control, he came down on one knee before her, though when he bent his head to her, she forgot.

His palms spread over her torso, fingers splayed out toward her sides, sinking lower until his thumbs came to tangle in the curls between her legs. He parted her gently, and she thought she would cry out when she felt the flick of his tongue against her secret opening. The touch was like wildfire. Wet and slick and shudderingly addictive.

Her fingers curled in his wet hair, the water pounding on his shoulders, her back hot against the cold shower tiles. She felt sensation build when he licked her again, nudging her thighs wider. His tongue worked magic, faster and deeper, her body climbing, but when she would have stopped him, just as he had stopped her, his lips closed over the sensation-filled nub and her body exploded.

She cried out as desire sizzled through her in racking waves. He brought his hand up to cup her. When finally her orgasm burned itself out, she felt so weak she didn't know if her legs would hold her.

He carried her out onto the thick bathroom rug, then wrapped her in a plush, oversized towel. The room was warm, and he rubbed her body until it tingled with heat.

He rubbed the towel over her hair. With a patience that stunned her, he found a dryer in the back of a cabinet, warm air blowing over her until her hair was dry. The attention was mesmerizing, the strokes and movements making her feel cherished. He even sat her down on a low, upholstered bench, the towel wrapped snugly around her, as he brushed out the long strands of her hair. When her eyes started to flutter closed from the languorous sensation, he set the brush aside and gathered her up in his arms.

Her breath caught when he carried her toward his bed. Like a princess prepared for the warrior. But when he laid her down, then came over her, he didn't nudge between her thighs. He pulled her up to the pillows, tossed the towel aside, then turned her until the sensitive skin of her back pressed against his naked chest. Then he held her close, holding her tightly.

They lay together for long moments, the only sounds coming from the faint rumble of a jetliner gliding by overhead. He still hadn't said a word, and other than to hold her and cherish her in the shower, he didn't caress her again. And when she felt his deep, steady breathing of slumber, she understood that he truly wanted little more from her than comfort.

Proof, perhaps, that two people could survive in this crazy world.

Chapter
Thirteen

The sound of water running woke Grace, and it didn't take more than a handful of seconds before she remembered she was in Jack's apartment. Again.

She groaned silently. These early morning, post-encounter regrets were becoming a really bad habit.

Squeezing her eyes closed, she wondered how yet again she could end up in such a position. Of course only a second later she remembered that all they had done was sleep, simply sleep, no sex.

Okay, so there was *some* sex, she amended, if a person wanted to get picky. In the shower, admittedly, for her more than for him, and she had loved it.

Instantly, she cursed herself for being so promiscuous, and even thoughts of *Sex and the City* couldn't erase her guilt—at least not entirely. But more than anything she felt awkward and embarrassed. Somehow that sensual shower seemed more intimate than sex on a dining room table with a stranger.

But something happened when the two of them came together, loss of control, giving in to a need that they both kept suppressed most of the time. Or should she say *she* lost control. It didn't escape her notice that Jack Berenger kept an iron grip on his emotions.

Hurriedly, she pulled on her clothes, gathered her coat,

shoes, and purse, then tiptoed downstairs just as the water turned off. She fumbled with the locks on the door, then slipped out into the hallway, telling herself that she would do some serious soul searching, but she would do it at home, alone, after she washed her face, brushed her teeth, and made sure she didn't have huge smears of mascara beneath her eyes.

She dashed barefoot up to her apartment, banging inside just as her phone started to ring.

Guilty, she stared, imagining Jack on the other line, standing in his bedroom, a towel around his waist, wanting to know where the hell she had gone. Gingerly, she picked up the receiver.

"Hello?"

"There you are!"

Her entire body seemed to deflate, and she sank down into the ladder-back chair. "Good morning, Suzanne."

"I've been calling for the last thirty minutes."

Sure enough, her answering machine blinked the number three on the readout.

"I was in the shower," she lied.

"What time will you be at the family meeting?"

"What family meeting?"

"Good God, Grace, don't you ever check your answering machine?"

"I got home late last night and didn't notice."

"You sure are gone a lot these days for someone who isn't employed or engaged. Anyway, Father's called a family meeting."

Grace sat up straight at this, her shoulders coming back. "What's wrong?" she asked immediately.

"I don't know."

"Is he ill?"

"Grace, I said I don't know. But as you can imagine,

Mother is frazzled over the whole situation. The meeting is at three. Don't be late."

They hung up, and instantly Grace pressed the button to play her messages. Three from Suzanne. None from her father, and none from her mother. But she was too concerned about her father for that fact to register.

Colebrook family meetings were reserved for the most important of issues. Mother had called them before, as had Suzanne. But Grace couldn't remember when or if her father had ever called their family together. Not even when he was remarrying, or taking on a new medical partner. Not when he sold his apartment and bought another a block away. Or even the time he planned a trip across the Atlantic Ocean in a helium balloon.

Then why would he call a meeting now?

Grace arrived at her mother's at 2:45. Berta, the maid, let her in. The apartment looked the same, only somehow different. Perhaps it was nostalgia, or perhaps it was the thought of getting old, she went to her childhood bedroom. She stopped short when she pushed through the door and didn't recognize anything there.

Confused, she stepped back out into the hall, looked around to determine if she had gone through the wrong door. But this was her room, or had been. Gone were the remnants of a child's life. The stuffed bears and chess club awards. No more school annuals, or bulletin board loaded with junky treasures collected over a lifetime, as if her childhood had been erased, replaced by a nondescript arrangement of dark cherrywood furniture and oil paintings hanging on the walls.

"There you are, dear."

Grace whirled around to find her mother, wearing cream-colored woolen slacks, a matching cashmere sweater set and pearls. Roberta's hair was swept away from her face, showing off high cheekbones and forehead, then gently curled under just below the curve of her jaw. She looked every inch the high society woman that she had shaped herself to be, the facade so masterfully constructed that not even the most discerning eye would see the reality of little Robbie Sue from Brooklyn underneath.

"Do you like it?" Roberta asked, glancing into the bedroom with a distracted air.

"Where are all my things?"

Roberta made some vague waving motion with her tastefully jeweled hand. "In the storage room, I think. I couldn't stand that clutter one more day. I asked if you minded. Remember?"

Barely, and only now that she was reminded. At the time, it hadn't seemed important. She was starting a new life. Why bother with the old. Only now, after the new life was disintegrating, did the fading Halloween masks and yellowing certificates matter.

"If you want all that jumble, I'll have it sent over."

What she wanted was her bedroom pieced back together.

Which was absurd. Most parents downsized their houses or used rooms for other children.

"How are you doing?" her mother asked, really looking at her.

Grace felt a blush of surprise, unused to her mother's attention.

"Are you okay?" she asked, as if she truly cared.

That was how Roberta Colebrook worked, blithely going about her way, oblivious to all but her own desires, until something happened and she remembered that there were people around her whom she loved. It was as endearing a trait as it was exasperating.

"I'm fine, Mother."

"Really?"

"Really."

"I worry about you. Did Donald call?"

"Yes."

"Was he nice?"

Grace debated her answer. "He was a perfect addition to my party," she equivocated.

"Ah, good," Roberta said. "I just want you to be happy—and settled. Sometimes I worry you want something that . . ."

Her mother hesitated, and she never held back anything.

"Mother, what? Tell me!"

"Sometimes I think you're looking for a fairy tale. You want a perfect life, but perfect doesn't exist, Grace. Not in men, not in careers. Not in friends or family. We can only try our hardest to live the best we can." Roberta squeezed her daughter's hand. "Does that make sense?"

A month ago, she would have been insulted. But today it made too much sense, and the moment of shifting and change that Grace had experienced after St. Luke's emergency room solidified. She had tried to find a life so different from her mother's, an orderly world, as if all the order could keep her safe. But safe from what? From feeling too much?

The truth was, for all her searching for order and safety, she had never found it, and every decision she made in the name of sanity and seemliness blew up in her face.

Standing in her old bedroom, the treasures of her childhood swept away as if they had never been there, Grace had a moment of shuddering insight that she had no idea who she really was. Her storybook character had started to fade, like colorful pages left out in the blistering sun. Was there something about her that made her desire for a child and a family of her own unreasonable?

"I hear everyone else arriving. I can't imagine what Calder wants. But we'll soon find out."

When they entered the living room, everyone was there. Suzanne Colebrook Harriman was three years older than Grace. She was as beautiful as their mother, always dressed to perfection, with two small children, a boy and a girl, born in that order, two and a half years apart, as if Suzanne had followed the perfect plan. She and Grace had never been close, and had only grown further apart since she'd married Herbert.

Grace hated to be callous, but the man was irritating. He was chubby, with little hair on top, and he had a laugh that Grace didn't know how Suzanne tolerated. Very much a huh, huh, huh, snort, huh, huh, huh, snort as his face turned a very bright shade of red.

Their father pushed up from his seat and pulled out a cigar.

"Calder, please," her mother said. "Not inside."

Just when he would have gone out onto the terrace, he saw Grace. For half a second she would have sworn he was surprised at the sight of her. But then it was gone, and she saw the familiar light that filled his kind brown eyes, and the crooked smile that seemed reserved for her alone.

"There's my girl," he called out, tucking the cigar away in his coat pocket.

"Hi, Daddy," she said, walking into his arms. How she loved this man, this genius of a doctor who turned wild and irresponsible the minute he walked out of the operating room door.

She sensed when Suzanne stood, sensed the all too familiar tension swirling around her. The older daughter might have been born with a supreme confidence, and she might have done everything first, and with great flair, but they all knew that Grace was their father's favorite.

But while Calder loved Grace, he had always been proud of Suzanne's accomplishments.

As an adult, on some level Grace recognized the possibility that he gave Suzanne what he could, when he couldn't give her the same kind of love he gave Grace. But love with no pride in her abilities had never seemed like much of a prize.

"Why the meeting, Daddy?" she whispered to him. "Are you okay?"

He held her at arm's length, his smile broad and hearty. "Did you hear that, Roberta?" he bellowed. "Grace here is concerned that I'm unwell. That is a true daughter. No wonder I have you so prominently represented in my will."

Suzanne blushed, and Herbert scowled.

Roberta waved the comment away. "Grace always did have a soft spot for you," she said with saccharine sweetness, her distracted air of only minutes ago gone, replaced with the nearly callous indifference that was the woman's trademark.

Seeing the two different sides of this woman juxtaposed in a matter of a few short minutes, Grace had the startling thought that her mother would have been a very different woman if she had married a man who had loved and cared for her, made her feel like the beautiful woman that she truly was. Then Grace had another thought—that no woman, regardless of how beautiful she was, could compete with the continually younger women that Calder Colebrook paraded under her mother's nose.

"I, on the other hand," Roberta continued, "have no such weakness when it comes to you, Calder. Given the fact that we are no longer married, I see no reason why I should be concerned with your health. My only concern is with your ability to live up to your legal obligations and provide my monthly income."

"Hell," he muttered, his broad beaming smile flattening to a hard line, "had I known you would never remarry, I never would have agreed to the terms that I had to support you until you did."

"Father, Mother, please," Suzanne stated.

"She started it," Calder grumbled like a child. "Besides, for someone who claims to have no interest in me, why the hell has she been lurking around my building like some kind of stalker?"

"Don't flatter yourself, you old goat."

"You're the old goat!"

"Enough," Grace interjected. She turned to her father. "Daddy, tell us why are we here?"

Calder and Roberta scowled before turning away from each other sharply. With tension running high, they all took their seats. When everyone was settled, Calder cleared his throat and suddenly became serious, very much the elder statesman.

"I think you remember my older cousin, Arthur," he began, crossing his legs and smoothing his pant leg in a way that on any other man would have seemed effeminate.

"The one who died decades ago?" Suzanne asked.

"The one who didn't speak to you for years?" Roberta added.

"That's the one." He shook his head. "What is it about young people that gets them so worked up about nothing that they can't see what is really important?"

He said the words more to himself than anyone, and Grace's concern started to grow. It wasn't like him to be in such a pensive mood.

"As his closest living relative," he continued, "I was recently contacted on his behalf."

"I thought he had a daughter."

"He did." He grimaced. "But Janine Colebrook passed away three weeks ago."

"Oh my," Suzanne said. "She couldn't have been much older than me."

"Younger, actually. Thirty. Car accident."

"That is horrible, Calder," Roberta said, "but what does this have to do with us?"

"Such compassion," he said wryly. "I'm touched."

Roberta flashed him a bitter smile, but didn't respond.

"The fact is," he continued, "Janine had a seven-year-old little girl. Her name is Ruth, and now that child is orphaned."

"What about Janine's husband, the child's father?"

"They're looking for him."

"Oh, that's right," Suzanne said pointedly, "she was an unwed mother."

Grace hardly listened. Her heart began to pound.

"That's all well and good," Roberta interjected, "but still I must repeat, what does this have to do with us?"

"The child needs a home."

Dead silence filtered through the room, and the rush of blood through Grace's ears was so loud, she was sure everyone could hear.

"And?" Roberta asked carefully.

Calder leaned back and steepled his fingers. "The state has asked me to take custody."

"Good God, you couldn't raise two daughters of your own with any skill, how can they possibly think you could raise someone else's child?" Roberta quipped.

"My thoughts exactly. She'd be better off with you."

Calder said the words directly to his ex-wife, and for half a second everyone could all but see the gears grinding in Roberta's head as understanding sank in.

"Are you out of your mind? Why in the world would I possibly take on someone else's child—a child I am in no way related to. Moreover, why would you possibly have to deal with this? While Arthur was living he hated you, wouldn't even speak to you. Need I remind you he wouldn't return your calls?"

Calder bowed his head. "No, you don't need to remind me," he answered honestly. "But I also haven't forgotten that I was the one who caused the rift."

"Ah yes, that's right, you slept with his wife."

Calder cringed. "Not in front of the girls, Robbie, please."

"Don't you Robbie me, mister. I will not make this easy for you. If you want to make some kind of postmortem amends to your cousin, then fine. But don't drag me into it. I'm sixty-five years old. I have a full and wonderful life, but I certainly don't have the energy to take on a child."

He sighed and turned to Suzanne. "What about you, Suzy? You're young enough, and she is your blood."

Suzanne stammered, her mouth opening and closing over unspoken words.

"I'm sorry, Calder," Herbert said, puffed up like a blowfish with his lips pursed and his chin thrust forward. "But Suzanne couldn't possibility take on the added responsibility of someone else's child. She has enough to take care of as it is."

Calder's long-held dislike of Herbert flared. "No, we wouldn't want Suzanne to miss a date with her hairdresser or her girlfriends for tea."

Suzanne gasped. Herbert's thin lips pursed so hard that they seemed to disappear. "You are in no position to cast stones, Calder," Herbert stated. "For as long as I have known you, you haven't exhibited one selfless bone in your body."

Everyone in the room held their breaths. No one but Roberta had ever spoken back to Calder Colebrook.

Calder eyed the younger man. "So," he finally said, sitting forward. "You have some balls after all. Glad to see it.

I always hated to think that my oldest daughter had married such a pantywaist wimp."

Herbert's mouth did that opening and closing thing again. Suzanne looked as if she might cry.

Roberta reprimanded her ex-husband. "Calder, what has gotten into you? Herbert has done nothing but provide a good life for our daughter, and Suzanne is a model wife and mother."

"They have a cushy life, one that I have provided for them."

"Father!" Suzanne barked.

"It's true, and Herbert knows it. I set him up in practice. I referred patients to him, and stood up for him to my colleagues when they thought he was nothing but a lightweight goof-off who had no business practicing medicine."

Herbert's face went a dangerous shade of red. But Calder didn't back down. "There is a little girl out there who needs us. A little girl who will be tossed off to some foster care system even though she has blood relatives who are perfectly capable of taking care of her. Someone from this family should have the decency to offer help."

"I'll do it."

The words were out of Grace's mouth before she could think. Everyone in the room turned to stare at her, and she felt the blood rise to her cheeks. But she knew it was right. If ever there was a child who needed her, this was it.

Her mind spun, and her heart whirled with excitement.

"You?" they said, gawking.

All eyes turned to her, and suddenly something came clear. She *hadn't* received a message from her father. Then she remembered the surprise she was certain had been on his face. He *hadn't* called her; Suzanne had only assumed he had. This conversation had not been meant for her.

With that, anger flared, bright and intense, like an explosion long held back. Strangely the intensity was exhilarating.

"Why not me?" she demanded.

Purpose and a great, nearly overwhelming joy coursed through her like a heady wine.

"I don't have to worry about hairdressers or teas," she said with calm determination. "Besides, I have a bit of money tucked away."

"Now, Grace dear," her mother said carefully. "A child is a big commitment."

"Commitment to children doesn't seem to be the strong suit for anyone in this family, so why pick on me?" she shot back.

Silence simmered through the room while her sister's eyes went wide, and her mother held her hand to her chest, though her father actually chuckled.

"I'm sorry," she said, hating that she had been unkind, "but why can't you see that I can do this?"

"For one," her father explained, "they want someone married—"

"*You* aren't married," she countered.

"It wasn't me they were interested in" he added, "at least not once they learned that your mother and I weren't married anymore. And now that I'm in the middle of a rather, er, messy divorce, they want me even less. Moreover, they are looking for someone who knows something about children. This child will no doubt be traumatized after the death of her mother. She needs someone around her who has experience."

"I've worked with kids for years!"

Her father's face filled with sympathy. "Grace, you've watched them through a two-way mirror. You observe, take notes. That's very different from actually raising a child."

The words were true, but hurt nonetheless. She had constructed a world that was carefully wrapped and unreal. So unlike the world in Jack's emergency room. But the truth made her want this child all the more, made her want to fight, because deep down she knew this little girl needed her.

"Social services want your mother or Suzanne," he added apologetically. "I don't think an unmarried twenty-nine-year-old who has just lost her job will fit the bill."

"That's ridiculous," she stated obstinately.

"Tell that to the state. Besides, don't get so worked up. It's only temporary, anyway. Once they learned about my marital situation, and I told them that I couldn't imagine Roberta or Suzanne would do it—though I had to try—they said they would find another relative or family that is more suited to the task than any of us."

"Then why not let Grace take her until then," Suzanne mused, an edge to her voice. "If she's so free, and thinks she can do it. . . ."

The sentence hung in the air unfinished, though the meaning was clear. Suzanne expected her to fail.

But they didn't know her, never had.

"I can do this, Suzanne," Grace said very clearly. "But more important, this child needs me, and I have plenty of love to give."

Chapter
Fourteen

It didn't take much more convincing before Calder promised to arrange for little Ruth Colebrook to stay with Grace until a suitable family could be found. Now Grace had a week to prepare.

Those long, desperate minutes in the ER were gone, the leftover feelings of despair pushed back by the promise of a child coming into her life. New purpose, deeper meaning. A sign that at every end of the road, a new path unexpectedly could pop open.

Twenty minutes after leaving her mother's, Grace stepped into her apartment and found herself stunned, excited, and amazed that she would be caring for a child. Questions rushed through her. What would Ruth be like? Sweet and cuddly. Sweet and shy. It hardly mattered. Grace would make this child feel safe and loved at a time when she must be so sad.

The answering machine blinked at her, and when she pushed the button, Jack's voice played through the room.

"Grace, are you there?" He sounded half exasperated, half amused. Then silence, before his voice lowered, that deep rumbling sound that sent shivers pricking along her skin. "Call me, Grace. We need to talk."

The message clicked off, and the machine rewound. She shook sensation away. She might have a bad habit of ending up in Jack's bed, but he had a bad habit of wanting to talk about it. She didn't return his call.

She didn't waste a second getting prepared for Ruth's arrival. First thing she had to do was return all the wedding gifts. She worked like a madwoman, and in less than three weeks from her derailed wedding, the deed was done. It was the end of February, and the relief she felt when the last box passed across the post office counter was enormous, but her only celebration was cleaning every corner and crevice of the apartment.

During that time, Grace made good on her other promise to avoid Jack, which wasn't easy considering he was making a determined effort to see her. He knocked on her door, called her apartment, even rang her buzzer from downstairs a time or two. But she didn't want to see him. Primarily because she was half afraid that with just one look she'd throw herself at him.

She would not fall into his arms again.

She remembered the hospital, remembered the trauma that had careened around her and in her head at all that had gone on. The intensity she had felt for life, for Jack. Wondering how she could survive this crazy world. Then the very next day, out of nowhere, she was given the chance to take care of a child. The despair turned to joy.

On the fourth day she finally opened the closet that contained the stairway leading to the attic that the real estate woman had said could be cleaned up and made into a master suite or extra bedrooms.

Grace walked up the very narrow staircase into the dim and dusty upper regions. At one time the entire brownstone had been a single-family dwelling, this attic reserved for the servants needed to run a household.

A century later, it was empty except for long-forgotten cans of paint and grimy glass windowpanes. She walked around the space, tiny puffs of dust billowing into the air with each careful step. She walked from room to room, going into the bath where the faucet chugged and sputtered but finally ran clean. With a little hard work, this place could be perfect for a child.

Not hesitating another second, Grace pulled on a pair of baggy jeans, a cropped sweater, twisted her long curly hair into a clip at the back of her head, then got to work. She washed floors and walls, cleaned windows until the sun came streaming in, and scrubbed the bath until her fingers were raw. She worked until every inch of the top floor was sparkling and clean. By the end of the day her body ached, but the entire apartment smelled of lemon cleansers and thick beeswax polish. She was exhausted but euphoric, until she realized she didn't have a stick of furniture for the room.

The phone started ringing just as she came downstairs. Her mother's voice whirled on the answering machine, and a thought hit her.

"Mom!" she blurted out as she grabbed up the receiver.

"Mom?" Roberta asked in her imperious tone.

"Mother, sorry. I need my old furniture."

"Heavens, why?"

"For Ruth."

"Ruth?"

"The little girl . . ."

"Ah yes, the little girl."

Grace prayed her mother didn't go to that place of selective memory—remembering only what was convenient. "I've just finished cleaning the upstairs, and now I need some furniture. As long as you aren't using mine anymore—"

"Grace." Her mother drew out her name with ominous import. "This child isn't going to be there for more than a few days. A few weeks at the most. It won't do anyone any good if you get attached."

"Mother," she stated, hating the hard bite of reality her mother's words made her feel. "What would you have me do? Make Ruth sleep on the floor?"

"What about a sofa?"

"Mother!"

Roberta sighed. "No, I suppose that wouldn't do."

"Good. Then could you send over my old things?"

"Well, I suppose eventually you were bound to want them. Age has a way of making a person feel nostalgic."

Grace heard an odd note in her mother's voice. "Are you feeling nostalgic?"

"Absolutely not. I'll have everything sent over. It shouldn't be more than a week or two."

"That's too long! I need it by the end of the week."

"Mercy, Grace. How do you possibly expect me to do that?"

"You're a miracle worker, Mother. If anyone can get it done, it's you."

"Yes, well, that's true. I'll see what I can arrange."

Grace could all but hear her mother's mind start to work and coordinate.

"I'll let you know when the delivery will be made." Her mother started to hang up.

"Mother, why did you call?"

"Oh, yes." Roberta grew awkward on the phone. "I just wanted you to know that I was proud of you the other day."

"You were? I thought you didn't want me to take care of Ruth."

"Truth is, I don't. But I'm proud that you are willing to step up to the task. You always were a compassionate child." Her mother sighed. "I just don't want you to get hurt."

A feather could have knocked Grace over. Moments like these were what reminded her of how much she loved this woman, even though she was a difficult one to figure out. One minute throwing a tantrum, the next showing a caring side that sometimes Grace felt the woman tried to hide. "Don't worry, Mother. I won't lose my head over this child. I know it's only temporary. But while she's here, I want her to feel welcome."

"All right. If you're sure."

"I'm sure."

They rang off, and Grace felt exhausted but elated. Next she called Mark, who promised to get her plenty of toys, adding that he thought he could rustle up a pair of Girlfriends' Feathered Mules. Spreading her arms wide, she twirled around, slowly, before she wrapped her arms close and hugged herself tight.

"I'm going to make this into the most wonderful room," she whispered. "A room filled with happiness and laughter. And love. Lots of love."

Her throat swelled with an emotion she had never felt before, so huge that she felt as if she would explode from sheer joy.

"Whether you stay for one week or one year, it doesn't matter. I promise I will take care of you. I promise that you'll feel safe."

Jack looked through his mail, separating bills from junk, then set it all aside. During the last week he had knocked on Grace's door, talked to her message machine, and once even found himself lingering outside his door when he thought he heard her coming up to the building. He should have been happy that he had seen neither hide nor hair of Grace Colebrook. But the fact was, he couldn't deny the urge he felt to see her.

He told himself he simply wanted to make sure she was all right. An impersonal visit. But no matter what he told himself, he knew it was more than that.

Thinking about the last night they spent together—her body coming to life beneath his touch—left him amazed and in awe of her passion. But it was the hours afterward, her lying in his arms, that wouldn't leave him alone. He couldn't remember the last time he had slept so soundly, waking rested, kissing her brow before going to the shower. Only to return to find her gone.

Now she was avoiding him. The realization didn't sit well with Jack, though he couldn't quite bring himself to admit it. He was used to getting what he wanted, and he wanted to see her.

Any other woman he knew would have called him a hundred times by now. Though hell, any other women he knew never would have left his bed.

If he had learned nothing else about Grace Colebrook, it was that she wasn't like any other woman he had ever known. Was that the appeal? The elusiveness? He had the reassuring thought that it was nothing more than that. But still he wanted her.

Hell, he didn't want to want her. Since he had known her, she had snuck out of his apartment, twice, had lied about her name—and tested the long-held control he'd had over his emotions. He had the glittering half-formed thought that this was the worst of her sins.

But still, he couldn't get her out of his mind.

With his boot heels ringing on the hardwood floor, he banged up the stairs and pounded on her door. He couldn't have been more surprised when the door opened after only one sharp knock.

"Well, well, well, look who we have here!"

It took a second for Jack to recognize Grace's cross-dressing friend, Mark. He had never seen him dressed as a man. Today Mark wore slacks and a sports coat, and a Harvard tie.

"Noticing the tie, I see. I read in that article that you're a Harvard boy, too," Mark stated.

"Yes," Jack responded, his single syllable as stiff as his shoulders were.

"Mark Beacher. I don't believe we've ever been formally introduced." He extended his hand.

They shook. "Jack Berenger. I'm here to see Grace."

"God forbid we exchange any small talk."

Jack must have grimaced, because Mark laughed.

"Let me see if she's receiving," Mark said, then shut the door before Jack could step inside.

Receiving?

Not more than a few seconds passed before the door reopened. Mark came out, shrugging into his coat.

"She doesn't want to see you," he said.

"Too bad," Jack responded. "She's going to see me."

Mark chuckled. "I agree. Sometimes Grace doesn't know what is good for her. Go in. I don't know what is going on between you two—in fact, I don't think either of you knows what is going on. But I think it might do you both good to figure it out."

Mark started past him on the landing. He stopped abruptly and was so close to Jack that his eyes narrowed. Standing there, Mark looked more like a boxer than a cross-dresser.

"Don't make me regret sending you in there. If you hurt her, you'll answer to me."

Jack was a full head taller than Mark, and he guessed that he could easily knock him senseless. But Jack respected his concern for this woman.

"I won't hurt her, you have my word."

Mark stared at him for a long time, as if taking his measure. "Fine," he said in the end. "And don't let her quips and jokes fool you. She is a sweet and very sensitive woman. She's in the kitchen."

Standing just outside the apartment, Jack waited until he heard the downstairs entry door rattle closed. Pulling a grim breath, he walked into the apartment. All was quiet. He took in the colorful pottery mixed with elegant art, a room that looked very much like its owner. A defiant mix.

He walked into the kitchen. She stood at the high counter that separated the sink and stove from a breakfast nook with a small oak table.

Unlike the last time he had been inside her apartment on the night of her dinner party, there wasn't a trace of a dirty dish or anything out of place. Sun drifted in through sparkling clean windows, and everything smelled of sunshine and lemons.

She looked out into the gardens below, her silhouette beautiful and highlighted by the sun. Something was different about her today, something was lighter. He felt it instantly.

He leaned his shoulder against the doorjamb, his boots crossed at the ankles, his arms folded on his chest.

"You look happy."

Jerking around, her eyes flashed dark and heated at the sight of him. Was she remembering how he had caressed her? Did the memory wake her up at night, as it did him? Did she feel a shiver of heat race through her when she thought of his tongue gliding across her skin?

But her excitement was brought immediately under check, and he would have sworn that she actually blushed.

"I told Mark to tell you I wasn't here," she said, though not before clearing her throat.

"He told me."

"He told you that I wasn't here, or he told you that I told him that?"

Jack shook his head, then pushed away from the door-jamb. "He told me not to get sidetracked by your quips and twist of words."

"The traitor."

"I'm starting to like the guy. He's a Harvard man, you know."

"Then go out and buy a dress, and I'll set the two of you up on a date."

"No thanks. He's not my type."

He took the steps that separated them until he stood before her, forcing her to tilt her head back to meet his eyes.

"You have a bad habit of sneaking out of my apartment," he said, his voice rugged and deep.

He saw the pulse leap in her throat, and unable to help himself, he reached out and ran his fingers along the porcelain column of her neck.

"We have a bad habit of ending up in situations we have no business being in," she responded. "I'm really not that kind of girl."

His laughter filled the high-ceilinged kitchen before it lowered to a rumbling deepness. "What kind of girl is that?"

She shot him a scowl. "You know what kind."

"The kind who is passionate and full of life."

"Days ago that 'full of life' part was giving you fits. I think you might have mentioned the word *irresponsible*."

"Did I say that?" he asked with a chuckle.

"Something to that effect."

"I must have had a reason."

"None that I could see. In fact, there are those who could argue the case that *you* are irresponsible."

"How so?" he asked, his strong fingers curling around the soft skin of her upper arm.

"I might be having more . . . relations with you than I should, but I don't have them with anyone but you."

"Glad to hear it."

"Ack!" She shook her head. "You, on the other hand, have a long line of women at your beck and call, thank you very much."

"You're welcome."

Grace screeched in frustration. "You talk about me never being serious."

"Okay, I'll be serious. I've been thinking."

"About what?"

"About you. About us."

"Us? There is no us. Just you and me living in the same building and needing to get along."

"We do get along."

"Barely, and only when we are—"

"Making love?"

"That only happened once! Okay, almost twice, but that is it."

"It has nearly happened several times since that first night."

He ran his thumb down her arm, the tip grazing the side of her breast, and her breath caught.

"*Nearly* being the operative word," she responded, forcing the words to be steady, knowing that had he even tried to make love to her the other night, *nearly* would have not applied.

She jerked away and strode determinedly around the counter. Suddenly she felt the need to eat. Lots. Preferably chocolate. She stuck her head in the refrigerator.

"Do you ever turn to anything besides food when you're upset?" he asked, coming up behind her.

"I am not upset." Drat. No chocolate. At least no chocolate that she could eat. She had made the most heavenly moist double chocolate fudge cake with fudge and walnut icing, but that was a surprise for Ruth, and she refused to cut it.

She considered the plastic container of sprouts, though not for long before she pulled out the lemon chiffon cake she had made the day before.

Nervous, jittery, or simply having the good sense to feel the need to flee with Jack standing so near, she steadied her hand as she piled a slice high on a delicate Wedgwood plate. Just as she took a bite, she looked up. "Oh, sorry," she mumbled, "would you care for a piece?"

Jack grimaced. "No thanks, I'll pass. Though you certainly make it look appealing."

She gave him an *it's your loss* shrug and took another bite. Jack made himself at home by going to the refrigerator himself and pulling out an unopened bag of bright orange carrots. Leave it to him to make her feel even worse by washing one, peeling it, then munching on it with his big, strong teeth.

"Mmmmm," he said. "You should try these sometime."

She glowered at him, then shoveled another bite in before the last one was swallowed.

He shook his head. "Tsk, tsk, Emily Post would be appalled."

"I'm not sure she would be any happier with you for barging into my apartment uninvited."

He conceded her point with a nod of his head and another bite of carrot.

"Now, where was I?" he asked, brushing his hands off after the last bite.

"Leaving," she stated hopefully.

"Nope, I believe we were discussing you slipping out of my bed."

Her face scrunched up. "You know, why can't you be one of those insensitive sorts of men who drive women crazy because they're always closed off and refuse to talk."

He opened his mouth to respond, but she wrinkled her nose, and waved his words away.

"What am I saying?" she groused. "You *are* closed off, distant, as close to the Neanderthal as Cro-Magnon man. It's just that you have to *talk* all the darned time. Or at least talk about things I have no interest in discussing."

"Like sex."

"Yes, like sex. It drives me crazy."

"Sex?"

"No! You!"

His face grew serious, and he crossed his arms on his chest. "We've gotten off on the wrong foot."

"What is that supposed to mean?"

"It means that we need to start over. We need to pretend that we haven't met before."

Without warning, she screamed. Jack—big strong, manly Jack—leaped off his feet at the shrill sound. "What was that for?"

"I always wondered what I would do if I found a stranger in my apartment."

His serious look turned foul, which quite frankly suited Grace a whole lot better. It was that crooked smile or deep, dark seriousness that got her into trouble with this man. When he looked at her as if he disapproved of everything about her, she could actually breathe and not get carried away with thoughts of what it felt like when his teeth nipped gently at her ear.

He started walking toward her, slowly, determinedly, like a predator stalking its prey.

"What are you doing?" she demanded.

"What does it look like I'm doing?"

"Like you are going to introduce yourself," she said hopefully. "Stranger that you are."

She stuck out her hand. He ignored it as he drew close. She would have made a dash for it had there been an inch of room between him and the kitchen wall. So she backed up instead, not stopping until her back bumped against the counter.

"Now, Jack," she said. "I'm not quite sure that this is the best way to start over."

"I was a fool to think we could."

"Fool? You? No way. Overly optimistic, maybe."

He kept coming.

She held up her fork as protection, a tiny bit of icing left on the tines, making it hard for her to look all that serious. "Don't come any closer."

"Or what? You'll fork me?"

The words hung in the air, the simple exchange of one letter telling exactly what he wanted to do.

They stared at each other for long seconds until Jack stepped so close that he could touch her. But he didn't. He stood there, looking at her, then said, "You drive me crazy."

"Is that your way of starting over?" Even she heard how her voice trembled.

"That's my way of saying that there is something between us—something I can't let go of. I want you." His palms closed around her arms again, the touch bringing a sensual heat coiling low. "You fill me in ways I don't understand."

Her heart hammered, and a great, grand place inside her wanted his words to be true. But the fact was she needed more than a man's simple proclamation that he wanted her.

Her father had wanted many women over the years, all women who played the game of cat and mouse extremely well. She had been playing that game, though not intentionally. She had to wonder if Jack was more intrigued by that than by her. What would happen if she gave in and said yes, take me, make me yours? Because the truth was, despite her father, or perhaps because of him, deep down she had always dreamed of finding a man so utterly devoted to her and so in love that he would want no other woman.

She had tried to convince herself that Walter was that man. An example of how people fooled themselves into seeing what they needed to believe. But Grace wouldn't fool herself anymore.

"What exactly does that mean? Why do you want me? Because you love me?" She said the words before she could stop herself.

Instantly his eyes narrowed, and he dropped his hands to his sides. She could all but feel the flash of tension that seared through him. His lips hardened into a straight line, and she could tell that he hadn't even given the word a thought.

He could want her, could want her badly, but that in no way needed to involve love. The realization hurt, though it shouldn't have. She was the one who had started them on this crazy path of sexual Russian roulette.

"Love?" he asked. "That's a word for inane pop songs with unimaginative lyrics."

She would have laughed out loud had she not been able to see clearly that he meant it. Suddenly all mischief evaporated from the room. His face closed up like blinds slipping down over a window that only seconds before had a view. She could feel how he moved away from her, not physically—he still stood close enough to touch—but mentally.

"Call it what you like, but I happen to like unimaginative

pop songs," she said, searching for the light, noncaring voice that she had mastered long ago, as she tried to slip past him. But just when she thought he would let her go, he caught her arm.

Their eyes met and locked.

She drew a breath. "I can't have desire without love, Jack. At least not anymore."

He stared at her, emotion like fire churning in his chest. But he didn't say a word. She nodded one time, then tugged free.

Jack watched Grace leave the kitchen. "Damn," he muttered under his breath. She had caught him off guard when she had asked about love, and he felt a need to explain.

Going after her, he found the living room empty, as was her bedroom. When he stood very still he could just make out the faint sound of a piano, tinny and somehow not quite right. He turned to the sound and caught a glimpse of a set of stairs he had never noticed before inside the closet.

Stepping closer, the music got louder as he peered up the narrow passageway and saw light gleaming at the top. The stairs creaked underfoot, his shoulders nearly brushing the walls as he climbed.

More sun greeted him at the top. Coming out of the dim light, it took a moment before his eyes adjusted. She sat on the floor in the middle of the room, her head resting against the top of the tiniest piano he had ever seen, plunking out some tune he couldn't place, seemingly unaware that he was there. He was surprised by this second floor, at once decrepit but clean, filled with an assortment of boxes, dainty white furniture. And toys.

The piano played on its own, a tiny player piano, the simple music trilling through the space. An old trunk spilled dress-up clothes in a tangle on the floor. Velvet capes and sequined wands. Low-heeled slippers trimmed with an explosion of flamboyant feathers across the toe. Toys for a little girl.

Jack felt his world rock beneath him as memories tried to seep into his mind, a band tightening around his chest making it difficult to breathe.

"I always wanted one of these."

It took a second for her voice to register in his mind.

"A piano?" he asked, watching mesmerized as a rolled sheet rattled through the miniature upright, making the piano keys play the songs.

She smiled, though there was something odd in her eyes. "Not just any piano. A player piano," she explained. "A friend of mine had one, and I absolutely adored it."

A child's player piano, and suddenly a memory tried to flare, bold and aching. He pushed it away.

Abruptly she flipped the switch, and the music grew distorted, then faded away. She rolled to her feet and moved from toy to toy. "I hope Ruth likes it here," she whispered.

"Who's Ruth?"

"A little cousin I'm going to be taking care of. She arrives tomorrow." She shot him a look. "I hope we can be civil to each other while she's here."

"Why wouldn't I be civil?" he asked coldly.

"Forget it. Just forget it."

But he couldn't forget. Not the toys in this room, or toys from long ago. And when he turned away, he barely made it out of her apartment before the memories hit him hard.

Chapter
Fifteen

Boston, Massachusetts—Years Earlier

"I'm pregnant!"

Jack looked up from the thick medical book he was reading in the library. He blinked in the semidarkness just beyond the circle of light provided by the reading lamp.

"Oh, Jack! Can you believe it? I'm going to be a mother."

A chorus of hushes echoed through the third-floor study area, as Jack could only stare. His young wife stood beside the reading table. She wore her usual pleated wool skirt, oxford cloth shirt with soft bow tie, and penny loafers. Her cheeks glowed with health and excitement.

"I just came from the doctor's office, and he confirmed what I suspected. We are going to have a baby!"

The words seeped in. At first Jack was stunned. They had been so careful. Then he was angry.

They had been so careful.

A librarian stood up from her desk. "Young lady, I am not going to tell you again to keep your voice down."

Marsha laughed, telling the stern-looking woman to hush herself.

"What do you mean you're pregnant?" Jack asked, his voice low and dangerous.

She didn't realize he was upset. She leaned over and

planted her elbows on the stack of books on the table. "We had sex, silly," she said, admonishing him like a coquettish flirt.

The librarian stormed over. "I've had enough of your shenanigans. This is not the place for such discussion."

Jack slammed his book shut and took Marsha's arm, and only then did she understand he was angry.

"Jack, what's wrong?"

They came face-to-face outside the imposingly modern expanse of Harvard's medical school library.

"What do you mean you are pregnant, Marsha? We discussed this. We've made plans. We were not going to start a family until after I finished my residency. I've just started my third year of med school."

Anger flared in her eyes. "We didn't discuss anything. You *told* me what we were going to do. You never asked what I wanted. I want a child."

"And Marsha gets what Marsha wants."

Four years ago, when they first met, her petulant demands had seemed cute and so very different from anything Jack had experienced in his life. At the time, she had represented a world far removed from his own—so like Harvard's ivy-covered redbrick buildings from the hells of New York City streets. He had wanted that life. Now he was paying the price.

"I'm not going to sit around until I'm old and gray before I have baby, Jack."

"You're barely twenty-one. We've only been married a matter of months."

"Old enough. Besides, all my friends are pregnant, and I'm not going to be the only one who isn't."

"Ah, just like you weren't going to wait around to marry me. Is that what our marriage about? We make plans—and you know that we did discuss this, and you agreed—then you secretly do whatever you want? You went off the pill, didn't you?"

She looked away.

Jack sighed and plowed his hands through his hair. "I have responsibilities, Marsha. To you, to my brother. I am working my ass off, and working nights as well. Sometimes I think you don't want me to make it through med school."

"Sometimes I wonder if it's worth it," she bit out. "You could work for my father. He'd love to have you come into the business. You'd be great at selling insurance." She started to get excited about the idea. "Just think. Daddy would pay you a huge salary, and then we could buy a fabulous house, and play golf at the club."

A cold shot of fury raced through him, fury at her, at the situation, and at himself. Did he want too much? Him, a poor boy from the wrong part of town? Was he fooling himself to believe he could be a doctor?

But he wasn't forced to answer his own questions. Or give up his dreams. As much as he hated it, Marsha's parents came to their aid yet again. If it hadn't been for Marsha's parents, Jack wasn't certain if he would have become a doctor. He owed them, and her.

Regardless of how it happened, seven months later, Marsha gave birth to an eight-pound, nine-ounce baby girl. Daphne Jane Berenger. They called her Daisy.

Jack had never felt a love so strong as the day the nurse placed his daughter in his arms.

Chapter
Sixteen

Ruth Colebrook arrived at the brownstone on West Sixty-ninth Street the following day.

As soon as the intercom buzzed, Grace dashed down and around and pulled open the front door herself with thoughts of all the love she would shower on this child. "Hello!"

Both a tired-looking woman and the little girl took a step back.

"You must be Ruth and Miss Bancroft. I'm thrilled that you're here. I'm Grace."

"Hello," the woman finally said, her hands on the child's shoulders as if to keep her there. "Ruth, say hello to your cousin."

Ruth scrunched up her face and stuck out her tongue.

Grace's eyes went wide, and for half a second she could only stare. The child stood on the front stoop stubbornly belligerent. She wore a badly mended, frightfully small sweater beneath a tattered coat against the early March cold. Her pleated skirt didn't match anything, her knee-high socks had seen better days, and her shoes had thick polish over the scuffs.

Not to be deterred, Grace bent down in front of the child. "Hello, Ruth. I'm so happy you're here."

"Good for you," the child snapped. "I'm not."

"Ruth," the state's agent said, "mind your manners."

"Why don't you mind yours? Your claws are jabbing into my shoulders."

Instantly, the woman's hands sprang away.

Grace knew that Ruth was seven years old. Size-wise that seemed about right, but with the expression and the miniature adult clothes, not to mention the words coming out of her mouth, she seemed more like she was 107. Though she probably felt that old after all she had been through in her short life. Grace's heart went out to her.

"Ruth," Grace said, "I was just getting ready to have some cake. Would you like some?"

This got the child's attention, and Grace was encouraged. How bad could it be if they both loved to eat?

"What kind?" she grumbled.

"Chocolate."

"Well, maybe a little."

The state's agent took that as her cue. "I'll leave you two to get acquainted. I want to get back to the office before traffic gets too bad."

Grace fought off a stab of panic that the woman would leave so soon. Shouldn't she come inside, make sure the child was in good hands?

Miss Bancroft handed Grace a legal-sized envelope. "Everything you need is in there. Phone numbers, names. Call the office if there's a problem."

"There won't be any problems," she stated optimistically.

Grace waved the woman good-bye, then she picked up Ruth's tiny suitcase and they started up the stairs.

"Geez," the child said with an irritated scoff. "Where do you live? On the roof?"

Grace chuckled. "Nearly. It's on the fourth floor. It's really a great place—if you can deal with all the stairs."

The apartment gaped open. Ruth passed through while

Grace shut and locked the door. When she turned back, Ruth walked from bureau to desk, table to credenza, where she found the T-shirt Mark had brought over.

" 'More Fluff than Stuff.' What's this?" the child wanted to know.

Grace blushed. "Just a shirt."

"I can see that. But what does it mean."

"Just a silly gift from a friend. A joke, actually, about me."

"Oh, great, they stick me with an airhead. Just what I need."

Grace forced a smile, then walked toward the kitchen. Just as she turned back she was surprised when Ruth slipped a tiny ladybug paperweight into her tattered pocket.

Standing there stunned, Grace had no idea what to do. Should she call her on it, or leave it alone?

Whatever remnant hope or illusions she'd had about how joyful it was going to be to take care of this child disappeared. Suddenly she wished she had thought to buy a book on child rearing. In a matter of five minutes, she already was at a loss. Instinct told her to leave it alone. At least for now.

Having little else to go on, Grace pasted on a smile and called out to Ruth. The child whipped around, a belligerent scowl plastered on her face.

"Yeah?" she challenged defensively, as if she was sure she was caught.

"How about that cake?"

Ruth's tiny brows riddled together in confusion.

"Yes, we'll each have a big slice of the most delicious chocolate you've ever had, and top it off with a tall glass of milk."

Hesitantly, as if Ruth didn't quite trust the developments, she followed Grace to the kitchen. "Milk's for babies."

"You're kidding!" Grace exclaimed. "I adore it. I can't imagine not having milk with cake."

"Yeah, well, you also got a shirt out there that says you're a dope. I want coffee."

Grace's head swam, and she would have sworn the agency had lied and given her a child far older than they'd claimed.

But through the muddle of thoughts, Grace knew it was her responsibility to do right by this child, regardless of how she acted. As for the coffee, when she had been young if someone had said she couldn't have something, it only made her want it more.

"Coffee and cake it is," she said, heating a cup left over from breakfast.

Ruth's eyes went wide when the steaming brew was set before her, then envious when Grace poured herself a tall glass of milk. Grace went about eating her cake. Ruth tentatively picked up the coffee, then set it down.

"It's too hot. I'll wait until it cools off."

"Good idea. Would you like a little milk while you wait?"

"Well, yeah," she said like she didn't really care. "Might as well. As dry as this cake is, I need something to wash it down."

A little angel, she was, Grace thought with a tight smile.

"So, tell me about your trip in to Manhattan," Grace said, returning to her chair.

"Trip? It was a ride, from Albany to this junk heap on a gross bus filled with gross people and that gross state woman who probably works as a prison warden on her days off."

"How old did you say you were?"

"Seven. You got a problem with that?"

"Oh, no, you just seem so . . . mature."

"What were you expecting, some crybaby? Some clingy little monkey who would throw her arms around you because she was so happy that you took her in? Forget it. I don't care where I am, whether it's this dump or some other. It doesn't matter to me." She stuffed a bite in her mouth, chocolate left behind on her lips.

They finished their cake, the coffee left untouched—as was Ruth's napkin. The child dragged her arm across her mouth, making Grace shudder.

"Let me show you to your room."

"Sure, whatever."

Grace took the battered old-fashioned, hard-sided suitcase in her hand and walked into her bedroom. The child followed. But the minute Grace opened her closet door that led to the staircase, Ruth stopped dead in her tracks.

"Hey, what is this? You making me sleep in a closet? I should have known that some relative I had never heard of had to be some kind of a lunatic crazy person." She crossed her tiny arms on her chest. "You're crazy if you think I'll be sleeping in there."

Blinking, Grace became flustered. "You're not sleeping in a closet. There's a bedroom upstairs. The stairs are in here."

Ruth looked utterly disbelieving.

"I swear. Look."

With eyes narrowed, Ruth took a few tentative steps to the doorway, hesitated, then holding firmly to the door-jamb, she peered around the corner. "Hey, there's stairs in here. Who the heck puts stairs in a closet?"

"I think when the brownstone was built the closet wasn't here. When they turned the house into separate apartments, they had to add a kitchen and a closet somewhere on this floor to make it into a separate space. One of these days I'll have regular stairs put in. But I haven't been here that long."

"What about locks?"

"Locks?"

"Yeah, on the door. No way are you going to lock me in some attic room until my hair grows ten feet long and my teeth fall out."

Grace shuddered, and couldn't help wondering what kind of books this child read. At least she hoped the ideas stemmed from books.

Taking the door handle, Grace displayed the knob, turning it back and forth. "See, no locks at all."

The child inspected the doorframe, as if looking for external barriers. "Well, all right," she said, heading up the steps like a doomed prisoner.

But once upstairs, Grace heard the gasp of delight, and felt it shiver through her soul.

Arriving at the top of the stairs, she got there just in time to see the child's amazement that even all her considerable effort couldn't hide entirely. Ruth touched every one of the toys Mark had gotten, marveling. But it was the canopied bed that Grace had slept in as a child, with lacy white eyelet coverings and the vanity, which Ruth liked best. How well Grace remembered the tiny white French provincial vanity, with silver-backed brushes, and delicate perfume bottles. It was the one thing her mother had gotten her as a child that she truly adored.

Tentatively, Ruth pulled up the top of the vanity, revealing a beveled mirror. She stared at her reflection, as if unfamiliar with the little girl who stared back. Carefully, she sat in the little throne chair with the gold velvet cushion. With nearly trembling fingers she picked up the time-worn but still beautiful silver-backed brush.

"Do you like it?" Grace asked quietly, feeling heartened.

Instantly the mood changed. Ruth stiffened before tossing the brush aside, slamming the mirror shut, and standing. "It's a room for a stupid prissy girl."

Grace breathed in through her nose. She felt like she
had been pushed into the deep end of the pool before she
knew how to swim. How to respond to this child? Again
and again, just in the few minutes she had been there,
Grace had no idea what to do.

"Sorry you don't like it. Can I help you unpack?"

"Nah. I'll do it."

"Fine. The bathroom is down that hall, and this is the
closet," she added, opening an antique white armoire.
"After you get settled, come find me. I'll be in the kitchen
making dinner."

Returning downstairs, Grace made a point of leaving
the door open, even went so far as to prop an upholstered
chair in front of it. Then she busied herself with the evening meal, turning on the small television so she didn't
have to think. When forty-five minutes had passed with no
sign of Ruth, Grace wiped her hands and returned upstairs.
Ruth was sound asleep on the comforter, the ragged little
girl on the pristine white.

With her heart beating hard, her throat tight, Grace walked
over, then carefully sat on the mattress. The child only
moaned and rolled over. In sleep, Ruth looked as sweet as
an angel. With her own hands nearly trembling now, Grace
reached out and gently smoothed Ruth's curly brown hair,
so like her own, her cheeks rosy and sweet. Tears burned in
her eyes as she knew that this was what she had always
wanted, a child to love. But Ruth wasn't hers, would be
taken away, and she had to remember that.

After one long, cherished moment, Grace stood and
pulled off Ruth's shoes, then pulled the comforter over to
keep her warm. Unpacking the little suitcase, she found

more of the same tattered clothes. But at the very bottom, she found a single snapshot, the edges torn from wear.

It was a woman, the image starting to fade, a hint of a smile curving on her lips as if she was afraid to give in and be happy. Grace didn't have to be told that the woman in the photograph was Ruth's mother.

She propped the picture on the nightstand next to the bed, and folded the clothes away in the bureau. Then she turned on the night-light she had found among Ruth's things before switching off the overhead fixture. With that simple photo, Grace had gained a piece of understanding. Like her mother, Ruth was afraid to be happy, afraid that things in life were fleeting. Her mother's death must have only proved that happiness really didn't exist. A difficult lesson for one so terribly young.

"Shopping?" Ruth demanded. "Why would I want to go shopping? Shopping is for stupid girls."

It was the next morning, and Ruth and Grace stood in the kitchen like combatants on either side of a war.

"While I have no doubt that you're anything but stupid, I thought it might be fun to get some new clothes," Grace offered.

The child became defensive, her chin jutting forward. "What's wrong with what I have on?"

Nothing if one didn't mind mismatched socks that looked like a seven-year-old had mended them, or the same sweater and skirt from yesterday. The only thing new about the outfit were the wrinkles from a nightlong sleep.

"I just thought you might enjoy shopping, then we could have lunch afterward." It would be her one splurge since losing her job, but one she felt was warranted. Ruth deserved a day of feeling special. Reservations for the Palm Court at the Plaza had already been made.

"Is there something else you'd rather do?"

The child sighed heavily. "No. Fine. We'll shop."

They went from store to store, but nothing was right until they found a flowered sweater and blue velvet pants. For the first time since she arrived, Ruth's eyes flickered with excitement. But even that was quickly covered. The only time Ruth couldn't quite squelch the light in her eyes was when the ornately garbed doorman at the Plaza held the door, allowing them to enter a world of gilded opulence. She actually squeaked her pleasure when they came to the Palm Court restaurant in the center of the hotel.

"Oh," Ruth breathed, her head falling back to take in the towering ceilings.

Ruth's pleasure grew, so much so that she even let Grace take her hand as they were led to their table. Chubby fingers curled around hers, giddy excitement pulsing through Ruth at such a new and wondrous place, an excited energy as they walked through the tables filled with elegantly dressed men and women. Only when they got to their table did Ruth seem to remember that she had no interest in being nice. With a jerk, she pulled her hand away, then slouched in the ornate chair the maître d' held out for her.

Ordering wasn't any easier. Eating was worse. The child swore she liked nothing, and pushed everything away except for the cream puffs that came at the end of the meal. She tore away the puffed pastry covering, scraping the chocolate sauce, whipped cream, and ice cream into a pile at the edge of her plate, then proceeded to get nearly as much on her face as in her mouth.

Grace cringed. But she wasn't discouraged. It wasn't surprising they would get off to a rough start. They didn't know each other. They had to grow comfortable together.

But three days later, an utter sense of discouragement hit her after taking Ruth to every possible New York City experience that might remotely interest a child, only to have it all thrown back in her face. Ruth did not like the glittering lights of Times Square, or the Central Park Zoo. The Rockefeller ice-skating rink made her scoff with disdain. She refused to get anywhere near the castle in Central Park, and she said "no way is any lousy fake artist sitting along Fifth Avenue going to make me look like some big-eared goofball." Not that Grace could blame her for that one.

On top of it all, Grace hadn't seen Jack since the day he had grown quiet and withdrawn in her apartment. It was foolish, really, that she should peer out the front window so often that Ruth had started asking what she was looking for.

Or the listening, turning expectantly every time she heard some noise in the building. Footsteps, she found herself hoping, coming up the stairs. But it never was. After all the effort Jack had made to see her after the day in the ER, now he stayed away. So much for his statement that he wanted to start over.

She told herself she was glad, that she didn't care. She ignored the fact that she didn't believe a word of it.

To make matters worse, she hadn't received a single response to the résumés she had sent out. In between showing Ruth around, Grace had made follow-up calls to each company. But she had gotten the same response—they would let her know if they were interested.

She refused to turn to her parents for help. Thank goodness she had rarely squandered a dime in all the years she'd had an income. So she was managing. But for how long?

Ruth had been there two weeks when Grace finally saw Jack. The weather had started its slow, arduous climb out of winter with the promise of brightness and warmth, those weeks at the end of March when the sky gives hints that soon it will melt away the winter gray of New York like ice in a spring rain.

Grace sat outside on the front stoop, the streetlight casting her shadow across the steps, the windows of her apartment open, Ruth already asleep. Grace felt spent and she was forced to concede that she wasn't helping Ruth. The child was more unhappy and belligerent than ever, adding pens and coins to her cache of stolen goods. Grace didn't know how either one of them would survive until a more qualified family was found.

Distracted, she didn't notice Jack until he stood before her and he said her name, didn't notice until she yanked her head up from where she pounded it on her knees.

"Jack," she said, her voice low and surprisingly sultry.

He looked handsome and wonderful, though on closer inspection he looked like he'd had a rough day.

"What's wrong?" she asked. "You look awful."

He smiled wryly. "I seem to recall you saying I was insensitive and a sorry example of what women had to choose from these days when I said you looked terrible."

"That's because you're a guy and I'm a girl, and guys can't tell girls they look terrible no matter how horrible they really look."

"Is that in a rule book somewhere? Maybe in that Emily Post's *Perfect Guide to One-night Stands* you mentioned."

Grace chuckled. "You're getting pretty good at this game," she offered.

He looked at her for long seconds. A dog barked in the distance, and a screech of tires sounded somewhere on Broadway. "Is that what this is about, Grace? A game where someone wins and someone loses?"

His words took her aback, startling her with a thought that was so new and horrifying that she couldn't think. Would someone win here? Would someone lose?

"I'm sorry," he said quietly. "I've been on duty for forty-eight hours straight, and I'm exhausted."

Grace remembered her day in the ER, and a shudder ran down her spine. "Working such long hours should be against the law."

"Tell that to the crazies who head out into the streets to find trouble the minute the weather starts to turn warm. The hotter it gets, the worse it becomes. It doesn't help that the hospital is short a doctor right now."

Despite the lines that creased his forehead and the shadowed hint of beard on his jaw and chin, he looked ruggedly handsome. The sensual heat of him rippled through her body, and it took some effort to focus.

"Why do you do it?" she asked suddenly, remembering the article about his renowned practice in Connecticut. "You don't have to work under those conditions."

His face darkened before he visibly calmed himself. "I do it because someone has to, and I'm good at it."

She remembered him that day, instantly coming alert, oblivious to all else but the precarious balance of lives all around him. "You *are* good at it." She considered him for a moment, his mastery at his craft, the way he felt the need to control every aspect of his life and emotions. "Are you one of those doctors who likes to play god?"

His brows slammed together. "No," he answered abruptly. But then he pulled a deep breath and looked somewhere inside himself. "But I do battle with Him," he said with a quiet determination. "Every day. Every minute. And many times I win."

The arrogance of his words shimmered through the air around them, charged, defiant, and a sudden thought whispered through her head. "Are you battling, Jack? Are you trying to win a life . . . or are you trying to prove something?"

The lines of his face grew fierce.

"Ah, Jack. Don't get that look."

"I don't know what you're talking about."

"I'm talking about the way your eyes darken that makes me wonder who you really are. Why you're here, why you work at St. Luke's. Why you are drawn to me but hate the fact that you are."

"I am no more or less than you see," he said, his tone stiff and unyielding. "As to why I am drawn to you, I can no more fathom the answer to that than you can."

Then he started up the stairs, his lips set, his jaw muscles taut. But he was stopped a few steps later when Ruth called out from the upstairs window. "Grace?"

Both adults craned their necks to the fourth floor.

"I'm down here, Ruth."

Jack stared up at the darkened window, no sight of Ruth, only the sound of her voice. After long seconds ticked by, he asked, "Ruth? The little girl who's staying with you?"

"Yes."

"Now *you* sound tired," he said.

"Me? Never."

He retraced his steps and looked at her, his reluctance nearly palpable as he placed one foot on the step in front of her, then leaned forward, crossing his forearms on his thigh. It brought them close, and he studied her. "How's it going? Really."

"Great. Fine. Wonderful, actually."

The tension from moments before was gone, and he gave her a wry grin. "I can see that. You look just like you feel *great, fine, wonderful, actually.*"

She rested her forehead on her arms. "Well, it's almost great, and it gets better every day," she lied hopefully. Surely it couldn't get any worse.

The door pushed open, and a sleepy Ruth appeared. At the sight of Jack, her normal belligerence melted into confusion, before confusion was replaced with the shy awe of a starstruck child. She hung on the doorknob, leaning her head against the edge.

Jack pushed away from Grace and stood at the bottom of the stoop. The two of them took the other's measure. After a moment he smiled. It was a different smile than Grace had seen on him before, different from the ones he offered her, different even from the ones he offered little Timmy and Marvin. It was a special smile that made him look very different from the hard and distant man she knew him to be. He looked almost like an oversized bear standing there, so big and tired, his grin wide and fatherly.

"Hi," he said.

"Ruth," Grace offered, "this is Dr. Berenger."

"Hi," Ruth mumbled in return, surprising Grace with her timid response.

"Call me Jack."

He took the steps until he stood just below Ruth, and extended his large hand. After a second, the child reached out, placing her small palm in his.

"Call me Ruth."

"Nice to meet you, Ruth," he added. "Those are some pretty great pajamas."

She looked down at herself, her chin planted in her chest. With both hands she pulled out the cotton top from between the sides of her robe, all of which had just been bought that afternoon on sale at Macy's.

"Ducks are the best," he added.

"They are?"

"Absolutely."

Ruth had thrown a fit when Grace had bought them, and had only put them on that night because Grace had refused to wash the ratty sweater and pleated skirt the child had clung to like a security blanket.

"Yeah, they are pretty great," she said, lifting her head and smiling.

Jack nodded. "I'm going to see if I don't have some duck pj's myself, then I'm headed for bed. It's been a long few days."

"Do you live with us?" Ruth asked on a startled breath.

"No, I live in the apartment below yours."

"Oh, wow," she enthused. "And you're a doctor?"

"Yep."

"Can you come over to visit?"

"Sure. But another time." He smiled and ruffled her hair, then headed inside.

Ruth and Grace watched him as he disappeared up the stairs, then through his apartment door.

For a few blissful seconds things seemed wonderful and glowing.

"He's beautiful," Ruth said in awe.

The door upstairs clicked shut.

"I guess," Grace answered, her tone a lament. "That is, if you like the tall, dark, and handsome sort."

Ruth crooked her head to look at her, then suddenly they both started giggling.

They returned to their apartment then, without another word, though every few steps they giggled a little bit more.

Chapter
Seventeen

Ruth fell in love with Jack Berenger with all the devoted, determined, and desperate passion of a lonely child who suddenly finds something in the world worth having. In some recess of Grace's mind she understood that this little girl would do whatever it took to see him again. But she didn't realize soon enough.

Three hours after seeing Jack, while she sat on the sofa in her apartment, Ruth lying upstairs in bed, Grace heard the first moan.

Tossing *The New York Times* aside, she felt a flash of panic as she leaped off the floral cushions and dashed upstairs to find Ruth curled up in a ball.

"Ruth, what's wrong?" Grace asked, frozen to the spot, staring at the child.

"I'm dying. The food you made me eat," the child moaned. "You've poisoned me, I can feel it."

Grace had eaten the same thing, but in that second with panic racing through her, that fact didn't register. "We'll go to the hospital."

Ruth rolled over and scowled. "The hospital? What about Dr. Berenger? Downstairs," Ruth stated in a series of punctuated syllables.

Had Grace not been so panicked she might have grown suspicious. But she was panicked. Relief filled her at the mention of Jack, and she flew out the door, down two flights of stairs, and all but fell against his door.

"Jack," she called, banging hard.

But no one came. She banged and banged, and finally she heard muttering and footsteps inside. After what seemed like an eternity, she heard the bolts turn, then Jack pulled open the door.

He stood there, his hair standing up in places, the design of his comforter marking his face. He still wore the same clothes, minus the shirt he'd had on when he'd returned home. Clearly he had fallen face first onto his bed and gone to sleep exhausted.

"This better be good," he half mumbled, half growled.

"Something's terribly wrong with Ruth!"

The change that came over Jack was instantaneous and fierce. Without bothering with shirt or shoes, he raced up the stairs. Grace was right behind him, then up to the top floor, nearly plowing into his back when he stopped in his tracks in front of Ruth's bed.

Grace sucked in her breath. Jack simply stared long and hard.

"Hello, Dr. Berenger," Ruth said, sitting up, her hair brushed for once, the covers folded demurely at her waist, her duck pajama top smoothed. "What brings you here tonight?" she asked, her smile sweet and angelic.

Slowly, Jack turned to Grace with a cold and grim expression. "What is this about?" he demanded.

But Grace was at a loss. She felt foolish and confused, and when she looked over at Ruth, the child smirked. Though when Jack turned back, the angel smile returned. Grace wasn't sure which was worse, the thought of how much this child must hate her, or the realization of how inept she was as a parent.

"I just thought . . ." she began, but nothing seemed right.

Jack dragged his hand through his hair. "I'm too tired to deal with this right now." He headed for the door, stopping just before taking the stairs, and gave both Ruth and Grace a fierce scowl. "I'm going back to bed and I plan to sleep until I can't sleep anymore. Don't wake me unless there's a fire."

Someone banged hard on his door. Jack muttered a curse, though thankfully this time he was already awake.

It was the next morning, and he was fixing breakfast. Wiping his hands on a towel then tossing it aside, he went to the door. Ruth stood in the hallway.

"You know that thing you said about the fire?" she asked, as serious and as calm as a judge.

"Yes," he replied carefully. But before Ruth could say another word, the smell of smoke registered in Jack's brain. Next came the sound of sirens screeching to a halt out front.

For a second time in less than twenty-four hours, Jack leaped up the stairs to Grace's apartment, Ruth following in his wake. Shock riddled through him as he burst into the kitchen just as Grace put out the last of the flames, her arms and fire extinguisher coming down in a shuddering sigh of exhaustion. But even with the fire extinguished he could see that the kitchen was charred and the entire apartment was filled with smoke.

"What happened?" Jack roared, concern making his voice sharp as he stared at Grace, who stood stunned, the hair around her face singed from the heat, her face streaked with sweat and cinders. As his heart pounded furiously, he felt the need to touch her, feel her, to make sure she was all right.

But Ruth came up behind him, her pajamas a mess, her hair a tangle, her eyebrows raised defiantly as she tugged on his shirt. "I told her I hated those gross eggs she likes to make for breakfast. I also told her I wanted cheese toast. Who knew that cheese could make such a mess."

Jack stared at this little girl who stared back, insolent, defiant, as if daring him to say one word to her. Slowly he turned to Grace. She stood like stone, her face a mask of disbelief. She didn't even blink when three of New York's Bravest fully decked out in fire gear stormed into the apartment.

Understanding that Grace was in shock, Jack took control. Over the next several hours, the fire department wrote up their report and Jack saw to it that her insurance company sent an adjuster. The kitchen would have to be completely redone, while the rest of the apartment would have to be rid of smoke damage. Most of the furniture could be saved, but everything, including rugs and draperies, had to be taken away and cleaned. The walls would have to be repainted, and the floors refinished, since the polyurethane coating on the wood just outside of the kitchen had melted.

By late afternoon, when the insurance adjuster had gone, Grace sank down in a kitchen chair and dropped her head into her hands.

"I have a friend who's in construction," Jack said, making mental notes. "I'll give him a call."

Grace murmured her thanks.

"In the meantime," he added, "you can't stay here."

Lifting her head, Grace looked confused.

For the first time, Ruth's face creased with worry. "Where will I go?" she asked, panic reddening her cheeks.

At the sound of Ruth's quavering voice, Grace's face cleared and she straightened. "You'll go with me."

"It wasn't my fault," Ruth stated, her voice both belligerent and scared.

"Hey, it's going to be okay," Grace offered, clearly searching for a kind smile. "Go upstairs and pack the things you need. In two shakes of a stick, I'll have everything arranged."

Ruth looked doubtful, her features creased with the kind of worry that said as clearly as words that she believed she was going to be left alone once again. With a trembling lower lip, she headed for her bedroom. Only when she was gone did Grace's smile falter. "I guess I'll have to call my mother."

Jack nodded his head. "That would be best."

With a cringing grimace, she found the cordless and punched in the number.

"Mother! Hi!" A momentary silence, then, "Mother, why do you automatically assume something is wrong? Nothing is wrong. Ruth's doing great. I told you I was perfectly capable of taking care of a child." Pause. "Of course, I'm sure. I just wanted to say hello, and tell you how much fun Ruth and I are having." More silence. "Yes, fine. We'll talk soon. Bye."

Grace pressed the OFF button, then slid the phone into its cradle.

"That's an interesting way to let the woman know that you'll be staying with her for a few weeks."

Grace squeezed her eyes closed. "I couldn't do it."

"I heard. But sooner or later she'll find out."

"You know," she began, her eyes popping open, "that isn't exactly true."

"What do you mean?"

"*Why* does she have to find out?"

Jack had the distinct premonition that he wasn't going to like the direction of this conversation.

"No one in my family has ever visited any of the apartments I've lived in. Why would they start now? And as often as I let the phone go to the answering machine, I could stay someplace else and just check my messages. They'd never have to know."

"Would you like to share where this someplace else might be?" Jack asked, his gaze narrowing with suspicion.

Grace folded her hands demurely at her waist and gave him a big, radiant smile.

"No way," he stated. "You aren't staying with me."

"Oh, Jack, please. You have that big apartment with just you banging around all by yourself."

"I like it that way."

"Come on, we won't be a bit of trouble."

"Grace—"

"Now, Jack, haven't you heard that saying: 'Like a good neighbor—' "

"Sure, so go live with State Farm."

"Jack!"

They stared at each other, and he saw the devastation seep back into her eyes.

"I can't go to my mother's," she whispered.

With a groan, he hung his head.

"It won't be so bad," she offered hopefully.

At this he muttered an oath.

"You won't even know we're there."

This got a snort.

"Please, Jack."

He lifted his head and shook it, completely unable to believe what he was about to say. "All right."

Grace cried out, leaping up to fling her arms around his neck. "You're a dream."

"Or a fool."

Jack shook his head, then reasoned that being around her full-time had to be the perfect solution to make whatever insane attraction he felt to her wear thin. Then, finally, he could regain control of his life.

* * *

Jack, Grace, and Ruth carted what belongings they would need down to Jack's apartment. Jack hadn't said much else to her, and clearly he wasn't happy about this turn of events. So for once Grace kept quiet and made a point not to make his bad mood worse.

For the first time Grace got a really good look at his place. Always before she'd had other things on her mind when they had crashed through his front door. But she wouldn't think about that, not now.

The ceilings were high, with beautiful crown moldings, his walls painted a bold gray, with the dining room decorated in a vibrant red. At the sight of the dining table a distinct rush of heat raced to her cheeks.

"What's wrong with you?" Ruth wanted to know, suddenly on alert for any impending disaster, her little hard-sided suitcase held tightly in her hand.

"Nothing," Grace said hurriedly.

By then, Jack had turned back to see.

"Sure something's the matter," Ruth added, her brow furrowed in consternation. "One look at that table and you turned all red."

Jack glanced from Grace's face to the dining table before a broad smile pulled at his lips. "I think she's rather fond of it."

Grace glared, and Ruth looked all the more confused, but thankfully she didn't ask any more questions.

"Why don't you show us to our rooms?" Grace said through gritted teeth.

This only added to Jack's amusement as he led them upstairs.

The upper floor consisted of three bedrooms, none of them very far apart, and for the first time Grace wondered at the wisdom of staying with this man, especially since he put her in the room closest to his.

"Don't get any ideas," she stated in a hiss when Ruth went into her new room.

"What kind of ideas did you have in mind?" he asked, his dark eyes blazing with heat, his lips curving at one corner as he stepped closer.

Grace squeaked, then raced after Ruth, ignoring Jack's deep rumbling laughter that followed her down the hall.

She stepped inside the room just in time to see Ruth quickly hiding the snapshot of her mother. Grace didn't say a word, only stood there as Ruth neatly unpacked the rest of her things.

"I've got to run by the hospital," Jack said, coming up behind her.

"You're leaving? So soon."

"Yes, unless you have a better idea," he said, the slow spread of his mischievous smile returning.

"Jack," she admonished, wiggling her eyebrows in the direction of Ruth.

He chuckled. "Then I'm off."

"When will you be home?"

He looked at her like she had lost her mind. "Why?"

"What time should I have dinner ready?"

His smile fled. "We aren't playing house, Grace. You worry about dinner for you and Ruth. I'll take care of myself."

"That's silly," she stated. "There is no reason for you to cook if I already am. Besides, it's my way of repaying your kindness. What time will you return?"

"Grace, I may or may not be back in time for dinner."

Grace and Ruth watched him go.

"He'll be here," Grace predicted.

Ruth looked at her like she was crazy.

Once unpacked, Grace and Ruth found themselves in Jack's living room, sitting side by side on the sofa, with no idea what to do next. For the last few weeks their days had been filled with Ruth's low-burning antagonism. Grace couldn't say that Ruth had warmed up to her, but the child no longer sent overly mature and exceedingly sharp barbs her way. Grace was thankful, she was, she only wished it had come about for different reasons. They were saved from having to decide what to do next when the phone started to ring. And ring. And ring.

By the time Jack returned nearly five hours later, Grace was not in the best of moods.

Jack stopped in the dining room where Grace sat on one side of the table, Ruth on the other, the expanse lined with a feast.

"Look, Jack," Ruth said. "We made you dinner."

At the sight, Jack's face creased with hard lines. "Thanks, but I'm not hungry."

Ruth's smile fell, and she returned her attention to her plate.

"Jack," Grace said, her tone overly sweet, "surely you can have at least a taste of the meal that Ruth and I slaved over, though not without a slew of distractions."

"What are you talking about?" He glanced around as if looking for some new catastrophe.

"Phone calls," Ruth supplied. "Millions of them."

"Ruth, don't exaggerate," Grace admonished. "There weren't millions. Only ten, maybe twenty. All from women."

"You answered my phone?"

Ruth leaped up and dashed to the kitchen, then returned with a list. "At first we did, but it got to be kind of a lot, so we let tons go to your machine. I wrote the first ones down, though." She started to read off the names.

"There was Brandy—"

Grace snorted. "Brandy? Probably the counter girl at Harvey's Deli."

"Janine—"

"Hatcheck girl at Sardi's?" she asked with cloying sweetness.

"Then Tiffany called. Three whole times."

"Ah yes, Tiffany. With a name like that, she's got to be a lap dancer from the Lower East Side."

Jack snatched the list away before Ruth could finish, then pasted on a glowering smile. "You're wrong, cupcake. They're a mortgage banker, clothes designer, and a Ph.D. specializing in handed molecules at Roche Pharmaceuticals. In that order."

Grace snorted. "I've seen the kind of women you date. I can't imagine any of them can spell *handed molecules*, much less specialize in them. Furthermore, my name is not cupcake."

Ruth giggled before she covered her mouth with her napkin. Grace pushed up from the table and took the extra plate to the kitchen.

"Looks like you're in trouble," Ruth whispered.

"I didn't do anything," he responded distractedly, listening to the clatter of cutlery in the kitchen. "I told her not to make dinner for me, and I certainly can't be blamed for the women who called."

"You should apologize, anyway, otherwise I bet she stuffs all the special little cakes we made in the garbage pail without giving anyone a bite."

Grace marched back in, and Jack muttered a curse. But after a long second of Ruth staring at him with big hangdog eyes, he sighed.

"I'm sorry, Grace," he said, his tone stiff and formal.

Ruth nodded her approval and rubbed her hands together in anticipation of cake.

Taking a deep breath, Grace looked at Jack. "Oh, I'm sorry, too. I'm being ridiculous."

"Good, I'm glad you see it that way. And as long as you're being honest with yourself, do you mind sharing what you are being ridiculous about? I told you I wouldn't be here for dinner, and if you plan to stay here you'd better get used to the fact that I come and go as I please."

Grace stiffened, then pursed her lips, only to storm out of the room once again.

Ruth groaned. "There goes our dessert."

Women. Lots of women. Not that it was any of her business, but Grace felt a frisson of something. Jealousy? No way. It was disgust. Jack Berenger was no different from her father, with his long line of women waiting in the wings. She rolled her eyes, gave a dinner plate a good wipe with the drying towel, and muttered about how he was worse than her father. Good God, she couldn't imagine how Jack had the time to keep up with them all.

She snorted as she put the last dish away. He had stamina, she'd give him that.

She had the flickering thought that since the day of the Krispy Kremes, she hadn't seen so much as a glimpse of a woman coming or going from Jack's apartment. Though clearly she hadn't been looking at the right times.

Jack had disappeared into his bedroom hours ago, and after Ruth finished eating two of the little individually baked and iced cakes, she took a quick bath, then crawled into bed. Grace snapped the dishwasher closed, turned the dial to wash, then headed upstairs.

The apartment was quiet, and not even the sounds of traffic made their way into the thick-walled confines of this masculine domain. On the second floor she checked on

Ruth, who was sound asleep, so Grace went into her own bedroom—only steps away from Jack's.

Suddenly her insistence that she and Ruth stay there seemed mad. What was so wrong with her mother finding out that her apartment had nearly burned down?

But she knew. Jack Berenger was far less intimidating than Roberta Colebrook, even if he did put her into a bedroom adjoining his.

She took off her clothes, then primly belted her flannel robe before going in to take a bath. Lost in thought, she pushed through the door, then felt her heart leap. It was the same bath she had been in once before, only now Jack stood in the center. He had just gotten out of the shower, his dark hair in wet slicks across his head. He rubbed a towel vigorously across his broad back and didn't realize she stood there until he tossed the terry cloth aside.

When he saw her, he stood very still, but didn't say a word. Clutching the edges of her robe together at her throat, she told herself to turn away. But she could do little more than take in his chiseled form. He was stunning, his broad shoulders, tapering into a narrow waist and hips. His manhood hung thick against his thigh, rapidly swelling at the sight of her.

"Did you lose your way?" he asked, his voice a guttural rasp.

"I'm afraid that happened a long, long time ago."

With both hands, he raked his hair back from his forehead, his chest and stomach muscles rippling. Still, Grace couldn't move. Her chest felt tight, a slow heat building inside her, sliding low when he took a step toward her.

"What are you doing?" she asked, her voice shaky.

"I'm not sure."

Grace tried to laugh, but the sound stuck. "Then let me enlighten you. You're walking."

"That I know."

"Toward me."

"I know that, too."

He didn't stop until they stood mere inches apart, the hair on his chest still damp, glistening in the golden glow of light. Her knees felt weak with yearning, and as much as she wanted to touch him, she wouldn't allow herself to let go of the thick flannel.

"The question is, why?" she managed to ask. "Why are you walking toward me when you've made it clear that I drive you crazy, not to mention that you can have an entire list of women as exhibited by the slew of phone messages you received today?"

"Were you jealous?" One corner of his lips tilted in a knowing smile.

"Absolutely not."

"I don't believe you."

"Then believe this—I don't care if you date every available female in all of Manhattan."

"Good to know." The half smile was still there, but his eyes took on a stern glow. "I assume we won't have any more scenes like the one we had when I got home tonight."

"Scene? There was no scene." She raised her chin, which only made his eyes glow brighter. "You were rude. I simply pointed out that your phone rings incessantly."

"All with women I haven't seen since the night I met you."

The words whispered through her head. "What about that woman I saw coming out of your apartment?"

"I brought her home, but all I could think about was you."

"You didn't sleep with her?"

"No."

A futile, foolish, piercing stab of satisfaction shot through her, and when a single drop of water rolled down his chest, she couldn't help herself as she traced the glistening bead. She saw his stern smile melt away, felt the shiver race through his body at the contact. Heat swelled through her, her heart starting a slow, heavy beat when he reached behind her and pushed shut the heavy door that led to her room.

Their eyes met, the meaning clear. But when she told herself she needed to leave, her fingers only continued their dangerous course down the trail of chest hair. He chuckled grimly, then he ran his hands down her neck, his thumbs skimming over her collarbone.

Her lips parted on a tiny breath, and a tremor shuddered through her when his hands trailed lower, parting the edges of her robe. She closed her eyes when he ran the backs of his fingers over her nipples. Slowly. Back and forth. Then the pads of his thumbs, circling over the tightening nubs. When she opened her eyes again, he was watching her.

"You like that, don't you?"

"I hate it," she managed.

His deep chuckle filled the room. "You'd like me to peel off this dowdy piece of flannel and cup your breasts, lift them high, and lave your nipples with my tongue."

"No way." The words tangled in her throat.

But when he slipped the robe from her shoulders, the material falling around her ankles, she only gasped, her body burning. She wanted this. She wanted him, and she knew he wanted her by the near growl that sounded in his chest at the sight of her.

Standing in front of him, she felt bold and so unlike herself. But it felt good, exhilarating, strangely powerful to have this man look at her with such hungry longing. Then he stepped close, running one hand down her spine to her hips, pressing her to his hard desire.

Instinctively she responded to his touch, arching to him. He bent his head, his tongue gliding hot and wet across her breast, searing her, until his mouth clamped on her nipple with such intensity that her body exploded with pleasure.

"You love that," he murmured arrogantly against her skin, his hand secure on her spine. "You want to wrap your legs around my waist, and lose yourself to me until you can't think at all."

Unable to do anything else, she started to reach up to tangle her fingers in his hair, but he caught her wrist.

"Why is that, Grace?"

She sucked in her breath when the words registered. Her body went stiff, and she tried to draw away from him.

"Why is it," he persisted, "that whenever something goes wrong I find you in my arms? What are you running from?"

Her mind reeled at the thought, her head spinning, before suddenly a calm came over her. "I think a better question is what are you running from?"

His dark eyes went cold. "I don't know what you're talking about."

"If I'm running, then so are you. Why else would you and I have ended up in each other's arms in the first place? That must be what I saw, what I recognized in you."

Abruptly he let her go, the muscles in his jaw taut.

They stood face-to-face, and despite the vulnerability she felt with her robe pooling around her feet, Grace refused to cower under his harsh glare.

But whatever might have been said next was lost when his expression changed, becoming alert, and he stepped away from her. "Ruth is up," he said, just at the moment she heard her name.

"Grace?"

"Oh, my gosh!" she hissed.

"Grace! Where are you?"

"I believe she's looking for you."

Grace shot him a murderous glare, then called out, "I'm right here." She jammed her arms through the sleeves of her robe that he held out to her, tied it securely, then slammed out the bathroom door, flattening her back against it, no doubt with a guilty bright red blazing across her cheeks.

Ruth stood there, her face set in ornery lines. "I'm hungry," she stated obstinately.

"How about some water?"

"What is this, prison? I want some more of those stupid cakes you made."

"Too late for cake. How about some hot milk?"

"How about make it cold, and mix it with chocolate. I saw that Jack had a big squeeze bottle of Hershey's syrup."

The thought brought a reluctant smile to Grace's lips. Hard to imagine the big, strapping man in the bathroom liking chocolate on anything.

"Yeah," Ruth said, as if reading her thoughts, "hard to believe."

Pushing away from the door, Grace said, "Go back to bed. I'll bring the chocolate milk."

The sound of little feet pounded down the hall, then the squeak of springs as Ruth must have leaped into bed. Within minutes, Grace threw on some clothes, went down, and made the chocolate, then was back upstairs. When she walked into Ruth's room, the child was looking at the photo of her mother. Grace felt her heart twist and her throat constrict.

As soon as Ruth saw her, she shoved the photo under the covers, as if she could hide it, folding her arms on top.

"Took you long enough," Ruth groused.

Grace walked to the bed and extended the glass. Ruth took it and drank it down nearly in one gulp, drips running down her chin. With deliberate effort, Ruth ran her arm across her mouth. Then she burped.

But Grace wasn't fazed. She understood that Ruth was scared, and the only way she knew how to deal with the emotion was to lash out. One minute she was happy, the next belligerent, never sad. All masks to cover up the very real and deep sadness this child felt.

Taking the glass, Grace set it aside, then sat down next to Ruth on the bed.

The child looked wary. The two of them had talked, bantered, argued, though they had never touched except for one brief moment in the Plaza holding hands. Ruth kept her distance, and Grace had no clue how to bridge the chasm. But something inside her pushed her on, wouldn't let her leave this alone.

"You don't have to hide your mother's picture."

"I'm not hiding it." Ruth scowled, then slowly pulled the photograph out from under the covers, staring at the image. "I'm not a baby."

"No, but no matter what age we are, we all miss people we love when they're gone."

"Yeah, well, I don't miss my mom." She took the picture and tossed it aside.

Grace was out of her depth, and she knew it. She wanted to smile and disappear back into her own room. But she wasn't a coward, she would muddle through, and pray she didn't make things worse.

"It's okay to be mad that your mom died."

Ruth looked at her like she were crazy. "Are you nuts? I know my mother didn't die on purpose."

"Exactly. But you can miss her and be mad that she's gone. I'm sure your mother loved you a whole lot, and she is missing you like crazy right now."

Silent minutes ticked by as Ruth's face screwed up with

trauma, the hard expression melting away. Suddenly the child scrambled for the photo, pulling it close to her chest like she had nothing else to hold on to.

"It's okay, Ruth."

Tears spilled over, down Ruth's plump cheeks, rounding over her chin. Grace's throat tightened, her eyes burned, and she barely held on. She spoke, the words catching in her throat, tangling with emotion for this child who missed her mother. She wanted to make some connection, though she didn't know how, couldn't find her way, making her wonder if she was ever meant to have a child of her own.

"I miss her so bad," Ruth whispered, her voice choked.

"Of course you do."

Without thinking, Grace pulled Ruth into her arms, and amazingly the child's hands reached out and held on tight, tears spilling over as she clung with all the fierce and determined passion she had poured into hating Grace up until then. Grace's breath caught with both sadness and joy as she soothed her. She rocked her until the sobs trailed off, rocked her as the moon moved through the sky.

When finally she felt Ruth relax into sleep, she held on for long minutes more, feeling for the first time in her life not the sensation of watching a child through a thick glass window, but the bliss of actually holding a child in her arms.

Chapter
Eighteen

If Jack thought being around Grace would make him tire of her, he was sadly mistaken.

Coming down the stairs the next morning, he stretched. The sun slanted through the windows at the back side of the apartment, casting long rectangles of light into the living room. Spring hinted on the horizon, the harsh winter being driven off.

He was still moved by Grace from last night. Her beauty, her embarrassment that stained her chest when he touched her, washed away by a desire that was intense and all consuming. The sensuality of her body arching to his touch.

Never had he felt such need, a need that he forced himself to control. A need that he refused to give in to. Because need made you weak.

Always before with the women he dated, he had never felt anything more than a simple appreciation for their beauty and intellect. He found release in their bodies, giving them pleasure, and easing his own strong sexual appetite.

With Grace it was different, had been from the first night he saw her sitting in that wedding dress in the snow. All he had to do was remember that night to feel heat pulse through him, a heat that seemed insatiable.

After she had settled Ruth for the night, it had been damn near impossible not to walk into her bedroom, pull her into his arms, and finish what they had started. Hell, he should have, then no doubt he'd feel less like a bull in heat this morning and more like the man who people claimed had ice running through his veins.

What kind of a fool was he to think that having her in his apartment and not giving in to his desire for her would get her out of his head?

She made him crazy, twisting him up in knots. But in the next second, inevitably she made him laugh or smile at some dismal joke or irreverence. A definite surprise coming from a woman with such a prim exterior. But it was only the exterior, he had learned again and again, that was prim. The innocent desire that burned in her eyes combined with the bold curiosity she gave in to could make even a celibate man forget his vows.

Noise came from the kitchen, and when he entered, all thoughts of desire and his need for control fled at the sight of Ruth standing on a chair at the counter, utensils, cakes, and dishes spread out before her. After he quickly determined that no heat was involved, Jack wasn't sure if he wanted to laugh or hang his head at the sight of her, dressed in her duck pajamas, with a dress-up feather boa wrapped around her neck that she must have brought with her from the overflowing trunk he had seen in her room at Grace's.

"Are you sure you should be cooking?" he asked, his voice kind but stern.

Ruth turned halfway around on the chair seat and smiled, clumsily pushing a stray wisp of hair back from her face with the palm of her sticky hand.

"Not to worry," she said in that way of hers that was far older than her meager years. She snorted a burst of laughter that sounded amazingly like Grace. "I'm not cooking anything. I'd hate for all three of us to be out on the street with no place to live. I'm making a surprise."

Jack peered over her shoulder and saw that she was icing tiny, three-inch or so, round cakes left over from last night. For a second he had the thought that she was putting faces on them. But then she turned back, nearly toppling over. Jack leaped forward, but she had steadied herself before he got there.

The sudden nearness surprised him, and when she turned her head back and smiled again, he was reminded of another little girl. His little girl.

Jack and Ruth stared at each other. Memories of another life tried to surge, memories murky and indistinct, memories he couldn't afford.

Suddenly Ruth's wide brown eyes, always so practical and disdainful since she had arrived, filled with an emotion that was much softer than Jack had imagined her capable of. "Grace said she wanted to be my mother," she half whispered.

The words startled him, and concerned him since they all knew that the situation between Grace and Ruth was temporary.

"When did she say this?" he asked with his best doctor's voice as he stepped away.

"Last night. Late. I couldn't sleep. I don't think she could sleep, either," Ruth added.

He knew that Ruth and Grace getting too attached would only traumatize the child even more when she was inevitably taken away. But then Ruth spoke again.

"Do you think you might want to be my dad?" she asked hesitantly.

The question hit him hard, like a stabbing pain to his heart. Ruth and Grace, two females that made his mind spin. Neither of whom he wanted, both of whom drew him—one as a man, the other as a father.

When he didn't answer right away, he watched Ruth's practical face fall in disappointment.

"It's not that I don't want to be your father," he began.

But Ruth waved him away and turned back to the counter, feather boa fluttering in her wake, her expression set as if used to disappointments. "Don't worry about it. I was only joking."

He knew she wasn't, but he didn't know what to say. He went to the kitchen table before a huge banging sound reverberated through the building.

"What was that?" he asked.

"Oh, yeah, those construction guys you hired got here early this morning. I buzzed them in, and they're upstairs now." She glanced at him. "I bet they get everything done real fast."

That was exactly what he had hoped for when he called his friend in Brooklyn, who promised to have the repairs done as soon as possible.

He headed up to Grace's apartment and spoke to the foreman, making sure they knew what needed to be done.

"Not to worry, Dr. Berenger. Max told us this job was top priority." The foreman gave him a knowing smile. "We're going to do a good job, and we're also going to do it fast. Max made sure we understood that."

When Jack returned downstairs he found Grace in the kitchen with Ruth. Grace walked across the hardwood floor, and for the first time he got a good look at the shoes that caused such a racket overhead. A small-heeled sandal-like thing with a strap over the toes and an explosion of feathers. Wild, outrageous. But making him smile. Yet another grim reminder that familiarity was doing little to make the attraction wear thin.

The realization wiped the smile right off his face.

At the sight of him, Grace's lips parted on a silent breath, and he knew she was remembering last night. His body surged yet again, and that made him even angrier.

She must have noticed the change—from desire to anger—but instead of being upset, it only seemed to amuse her.

"Good morning," she said, smiling as she looked down at her feet. "Do you like them?" She extended her foot, showing the briefest glimpse of slender ankle below the elastic band of her sweatpants bottom. Her smile turned wry. "I was in a hurry when I packed. Not that I really have anything that goes with my new shoes. . . ."

The words trailed off as she turned away and found a cup in the cabinet as if she had lived her whole life in this kitchen. She looked around for coffee.

"I would have made some," Ruth explained, "but no sense in trying my luck." She wrinkled her nose, and seemed to consider. "And here," she added, suddenly looking concerned.

Ruth reached into her oversized pockets and pulled out the ladybug paperweight and a jangling mix of items that belonged to Grace. "I took these from your apartment."

Grace looked at Ruth as the child squirmed, clearly ready to be sent away. "Thank you for returning them, sweetie," was all she said, then she gave her a hug.

Ruth's rosebud mouth rounded in surprise.

"I have eyes in the back of my head," Grace answered, ruffling Ruth's hair. "You can't get anything past me."

Jack strode over to the coffeemaker and put a pot on so that Grace couldn't make herself even more at home by doing it herself. He felt childish, but he figured he needed all the help he could get.

"Oh my, look at this," Grace exclaimed. "You've iced it so beautifully!"

Jack glanced over at Grace and Ruth in time to see the miniature round cake iced with eyes and a nose, ears and a mouth. The ones Grace had made last night had delicate flowers budding along the edges. Ruth had turned hers into a face.

"I made it for you," Ruth told her shyly.

Grace hugged Ruth again. "I adore it. Now let me make one for you."

Jack was amazed as she whipped up a face on the next cake that was both fun and charming.

"Voilà!"

Ruth squealed. "It looks just like me!"

"As mine looks like me."

"Thank you, Grace," Ruth said, then she dashed out of the kitchen to get cleaned up.

Grace watched her go. Seconds passed before she turned back and Jack could see the simple happiness on her face. She didn't look at Jack; she went to the table, then stared into her coffee.

"Things certainly have changed since yesterday when she nearly burned down the building," he commented.

Her head came up, and even his sharp voice didn't erase the contented smile. "They have, haven't they? By the way, thanks for dealing with the construction workers. I heard them banging away this morning."

"You're welcome." Jack poured himself a cup, then went to his seat. He needed to get to work, but he couldn't bring himself to leave. Yet. He would. But it wouldn't hurt to sit there for a few minutes, he reasoned. "What caused the change?"

She tilted her head and smiled at him like the imp he knew her to be. It was all he could do not to laugh out loud.

"I guess I must have a natural mother's instinct. Kind of like having eyes in the back of my head."

"Ah, is that it?" he asked, unable to keep the irritation

around him for long. "Ruth tells me that you are going to ask for permanent custody."

"I know, I know, it just came out. But I want this." The impish look turned serious and wistful and desperately hopeful. "I didn't dare think about it when we weren't getting along. But, now . . ."

She let the words trail off.

"But now, what?"

She shrugged, running her finger along the rim of her cup. "But now we're forming a bond. I can feel it."

"And you believe that because she made you a cake?" he asked, and even he could hear the exacting edge in his voice.

Defiance resurged, mixed with something vulnerable. Yet again he was struck by the changes in her. One minute laughing, the next desperate and fragile, like spun crystal ready to shatter.

"I want this," she whispered, her voice nearly breaking. "I want to keep Ruth, and Ruth needs me."

He stared at her hard. "The state might not agree," he said.

"Why wouldn't they?" Her posture took on a defiant stature, her eyes narrowing with insult.

"For starters, you don't have a job."

Concern flashed in her eyes. "I sent out another round of résumés last week. I'll get a job. I'll prove to the state that I can be a great mother to Ruth."

"How will you do that if you haven't even thought to enroll her in school?"

Her head came back. "Oh, my God! I didn't think! It never occurred to me!"

"What else hasn't occurred to you, Grace? There are hundreds of things a parent has to think of. School is just one. Think about that."

Jack took one last sip, then left the apartment just as Mark arrived.

"What's wrong with him?" Mark wanted to know, clicking into the apartment in size twelve Ferragamo pumps.

Grace stared at the door a second longer before following Mark. "I guess he woke up on the wrong side of the bed."

"Whose bed, is what I want to know."

"Funny," she said, though when Mark looked back at her with a thick raised brow, she couldn't meet his eye.

"You might not have been in his bed last night, but I can tell from the guilty look on your face that something went on . . . that, or you *wanted* something to go on."

Grace glared, and Mark burst out laughing, the deep guttural sound, as always, at odds with his sleek woman's suit. He chuckled all the way into the kitchen, where he went from cabinet to cabinet looking for a cup.

"Why aren't you at work?" Grace asked.

"I called in sick. And I am sick. Sick and tired of listening to that maniac Jay scream. I figured I deserved a day off." As soon as he had poured the coffee and turned back, his laughter cut off. "What are these?"

Leaning against the doorjamb, Grace watched as he picked up each of the cakes.

"Ruth made one for me, and I made one for her." She hesitated, silly tears welling up. "I'm going to ask for custody."

He glanced over at her. "Really?"

"What do you think, Mark?" she asked, her voice shaky since she wasn't sure what she would do if he didn't believe in her, either. "Do you think I can do it?"

"Of course you can. I don't know anyone more suited to being a mother."

A relieved sigh seeped out of her. "Thank you."

He kissed her forehead. "You're welcome. Now enough about you, let's talk about me. I'm miserable."

Grace choked out a laugh through her tears. "What's wrong now?"

"Work's wrong. It gets worse every day. Jay still hasn't come up with a single new idea, and Kendrick is getting antsy that we have nothing in the pipeline."

"Nothing?"

"Nothing to speak of. Everything Jay comes up with has already been done, and I swear Kendrick is starting to sweat. Of course it serves him right, but what if Kendrick Toys starts to tank? What would I do if I didn't work there? I've seen how hard it's been for you to find a job."

She hated the reminder.

Mark took a sip of his coffee, realized it was still black, then found sugar and milk. Once the brew was more light brown than black, he tilted one of the plates and studied the cake.

"You know," he mused, "you should sell these on eBay."

"My computer is in storage. Besides, I don't have time to play around. I've got to enroll Ruth in school."

But Mark wasn't listening. He clicked out of the kitchen, coffee in hand, and looked around. "Hmmm," he said, then headed for the stairs.

"Where are you going?"

"To find a computer. Surely that big manly man has a computer in here somewhere."

"You can't do that!"

"Of course, I can." He marched up the stairs, with Grace running after him. He went from room to room, stopping in Grace's. "Hmmm," he said, suddenly distracted. "Tiny, but"—like a homing pigeon, he found the bathroom and the connecting door—"isn't this convenient. A little late-night rendezvous?"

This time Grace blushed a dangerous shade of red.

"Ah-ha! That's what happened last night."

"Stop it, just stop it, and get back downstairs."

"Tsk." He strutted into Jack's bedroom. "Nice. I could have some serious fun in that bed. Too bad he's straight."

Very straight, she thought, remembering all too well the feel of his hands on her.

"Grace," Mark quipped, waving his hand in front of her eyes. "Are you there?"

Her grin was strained.

Mark only laughed, then turned away. "Bingo. Here we are."

A computer sat on the desk in front of the window. Without hesitation, he strode over and turned it on.

"You can't do that!"

"Stop being such a sissy."

Mark handled everything, and within the next couple of hours they had taken photos of the cakes and had signed up to auction them off. After that, he posted notes about the miniature cakes on every electronic bulletin board he could think of.

Ruth was amazed by Mark and by the computer, and thrilled about the prospect of selling her creation. She didn't like the idea of going to school nearly as much.

"You're going to love it," Grace promised. "There's an elementary school a block away."

On their way to enroll, Ruth grumbling, Mark saying Grace was no fun at all since she wouldn't go out to lunch before going over to the school, they met a woman hurrying up the outside steps. She was stunningly beautiful, wore tight spandex leopard-print pants, a top that displayed ample breasts, and blond hair so bright, it had to be fake. The very picture of the kind of female her father would date.

"Hello," the woman greeted them, her voice sultry, passing them by and going straight for the buzzers.

Grace, Mark, and Ruth watched as she rang Jack's bell once, twice, then a third time.

"He's not there," Ruth explained.

"Oh." The woman looked utterly disappointed. "Are you sure?"

"Of course I'm sure," she stated, her tone possessive. "I know, because we live with him."

The stranger looked stunned at this, and concerned, her perfect high forehead furrowing.

"Can we help you?" Mark asked with a coy voice and a once-over that should have made the woman blush.

She only preened, then gave Mark a once-over herself. "Nice suit. I saw Ivana Trump wearing one almost identical last week."

"Really?" Mark said, his hand coming up to his chest, flattered, whatever intimidation he had attempted going by the wayside.

Grace grumbled that he was so easily won over.

"It's an Olivier Theyskens," he explained. "Cost me a fortune. What color shoes did Ivana wear?"

"Bone, as I recall."

Mark sighed dramatically. "I knew it. I went back and forth wondering if I should go with the taupe or the bone."

"The taupe looks fine."

Displaying the gigantic pumps, Mark asked, "Do you think?"

"Excuse me," Grace interrupted, hating to admit the exact kind of jealousy toward this woman she had denied. "I'll leave you two to chat. Ruth and I have to get to school."

"Can you tell Jack that Tiffany came by?" the woman

called after them, then added with a hopeful note, "Maybe you can ask him to call me."

Ruth reached up and took Grace's hand as they headed down the sidewalk. "Don't count on it," she muttered.

Grace squeezed Ruth's hand, then they both burst out in a fit of giggles.

It was late afternoon by the time they returned. But everything was set for Ruth to start second grade the next morning. Ruth had grown quiet and sullen, and Grace couldn't get a single smile out of her until she offered to turn on Jack's computer to see what had happened at eBay.

"Wow!" Ruth cried, hopping up and down at the staggering sight of all the bids. "We're going to be rich!"

Grace was floored. The simple little cakes were a hit.

Ruth chattered excitedly all through dinner, asking every few minutes when Jack would be home. Grace didn't know, and knew better than to have expectations. By the time she tucked Ruth into bed, though, she had started to wonder.

It was late when keys rustled in the lock and the front door pushed open. The apartment had grown nearly dark, only one light casting a soft glow from the kitchen to the living room. Grace sat on the stairs and heard his footsteps, heard keys drop into the tray on the entry hall table. He didn't see her, and she watched as he flipped on a light and started looking through the mail. Heading for the kitchen, he stopped mid-stride when he noticed her.

For half a second he looked surprised she was there, then he smiled, that half smile that made her think of a mischievous boy. Changing directions, he came over to stand at the bottom of the stairs, one foot up on the step, and leaned forward, his forearms resting on his thigh.

Like so many times before, he looked handsome and tired at the same time, and it was all too clear why patients and women would flock to him.

"What are you doing?" he asked.

"Sittin'."

"Sitting?" His smile broadened, and he glanced upstairs. "Where's Ruth?"

"Sleepin'."

"You're a regular font of information tonight."

"Yep."

His smile disappeared. "I'm sorry about earlier today."

She tilted her head. "What about earlier?"

"When I questioned if the state would approve of you or not."

"Approve of me?" she gasped, sitting up straight. "That's what you meant?"

"To think I actually worried that I had hurt your feelings."

"You *did* hurt my feelings. Only I didn't know it until right now. The fact is, I will be a good mother. I was a great mother today. For your information, Ruth starts school tomorrow."

"I'm glad to hear it," he said softly.

"Are you?" she challenged. "I don't think you want me to win."

"It's not a matter of what I want, Grace, or even what you want. It's what's best for the child."

"*I'm* what's best for Ruth! I love her. I'll take care of her." She pressed her eyes closed. "You have no idea what it's like to want a child so bad it hurts." She glanced back at him. "You don't know how hard it is to see a child smiling at her mother, extending a melting ice-cream cone like it's a precious gift." She hugged her knees. "I can take getting fired, or even finding my fiancé having sex with someone else. But it's not having a child to love and keep safe that leaves me reeling. I'm reminded of it everywhere I go. The children's shop windows filled with dainty little dresses and duck-covered rain boots. Matching plastic umbrellas with tiny yellow handles."

"It sounds to me," he said quietly, "like it's the trappings of motherhood you want. There is more to being a mother than picture-perfect moments."

A shuddering violence jerked through her, and she marched down the stairs to face him. "Yes, I want the trappings. Sure, I want the little boots and plastic umbrellas! But I also want the Band-Aids and temper tantrums, and whatever else comes with the job. I want the good, yes, but I'd give everything I've ever owned to have the bad as well."

She drew a deep, strengthening breath. "Do you know why I really wanted to marry Walter?"

His gaze went hard, and he took a step back.

"Because he would have given me a child. The truth is, deep down, I knew he slept around, but I denied it, even to myself. I refused to open my eyes, because I wanted a child more than his love." As quickly as it came, the fight seeped out of her. "But in the end, even I couldn't overlook the sight of his bare backside as he slammed into a woman on my wedding day. It was more than a slap in the face. It was a shout of warning that I couldn't do that to myself, or to a child. I will not re-create my own childhood. That would have been the cruelest joke of all."

The semidarkness surrounded them, her heart pounding fiercely as Jack looked at her with an expression she couldn't read. "I want a child, Jack. I've dreamed of having a child to love and cherish for as long as I can remember. And Ruth needs a mother. I see the hunger in her eyes, the wish for love and safety in a world that no longer makes sense. Maybe I don't have the ideal life right now, but I'll find another job. I'll provide Ruth with a safe and stable world, a real world, where toys are Easy-Bake ovens, not porcelain dolls that you can see but not touch, and games aren't finding new ways to sneak your father's latest mistress out of the apartment when the doorman frantically buzzes that your mother's on the way up."

The words spilled out unexpectedly, heatedly, and when she realized what she had said, she cringed. But if she thought he would shake his head in disgust, she was wrong. That protectiveness she had seen in him before surged, his gaze growing fierce, his shoulders seeming to broaden like a warrior readying for battle, his hands braced on the stair banisters. "Your parents should be shot."

Foolishly, she felt the rush of gratitude, followed quickly by the fact that she knew the past didn't matter. She placed her hand over his in an intimate gesture that surprised them both. She felt a bone-deep shuddering within him as he stared at her fingers spread over his, small over large.

"They did the best they could," she said after a moment. "But don't you see, marriage and thinking of enrollment on the first day a child arrives doesn't make the parent perfect. My parents were married; I never missed a day of school. Did that make them ideal? No. It only means that everyone tries to do the best they can. All I'm asking for is the chance to do the best that I can for Ruth." She hesitated. "How can that possibly be wrong?"

Chapter
Nineteen

Early the next morning, Jack's bedroom door flew back on its hinges, banging into the wall, bringing him out of a deep sleep like a bolt of lightning leaping out of the sky.

Ruth dashed to the computer. It didn't matter that Jack sat there, stunned, the sheet barely covering his waist as he tried to assimilate the emergency. She turned the machine on with the prowess of a child who wasn't intimidated by technology, and before Jack could clear his head from the murky depths of sleep, she had it up and running.

"Oh, my gosh! The bids are up to fifty dollars! Grace!" she squealed.

Grace dashed into the room, groggy and disoriented, panic racing through her. "What?" she stammered.

"Everyone wants a cake! And look!" She had pulled up Grace's e-mail as Mark had showed her, and found a whole slew of notes from people requesting cakes for themselves.

"What?" Grace repeated, trying to comprehend the fact that the squeals were not of danger. Ruth was just excited.

Once she realized there was no emergency, Grace suddenly became aware of Jack, his hair sexily disheveled, his chest bare, shoulders broad.

"Good morning," she offered, her voice catching in her throat. She remembered how she had stood before him, her robe pooling around her ankles. Her body tingled at the memory of his words and his touch.

"Is it?" he asked dryly. "I'm still recovering from the jolt of adrenaline that shot through me when the door burst open. What is going on?"

Grace wrinkled her nose. "I forgot to mention that we borrowed your computer yesterday. I hope it's all right."

"The computer? Well, sure. I rarely use it."

"Okay, good. I was worried, but Mark insisted. We put the cakes up for sale."

"You're kidding. Who would buy a three-inch cake with a face on it over the Internet?"

Grace walked over to the computer in her flannel pajamas and bare feet, placing her hand on Ruth's shoulder, who peered at the screen. "Ask that to the five people who put bids in," she said, as surprised as he was. "But the fact is, it's all in what you call something. Five people bid on Sweetie Cakes—a very different proposition than a simple cake with a face on it." She turned around and took in his silky hair that just then stood up on one side, and the pillow mark down one cheek. "Though if we had put *your* face on it, that might have been a different story," she teased.

Ruth glanced back and then giggled before returning to the screen.

Jack flashed an arrogant grin. "With my face on it, you'd have a lot more than five bids."

"Look at this!" Ruth cried excitedly. "We have an e-mail saying someone wants a hundred cakes!"

"You were saying about your face," Grace asked, crossing her arms.

Jack laughed out loud, the sound sliding down her spine, filling her with warmth. "I stand corrected. Now, if you'll excuse me, I'll get up. You're welcome to stay, but I doubt it would be a good idea for Ruth to get an anatomy lesson."

"Anatomy?" Then she looked down at his chest, felt the warmth turn to heat, then squeaked, "Oh."

"Or better yet," he said for only her to hear, his dark eyes turning velvety as they ran the length of her primly paja-maed form, "why not send Ruth to change while you stay and make sure I'm fully awake."

Grace's mouth fell open, and Jack's lips tilted with a sensual grin.

"Come on, Ruth," she said hurriedly. "Let's leave Jack alone."

Ruth galloped out ahead of her, chanting and cheering the whole way back down the hall, then slammed into her bedroom to dress.

In the doorway, Grace stopped. "By the way, your lap dancer came over yesterday. She wants you to call."

That wiped the smirking smile right off his too-handsome face.

"Lap dancer?" he asked ominously.

"You know." Her voice went overly sweet. "Tiffany."

He shot her a caustic scowl, then whipped the covers back, revealing his nakedness. "You mean Tiffany who has a Ph.D. in handed molecules?"

Grace swallowed hard at the glorious sight of him. "You say tomato, I say tomahto." She focused on his face. "I think we really bonded."

Stepping into a pair of warm-up bottoms, his muscles rippling, he said, "I don't like the sound of that."

"A little insecure, are we?" She looked at him through lowered lashes. "Seconds ago you were bragging about your staggeringly valuable good looks."

"Don't you forget it," he quipped, his grin returning.

He walked across the room until he stood before her, his

movements slow and easy. With one effortless motion, he tugged her back inside and pushed the door shut, pulling her into his arms as if they had lived together for a thousand years—as if so early in the morning he hadn't had time to remember to keep her at a distance. He wanted her and he took, his eyes glittering like black fire.

"I can't imagine what you and Tiff could bond over," he said.

She tried to concentrate on the familiarity of him calling the woman Tiff; she even tried to be insulted, but she never got much further than thinking about how very close he was. "Why is that?"

He ran his fingers ever so gently along the flannel ruffles of her pajama top, the sensation so exquisite that she felt as if he had touched her much more intimately.

"Let's just say the two of you are different," he said. His voice was guttural, sexy, as he stepped closer, his body guiding her back against the wall.

Her breath caught. "Different how?"

"I don't know." He didn't appear to care as his fingers drifted along the flannel over her collarbone. "You just are."

"Good different?"

He shot her a curious look before bracing his hands on either side of her, then dipped his head. "What does that mean?" he asked, nipping at the lobe of her ear.

"You know," she stated breathlessly. "Good as in better."

"Better than what?"

His tongue traced the delicate shell, and she sighed. "Better than me."

He leaned back and made a great show of pondering, a devilish glint starting to show in his eyes. "No, just different."

"Ah, back to different again. Leave it to a man to be evasive and noncommunicative." She forced herself to concentrate as he wrapped her in his arms, pulling her close until she felt his shaft hard and insistent against her. It was difficult to think, much less speak. "Clearly you're bothered that I talked to her. I wonder what you think we might have said?"

"I am not bothered. Be as friendly as you want, just leave me out of it."

He lifted her up, then slowly let her down, her body sensually gliding along his, and he groaned into her hair.

"Why not, it's fun," she managed. "Are you sure she's not a lap dancer? She sure seems to like sex."

Abruptly he froze, then after long seconds he stepped away. Her body screamed out against the sudden lack of heat. He raked his hair back with his hands, his chest and abdomen going taut in that way that made Grace's knees fuse and her heart skip a beat.

"You talked about sex with Tiffany?" he asked, his eyes narrowed.

Grace could do little more than stare at the swirls of hair on his chest that tapered down, disappearing beneath his waistband. "Maybe yes, maybe no."

"What did she say?"

"See, you are concerned." She tilted her head, hardly able to believe she was baiting him. "Do you wonder if you measure up?"

"No, I do not. In fact, forget it. I've had enough of this crazy conversation." He retraced his steps, snapped up a terry cloth towel, and slung it over his shoulder, his jaw set.

"She didn't really talk to me about sex," she called out, feeling guilty. "But if she did, I'm sure she would have said you were great, really great."

He looked back at her just as he got to the bathroom, a

wickedly devilish smile pulling at his lips in a way that made the heat surge back through her body. "I never doubted it," he said.

Then he shut the door between, and she choked out a spurt of laughter as the shower burst on.

Grace threw on a robe over her pajamas, then hurried downstairs to make Ruth breakfast. "Guess what today is," she said with great enthusiasm.

Ruth's face took on a hint of its former belligerence.

"Your first day of school!"

"I don't wanna go," Ruth mumbled, her arms crossed stubbornly on the table.

"You're going to love it. You'll meet lots of other kids and make tons of friends and learn really great things."

"I wanna stay here with you."

Grace's heart felt like it would burst with joy. She had contacted a lawyer who put together the petition for the child welfare agency, asking for custody. The pieces were falling into place. Or they would be, she thought dismally, if Walter hadn't started leaving increasingly insistent messages regarding the money he said she owed him. Where exactly she would come up with an extra fifteen hundred dollars, she didn't know.

Why, why, why hadn't any of the toy companies called her back?

She hadn't been able to get so much as an interview with any of the companies she had sent résumés to, and she still refused to ask her family for help. Which left her with only one alternative.

She made Ruth a bowl of Cream of Wheat mixed with brown sugar and cinnamon, a slice of toast, and a tall glass of orange juice, then found Jack's newspaper out on the front stoop. By the time he came downstairs, his hair slicked back from the shower, she had a pen in hand, a cup of coffee at her elbow, and was circling any job that looked interesting.

"What are you doing?" he inquired.

"Job hunting. What are you doing?" she added when she saw that he held part of the computer.

"I thought it might be better if Ruth had the computer down here."

Ruth leaped up. "I'll clear a spot!"

Indeed, in a matter of minutes Jack and Ruth had the computer set up in the living room on a desk that was more decorative than utilitarian. Ruth sat on her knees in the fancy leather chair and called out another whoop of delight when the machine flashed on.

"More e-mail! People want cakes."

"Ruth, you've got to get upstairs and brush your teeth. We have to leave here in thirty minutes. You don't want to be late for your first day of school."

"Look at this," Ruth exclaimed, ignoring her.

Jack walked over and looked. "She's right. There really are a lot of requests."

"See, I can't go to school! We have to make cakes!" Ruth cried. "We're going to be rich!"

"Ruth," Jack said kindly, "you can't make cakes and send them off to people in the mail."

Tilting her head, Ruth wrinkled her nose. "Why not?"

That's when it hit Grace. "Yes, why not?"

"They'll be old and stale and falling apart before they ever get anywhere."

Pushing up from the chair, Grace started to pace. "Not if we seal them in plastic," she said to no one in particular, her mind starting to spin as it used to when coming up with new ideas. Only this time it had nothing to do with toys.

"Grace?" Jack asked, his tone warning.

Ruth came up on her knees and faced the back of the leather chair, animation brightening her cheeks.

"We could offer a whole slew of the cakes on a Web site," Grace said, her eyes glittering in concentration. "Mama Cake and Baby Cake." She stopped and closed her eyes for a half second, then burst out, "You're a Piece of Cake. You Take the Cake. Ack! She's No Angel Cake!"

Ruth cheered. "You're My Cupcake!"

Grace laughed. "Perfect. There's an endless number of cakes we could make." She resumed her pacing. She was in her element, ideas flowing so fast, it was hard to keep up. "We'll set up the Web site. SweetieCakes.com. Though I'm sure that's taken." Then it came to her, defiance and pride swirling through her. "We'll call it MoreFluffThan-StuffCakes.com."

Jack looked at her long and hard, a fierceness flaring in his eyes as he took the steps that separated them. She had to tilt her head back to meet his gaze. She could hardly concentrate on his words because she could feel his heat, his strength, the scent of man wrapping around her.

"You might drive me crazy, but anyone who knows you at all knows that you are more *stuff* than fluff. If you're dead set on selling cakes over the Internet, I say you call it StuffCakes."

The words filled her heart, and she saw in him a gentle caring that she hadn't guessed at before. It was as startling as it was amazing. "Thank you, Jack," she said softly. "I can't imagine a greater compliment. I'll cherish it always." She hesitated, then scrunched her shoulders. "But I'm not sure that 'stuff' has the right sound to it." Suddenly another idea hit. "Though maybe just plain FluffCakes might work."

He reached out and ran his finger along her cheek as if

he couldn't help himself. "As long as you know it's the cakes that are fluff and not you." Then he tapped her nose. "I've got to get to the hospital."

He told Ruth to have a productive day at school, then headed out, the door clicking behind him, and Grace twirled around the room like a teenage girl who had just been invited to the prom.

For the next few hours, Grace felt like she was dancing on air as she dashed around to get dressed, then walked Ruth over to the elementary school. Ruth, however, dragged along, muttering and groaning, swearing that she was going to hate every second of second grade and would probably die of boredom.

The school was crowded with little kids and brightly colored pictures hanging on the wall. The principal insisted Ruth was in good hands, and told Grace it was time to leave. She left with a lump in her throat at the sight of Ruth marching down the hall next to the cheerful woman as if she were going to an execution.

The rest of the day Grace ran errands, but she could hardly concentrate, returning a full thirty minutes before the final bell.

When Ruth came down the steps, she pronounced that she had hated second grade even more than she thought she would. It was best, she added in her very knowing voice, that she didn't return.

It took the remainder of the afternoon and well into the night to convince her that not going back wasn't an option.

After that, the days took on a routine—walking Ruth to school, working obsessively to make FluffCakes a reality, building a Web site, and checking with workmen in regard to the progress of her apartment. But she didn't allow herself to think about the day she and Ruth would move home, and refused to think about those rare moments of being with Jack, seeing the heat that flared in his eyes at the sight of her.

The confidence she had lost started to rebuild slowly, brick by brick, as purpose drummed through her veins. She made plans, drew up ideas, and created cakes. She made some with blue icing eyes and green icing hair, while others had green eyes, blue hair, and orange lips. Some were outrageous, some were sweet, but all were fun, each wrapped in plastic and placed in small boxes, with curly ribbed ribbons and tiny tags that gave the name of the cake along with the address, FluffCakes.com. Then she secured them in a sea of Styrofoam peanuts inside a shipping box, and sent them off within hours after they were done.

Mark cheered her on at every turn, believing in FluffCakes.com so much that he arranged for her to do an interview with *Entrepreneurial Weekly*.

It was the end of the first week when the buzzer rang. Jack wasn't home, Ruth was busy surviving her third day of school, and Grace sat in front of a table lined with little cakes, every part of her being humming with optimism.

Wiping her hands, she went to the door. "Who is it?" she called down.

"Oh, hello. It's Hugh Berenger."

She buzzed him in and opened the door.

"Hello!" he called out as he came up the stairs. "I wondered who Jack had answering the door. It's Grace, isn't it?"

"Yes, but Jack's not here."

"All the better," he said with a teasing glint, "you're more interesting."

"If that's a come-on line, I'm not interested," she said wryly. "I have enough trouble with Berenger men as it is."

Hugh laughed out loud. "No wonder Jack's so smitten with you."

"Jack, smitten?" Was he? She couldn't imagine.

Ever since the day he had told her she was more stuff than fluff, he had spent more time than ever working, as if his control had slipped and now he was making a concerted effort to stay away to ensure it didn't slip again.

She rarely saw him anymore, frequently only heard him come home during the wee hours to fall into bed, then leave before either she or Ruth woke up. When she had spoken to the construction workers that morning, she'd learned that they had seen him several times. She had the sneaking suspicion Jack was bribing them to get the work done even sooner than planned. He might want her in some deeply sexual way, but he also wanted her gone. That need had grown with each day she had lived in the room next door to his. "Are we talking about the same man?"

At this, Hugh laughed louder. "Jack, Jack, Jack. Never one to show his emotions. But that's not why I'm here. We've been trading messages, and he left one saying to meet him here at eleven, eleven-thirty at the latest."

"Then by all means, come in. I hope you don't mind if I keep working. I have an entire batch of cakes I need to get out this afternoon."

"That's right, I heard about your endeavor," he said, following her into the kitchen. He sat across from her and picked one up to have a look as she got back to work. "They're great."

"Thank you," she replied as she pulled a cake in front of her and started to ice.

Hugh considered her for a second, then picked up a baker's bag of icing. "Do you mind?" he asked.

"Well, no, I could use the help."

It took him only a second to figure out what he was doing, then they worked in companionable silence, making their way through the long lines of cakes with gratifying speed.

"How did you hear about this?" she asked when they got to the end of a row.

"From Jack." He looked over his latest effort and nodded his approval. "He sounded proud."

"He sounded put out, is more like it," she groused. She didn't add that he was avoiding her like the plague. "I've had his oven working overtime."

Hugh chuckled again, then glanced at her.

"What?" she demanded after long minutes ticked by.

"You love my brother, don't you?"

A squeeze of icing ran amok on the cake. "Love?" Sexual cravings of a madwoman, okay. Going loopy over his too-good good looks, agreed. But anything deeper? She couldn't afford anything deeper with the man who refused to let her into his life in any meaningful way. "I can't imagine two people who are more mismatched than Jack Berenger and me."

"Why is that?"

"What are you? Mr. Fifty Questions?"

He shrugged. "If I've made you uncomfortable . . ."

His words trailed off in that aggravating way that implied she had something to hide and far be it from him than to press. The cad.

"I am not uncomfortable. It's just that Jack is just so . . . controlled."

Hugh bent his head over a cake, his lips set in concentration as he finished off a set of eyes. Then he sat back and studied her. "I've always believed Jack would meet someone who could break that control."

"What are you talking about?"

He shrugged, then started on another cake. "Jack has always been exacting. But I guess it's hard not to be, growing up like we did."

Despite the minutes that ticked away before the order had to be completed, Grace could hardly concentrate on the icing. "How did you grow up?"

"Poor, with a well-intentioned but misguided father who never amounted to anything. Worst of all, he blamed his failings on anyone and everyone but himself. Then there was our mother, who worked herself to the bone to keep shoes on our feet and food on the table." He picked up a bag of bright green icing with sparkles. "Jack swore he would get a job and make enough money so that our mother would never have to work again."

"Then he succeeded."

"Yeah, he succeeded." A heavy sadness laced the simple word. "But not soon enough. She died before he finished medical school. He was devastated. We both were. But it was like Jack blamed himself."

"What did she die of?"

"Weariness? A lifetime of burden? Who really knows. They say it was cardiac arrest. I say her heart finally gave out on her. She was sick long before she died."

Grace thought of the darkness she had seen in Jack's eyes, and she wondered if this was the cause. "Is that why Jack wanted to become a doctor? Because she had been sick for so long?"

"Maybe. I just know that he's had more than his share of hardship and responsibility." He looked up from the cake. "Did he tell you he put me through college?"

"Really?" The thought surprised her at first, one brother putting another through school. But then she thought about the reality of Jack, the pride, the protectiveness, and she knew that it was true. "Jack doesn't answer questions about his past, at least not when I ask."

"He's a very private guy," Hugh continued. "He got a scholarship to Harvard. I'm ten years younger than he is, and by the time I graduated from high school, Mom was getting sick. She made him promise he would help me with college. God, it was hard on him. He was married by then, still trying to finish his training. But he never made me feel guilty, or that I was a burden." His brow furrowed. "I don't know how he managed. I'm not sure I would have been able to do it."

Grace reached over and touched his hand. "Why are you telling me this?"

His distant smile evaporated. "Because I owe Jack, and Jack deserves to be happy. All I know is that since he met you he has seemed more . . . alive than he has in years." He hesitated. "I think you just might be the person to help him see that letting his control slip once in a while is okay. He doesn't have to carry the responsibility for the whole world. Maybe then he can start to live again."

The words whispered over her like a chill as a piece of understanding about Jack slid into place. "Can a person ever really change?" she asked quietly. "Will Jack ever let his need for control truly slip? And if he does, what will happen to him?"

The questions hung in the air unanswered when they heard the front door click open, followed by the jangle of keys in the tray on the entry table.

Seconds later, Jack entered the kitchen, and he hesitated when he saw her, that same sensual heat flaring in his eyes. But the heat quickly changed to an unrestrained delight when he noticed his younger brother.

"I see she's recruited you," Jack said, a teasing half smile crooking the corner of his lips.

"Actually, I asked. And let me tell you, I'm a damned

good icer, if I do say so myself. No doubt better than you," Hugh challenged.

Grace could see the love the brothers shared, as well as a friendly competitiveness that instantly sparked between them. Jack didn't need another word of encouragement. He pulled his stethoscope from around his neck, set it aside, then sat down, preened to Grace, and got to work. In minutes he held up a cake. "I call it You Can't Ice Worth Crap Cake."

Grace's eyes went wide. Hugh laughed out loud, then demanded, "Give me another." He snapped up a cake, then bent his head in concentration. Soon he held up his own. "Kiss My Pound Cake."

In a matter of minutes, these two incredibly masculine men had a half-dozen cakes apiece iced and named, each more profane.

"Stop!" Grace said sternly, like reprimanding two little boys. "It's nearly noon, and I need cakes that I can actually send!"

The men chuckled, then she couldn't believe it when not only Hugh but Jack got serious. They iced, and she wrapped and packed, and by twelve-thirty, with an hour and thirty minutes to spare before she had to pick up Ruth, she had the order complete.

Hugh leaned back and stretched. "Boy, that'll put a cramp in the ol' fingers."

"Thank you both so much," Grace enthused.

"What are you going to do with Cretin Cake?" Hugh wanted to know.

Grace smiled wryly. "You are welcome to all the curse cakes."

Jack rubbed his hands together, then stood and went over to the refrigerator and pulled out a carton of milk. "If you insist."

They polished off four cakes apiece and two large glasses of milk before Hugh leaned back with a contented sigh. "You sure know how to bake."

Grace blushed. "Thank you." Then suddenly an idea popped into her head. "I could make your wedding cake."

That wiped any trace of contentment right off Hugh's face. "Ah, the wedding. It's off. That's why I wanted to talk to you," he said to Jack.

"I'm so sorry." Grace instantly grew concerned.

"Thank you, but Jack was right," he said. "Nadine was only interested in me when she thought I was loaded. I realized a little late that she thought I was a partner at CPJ Ventures, not just an associate."

"But an associate works into being a partner," Grace stated defensively.

"Yeah, but she wasn't interested in the journey. She expects to marry someone who's already there."

Jack nodded his head solemnly, looking like a stern but caring parent. "I'm sorry, buddy, really."

"When we started making wedding plans, hers included a sit-down dinner for two hundred at the Four Seasons. Mine included a quaint meal for four at the neighborhood pub where we met. We couldn't find a happy medium on that or anything. Hell, she even refused to tell anyone we met in a pub. I refused to make up some new, fake history. I haven't seen her since, and that was a week ago."

"Are you okay?" Grace asked kindly.

"Hey, better than okay," he responded, shaking off any anger. "I'm glad I found out the truth now, rather than later. I should have listened to Jack in the first place. My big brother's always right."

"I really am sorry that I was right about Nadine."

"I know you are, Jack."

The men looked at each other, and Grace could see a wealth of love.

"Hey, listen," Hugh said, a trace in his voice that he wasn't as okay as he'd said. "I was thinking maybe we could head down to Chelsea Piers to hit some golf balls."

Grace could tell that Jack was exhausted, but he only smiled and stood. "Sure, I'll get my clubs."

Minutes later, they headed for the door. Grace watched, and at the very last second Jack turned back to look at her—just look, long and hard, as if searching. For a second he seemed on the verge of saying something, and from the expression on his face she had the startlingly clear thought that he was going to say that he had missed her these last few days. But then the dark intensity disappeared, and he smiled.

"Thanks for the cake," he said.

Then he was gone, leaving her alone in the kitchen with her heart in her throat, unsure if she wanted to laugh at her fanciful thinking or throw a bowl of icing at the closed front door.

Chastising herself for wanting to do either because of the man, she made quick work of loading her cart with cakes. She had plenty of time to send off the boxes, then return to clean the kitchen before she had to pick up Ruth. But when she returned to the brownstone, she gasped when she found the child sitting on the front stoop.

"Ruth, what are you doing here? School isn't out yet," Grace said, hurrying forward, her mind racing.

Ruth's lower lip trembled, her fists balled angrily in her lap. "I'm not going back. I hate school."

"What happened?" Grace fell to her knees.

"Nothing happened. I just hate it there. The kids are mean, and the teacher is stupid. So I left and I'm not going back."

"You just walked out?" Grace was stunned. "How could you have just walked out?"

"Any idiot could sneak out of that place, and how hard is it to walk a block?"

Once Grace determined that Ruth was not hurt, she gathered her hands in her own. Her voice became stern, to cover the start of fear she had felt. "Sweetie, you can't just leave. A seven-year-old has no business walking the streets of New York alone. Besides, you have to stay in school. The state requires it. You want to stay with me, don't you?"

"Well, yeah."

"Then you have to go to school."

Ruth grumbled, "I told you, I hate that place."

"Unfortunately, the state doesn't particularly care if you like it or not. Ruth, promise me you won't sneak out again."

Ruth considered at length, then sighed. "All right. I'll go back. But that doesn't mean I have to like it. And if that ratty ol' Billy Walker says he's going to marry me one more time, I'm not going to be responsible for what I do."

Grace hugged her tight, then straightened from the steps. "It's too late to go back now. I'll call the principal—and let her know what I think of her security measures—then how about we have some cake?"

"Sounds good." Ruth pushed up and gathered her sweater and backpack Grace had gotten her. Then she remembered something. "The postman came while I was sitting out here. I got the mail." She pulled out a stack of letters and extended them.

Two caught Grace's eye, and she felt a shudder of tension race through her. One was from a lawyer she knew Walter used, and the other was from New York's child services agency.

Chapter
Twenty

Grace needed a lawyer or fifteen hundred dollars to get Walter off her back.

The letter fluttered from her fingers as she absorbed the news. If she didn't reimburse her former fiancé, he would take her to small claims court. She could hardly believe he'd go that far. But she knew without having to be told that it had more to do with his pride than the money. She had left him at the altar, and this was his way of retaliating.

Picking up the second envelope, she read the official notice informing her about the unannounced visit that would occur sometime in the month of May. The state wanted to see how Grace took care of the child.

A low, steady pulse of stress started to rise.

Up until then, FluffCakes and Ruth had been more of a dream than reality. Now, suddenly, she was truly being given the chance to make them both real. With that reality came the churning anxiety of finding a way to make it happen. As much as she didn't want to admit it, she knew on paper she didn't look like the ideal candidate to adopt a child, not when she didn't have a job or an income. Which meant she had to make FluffCakes succeed.

But sitting at Jack's kitchen table, she figured and refigured her bank balance and the projections for cake income. Even if the orders continued to grow at the rate they

were and she continued to fill them at the rate she had
been, it would still be two more months before she'd be
able to hire a full-time baker. Without any help, and with
orders coming in faster than she could fill them, it didn't
take a rocket scientist to realize that it was only a matter of
time before people would start canceling their orders. She'd
be finished before she'd ever really begun.

Carefully, she refolded the letters and set them aside.
She'd just have to bake faster, ice quicker, even enlist Mrs.
Neimark's oven downstairs, she thought with a firm nod of
her head. Determination replaced anxiety, and Grace moved
into action.

First she called the school, had a meaningful conversation with the principal about security, after which she went
upstairs to her apartment to confirm that the work would
be complete by the end of April. The following day, she
headed down to the Diamond District to sell the ring,
going to every reputable dealer there, only to learn that the
sorry piece of jewelry wasn't worth more than a thousand
dollars at best. Yet again, she was faced with how little
Walter had thought of her.

But she held on, she would not be discouraged. She returned home, tucked Ruth in for the night, then filled orders
until she fell asleep at the kitchen table, dreaming of miniature cakes with faces that came to life and laughed at her.

In the morning she woke more exhausted than before,
her edginess mounting. She barely remembered Jack
coming home in the night, picking her up in his arms and
carrying her to her bed. Like a dream, he had hovered over
her, one single finger tracing her cheek before he pulled
back, the fleeting thought churning sluggishly through her
sleep-filled brain that his need for control increased in di-

rect proportion to the ease that had started to grow between them.

When she got out of bed, Jack was still asleep. Bleary-eyed, she walked Ruth to school, only then remembering that her interview with *Entrepreneurial Weekly* was scheduled for eleven-thirty that day. With footsteps like lead, she dragged herself upstairs to her own apartment, stepped between saws and sawdust, then peeked through the plastic that covered her clothes and tried to find something really great to wear for the interview. But since her entire professional wardrobe consisted of plain, sensible suits, she had little choice but to go with just that.

For half a second she entertained the idea of charging something chic and stylish that would make people look at her and say, *Wow, isn't she successful-looking?* But in the end, common sense won over. She staggered back downstairs to Jack's with four different outfits. When she heard stirrings in his bedroom, she decided to ask Jack which of them she should wear.

But by the time she had determined what to try on first, and came out to knock on his door, he was dressed and gone, the smell of shaving cream and soap all that was left behind. Tired, nervous, and now irrationally disappointed that she hadn't seen Jack, she left the brownstone in the serviceable blue suit rather than the serviceable brown suit that she had worn a thousand times before.

Blue or brown, however, hardly mattered when, two hours later, she exited the magazine's Midtown office building, wanting to cry. The man had questioned her, never smiling, grilling her like a common criminal, making her certain that he thought FluffCakes was an idiotic idea.

Maybe he was right. The truth was, no matter how hard she tried, without help she knew she couldn't get the orders filled fast enough to get the cakes to their destination in a timely manner. On top of that, her savings were dwindling faster than she wanted to admit. She had to face the fact that her cake business wasn't succeeding. *She* wasn't succeeding. That's when she got mad. At Walter, at the interviewer. At her fear.

She would not be defeated by this. She would not give up, even if it meant going to her family for a loan.

In that second she understood what she had to do. Barely seventy-two hours after the letters arrived, Grace called her mother and asked if they could meet.

Rain threatened the following day as Jack drove down Sixty-ninth Street, heading for the garage. He'd had an early morning meeting at Beth Israel Medical Center and decided to drive. For days now he had been consumed with work, coming home late, leaving early. As the weather turned warm, the hospital's ER was inundated with criminal shootings, gang warfare, and car accidents. To compound the situation, St. Luke's was short a doctor again, so Jack spent much of his time on call.

It had felt good to get out and drive, turning up the stereo, speeding along on the deserted early morning streets on the way to Beth Israel. He didn't have to be back at St. Luke's until that afternoon to check on an elderly patient he had admitted yesterday.

As he drove in front of the brownstone, the first drops of rain starting to fall, the door opened and Grace stepped out. He smiled when he made out the curse she muttered as she rummaged in her bag for an umbrella, then hurried down the steps.

With quick efficiency, he pulled over and rolled down the window. "Do you need a lift?"

Ducking, she looked inside. "Jack?" she said, surprised. "Get in."

Not needing a second invitation, she leaped in, banging the door closed just as the skies opened up. For half a second they looked at each other and he felt a ridiculous amount of pleasure at the sight of her. In the close confines, he could smell the hint of her perfume, more a subtle scent of soap and innocence.

She smiled at him, and his gaze drifted to her lips, full and red. He wanted to dip his head and taste, lose himself in the sweetly exotic essence of her.

"How are you doing?" he asked just as she said the redundant same thing.

They chuckled.

"Last time I saw you," he said, "you were facedown in a bowl of icing."

"I was not!"

"Okay, just facedown close to a bowl of icing. You probably don't remember that I carried you to bed."

A gentle blush rose in her cheeks, and desire hit him hard. It was always that way with this woman. Intense, automatic. Tilting his ordered world.

Abruptly, he turned away. "Where to?" he asked.

"If you're sure, I'm going to my mother's on Fifth Avenue."

The car surged powerfully beneath them as he accelerated, turning north on Broadway, then heading for Eighty-first, where he could cut across the park. Traffic was bad, slow, and wet, and he concentrated on driving, the only sound coming from the rain pounding on the windshield and the wipers gliding back and forth across the glass. Not until they swooped down the ramp and green trees lined the way did he speak again.

"How's Ruth?"

"Good, except she hates school."

"She'll get used to it."

"I hope. She snuck out the other day."

He glanced at her, lifting his brow in question.

"Yep, she just waited until someone turned his back, then away she went. I found her sitting out in front of our building. This morning she looked a tad mutinous when I dropped her off, and I'm praying we won't have any more reenactments of her last escape. I can't afford any mistakes if I want the state to let me keep her."

They pulled up to the red light at the park exit and Fifth. The intersection was filled with wall-to-wall taxis and black livery sedans. "How's that going?" he asked.

She sank down against the plush leather. "I'm about to find out. I'm going to my mother to borrow money. Cake payments haven't started coming in yet. If I don't get money in, I can't hire anyone to help me, and if I can't hire anyone, I can't fill the orders fast enough. Kind of a catch-22."

The light turned green, and he accelerated, using one hand to turn right down the avenue, not saying a word as she directed him to the front of the large, ornate, prewar apartment building. The short burst of rain had ceased, leaving a low-cast line of clouds. With a sigh, he slid the car into park, then turned to face her.

"I know this isn't any of my business, but I think you have to make a choice, Grace. Either you make FluffCakes work . . . or you fight for Ruth. I don't see how you can do both, at least do them both and do either of them well."

Her eyes narrowed, and she pushed up. "How can you say that? Women work and raise children all the time!"

"Under the best of circumstances it's a struggle. But starting a business isn't an ordinary job. Can you afford such a struggle right now while you're trying to prove that you're capable of providing a stable home for Ruth?"

Harshly she looked away, and he understood that she was afraid he was right. He wanted to hold her, make the sadness in her eyes go away. But life wasn't easy, and frequently choices had to be made.

"Why don't you want me to succeed?" she whispered.

The words surprised him.

"Adopting Ruth is a dream, Jack. And sure, starting a business isn't an ordinary job, but if I can make it happen, it gives me the freedom to bring in an income and be home to raise a child. I'm close, so close, I can taste it. Is it really so wrong for me to want my dreams to come true?"

Whatever lightness he felt when he saw her evaporated, leaving behind the simmering anger he had lived with for nearly two years now.

"Don't you believe in dreams, Jack?"

Sharply he looked away, his hands curling around the steering wheel, his mind drifting back to life in Brooklyn. That apartment. His parents. His father's futile rage at an unfair world that he swore didn't appreciate his abilities. "I did once. Growing up. I was streetwise and arrogant, full of dreams that I could live a different life from my father's. I worked relentlessly until I had it all. The thriving career, an expensive house, a beautiful wife, and a daughter."

He felt as much as heard her gasp of breath.

"A daughter? Oh, my gosh, Jack. I had no idea."

The image of Daisy leaped to life in his mind, twirling around, smiling. *Do you love me, Daddy? Forever?*

"My Daisy." He felt the joy of his daughter. "Bright and wonderful. I miss being with her every single day." He turned to face Grace. "Despite all my efforts, despite all my dreams, I wasn't any better of a father to my child than my father was to me. I was just a different father, making different mistakes with both my wife and my child. I failed, Grace. I failed because I was too busy trying to have it all. Just like you want it all now."

He expected defiance or anger, wanted to feel them both because that was safer. Instead, Grace reached out and laid her hand on his arm, a determined certainty in her expression.

"I don't believe you failed anyone," she said. "If I had to guess, I'd say it was a case of you not being perfect. But who is, Jack? No one. I saw you in the hospital, working so furiously, like you're competing with God, refusing to let Him take anyone from you."

Tension rose like a knot, her bone-deep faith in him shaking him to the core. He had lived a life of caring for his mother and brother. Then his wife and daughter. He had been the one to listen and to shore them up when they had concerns, and had done it without thought or reservation. It had never occurred to him to share his own concerns, or gain anything in return.

"None of us are perfect, Jack. Don't expect yourself to be any different."

They seemed to be separate from the world, cocooned in the car, that ease she brought to him wrapping around him, and he had the fleeting thought that he could lose himself in her faith for a lifetime. But the moment was shattered when someone knocked sharply on the windshield.

"Grace," came the muffled sound. "Is that you in there?"

Grace's hand froze, but she didn't pull away. "It's my mother," she explained with a grimace. "I'd best go." She started to turn away before glancing back. "Thank you for sharing Daisy with me. Maybe later you'll tell me more." Then she pushed open the door. "Thanks for the ride."

She hurried around to the sidewalk. "Hello, Mother."

"I thought I recognized you." She leaned down and peered into the car. "Who else is in there?"

"Just a friend." Furtively, she waved at him to go.

"If it's a friend, I'd like to meet him." The woman knocked on his window.

Grace squeezed her eyes closed, and Jack extracted himself from the leather seat.

"Mother," Grace said reluctantly. "This is Jack Berenger. Jack, this is my mother."

"Please, call me Roberta," she said, handing off a slew of expensively logo-ed shopping bags to the doorman without so much as a glance. "How do you know Grace?"

"We're neighbors."

"Really?" she said with a speculative gleam. "How neighborly of you to give her a ride across town."

"It was raining," Grace explained, taking her arm and trying to tug her away. "See you, Jack. Thanks again."

Roberta Colebrook disengaged from her daughter. "She never mentioned she was hiding such a handsome man." She tsked. "Shame on you, dear."

Grace groaned. "My mother is an incorrigible flirt."

"Now, really," her mother admonished, before her smile returned. "I don't flirt."

"Of course not. Prancing around in leotards in front of my junior high boyfriend was a regular motherly thing to do."

"He was not your boyfriend. As I recall, you asked him to go steady, and he said no. Always a forward one, our little Grace."

Grace cringed, and Jack felt his gaze narrow.

"So glad you cleared that up, Mother. Now, can we go inside?"

"It was nice to meet you," he said.

"Nonsense. You can't leave now."

"Mother," Grace warned.

"Don't get that tone with me, young lady." Then she tittered. "I never taught her to be rude. And I would be rude if I didn't invite you up for tea so we can chat. Besides, how can I possibly get all these packages upstairs without a little help from a strong man such as yourself?"

Jack knew he was being manipulated, but he'd also had it bred bone deep in him that he should never be impolite to a lady.

"I'll help," Grace interjected.

But Jack had already shut and locked the door, then took the packages from the doorman. Roberta preened. "Hans," she said to the doorman. "Watch Mr. Berenger's car, please. If one of those pesky traffic patrols comes along and wants to ticket it, call up to the apartment."

Then she led the way through the marble-tiled foyer into the brass and crystal-chandeliered elevator.

When they arrived upstairs, Grace halted just inside the living room door. "Suzanne, what are you doing here?" she asked.

Jack noticed a woman who probably was close to the same age as Grace, though she looked much older and much younger at the same time. He immediately recognized the signs of early-stage plastic surgery, which made her look younger. But it was combined with the attire and demeanor of a woman far older. It was an unsettling combination.

"Mother called saying that you had some kind of an emergency," Suzanne explained, looking at Jack and not her.

Where Roberta had been coyly flirtatious, Suzanne took his measure, as if itemizing his clothes, tallying their worth. She reminded him of Hugh's Nadine.

"Mother," Grace countered with clenched teeth, "I didn't say anything about an emergency."

"You might not have said the words, but I know these things. I can't remember the last time you called saying you needed to talk. So I knew."

"We both knew something had to be wrong," Suzanne added. "Seems like everything is going wrong for you these days."

"Now, Suzanne," Roberta said. "Let's not get into that now. Grace has brought such a nice man with her, and we wouldn't want to scare him off."

"Mother!" Grace cried.

Roberta ignored her. "Suzanne, this is Grace's new neighbor, Jack Berenger."

Suzanne extended her hand, her smile impatient. "It's a pleasure to meet you." Then abruptly she turned to Grace. "I can't stay. I have to be at the museum within the hour. Tell us what's wrong."

He would have been amused at the curt dismissal if he wasn't struck by the fact that this was Grace's family. He had an unexpected appreciation for why she had wanted to stay with him instead of her mother.

"It was nice to meet you both," he said to the women.

He glanced at Grace, feeling a strange urge not to leave her. But knowing this wasn't his place, he headed across the room for the door, wanting out of there. But he hadn't taken more than a half-dozen steps when Suzanne spoke.

"What kind of trouble have you gotten yourself into now, Grace? Good Lord, I've never seen such a mess in all my days. How my mousy little sister has managed to walk out of her own wedding, get fired from her job, and even have a party where she makes a disaster of her kitchen, then runs poor Donald off to tell every one of Mother's and my friends about the whole sordid affair, I'll never know."

His footsteps hit tile just when he saw the burn of mortification sear Grace's cheeks. Jack felt a burn as well, the burn of anger. But this was none of his business, he reminded himself. Grace was not his concern.

"Has something happened to Ruth?" he heard her mother ask with a sigh, just as he stepped into the cavernous foyer. "I told you that taking care of this child would be too much for you."

Keep going, he told himself. But when he caught a glimpse of Grace's reflection in an entry hall mirror and saw her raise her chin as if drawing strength, the memory of her delicate hand resting on his arm sparked in his mind. And those simple, determined words. *I don't believe you failed anyone.*

"Ruth is fine, Mother. I've come over today to ask for a—"

"Grace." He cut her off.

She froze, and their eyes met in the mirror, her expression a mix of confusion and embarrassment.

Cursing himself for a fool, he turned back, leveling his hard, cold stare on her relatives. At the sight, Roberta gasped, and Suzanne sat back against the dainty sofa with a start of surprise.

"Based on your description of Grace," he stated, a whiplash sharpness edging his voice as he retraced his steps, "we must not know the same woman. The Grace I know walked out on a man who was found with his pants around his ankles. The Grace I know got stuck with an unforgivably rude guest who deserved to be tossed out the fourth-floor window. And the Grace I know came here to tell you about the incredibly inventive business she has started. She has orders coming in so fast that this dot.com will undoubtedly be a bright spot in the otherwise dismal dot.com industry. You should be impressed." Slowly he turned to Grace, emotion filling him. "I know I am."

Utter astonishment creasing her face, Grace stared at him.

"Your mouth is gaping," he whispered wryly. "Not the best way to give my assertions credibility." Then he took her hand and pulled her after him, leaving her mother and sister startled and speechless.

Grace was the same, not saying a word until he had them slammed back into the car and wheeling across the park at Sixty-sixth Street.

"Jack . . ." She hesitated. "Jack," she began again. "I appreciate what you did back there, at least I appreciate the kind words, but I will not give up on FluffCakes."

His brows slammed together as he pulled up in front of their building. "What are you talking about?"

"My mother and sister might be hard to take, but if I ask, they will help me—and right now I need help. After your display, regardless of how gratifying it was, you only managed to keep me from getting what I needed."

He muttered an oath. "That wasn't my intent."

She looked doubtful, and he swore again when he glanced at the clock in the dashboard.

"I'm late. I have to check on a patient." He leaned over and popped open her door.

"Just like that?" she demanded. "You ruin my chances for getting a loan, and you have nothing else to say?"

He was so close that if he moved ever so slightly he would touch her. She made him crazy, filling him with the need to protect her and keep her safe. But could he afford to give in to the need?

"Don't do anything until I get back," he commanded. "I'll figure something out."

Reluctantly, she stepped out onto the curb in stunned confusion. After a moment's hesitation, he forced himself to pull away. But when he glanced in the rearview mirror, she stood there watching him, her features lined with hurt and betrayal, and he felt the vise around his chest slip a notch tighter.

It was late when Grace heard Jack come home. She had put Ruth to bed hours before, and now she was ready to crawl between the sheets herself.

She still hadn't completely absorbed the fact that he had defended her to her mother and sister. The feelings of hurt and betrayal had faded, replaced with a shiver of gratitude and amazement. But added to that was the news that Jack had a daughter.

Knowing how private he was, she felt they had made a small step together when he had told her about Daisy. With time, would he tell her more? Should she push? Or let him tell her in his own time?

Pulling the covers up to her chin, she listened as Jack walked into the kitchen, then tugged open the refrigerator, the clatter of a plate, the sound of the microwave coming on. She listened, imagined him moving around the kitchen with quiet control, before she heard the light switch flip off and he headed up the stairs.

Her heart pounded when his steps stopped outside her room. But he didn't come in, he continued on as if that ironclad control wouldn't allow him anything more. Shortly after, the shower came on. The water seemed to run forever, but finally it turned off, and just when she thought he would return to his room, the adjoining door clicked open.

He stood in the doorway, the hard carved muscles in his body rippling, his hair slicked back, a towel wrapped around his waist. He looked rugged and sexy, but commanding and contained as well, as his dark eyes took her in.

"Hey," she said softly.

"I'm sorry about today," he said. She could tell the words cost him. "I shouldn't have interfered."

"That's all right. About an hour ago, I realized you might have put me in a better position with my mother. When I go back and tell them about FluffCakes, my plan will have some credibility after you said how great I'm doing."

"I don't want you to go back."

"What?"

"I've thought of little else all evening, trying to come up with a way to help you. I realized the only way I can is to give you the money myself."

"You? I can't take money from you!"

"Consider it a loan. Whatever. I don't care." The harshness faded, and his eyes grew troubled. "After your talk of dreams, then listening to your sister walk all over you, I realized that whether my dreams succeeded or failed, it was those dreams that kept me alive when I was growing up. There's no reason for yours to be dashed. At least not while I have the ability to provide the money you need."

Even in the semidarkness she could see the severity in his features. "Go for it, Grace. Dream. Fly. Don't let people like me make you forget that hopes and dreams are what keep us alive."

They stared at each other across the room, her mind spinning with thoughts and a great surge of gratitude, and the need to say so much to him. But she didn't know where to begin. After a moment, he started to leave.

"Jack?"

He stopped and turned back. But what to say?

"I . . . brought your mail in and set it on the table."

"I found it. Thanks. I also found the plate of leftovers you set aside for me."

She curled her fingers around the edges of the covers. "I hope you didn't mind. I don't want you to accuse me of trying to play house again."

The minute she said the words, his expression changed, softening as he must have remembered the night she had made the extravagant meal even though he had told her not to. Slowly, he walked toward the bed, and her stomach began to flutter.

"Me, accuse you?" he said, his voice rumbling deep in his chest, a smile tilting on his lips. "Never. But if you really want to play something, how about Doctor?" He placed one knee on the mattress, then stretched out on his side next to her, his head propped up on his hand. "Let's see, who will be in charge? All right," he said with great production, "if you insist, you can be the doctor."

He flopped on his back, his eyes closed, the damp towel barely covering him.

"Good thing you're here, Doc," he said, groaning, though the effect was ruined when he popped open one eye. "I've got a pain."

Grace choked on her surprised laugh. "You've taught me all about pain—the kind in the hindquarters," she quipped.

Jack laughed out loud, then rolled back onto his side, his face becoming mock indignant and gravely professional. "You're doing a terrible job of upholding your doctor's Hippocratic oath," he claimed. "So I guess I'll have to be the doctor. Let's see . . ."

All traces of teasing fled, replaced by a heated glint as he tugged at the covers. Grace giggled and held tight.

"Now, now, Miss Colebrook, don't be shy."

"I'm not shy. I'm just healthy as a horse, and don't need an exam."

"I'll be the judge of that."

When she wouldn't let go of the sheet, he slipped his hand underneath from the side. She yelped when he caught her leg.

"Hmmm," he said solemnly, running his palm up her calf to the sensitive spot behind her knee. "We might have a serious case of crooked legs and knobby knees," he explained.

"My legs are not crooked or knobby." She whipped one out from beneath the sheet and held it up in the air. "Straight as an arrow," she stated proudly.

"Ah, yes," he said, his gaze running the length of the body part in question, "my mistake. But we can't take any chances. I'd best check the soundness of your hips. One can never be too careful with such a pivotal joint." His hand slid down her leg with sizzling intensity, slipping beneath the silky material of her nightgown before she could react.

With a gasp, she felt his palm slide to the intimate curve, then she slammed her leg down, catching his fingers underneath the fullness of her bottom.

"Hmmm, the location of your pain," he said with a scholarly nod.

Then before she could roll away, he had her out of the sheets, flipped over and on top of his hard chest, the towel falling away, while his hands very sensually examined the curve of her hips.

"Mmmm," he murmured, pressing her close to his growing hardness, "nothing wrong here."

Then as suddenly as it had begun, all humor evaporated. She watched, amazed, as a battle waged on his face, his desire for her fighting with the control he forced himself to maintain. He wanted to give in, and he did.

He groaned, the sound desperate and despairing, as he

rolled her over and covered her mouth with his, their lips slanting together, his hand sliding between the mattress and her back until he held her close.

But when he pulled back and their eyes met, she couldn't help asking the question that had circled in her mind. "Why did you do it?"

"Do what?"

"Defend me to my family."

Jack looked as if he wouldn't answer, his large hands coming up to frame her face. "Because I wasn't going to stand by and listen to them treat you like that. They have no idea who you really are."

Very quietly she said, "Not too long ago, that could have been you saying those things."

"That's because I didn't know any better."

Tears threatened, her throat tight. "What if they actually do know me?" she whispered. "What if they're right? You're giving me the means to make FluffCakes a reality. You defended me to my family. And I'm being given the chance to prove I deserve to adopt Ruth. But what if I can't do it? What if I fail?"

His gaze grew fierce, and he smoothed back her hair. "They aren't right. And the truth is, you only fail if you don't try."

Her tears spilled through her lashes, and she could feel the shift in him. For one long second he held her tight in the strength of his arms. Then slowly she sensed that his control seeped back, that moment of him giving in vanishing, the walls he kept around himself returning. After allowing himself to hold her for one more second, he kissed her forehead and stood up from the bed.

She felt cold where his heat had been, and when he got to the door, she called out. "Jack?"

"Yes."

"Thank you," she whispered in the city's glittering darkness.

"You're welcome."

"I hope you don't regret your decision."

The faintest trace of a smile returned. "So do I."

Chapter
Twenty-one

*FluffCakes.com Gives Competitors
A Run for the Dough*

Life took a dramatic turn the following week when the phone rang. May 1 was fast approaching, and Jack was busy at work while Ruth was trying to adjust to school.

"Grace!" Mark cried out over the line. "Have you seen it?"

"Seen what?"

"Entrepreneurial Weekly."

"It's already out?"

"I have a copy right here."

"Oh, God. What does it say?"

She held her breath until he read the headline out loud, then she squealed. "Oh, my gosh! He loves Fluff-Cakes.com!"

Mark chuckled. "To think you said he hated you."

Within a few short hours after the article hit the stands, orders started pouring in. Beyond that, the vice president of a venture capital firm called, wanting to make an investment. Bill Header, New Jersey's Mattress King, had his personal assistant order one thousand Bed Head Cakes to send out as promotional gifts.

She could hardly believe her luck when she started getting calls from industry magazines and from *The New York Times*, whose business editor had received a special-order cake she had filled called, Can't Write Worth Crumb Cake from a disgruntled interviewee.

Once the reporter got over the insult, he grudgingly realized that FluffCakes.com with its little cakes was fast becoming a sort of three-dimensional greeting card, and the newspaper wanted to interview her. In an age of dot.com disasters, an Internet site that sold an old-fashioned product was making good. *The New York Times* wanted to report the story.

It was the last week of April, on Saturday, and Grace and Ruth were making cakes, singing along with old Carole King, sort of old Journey, and really new music by Train. Ruth had mastered the art of dancing and icing, the knife swishing back and forth in tempo to her hips. It took a second before they finally registered the insistent buzzing at the front door.

Grace was surprised to find Cecil Kendrick on the landing.

"The construction workers said you were here," he explained when she let him in.

The timer went off in the kitchen, and she dashed away to pull out the next round of cakes. Cecil followed, saying an awkward hello to Ruth.

Grace had seen few people in her life who looked as ill at ease as her former boss. "Is something wrong? Has something happened to Mark?"

"No, no." He smiled wanly. "Mark is fine, and nothing has happened . . . other than I fired J. Hastings Rodman yesterday."

Her mind went on overdrive as she absorbed the facts. "Really? Fired?" Her brows knitted. "I'm . . ."

She was what? She had no idea. The fact was, she realized now she hardly cared. "What does that have to do with me?"

"I just thought you might like to know." He squirmed, then noticed a row of newly iced cakes.

"So," he mused, "these are the cakes."

"Yep." She shoved her palms in the back pockets of her jeans and rocked back on her heels.

He strode over to the counter. "What is this one?"

Ruth tilted her head and screwed up her lips as she got a better look, then laughed gaily. "That one's called"—she didn't notice Grace standing back and frantically waving her arms—"You're a Dope Cake. Grace came up with that one. She says it's a great cake to give to a stupid boss."

Grace's arms froze when Cecil turned to look at her. She smiled and snorted. "Kids. Gotta love 'em."

"Yes, well, um," Cecil said, clearing his throat, "the reason I came by is to make you an offer."

As soon as he said it, she knew he wanted her back. A visceral thrill made her blood pump with gratification that she was vindicated. But the question was, should she take the job?

Three weeks ago she would have agreed so fast, heads would have spun like Linda Blair's in *The Exorcist*. But three weeks ago FluffCakes wasn't working. Now it was. Payments had yet to start filtering in, but they would, soon. It might be touch-and-go for a bit longer, but she believed she could make it.

She thought of Jack's words. *Go for it. Dream. Fly.*

"Cecil, thank you, but—"

"Hear me out," he interjected, holding up his hands in surrender. "I want to buy the rights for FluffCakes.com from you, and bring you back to Kendrick Toys."

She could hardly get her brain around what he was saying.

"Kendrick Toys needs to diversify," he explained, "and I believe FluffCakes is a way to do it."

Hardly able to get sound out of her mouth, she mumbled something he took for agreement when he made arrangements to meet at his office on Monday. By the time he left, Grace stood stock-still.

She felt confused. Should she return to Kendrick Toys? Seconds ago, the answer had seemed clear. But now, when faced with the reality of a real, live job and guaranteed income, she wondered if she could afford the risk of turning Cecil down. What if her savings ran out before payments were received? And she couldn't take money from Jack for long.

Lost in thought, she didn't notice when Ruth pushed up quietly from her seat and headed for her bedroom. But it wasn't long before she realized the child was gone.

"Hey," Grace said quietly when she came into the room. Ruth was lying on top of the bed covers.

"Hey."

"Is something wrong, sweetheart?"

"No." Ruth rolled away, pulling a tattered stuffed animal that Grace had never seen before, tighter into her arms. "I'm just tired."

"Are you sure?"

"Yeah."

Grace nodded. "Then a nap will do you good." She turned to go.

"Grace."

"Yes, sweetie?"

"Is that man going to take our cakes away?"

Grace tilted her head. "No. If we do sell it to him, he'll pay us money, and I'll go to work there and run it from a big fancy office."

"Where will I be?"

Emotion swelled in her veins like honeyed syrup, thick and slow, intensely sweet, though concern rose as well. Grace returned to the bed and sat down. "You'll be right here with me."

"At your office?"

"No. You'll be in school."

"I'd rather make cakes with you."

Reaching down, Grace hugged Ruth tight. "You're going to be with me, even if you're at school."

"Forever?"

Grace realized too late what a precarious edge she walked. She prayed she would win full custody of Ruth. Part of her knew to be careful. But another part of her, the part who had been desperate to know that she was loved when she was a child, spoke up.

"Forever," she confirmed.

"You promise?"

"Of course, I promise."

Now more than ever she had to make sure she gained custody, because she refused to break her promise.

Grace walked into the offices of Kendrick Toys with her head held high, though she shook inside. She had been up since five, preparing. Hair, makeup, clothes. Based on the reaction, her efforts had paid off. More than one person murmured that she seemed different somehow. Nodding to several people, she conceded that she was different, very different from the woman who had been escorted out of the building nearly three months before by a security guard.

As soon as she entered the conference room and sat down, Cecil didn't bother with small talk.

"I want you back. And I'm willing to pay six figures for

the rights to FluffCakes," he said, leaning forward, "and Kendrick Toys takes on all responsibilities for manufacturing and distribution."

"Six figures?" she asked, her voice low in disbelief.

Cecil didn't recognize the sound of disbelief though. "All right, the number is negotiable," he amended. "But either way, I will do whatever it takes to get FluffCakes.com under the Kendrick Toys umbrella."

Grace listened, her head spinning, and she knew that this deal was the answer to her money concerns.

But at what cost?

Would the state be any more willing to give her custody of Ruth if she had to work sixteen hours a day doing for someone else what she was already doing for herself—and starting to succeed?

On top of that, could she return to Kendrick Toys and disregard the fact that the man who wanted to hire her back had laughed when someone said she was more fluff than stuff? Would he bring her back only to fire her again?

Like a doorway opening up, clarity came to her. She thought of Jack and the change that settled over him when the hospital intercom shuddered with a Code Blue warning. He knew exactly what he had to do. He didn't question; he didn't doubt. That was the mark of someone who understood his place in life—something Grace had never known. Until now.

She surprised herself and them when she pushed her chair back from the elegant mahogany table and stood, feeling a combination of freedom and fear.

"I appreciate your interest, Cecil. But FluffCakes.com is not for sale."

"Are you crazy?" the man bellowed, every ounce of good nature evaporating like it had never been real. "How do you possibly think you can succeed on your own?"

His condescending attitude made her bristle, and she leaned forward, planting her hands on the table. "I already am succeeding, proof of which is in the fact that I am here right now." She straightened and headed for the door. At the last minute, she turned back. "But I do thank you for the opportunity."

Cecil's bushy brows furrowed.

"If you hadn't fired me so unfairly, Ruth and I never would have come up with FluffCakes.com."

She left him as she found him, in silence at the table. As soon as she opened the door, she came face-to-face with a circle of people who had been listening in the hallway. Mark hovered nearby, pretending to be busy with a stack of files at a file cabinet, rushing after her when she started to leave.

"What happened?" he wanted to know.

"She said no," Herb from accounting announced proudly. "She stood up to Kendrick."

"You aren't coming back?" Mark demanded.

A luminous smile broke out on her lips. "Nope, I turned him down."

The small crowd broke into spontaneous applause while Mark stood speechless and Grace exited the building feeling like a warrior queen.

It was later, much later that night, when Grace headed for bed. Her apartment would be ready in the morning, the floors dry enough that they could return. Their belongings were packed, some downstairs at the door, the rest still opened and lined along the wall in her room, nearly ready to go.

Ruth was sound asleep, and Jack was going over patient files at his desk. During dinner they had celebrated Fluff-

Cakes's success, and she could see the belief and faith in Jack's eyes, even if she also saw that all-too-familiar distance he kept between them.

Now, in her room, there was no noise, no cars in the distance. All was dark as she slipped out of her clothes, then walked into the bathroom. She turned the lights on low, the dimmer switch nearly off as she ran water into the massive marble tub that stood next to the glass-encased shower, and poured some of Ruth's bubble bath into the water.

Securing her long dark hair on top of her head, she slid into the water and sighed as the warmth seeped into her muscles and bones. She closed her eyes, emptying her mind, easing herself deeper.

When she heard the door open, it was as if she had been waiting. Though she shouldn't. If Jack could keep such tight control around his emotions, she should be able to, as well.

She opened her eyes. As always, he took her breath. The dark hair, the fathomless eyes.

He wore soft, faded blue jeans, hanging low, the top button undone, and nothing else. No shirt. No shoes. Only a light smattering of dark hair on his chest that trailed down his abdomen in a fine line, then disappeared beneath the waistband.

Heat shimmered through her, making her yearn, and she was thankful for the bubbles that covered her breasts.

"I saw the suitcases and boxes downstairs. You're ready to go," he said quietly.

"Yes, you'll be rid of us in the morning." She tried to grin, but her heart fluttered at the way he looked at her. Then her breath went still when he walked to the opposite door and locked it.

She wasn't sure what she expected, but she was surprised

when he sat down on the floor next to the tub, one knee up, the other crooked beneath him. He leaned forward and rested his chin on his fisted hand. All at once he looked manly and boyish, mischievous and inordinately sad.

"I'm proud of you," he said, looking into her eyes, making it impossible to look away. "You never gave up. You didn't give in when your life was spiraling out of control. Now you are rising from the ashes to succeed."

"I couldn't have done it without your help. Letting us stay with you while they repaired my apartment. Lending me the money at the exact moment I needed it most."

She moved slightly, the water sloshing, the curve of her breasts rising from the bubbles.

"What am I going to do with you?" he asked.

She shrugged, her shoulders coming out of the water. "Have you hated having us here?"

"Yes," he said softly as he shook his head no.

His gaze had shifted to her shoulders as he sat up, then touched the pulse in her neck—barely. The tips of his fingers grazed her skin, then drifted along her collarbone, down her arm, into the bubbles. She watched as his hand disappeared into the water, down until his fingers touched hers.

For half a second he let their fingers twine before he moved on, his hand drifting to her stomach, his palm cupping the gentle curve. He looked at her then. Questioning. Wondering. Deciding where they would go from there.

She didn't know. Couldn't think of anything beyond now, this moment. Wanting to feel his hands on her. Feel the heat of him.

He didn't wait for an answer that she didn't know how to give, before his hand skimmed up, the bubbles gathering against his forearm, his palm grazing the tips of her breasts— back and forth, over each—and her eyes drifted closed.

With seductive expertise, he filled her body with sensation. Then his hand grazed down, lower and lower, and her eyes went wide when his fingers found the curls between her legs.

"Jack!"

"Shhh," he whispered, his own breath catching.

"This isn't right—"

But the words cut off when his finger whispered between the curls, finding the heat of her, grazing, brushing, and she sucked in a silent breath.

"Lie back, Grace," he told her, his voice commanding but gentle.

"Jack," she said, her voice both a lament and a question.

"Lift your knees."

She groaned her mortified ecstasy, instinctively obeying, the bubbles clinging to her knees, then slowly sliding back to the surface. "Jack, really."

"Really, what," he said, his voice gruff as he traced circles at the entry of her body, making her yearn for the exquisite feel. And when he slipped his finger inside her, sensation exploded, swallowing her whole. It was this she had been waiting for, wanting.

Her mouth fell open, but no sound came out as his finger started to move . . . slowly, in and out, the water sloshing ever so softly against the sides, the bubbles caressing her skin as they ebbed and flowed with the water.

Sensation built and grew, crashing in on her, and she felt her hips begin to move. She couldn't believe what she was doing, but still her body sought what her mind told her not to want.

Then she forgot. About being embarrassed. About propriety. About sanity and seemliness. And when he slipped a second finger inside her, he had to gently press his other hand over her mouth to keep her quiet.

"You don't want to wake anyone."

In some recesses left of her working brain she was appalled, but very little of it was working right then. Her whole being was centered on the building fire at the core of her soul, the mounting need that had to be satisfied.

He couldn't stop. She couldn't stop, her body moving, her eyes closed. His fingers worked their magic. But just when she thought she couldn't take it anymore, was certain that her body would explode with the pleasure she sought, she fought for control.

She gasped and struggled, pressing her thighs together. When she could breathe, and she looked into his confused and passion-burning eyes, she said no.

"Not this way," she managed.

Then she stood up in the tub.

Chapter
Twenty-two

"Not again," she whispered.

His countenance darkened, his back muscles straining and defined as he braced one hand against the tile floor and pushed up.

"You can't keep doing this to me, making me feel, but not giving in yourself. No more, Jack. No more of your ironclad control."

She stepped out of the tub, taking up a towel and drying off. He watched her, every muscle tense, his reflection caught in the mirror, angry and lost. When finally she stood there staring back, the soft gray towel clutched to her chest, the ends trailing down in front of her, he said, "I'll leave, then."

"Why?" She whirled around to face him. "Why do you have to leave?"

"Because."

"Like that's an adequate explanation? It's not enough by a long shot."

With jerking movements, she secured the towel around her, holding it tightly at her chest. "You want me, I know you do. But you won't lose that furious control you secured around yourself like a shield." She took a step closer, so close that she could touch him, but she held back.

She saw anger mix with pain on his features.

"Why do you do this, Jack? Why won't you let yourself feel? With the exception of that first night, you never let things go any further than you giving me pleasure. I'm tired of it."

Anguished, she watched myriad emotions play havoc with the chiseled planes of his face as his anger melted to despair. Drawing a deep, ragged breath, his jaw cemented.

Without a word, he started to step away and would have left her then, but she couldn't let him go. He was like a drug that she didn't know how to give up. She wanted him to wrap his body around her, like a white picket fence around a safe green-grass yard.

She wanted him, but it was deeper than that. She needed him in some elemental way that was beyond physical—as if this man who on the surface was everything she didn't want was deep down what she had wanted all along.

As he looked into her eyes, she had a startling insight of what it was that had drawn her from the very beginning. Not desire. Not passion. Yes, those had been there, burning her up. But more than that, first and foremost, he made her feel safe.

Despite the women who could easily come back into his life, despite the fact that he clearly wanted no commitment. Despite the unavoidable truth that he had been a stranger when he'd walked out into the night. At some deep level she had recognized that he was a deeply caring man. He made her feel as if she had an ally—for the first time in her life.

With Jack she had been herself, a self she hardly knew existed, and he had come to accept her, had been drawn to her from the beginning. He had sought *her*, not Calder Colebrook's daughter, or Suzanne Colebrook Harriman's sister. He had come out into the night with no preconceived notions about who she was—then hadn't been able to let her go completely.

In that moment she understood. She loved him. She loved him in every way, for all that he was. For his dedication, for his willingness to help even though he didn't need to. For the honor that she saw in him every day. But was love enough? Could he ever feel more for her than unwanted desire? When passion was swept away, could he love her in return? But most of all, could she overcome whatever it was that brought the darkness into his eyes?

She looked up at him, trying to find some truth, some insight. But his face was an unfathomable mask, no answers staring back. His gaze was hard, his eyes narrowed.

Her knees felt weak, and when she reached out, her hand trembled as she pressed it to his bare chest. She had to find a way to break through his control. She understood in that moment that it was this restraint that stood in her way, and she had nothing to lose. Not after she had realized that she loved him. Whether he walked out on her now, or after she had thrown herself at him even more boldly, wouldn't matter. If he did, she would have lost. She wasn't going to lose without a battle for what she wanted to believe was below the surface of his hard control. A caring for her that he didn't know how to give in to.

With that, she dropped the towel, the terry cloth puddling on the small rug between them. Trembling inside, she reached up and pulled the pins from her hair, the long wild tresses tumbling around her shoulders. Jack looked on. His features became a sharp blank, giving her no clue to his feelings. He didn't move, he didn't seem to breathe, he simply stood before her, seeming formidable, seeming more unapproachable than ever before. But she wouldn't lose her courage.

She was sure he could see her pulse pounding frantically in the line of her throat, but she stepped closer anyway. Still, he didn't move. But when she lifted her chin and pressed the palm of her hand to his heart, she felt a shudder run through him, saw the dark heat in his eyes flare.

"Please don't leave me," she said.

He stood like stone, his jaw tightly furious, and her conviction tried to waver.

They stared at each other for a lifetime, a battle of wills waging war. It was clear from the look in his eyes that he was holding on by a thread. Then a horrifying thought occurred to her.

"Do you really not feel anything for me?" she whispered.

Suddenly, his steely restraint boiled over and his hands came up to grip her forearms, his countenance fierce. "God, I want you. You do things to me. All I have to do is see you and my body grows hard. But I don't *want* to feel. I've spent a lifetime making sure that I don't. Then you walked into my life, turning my world upside down. I want you." His voice was ragged. "I want to be inside of you. I want your legs wrapped around my waist and your breasts arched into my palms. I want to lose myself in your blue eyes that look at me with such innocent and passionate wonder. But I don't want more than that. I don't want the commitment." He drew his head back, the cords in his neck straining. "I care for you too much to make love to you again, then walk away."

With a measured command that she could feel slicing through every muscle in his body, he let go of her.

"I'm an adult, Jack," she said with fervor. "Let me worry about what's best for me."

But he wouldn't listen, that deeply ingrained sense of honor etched on his face. He would walk away from her, leave her standing in this bathroom alone and mortified that she would be so bold.

"Don't do this to me," she whispered, her voice breaking. "Don't make me beg."

He stopped, and she could feel the rigidity in him like glass ready to shatter.

"I love you, Jack."

She felt as much as heard his sharp, shuddering intake of breath.

"I love you as I have never loved before," she added, her voice soft but determined.

His face took on a haunted darkness, looking like an animal caught and desperate.

"I love you because you fill my heart. I love you because I feel whole when I'm by your side. But most of all I love you for the honorable man you are."

With that, he gave in, his strangled cry echoing against the marble walls. They came together like two lost souls, his groan reckless as he pulled her close.

Their embrace was frantic, each surrendering, each forgetting all else. He ran his hands over her body, like he couldn't quite believe she was really there. The heel of his hand grazed the side of her breast before he cupped the soft underswell.

Their mouths came together in a clasp of passion, lips slanting, neither able to get close enough. The touch was like fire, burning and hot, consuming her, before his lips trailed back along her jaw.

A shiver of yearning coursed down her spine as he nipped at the shell of her ear. She couldn't get close enough, pressing her body into his like melting into heat.

"Yes," he breathed against her temple.

He moved her ever so gently, back and forth, so the swells of her breasts brushed against the crisp hair on his chest. She wanted to touch him, taste the heat of him. But most of all, she wanted him to feel.

"How do you do this to me?" he groaned. He kissed her on the forehead. "It always comes back to that. I can't stay away. I want you. Now, not later. I want to sink inside you, feel your warmth. Ever since the first night," he accused raggedly. "Sex and wanting, and not knowing how I can breathe without you. You make me want to rewrite life."

That was her undoing.

She ran her hands up his arms to his shoulders. She relished the texture of hard sinew beneath her fingers, she savored his jagged intake of breath.

"Grace," he groaned against her ear, her name a curse, "I want you as I have never wanted anything in my life."

She could feel his yearning in his pounding heart. This strong, good man wanted her. With joy singing through her mind, she touched him as he had touched her, barely, softly, her finger circling the deep brown nipple.

He closed his eyes, and he drew a deep, shuddering breath. The power she had over him stunned and amazed her. His mouth tightened into a hard line when her finger drifted over to the other nipple, circling once, then following the thin line of hair that trailed down, stopping at the soft jeans that hung low.

He coaxed her lips apart, tasting her. Cool air swept across the bare skin around her neck, his breath sending shivers through her as he ran his fingers down her spine.

His eyes flared, and he groaned the second she reached between them to the metal buttons of his jeans. When she had worked them free, he kicked them away. Then, as if he could do nothing else, he wrapped her hand around his hard shaft. She gasped at the feel of him, velvet and steel.

His body leaped at her touch, and she felt a rush over the strong sense of satisfaction that he was not immune.

She stroked him with maddening slowness, her fingers tight until he groaned into her hair and grabbed her hand. His expression was grim. "You bring me to my knees."

With the same furious control he had used to keep her distant, he turned her around, bringing her spine to his chest until they faced the mirror, two strangers staring back. His warm hands drifted up against her bare skin, slipping higher and higher until he cupped her full breasts, pressing the soft pertness high.

A sigh escaped her lips, and she felt his body shudder behind her, the hard length of his desire bold against her buttock.

"Do you like this?" he whispered in her ear, slowly moving his hips across her.

She only managed to open her mouth in a silent moan as he brushed the flats of his palms across her nipples.

"I think you do," he murmured, his voice a deep brush of sound. "I think you and I were meant for this. I was meant to be inside you."

She gasped when his hands drifted low, grazing over her abdomen, slipping between her legs.

Her mouth opened on a silent cry, her hair tumbling madly, his erection insistent.

"You are so soft," he said.

He stepped every so slightly to the side, bringing them face-to-face with the mirror. Running his hand down her back, he gently bent her over the marble counter.

The sight of her brought heat flashing through him with raw intensity. He trailed his hand lower, cupping her bare bottom, his fingers sliding low and deep inside her in one erotic thrust.

He felt her body shudder with desire, and when she tried to stand, he gently pressed his hand to her back, his fingers sliding deeper. He stroked, moving in a slow, steady rhythm that made her body pulse.

Her breathing grew ragged, and Jack couldn't believe the passion Grace showed. It was like a burning that she gave in to, however reluctantly, that matched the burning that always surfaced inside of him whenever he saw her. She was slick with desire, and his erection was nearly painful. When her hips started to move, they brushed against him until he thought he would embarrass himself like an adolescent.

With tautly held control, he withdrew from her, and couldn't help but chuckle grimly when she squeaked her protest. Then he turned her to face him. He knew he was well built, but the awe in Grace's eyes went beyond the physical. Whenever she saw him, it was the same. Each time he saw amazement in her eyes—but it was an amazement that he was sure had nothing to do with his body, but rather something deeper.

She did love him, he saw it so clearly. The truth. The honesty.

With reverence filling him, he swept her into his arms. She grasped his neck as he carried her into his bedroom and laid her down on the bed, following after. Never once did she let go.

He kissed her again, his lips traveling lower along her collarbone, then over the swell of her breast, but not stopping. Suckling and nipping, then the flick of his tongue before continuing on, his kisses trailing over her abdomen.

Each of them was breathing hard now as he pulled up her knees. His fingers scorched a path up from her ankle, along the inside of her thigh, until they grazed the silken folds between her legs. He groaned when he felt her wetness. He circled, teasing, but never entering, just grazing. He could feel when she gave herself over to sensation. But then he startled her when he pressed his tongue to the center of her being.

He felt her surprise and her resistance, but he circled his tongue, dipping, and she cried out in pleasure, her fingers tangling in his hair. They grew frantic once again, each desperate to find release in the other. Then he came over her. Supporting his weight on his forearms, he framed her face with his hands. Their eyes met, locked, and they never looked away as he nudged her knees apart. Then he filled her as he had wanted, as he had dreamed about every second since the night he'd found her in the snow. He sank deeply inside her, but still didn't look away.

She took him completely, raising her knees, inhaling a deep, shuddering breath when he sank even deeper.

Then he began to move, slowly at first, because she was so tight—so tight that it took every ounce of concentration not to thrust hard and be done with it. But soon she wasn't satisfied with the pace.

"I can't wait," she breathed.

Sensation shot through him as she arched her back, her eyes fluttering closed.

With that, he buried his face in her neck, calling out her name as he gave in to the primal need and thrust inside her, again and again. He cupped her hips, pulling her body up to meet his bold, fevered thrusts until he felt her body explode with sensation. Only then did he give in, taking what his body demanded. Taking his release in a moment of pure surrender. To her. To fate. To the fact that he didn't know how he could live with her.

Or without her.

Chapter
Twenty-three

Reality surged back like a wave crashing against the shore. Jack shielded his eyes against the sun that streamed through the windows. His mood was dark and grim as he lay alone in bed.

He had lost control last night, giving in to the terrible need he had steeled himself against since the moment he had met Grace. Just thinking about her now made his shaft grow hard. He wanted to bury his face in her hair, hold her tight, seek peace in the scent and taste of her.

And that was impossible.

He wanted no commitments, he had told her as much. When he moved back to New York, he had hated the permanence of buying the apartment. But he had enough business sense to know that renting was like throwing money down the drain, given his income. So he had bought, but he had wanted no other ties.

He knew that, held to the thought with a furious determination. But when she had uttered those words, *I love you*, his last shreds of control had vanished. Even now he felt shaken by the insatiable need he had given in to.

Despite the early hour, he found Grace on the phone, and he felt his chest constrict. When she saw him, her cheeks blushed pink, her lips love swollen from his touch, and she smiled at him.

"I had a message from the editor of *Fortune* magazine," she explained almost shyly.

She murmured a contented sigh when he allowed himself one shuddering touch and he leaned over to press a kiss on her forehead.

"I'll be down in a minute," she added.

Jack showered and dressed, then took the stairs to the kitchen with controlled and measured steps. He stopped in the doorway when he saw Ruth sitting at the table, a bowl of icing and a cake in front of her, her head bent in concentration as she worked on one of the cakes that had become such a part of their lives. For long seconds his mind slipped and spun, careening back in time—back two years ago, then further. Back to years before, to another child's head bent over in concentration.

"What's wrong, Jack?"

He blinked, his heart beating hard, his palms damp. It took a moment for him to realize it was Ruth who spoke.

"Are you okay?" she asked, clearly worried. "You're not going to die, are you?"

He forced himself to focus on Ruth. "No, I'm not going to die."

She looked down at a cake that she was icing in front of her. "Good," she whispered.

He started to go to her, understood that he needed to reassure her that everything was all right. But he stopped in his tracks when she extended a cake in the palm of her hand.

"I made this for you," she said softly.

He stared at it. A round cake iced with dark hair and dark eyes, just a hint of a smile. His heart surged again, memories swirled. A little girl's hand extended. The gift.

"It's Doctor Daddy Cake," Ruth added.

She sat there, so young, so hopeful. So fragile. He had learned that. For long seconds he couldn't seem to breathe, a deep, abiding pain and uneasiness trying to overwhelm him.

Her hand faltered when he didn't reach out, but thankfully he had the presence of mind to accept the cake.

"Thank you, Ruth." He inspected it without really seeing. "It's great."

Placing his free hand on her head, he smiled as best as he could, then sat down at the table. Contented, relieved, she picked up another baker's tube of colored icing, all the while chatting away. Jack tried to clear his mind, but the cake sat on the plate before him, and the vision of Ruth's hand extended circled relentlessly. Ruth's hand that slowly shifted to another hand, another life, to another child.

Daddy, you're home!

Jack closed his eyes, willing the thoughts away.

Look what I made for you!

He couldn't breathe, the restlessness he had hoped to put behind him swirling up like a swallowing mist. Daisy. But it was Ruth who had come to live in his world every day.

It's my footprint! That way you'll have it forever!

Where was it? he wondered. What had happened to the art and the kindergarten gifts?

Oh, Daddy, I love you so much.

Then chubby little arms wrapping around his neck, turning to older, teenage arms hooking with his, those knowing smiles, and his wife shaking her head, saying he was spoiling their daughter.

He knew now that he had.

With a jerk, he pushed up from the table. But he didn't get farther than the doorway when Grace appeared.

"Grace!" Ruth leaped up and launched herself into her arms.

"Good morning, sweetheart."

"Can you believe it?" Ruth asked. "Any day now the state will do their visit, then we can go to court to make me official!"

"I'll take your things up to your apartment," Jack stated. "Can I have the keys?"

"What? Well, yes." Grace sensed the tension that sliced through him, though she didn't understand the change. She retrieved her keys. "I know you're busy. I can take everything up after I take Ruth to school."

"No need," he said tightly. "I'll do it now."

He walked past her without a word. Ruth's brow furrowed, and she bit her lip.

"Thank you," Grace said, watching him disappear through his front door with a suitcase in either hand.

Ruth was quiet most of the way to school. Grace tried to make small talk, but it was a struggle.

"When you get home this afternoon, I have a surprise for you in our apartment."

"Will Jack come to our apartment?"

"Of course he will, to visit," she clarified. Though she wasn't sure if that was true.

She didn't understand what she had seen in Jack's eyes, and as they got closer to the school, she wondered if she had made a grave mistake last night. In forcing him to feel, had she once and for all pushed him too far? Did he resent her now?

Once Ruth was safely inside, Grace returned to help move the rest of the things. But Jack was gone, the boxes and suitcases put away in hers and Ruth's bedrooms, with all the cake stuff in the kitchen. For long minutes she stood there, the smell of polyurethane mixing with the slight breeze drifting in through the open windows.

She had always loved this apartment, the yellows bright and the blues soothing, but suddenly it felt small and lonely. Pushing the thought aside, she told herself that this was where she and Ruth needed to be.

She tried to calm her mind with thoughts that she was prepared for the unannounced visit. She was determined to make her case before the judge to prove her abilities to adopt Ruth. Everything was going to be fine, she told herself minutes later when she stepped onto the subway to head downtown to buy more supplies, though a slow bead of anxiety swelled in her mind.

Ruth sat quietly, waiting until the lunch monitor's back was turned. Then she stood, walking stiff and quick so she wouldn't attract notice, and with a few careful maneuvers, she was out on Sixty-eighth Street, running so fast her heels made her pleated skirt fly up in the air. This school stuff was for the birds. She'd just have to have a heart-to-heart with Grace and let her know that it wasn't working out. The kids were dumb, and the teachers taught stupid stuff. They had to learn about some gross plague today. Right before lunch. What were they thinking?

The weather was great, only a few puffy clouds in the perfectly blue sky, and maybe, just maybe, she could get Grace to take her to the park. Ages ago she had said she didn't like it there, but that was just because she didn't like anything back then. Now she did. Just not school.

But she came to a dead stop when she saw someone standing at the front door of the brownstone. Ruth gasped when she recognized the state lady who had brought her there a million years ago. Maggie, or Mary. No, Margery.

Ruth watched as the woman pressed the buzzer again, and she figured getting caught out on the street alone by this woman couldn't be too good.

As quietly as she could, Ruth started to sneak away just when the woman looked up. Their eyes met, the woman's at first confused, then surprised.

"Ruth? Is that you?" she called to her.

"Ah, no. I'm not Ruth."

"Of course you are." The woman marched down the steps, briefcase held rigidly in her hand. "What are you doing out here?" She looked around. "Where is Miss Colebrook?"

"Ah, well, um, she's upstairs, yep, upstairs sound asleep. She isn't feeling great, so I don't think we should wake her."

"You mean to tell me you are out here alone while she is upstairs ill? And why aren't you at school?"

"Me, school?" She had to think. "Sick! Yep, I'm sick, too." She leaned forward and coughed, then moaned. "I've got the plague. The really contagious kind, where you shrivel up and turn all black and blue," she added, looking at the woman through lowered lashes. "I had to come home because they won't let me even stay in school because I'm so sick!" She coughed again and moaned a bit for good measure. "I better get inside before I give it to you. You can tell me what you want, then I'll tell Grace when she gets up."

"What I want is to talk to her." Margery pulled back her shoulders. "I am here for my visit to evaluate the abilities of Miss Colebrook as a mother."

"You should have called first," Ruth stated.

Margery blinked. "This is the unexpected visit, about which Miss Colebrook was notified."

"Well, then, I'll let you two visit, and I'll just be going." She flashed a chubby hand in the air. "See ya."

"You're not going anywhere, young lady. We are going to talk with Miss Colebrook." She took Ruth's arm and marched back up the steps, and started to buzz.

Ruth realized that Grace must not be home. Her brain scrambled as she tried to come up with a plan.

When no one answered, Margery looked at Ruth. "How did you intend to get in?"

Truthfully, she hadn't thought that far ahead. But if worse came to worse, she knew there was a key.

Not knowing what else to do, Ruth found the hiding place behind a loose piece of cement. They had put both Jack's and Grace's keys in there after Grace said something about not wanting to get locked out again. Ruth wasn't sure which was which, since they both looked the same. So she took both out, then forced a smile, praying for a miracle.

They got inside, and walked up the steps. Ruth prayed all their stuff was back in the old apartment since she knew this lady would have a fit if she took her to Jack's. On the fourth floor, Ruth tried one then the other key, and finally got the door open.

"What's that smell?" the woman asked.

"Paint and stuff." But as soon as the words where out, all worry evaporated. "Look! A stairway! A real live stairway up to my room!"

It was grand, and somehow had been installed when the men were doing the work. Ruth raced up the steps, turned at the top, then proceeded down like a princess. At the bottom, without thinking, she raced into Grace's bedroom, the reality of her precarious situation only returning when she realized the room was empty.

"Young lady, stop that this instant and wake your cousin.

I am not leaving here until I get some answers," Margery finished grimly.

The excitement in Ruth's heart burst like a balloon blown up too big. "I can't wake her up."

The woman's eyes narrowed.

"She's not here." Ruth bit her lip.

"You mean to tell me you are walking around New York City alone and sick?"

"Okay, I'm not really sick. Grace would never leave me alone if I were sick!"

"She just lets you wander around alone when you *aren't* sick."

Ruth rose to Grace's defense. "Oh, no, ma'am. She doesn't know I was wandering around alone."

"She doesn't?" the woman asked ominously. "Where does she think you are?"

"In school, of course. Grace is the best kind of mom. She loves me. She tells me I have to go to school. But I hate it, and sometimes it's hard to stay. She made me promise never to sneak out again."

"Again?"

Ugh. Talking to adults was really tricky. "This is only the second time. But today I really, really wanted to see what my surprise was." She pointed to the stairs. "This must be my surprise! When the men were fixing the apartment, they made me some stairs!"

The woman crossed her arms. "Why was the apartment getting fixed?"

Oh, no, not again. Something else she shouldn't have said. "Well, I kind of started a fire in the kitchen. Just a little fire, really, but it's amazing how such a little burning cheese can really mess things up."

Margery scowled, took out a pad of paper and scribbled

some notes, slapped it shut, then shoved it into her bag. When she walked over to the couch and sat down, making it clear that she wasn't leaving until Grace returned, Ruth started thinking that maybe learning about the plague right before lunch wasn't so awful. Too bad she hadn't thought of that before she'd hightailed it out of school.

Chapter
Twenty-four

Grace balanced a bag of baking goods in one arm as she came up the brownstone steps. She managed to get inside, then secured the bag between her hip and the wall as she fumbled with the mailbox key. As soon as she opened the box, mail spilled onto the floor in a gush.

She stared at the scatter of mail as she tried to understand. With her heart in her throat, she set the bag down, then knelt, picking up envelope after envelope. One from the Mattress King. Another from a company in Missouri she had sent cakes to. Ripping one open, she pressed her eyes closed. A payment. Then she tore open another and another, tears streaming down her cheeks. Payment after payment.

It was really, truly starting to work.

She managed to get the mail stuffed into the bag, then headed upstairs. Out of habit she nearly stopped at Jack's apartment, but remembered, then continued on. Up and up, like she was flying, because she was so happy.

But the second she opened the door, she nearly dropped everything when she saw the woman she instantly recognized as the state's social welfare caseworker. The woman didn't look happy, Grace realized with a frisson of nerves.

"Miss Bancroft?" she asked, confused as to how she got in.

"Yes."

Then she saw Ruth walk out of the kitchen, and understanding hit her square in the chest. "Ruth, you didn't."

Her young face scrunched up. "I'm sorry." Then tears welled. "I know I shouldn't have left school. But somehow it just happened, and I found myself here." She looked at Margery. "With her."

Grace's brain raced. "Ruth, please go upstairs while I speak with Miss Bancroft, then you and I will talk about school after that."

With a mixture of relief and doom etched on her face, Ruth dashed up the new set of stairs, stopping halfway up. "Grace?"

"Yes?"

"Thanks for the stairs."

A trace of a smile surfaced. "You're more than welcome. Now go on."

Ruth hurried the rest of the way up the steps, and Grace just barely caught sight of the child's fingers crossed in hope.

Margery looked around. "Ruth told me about the fire."

Grace nodded truthfully. "It was an accident. Can I get you some tea?" She headed into the kitchen, where she set the bags down, removing a new set of cake molds and icing bags, busying her hands in an attempt to give her a moment to think.

"No, thank you," the woman said. "I think it's wise that we get right to the point. I have grave concerns about the situation here. A child burning up kitchens, sneaking out of school, home alone."

"Please, Miss Bancroft, let's sit down and discuss this."

"I didn't come here for a social visit, Miss Colebrook. I came to observe the environment in which you are caring for Ruth." She glanced over at the table. "Ah, the infamous cakes."

The sound of footsteps on hardwood floor rattled in Grace's brain as the social worker strode across the room when she saw the line of baking things. "You know about the cakes?"

"Of course, I do. You signed documents allowing the state to verify your financial status."

"Then you've learned how popular they are," she added.

"Popular? I have no idea. What the state has learned during its investigation is that you are making cakes that haven't brought in a penny as far as we can discern, this after you were fired from your job. Additionally, a claim has been filed in court for fifteen hundred dollars by one Walter Reed, and what savings you had managed to accrue has all but dissipated. Though we did notice a sudden deposit three weeks ago—too much, I would think, for a simple cake. I know the judge will be interested in learning where that money came from." The woman's fingers curled around the handle of her leather briefcase, her polyester suit giving off a shine where the sun hit the fabric. "He will also want to know if you are even looking for a job."

Grace wanted to close her eyes, not see, as if she could will this woman away. "I have a job, Miss Bancroft, with my cake company. Besides that, my bank account is on the verge of a drastic change. A good change."

She pulled out the payment checks and extended them. But the woman sighed, her chin tucking close to her chest in stern disapproval. "Miss Colebrook, while I applaud your entrepreneurial spirit, this is not a situation in which I can recommend a child like Ruth, who has already been through so much, should be raised. I must tell you that based on what I have seen, my recommendation will be that the child be placed with a more suitable family."

The words raked Grace's brain, sucking the breath out

of her so quickly that she nearly buckled over. "But you can't take Ruth away. She's mine."

"No, Miss Colebrook. She is not yours, and she never was. As you well know."

"But I am her family now. I'm the best she has."

" 'Best' isn't an unemployed single female who allows the child to run wild through the streets of New York City. Good heavens, Miss Colebrook, you are being sued. Besides which, for all that I have been able to ascertain, your immediate family plays virtually no part in your life. You have no backup and no husband, Miss Colebrook. I don't see how you can possibly consider yourself an adequate candidate for adoption."

"But I love Ruth, and she loves me. She's happy here."

At this, the woman set her lips, then sighed again. "I'm sure you are right. But love and happiness alone is not enough."

"Then look at these checks. I'm fine financially."

"I am not convinced you are going to be fine. The truth is, there is more to stability than money. If you truly want to adopt a child, Miss Colebrook, you need a husband. A father for Ruth."

"That's ridiculous," she snapped, frantic to find sense. "Nearly half of all families today are single-parent homes. Moreover, single celebrities adopt all the time."

"You are neither rich, nor a celebrity." She pulled an official-looking letter out of her briefcase, then handed it over. "Our findings will be presented to you by the judge in one week from today at two. Given this situation, I must advise you to bring Ruth to the courthouse with you at that time."

Suddenly Grace got mad, at this woman, at the court, at a life that constantly became too difficult to maneuver. "You can't do this. I am a good mother. I have been a great mother. Ruth is happy with me. I'm the one who knows that she gets scared at night, and that she likes chocolate sprinkles on her ice cream. She will be devastated if she is uprooted yet again by uncaring people who claim to be looking out for her welfare."

The woman looked at her long and hard, as if she wanted to say something else. But in the end, she walked to the door. "I'm sorry, Miss Colebrook." She hesitated. "I truly am."

At two in the morning, Jack sat at his desk in the bedroom, moonlight finding its way through the clouds overhead. Unable to sleep, he tried to concentrate on the file he was going over. But it was Grace who plagued his thoughts.

Hell, he missed her. She was gone, along with Ruth, leaving no trace that she had even been there. Except for a single cake. Doctor Daddy Cake.

He told himself it was best this way. Then why was he sitting there unable to get her out of his mind? He hated the control he had lost when she had stood up in the bathtub, felt as if he was drowning with hope and happiness, grief and loss. But he couldn't deny that he missed her. All of her, the wit, the laughter, the brown curly hair and painfully blue eyes. He was drawn to Grace, who was like stars in the sky broken apart, shining brightly, too brightly, when what he wanted was an ease in the velvety darkness of night.

She made him laugh, she made him think. She mitigated his churning unease.

Footsteps overhead pounded their way into his thoughts. Not the clicking heeled shoes he had heard those first days, but rather regular shoes, back and forth, across the floor. Like pacing.

He knew Grace wasn't one to pace in the middle of the night. When she went to bed, she fell asleep hard and fast, barely moving until dawn. Too many times he had pushed through to her room in his apartment and watched her sleep.

In rest, her beauty softened, the intensity of her melting into the trailing white sheets. In sleep, the quips and hints at wildness evaporated, leaving the vulnerability behind, filling him with the need to protect her.

The footsteps pounded back across. Cursing himself for a fool, he left his apartment and went to hers. He knocked, then knocked louder, and only when he wouldn't let it alone and knocked again did she finally pull open the door.

Grace. Wild and startling, feral as she looked at him, her hair curling about her head and down her back. The vulnerability so apparent in sleep gone.

Jack felt the force of her presence as the sound of Elton John's "Tiny Dancer" seeped out into the hallway.

"What's wrong?" he asked quietly.

"Nothing's wrong."

"I don't believe you."

Her eyes darkened, then she retreated into her apartment.

After a moment, he followed her inside, leaning back against the door as he clicked it shut. He stared at her, watched as she went to the stereo, fast-forwarding to another CD. Journey's "Only the Young" started up.

"Where's Ruth?" he asked.

"Upstairs. Asleep." She went to the sofa, sat, then stood to straighten the already straight coffee table.

"Grace . . ."

The minute he said her name, the whole of her body tensed, and he saw her eyes well with unexpected tears. Abruptly she turned away and went to the darkened window, staring out, her hands clutching the casement as if holding on to a lifeline.

He came up behind her, wanting to touch her, but not

giving in. He could see her reflection in the glass, the trauma on her face, control barely managed.

"Tell me, Grace. What's wrong?"

Her eyes pressed closed, her fingers curling into balls, her head bowing, fighting emotion, fighting hard. In that moment he remembered her words from that first night.

I know you. Then seconds later, *We are two of a kind.*

He hadn't understood it at the time, but now he did. The desire for control, the need not to feel. He thought of the family she had grown up in. Untouchable china for toys, and sneaking out mistresses substituting as games. A mother who flirted with Grace's friends, implying that she had a better chance of winning their attention than her daughter did. Could Grace afford to feel any more than he could? Probably not, but she had, for him, for Ruth. He had the sudden thought that perhaps this delicate woman standing before him was braver than he.

Giving in, he touched her. He placed his hands on her shoulders, and he felt her deep, ragged breath.

"I'm here, Grace," he said.

She whirled around to face him. "Are you?"

"I am. Tell me what's wrong."

Her tears spilled over, and she let him pull her close. She cried into his chest in sudden, fiery, great, gulping sobs. Not pretty, not practiced. Real. Just like Grace.

A world of emotion swelled inside him as he wrapped her in his arms, murmuring against her hair. He offered her comfort, holding her, not thinking.

The CD changer clicked and switched, the sound of Journey's "Faithfully" swelling in the room, surrounding them. He kissed her then, just a brush of lips trailing up her jaw to her eyelids. Her palms flattened against his chest, as if pushing him away, before her hands curled into the edges of his shirt.

When her fingers grazed his skin, the touch was like fire, and without knowing how comfort turned to passion, their lips met. Like a dying man who suddenly found himself craving the noose, his hands slid down her back. He felt her gasp deep into his soul when he cupped her hips and pulled her against his aching arousal.

"Let me love you," he rasped.

But with those words, the world came crashing down. She cried a curse, her hand pushing. "No! Not again! I thought that would make things clearer between us. It only made it worse." With a jerk, she whirled away.

She started to pace, back and forth, in front of him as he regained control of his raging desire.

"Damn it, Grace. Tell me what's wrong."

Aggravated, she dragged her forearm across her eyes. "I was so close to making everything work that I could taste it. I was filling orders; I was getting press. Money had just started to come in. You should see all the checks."

He touched her chin. "Then what is it?"

"The state came for their visit today."

"I'm sure you impressed them."

"I'm sure I didn't. Not when they found Ruth home alone. I have to go to court in a week, and I'm afraid the state is going to take Ruth away."

His head jerked back, and he stared at her as her tears resurfaced, devastation creasing her brow. He didn't know what to say, didn't know what he felt.

Instead of words, he pulled her back to him, holding her tight as if he was afraid she would slip away.

"I'm sorry," he said raggedly.

"Sorry doesn't help!" She jerked free. "Sorry never helps!"

"Fine. If you want Ruth, I've told you before, fight." He

grabbed her forearms and looked her in the eyes. "You are many things, but never a coward. Don't be one now."

Her mouth opened on a silent breath, as if trying to find a way to believe. "But how?"

"The fact is you have turned a simple cake into the hottest food product to hit since frozen yogurt burst onto the scene."

"Turning cakes into a business has nothing to do with being a good mother."

"Of course it does." He looked at her intensely. "It makes a difference because you did it for Ruth. You did it out of love. Now that love is turning into a means to support her."

"The state doesn't believe that."

"Not yet. But you will make them believe it. You will go to that judge and you will prove that you are capable of raising Ruth. You will show them what you have accomplished in a very short period of time. They will see that you and Ruth belong together."

She tugged away from him. "Don't you think I already told the woman that?"

"Now tell the judge. I'll help. I will go to court and tell them what a great mother you have become. I'll do whatever it takes to make sure you gain custody of Ruth."

"Even if it means marrying me?"

Chapter
Twenty-five

Startled silence filled the century-old space, echoing against the plaster walls and hardwood floors. For long seconds Grace swore that Jack didn't breathe. She knew she didn't.

The words had burst out of her, and she felt the biting sting of regret and embarrassment when he continued to stand there without saying a word.

"I'm sorry," she stammered. "It's just that the state's caseworker said my biggest problem was that I wasn't married. In essence, no father for Ruth, and I thought . . ." The idea took hold and wouldn't let go, no matter how crazy it was. "Listen, it doesn't have to be a real marriage. Just real enough so I can gain custody of Ruth. Kind of like two people marrying so that one can get a green card. I saw it in a movie."

"That's illegal."

This time he was the one who started to pace, and with every step he took across her living room floor, her distress and chagrin turned to desperation. "Not five seconds ago you offered to help."

He whirled to face her. "Sure, I'll help. I'll write you another check, I'll beat up Walter, I'll testify before a judge. Hell, I'll even bake those damned cakes for you." He stopped and regained a measure of control. "But some sham of a marriage isn't going to help anyone in the long run."

"Right now, I'm only interested in the short run!"

He turned away and resumed his pacing, dragging his hands through his hair. "I can't. I'm sorry, Grace."

Yet again, just that, no explanation.

"You can't or you won't?"

"Does it matter which?"

"Yes! Yes, it matters." She lowered her voice, not wanting to wake Ruth. "Tell me, Jack, once and for all, tell me what are you running from? Me? I doubt it. You were running long before I met you."

His jaw went tight with fury. "I've told you, I'm not running from anything," he bit out.

"Oh, Jack, aren't you? You used to be some incredible surgeon in Connecticut. And from what I can gather, for months you dated an assortment of women, never committing, moving on to the next when one got too attached. You bury yourself in your work."

"The ER takes up most of my time."

"I don't think that's it."

The danger in him grew exponentially. But Grace didn't back down. She had come too far for that.

"Why do you hate that you need me?"

"I have to go."

"Stop running!" She drew a deep, calming breath. "Whether you're willing to admit it or not, you care for me, and I know you care for Ruth."

On the verge of exploding, he turned away from her and took the remaining steps to her apartment door.

"You know what I think it is, Jack? You're afraid. Of commitment, of permanence, of obligation. But more than that, you're afraid of being hurt."

He still faced the door, but she could see the tightening

of his jaw. She understood in some recess of her mind that she was treading in dangerous territory. But she was unprepared when he finally turned around, his eyes black orbs of desolation.

"Jack," she said softly, "I would never hurt you. Will you please trust me enough to help me understand why you keep people at a distance?"

The coldness in him cemented into something that was at once furious and despairing. She understood in that moment that she had pushed him to some limit he had always kept at bay.

Her need to push him vanished. She wanted to wrap him in her arms, press his strong body to hers so the look on his face would disappear. She wanted to take back her careless words. But it was too late for that.

"My wife used to say that Daisy was a daddy's girl."

She wasn't sure what she'd expected him to say, but this wasn't it. She started to go to him, but there was such raw pain in him, she didn't know how to move.

"She *was* a daddy's girl," he said, his voice accusing. "I spoiled her. She had me wrapped around her little finger."

"Then she was a lucky child."

"No." He said the word forcefully. "I should have been stricter." He looked as if he would break apart. "Just as my wife told me hundreds of times."

"Damn it, Jack. You have to stop being so easy on Daisy. She's unmanageable."

"She's a teenager," Jack said with a grin. He pulled his tie into a perfect Windsor knot at his neck. He had a full schedule of patients that day, including a governor who sought his expertise.

Marsha crossed her arms, the bell-shaped sleeves of her robe sliding down to her elbows. "She's an unmanageable teenager. Just yesterday the neighborhood patrol brought her home for smoking with that Lancaster girl. Out smoking when she was supposed to be over at Hattie Merriweather's house getting ready for the canned goods drive."

"A project that you didn't bother to ask her if she wanted to be a part of."

"She would have said no."

"Exactly. So you did it anyway, then you get mad when she doesn't show up."

"Doesn't show up, then goes off smoking right here in our neighborhood."

He cast her a wry glance. "Which bothers you more, Marsha? The smoking, or Daisy embarrassing you?"

Her shoulders stiffened, and Jack sighed, hating the age-old argument. In his opinion, Marsha cared too much about what others thought of her. But he knew it was fruitless to try to change her. "Hey, don't get so upset. What teenager doesn't experiment with smoking?"

"I didn't!"

"Yeah." He smiled, remembering the young woman she had been when they'd first met. "But you were a brain who had more relationships with books than with friends."

His wife stiffened. Jack sighed, then walked over to her. "I'm sorry. I love who you were and who you are. But neither of us can expect our daughter to be like us. We can only let her find her own way."

"Her way to trouble. Just because you were wild as a boy and turned out all right doesn't mean that Daisy will do the same. She needs more to do than hang out with friends at the mall. When you were young you had something to fight for, dreams to achieve because you had so little. Daisy has it all; she has nothing to fight for. And a bored teenager is headed for trouble. That's what you don't understand."

Marsha turned and left the bedroom. Jack's eyes narrowed against her words, and for the first time he wondered if she was right. He followed her to the kitchen, and they ate in silence, Daisy's place empty.

"Daisy," Marsha called out to her. "If you don't hurry, you're going to be late."

They heard the faint bass from their daughter's stereo thrumming through the floor.

Marsha would have gone up to get her, but she was saved the effort when a horn beeped outside. Miraculously, the stereo switched off, and the sound of footsteps raced down the stairs.

Daisy burst into the kitchen like a ray of sunshine. Her dark hair and blue eyes, her lips that were full and always smiling. She had always been a happy child, and still was. But for the first time, Jack noticed the clothes she wore. Not revealing, just lots of color and layers, and pieces that didn't go together. When she leaned over to grab a piece of toast, sunlight hit her, and he saw the streaks of purple in her hair.

The love he felt for this child filled him to an almost painful point. He also understood that for years now he had let her get away with so much, too much, because he couldn't stand to see that smile disappear. He loved her, and he wanted her to be happy.

The horn blared again.

"That's Cissy. Gotta go."

She raced for the door.

"Daisy?" he called out.

She stopped and turned back. "Yeah, Dad?"

No more Daddy. When had that stopped? When had she ceased to be his little girl?

He hesitated. What did he want to say? That he loved her? That he wanted her to still be young and innocent and not have purple streaks in her hair?

"I'm heading to the office now. Ride with your old man, and we'll catch up. Like old times."

Daisy rolled her eyes and laughed, then dashed back to him, circling his neck, the piece of toast still in her hand, her backpack slung over one shoulder. "Old man? God, you are so retro." She kissed him. "Thanks, but Cissy is waiting. See ya."

Then she was gone, out the door, the bright red two-door BMW bouncing over the dip between the drive and street.

"I wish you would put your foot down with her."

Marsha's voice was bitter.

Jack felt disjointed, the world around him foggy and odd. How had he not seen the reality of his child before?

He hardly realized when he finished his breakfast, taking a last sip of coffee before he stood and distractedly kissed Marsha good-bye. He pulled on the navy blue sport jacket, found his keys, and walked to the garage. When he steered the Mercedes over the dip in the drive, he went slowly, thinking he should get it fixed.

He held the wheel in a tight grip as he turned out of the safe confines of the affluent neighborhood Marsha had chosen, onto the main street that led to his office. It was Monday, always a full day, busy, with no time to think. He always prepared as he drove.

But his thoughts ceased completely a half mile away from the house when he saw the tangle of cars. Some stopped, people getting out. One car was flipped over.

Jack felt nothing. No thoughts. No breath. No realization that he put his car into park, leaving it where it was and starting to walk toward the growing crowd. The closer he got, the louder the voices became. Screaming, crying out. Someone yelling that they needed an ambulance.

Then he ran, his silk tie swinging crazily back and forth

*across his chest in cadence with his steps. Numb. But at the
sight of the red BMW, shock exploded in his mind.*

"No!"

*His voice echoed through the streets. He pushed people
out of the way and he raced to the car. At first he didn't see
anything other than twisted metal and red paint. Then he
saw Cissy lying lifeless a short distance away. Years of experience told him she was dead.*

*Then he saw Daisy, her blue eyes wide, tears streaking
her face. Relief shot through him. Selfishly, all he could
think was his baby had survived.*

*The minute she saw him, he saw the relief in her eyes. It
wasn't until he dropped to his knees beside her that he saw
the blood. Too much. Everywhere. She was wide-eyed with
shock, not relief.*

*She lay half in, half out of the upturned car. Then she
uttered the words that would stay with him for the rest of
his life.*

"Daddy," she whispered when she saw him. "Save me."

*He worked like a man possessed. With gravel biting into
his knees, he made a tourniquet with his tie, his white
handkerchief pressed to the wound in her neck to stop the
bleeding. But nothing helped. The perfect square of white
turned red, blood seeping, not stopping, until her body
went limp in his arms, breath expelled in a whispering
shudder, and her eyes fluttered closed.*

*"No!" he cried, rocking on that street, his child lying
lifeless in his arms.*

When Jack's choked voice broke off, Grace wrapped her
arms around him and could feel this strong man crumbling.

"I didn't save her," he stated coldly. "I couldn't save her.
Me, known for my skill. Me, who loved her so much. And I

couldn't save her. She died in my arms on that crowded street."

Grace pressed her eyes closed and whispered, "So you've been trying to make up for it ever since."

He didn't respond; he remained rigid.

"You work in the ER in hopes of saving people. And when you saw me out your window, you came out because you wanted to save me, too." She tried to draw strength. "But you always have to keep a safe distance. Saving strangers is safe. What a shock it must have been when you saw me again after that first night."

He pulled open her door, forcing her to let go.

"You can't save everyone, Jack."

For long seconds, he didn't respond. "Maybe not, but I can try." Strength and that hated control returned to his body, and he looked back at her. "I'm sorry, Grace. But the truth is, every child needs the kind of mother and father that neither you nor I will ever be."

Then he left her alone in the apartment; the only sound remaining was the click of the lock when the door swung closed with finality.

Chapter
Twenty-six

Days ticked by, and Jack spent most of his time at the hospital, sleeping on the makeshift bed in his office. Staying away. When Hugh called, Jack was short, giving truncated responses to his brother's questions. He didn't want to talk, even to Hugh.

Jack lost himself to the work, the sirens, the paramedics wheeling in patients, the nurses' and technicians' knowledgeable efforts. As much as he hated the broken lives of accident victims, he almost relished the radios going off announcing an ambulance coming in. The whirl of sirens, the *whoosh* of automatic doors gasping open, followed by the frantic but controlled staccato burst of vitals that were reeled off for each incoming patient.

He needed to find a way to get back into the habit of working without feeling, of putting one foot in front of the other. The pattern he had perfected before finding Grace.

Or had he perfected it?

He had been there a week, rarely going home, when a lull came in the workload. Given that he wasn't supposed to be on duty in the first place, and his head nurse was starting to question what was wrong, he forced himself to leave. With his head bent, he wanted to out-walk his raging thoughts—just as he had the day he'd met Grace. It all came back to him. The shimmering tension, the unease, until he had looked out his window and had seen her. She had made him forget.

No, not forget. Through Grace he had found a way to push the reality of Daisy's death to the back of his mind. With Grace's irreverence and suppressed passion, she had managed to cease the endless thoughts of his divorce nine months after Daisy died, when both he and his wife understood that they were tearing each other apart. Guilt, fury, despair, and neither of them willing or able to help the other.

But deep down, all along, he had known that pushing the thoughts aside was unacceptable.

He realized now that the escape he had sought ultimately made the guilt and despair worse. Because when it did circle back, as it inevitably always did, he felt worse that he'd had any moments of peace at all. How could he be happy when his child was gone?

Just over a year ago he had fled Connecticut and returned to New York City. Every hospital in town had offered him a surgical position on staff. He could have written his own ticket anywhere.

But he had surprised everyone when he had taken the job at St. Luke's trauma unit, which received its patients from some of the most dangerous parts of Manhattan.

Had he been trying to undo his failure, as Grace had said? Had he been trying to save people and keep his distance?

Answers didn't matter, because whatever the underlying cause, he knew he had been running, running from the sight of that overturned car. From his baby shuddering in his arms, and those horrible life-changing words. *Daddy, save me.*

Then his wife at the hospital afterward, cold and dead inside, looking at him with blank, staring eyes, asking one mind-shattering question. *Do you believe me now that you weren't strict enough?*

Traffic on Broadway was busy, but not wall-to-wall where cars were forced to creep along, rather a solid mass of vehicles that hurtled dangerously forward from light to light. With his mind in turmoil, his heart tight and aching, Jack stepped off the curb. The sound of horns blaring and wheels screeching filled the air before he looked up and only then noticed the DON'T WALK light strong and steady. He stopped, halted abruptly, a cab mere inches from him. The cabbie yelled and shook his fist. But the shouting faded away at the look in Jack's eyes.

What had the cabbie seen? The despair? The lack of caring if the car had stopped or not?

The yellow cab raced away, moving so close that the gust from its wake rippled against Jack's face.

Finally the light turned, and the WALK sign flashed on. It took a second before Jack's brain registered that he could go.

In the center island that divided the thoroughfare, he passed three old men sitting on the wood-slat bench. They sat back with their legs crossed, talking about world events, the crush of trees and flowers making the ten-foot space seem like an island of green slicing down the unrelenting pavement of the city—as if everything was right in the world. But nothing was right.

Eventually, Jack came to his garage, and he pulled his car out of the darkened recesses, merging with traffic. He needed to drive. Needed to feel the ease of pavement rolling beneath, and the cocoon of the leather seats against the harshness of the streets.

He drove until he finally pulled onto the West Side Highway. He continued on, driving without thinking. Emptying his mind—until an hour later he understood where he was going, what he was doing.

He arrived at the cemetery nearly two hours from when he'd pulled out of the garage. All day the thought had been there, teasing at the edges of his mind. The second anniversary of Daisy's death.

Those who said that time healed didn't understand the intensity of an anniversary of a loved one who was lost tragically. Beyond that, did any parent get over the death of a child?

Pulling the BMW over to the side of the narrow, curbless road that wound its way through the manicured cemetery, Jack got out of the car. He stood for long moments, unable to move, wishing there was no reason for him to be in this place. Then he walked through the bronze plaques and headstones, his hands deep in his pockets. He wasn't surprised when he found Marsha standing in front of the grave.

She hadn't seen him in over a year, but she gave no start of surprise when he walked up beside her.

"I thought you'd come," she said, never looking away from the carved granite marker in the earth.

His breath sighed out of him as he stood next to this woman who had shared so much of his life. "Of course." Then silence, the breeze rustling in the trees. "How are you?" he asked.

Marsha shrugged, the gesture at odds with her expensively tailored suit, hat, and medium-heeled shoes. She looked like the wealthy wife of a prominent doctor she had been for so many years. "I miss her," she whispered.

"I know. So do I."

They stood in silence then, each lost in their own thoughts, until finally she asked, "Do you ever think about what we would be like right now . . . if she were still alive?"

"Sometimes."

"I wonder if we would still be married."

"What? Of course we would be."

"Probably," she conceded.

Jack could tell from her voice that she didn't believe it.

"What do you think she would be like now?" she asked.

"Don't do this, Marsha."

"I'm not being morbid. I just like to think about her, growing up, turning into a young woman."

"She'd be beautiful and full of life," he said. "Just like her mother."

"Thank you."

He could tell that tears were tightening in her throat. Out of habit born from the years they had spent as husband and wife, he reached over and took her hand. She grabbed it with both of hers, hard, holding on like holding on to life itself. Then she was in his arms, crying against his chest.

"She was my baby."

His throat worked as he held on to control. He wouldn't cry. He never had, having understood from living in a world of people's grief that it never did any good.

"It's going to be okay," he said, not believing it.

She cried for what seemed like an eternity, her tears seeping into the starched shirtfront, until finally she took a deep breath and stepped back. For the first time since he'd arrived, she looked at him. "It *is* going to be all right."

His thoughts snagged at her tone, laced with conviction.

"It's time to move on," she stated. "For both of us."

His chin came up, and he looked at her in confusion. "What are you talking about?"

"I've mourned for two years. I haven't lived for two years. I have locked myself away and thought I would go mad. But I can't anymore. I want to live."

"You should," he said carefully.

"But I mean I want to start a new life." She hesitated. "I've met someone."

His eyes narrowed against the sun.

"I'm not strong like you, Jack. I don't want to be alone for the rest of my life."

"Who is it?"

"A lawyer here in Greenwich. I want to be happy again, Jack. I'm tired of feeling like I'm dying. I'll never forget her. But I need to start living again. Can you possibly understand that?"

He didn't answer, couldn't. Hot anger burned through him. Or was it jealousy that she could find a way out of the hell of torment they had been through.

"I think you should move on, too," she added. "I don't see how ceasing to live helps Daisy."

Then she hesitated, and he knew there was something else.

"I know about Grace Colebrook."

"What are you talking about?"

"The woman you met, and the child. Ruth, isn't it? I also know that you walked out on them."

"Have you been spying on me?"

"Absolutely not! Hugh told me."

"Hugh?"

"We keep in touch. He was my brother-in-law, after all, and he was a big part of our lives all those years you put him through school." She looked at Jack.

"He needs to mind his own business."

"He loves you. Worries about you. He even worries about me, for that matter. He introduced me to Lowell."

Agitated, he dragged his hand through his hair. "God, how didn't I know anything about this?"

But as soon as he said the words, he knew that all he felt was relief. Yes, relief, that finally Marsha would be cared for. He realized then that Hugh had understood that Jack would not be able to go on with his life until he was certain Marsha was taken care of. They might not be able to stay together, but she had been his wife, the mother of his child.

"You know now," she answered, sadness mixing with hope on her face. "I'm happy again. I think of Daisy every single day, I do. But I'm not even forty yet. I'm not ready to be buried. Don't make me feel guilty for needing to move on. I loved her, just as much as you did, Jack."

He felt his heart harden as he remembered that day in the hospital.

"You were a good father, Jack. A wonderful father."

A chill ran down his spine, and he felt as if his effort to fight back tears would break him in two.

"And Daisy loved you," she added.

Blood rushed through his ears, pounding in his temples. "I never should have let her get in that car. You said so yourself."

"You didn't know what would happen." Marsha's face grew aged and old, making her look well beyond her years. "I realized that I blamed you because that was easier to do than open my eyes and accept responsibility. She was my daughter, too. We both let her get in that car. We both let her have friends like Cissy. But it was easier to blame you."

Jack stared out into the distance, his hands firmly at his sides, tension racing through him.

"I'm sorry, Jack. Can you forgive me? You loved Daisy so much, and it always made me feel like less of a mother that my love never seemed to measure up." She sighed. "I was jealous because from the very beginning she always loved you more. Most of all, *that* is what I blamed you for."

And then the tears came, fought off for two long years, breaking free, streaming down his cheeks in silent, burning trails. Marsha cried then, too, wrapping her arms around him. "You were a wonderful father. You are a good man, and you deserve more than I ever gave you."

The sun shone overhead, bright and burning.

"Go to your Grace, don't lose her because you can't allow anyone else into your life. Let yourself love little Ruth. It sounds like they deserve your heart. I know you deserve theirs."

He remained rigid.

"Oh, Jack," she said, a sigh winging out of her. "Can't you understand that loving another child doesn't mean that you loved Daisy any less?"

Chapter
Twenty-seven

Jack hurtled down the long expanse of the New England Thruway, speeding back to New York.

He had walked Marsha to her car, then wished her good luck with her new life, before leaving. He had to get back, had to find Grace and make things right.

How had he ever left her?

The question exploded in his mind, making him ache. But the pain was set aside with the knowledge that he would not rest until he had Grace by his side.

He would propose, he would marry her, and his heart tripped with something new. A lightness, the light of hope.

But then he remembered that the hearing was scheduled for today. He glanced at the clock on the dashboard and saw that it was two. The hearing would already have begun, and he was more than an hour away.

Sick dread raced through him, and he pressed the accelerator hard, the car surging beneath him with a controlled power. But deep down he knew it wouldn't matter when he got there, he would be too late to help in the one way Grace had truly wanted.

Frustration snaked through him, frustration and regret. But on the heels of that came the determination of a man who was used to making things happen. He would do whatever it took to help Grace get Ruth back. He would do what he had to do to get an appeal. He would testify as he had promised. Then he would build a life for both Grace and Ruth, and never let either of them go again.

One hour thirty minutes and thankfully no tickets after walking Marsha to her car, knowing it was too late to go to the courthouse, he wheeled up in front of the brownstone on Sixty-ninth Street, double-parked, then barreled into the building. He dashed up three flights of stairs to bang on her apartment door.

When no one answered, he banged again, calling out her name. But still nothing.

Finding the key under the umbrella stand in the hall, he let himself in. Music filtered out from the kitchen. A sad, haunting melody. But no sign of Grace.

"Grace?"

He followed the music to the kitchen. He stopped in his tracks at the sight of her at the counter, looking out into the back gardens, food in front of her, a knife held forgotten in her hand. But most of all, Jack noticed the tears streaming down her cheeks.

She had lost.

"Grace," he said, turning the CD down.

She whipped around to face him, and at the sight, there was no relief. No joy. Only the tears and a cold finality.

"We'll get her back," he stated raggedly.

Her brow furrowed, and she looked at him without an ounce of forgiveness. No more vulnerability, no more cast to her glance as if she knew him.

"I'm sorry it took so long for me to see straight," he added forcefully, needing to make it right. "I will do whatever it takes to help you bring Ruth back where she belongs."

Still nothing.

"Let me help."

She set the knife down and wiped her hands. "I don't need your help, Jack."

The words came out of her mouth with a calm, unfeeling inevitability. He had offered too little too late. But then he heard footsteps running over hardwood, the vibration sliding up his spine. Then his name.

"Jack! You came back!"

Ruth skidded into the kitchen and catapulted herself into his arms. He caught her securely, and held her tight in a way that he had never let himself hold her before, relishing the feel of this child in his arms.

"We won!" she cheered. "I don't ever have to leave." Her cheer turned to a brief concern. "Isn't that right, Grace?"

"You bet, sweetie. That's absolutely right. You're stuck with me forever."

Jack tried to assimilate the news, as, for the first time, he noticed the onions Grace had been chopping. "How did it happen? What did you tell the judge?"

"I told him that I was a good mother, and that I could provide Ruth with stability and safety. I also showed him the balance sheet on FluffCakes.com, the article that ran in *The New York Times*, and my business plan. Then I showed him the valuations on the engagement ring Walter has made claims about, proving that I was the one who got swindled. I impressed him," she stated proudly, defiantly. "On my own. Without your help. Without anyone's help."

A surge of pride swelled inside him, elation seeping into those cracks and crevices that had up until then been filled with guilt. "The truth is," he told her, his voice intense, "you haven't needed anyone's help since the night I met you."

She looked at him as if she didn't know what to make of this turn of events, and she tensed when he reached out and took her hand, looking at her fingers. "Marry me, Grace. Marry me, because I can't live without you. Marry me for all the right reasons."

"What would those be, Jack?" she asked sharply. "So you can save me, too? Well, I don't need saving, as you pointed out yourself. I don't need anyone's help."

She jerked her hand away, then walked out of the kitchen. Ruth looked at him, an eyebrow raised as she silently implored him, *Go after her.*

His brow furrowed, and a burning fire fueled him. "Grace, don't go. Please."

At this, she hesitated, but didn't turn back.

"I know you don't need saving—you never did." His voice lowered, and he felt emotion tighten in his throat. "I was the one who needed to be saved. I was the one who had to face the fact that I was running away from life. You made me see that. But what I've also come to understand is that I was unwilling to admit that I might need you more than you would ever need me."

Her head came back, the tension in her shimmering through the high-ceilinged room.

"I can't change the past," he said. "I can only move forward with you and Ruth, if you'll let me. There is nothing more that I want."

But she remained tense, unyielding. Taking the steps that separated them, he wouldn't give up.

"I was wrong to think that I couldn't be a father to another child. You are a wonderful mother who never gave up, even when everyone seemed determined to defeat you. I admire you, Grace."

He could almost feel the sharp breath she inhaled.

"But more than that, I love you." He understood in that moment that until then, he had never said it, and he understood as well how deeply his words were true. "I love you and I love Ruth, and I will do whatever it takes to make us a family. I won't give up, Grace, because I do love you. With all my heart. As I have never loved a woman before."

Slowly she turned around to look at him, and he saw the aching glimmer of hope that filled her eyes.

"You are brave and good," he repeated, taking a step closer. He knew that he was asking her to be vulnerable to him, vulnerable enough to open her heart once again. "I love you, and I would be honored if you would be my wife."

A joy- and tear-filled smile broke out on her face, and just when he thought she would come to him, they both remembered Ruth. When they looked at her they saw she had her eyes squeezed closed and her fingers crossed in hope.

"Yes, I'll marry you, Jack Berenger, for all the right reasons," Grace said.

With that, Ruth's eyes popped open, and she whooped her delight. "Finally, the two of you got it right."

Epilogue

"Mom."

The single syllable stretched out and became a multi-syllabic lament.

"Yes, Ruth?"

"Dad won't let me do anything."

Ruth stormed into the sunny brownstone kitchen filled with bright white cabinets and multicolored dishes, a kitchen that had once been lined with granite and steel. Grace wiped icing from her hands on a linen towel, then cupped her daughter's face, stroking Ruth's tousled hair back from her forehead with a smile. "Granted, he is a tad overprotective, but only because he loves you."

Ruth groaned dramatically, in that way that teenagers around the world had perfected. At thirteen, Ruth was definitely becoming a teenager.

Grace grimaced inwardly, but smiled at her child. The love she felt for this young girl who had come into her life and changed it so dramatically still had the power to bring tears of happiness to her eyes just by looking at her. Grace had known they were meant to be together, and the years had only proved her correct.

"All of my friends get to go to Chelsea Piers on Saturdays," Ruth lamented. "But Dad won't let me go."

"How about if your father took you?"

Ruth made a face of utter horror. "Dad, me, and the girls—I don't think so."

"Ruth," Grace said sternly.

Instantly, Ruth became contrite. "I know, I know. I love him, and am so totally glad that he cares. But I'm not Daisy, and I'm not going to turn into Daisy."

Jack's first child was celebrated in their household, but no matter how many years passed, Grace's dear husband never was able to put his guilt completely behind him. He watched over Ruth, refusing to make the same mistake twice. They didn't like to remember the day Ruth had come home with grape Kool-Aid accidentally spilled in her hair, the purple streak reminding Jack of Daisy.

Grace loved Jack for his concern, and shook her head in dismay at the same time. It had only gotten worse after little Jackie was born.

Grace was nearly felled by the love that surged inside her over the thought of their four-year-old son. She loved him no more than she loved Ruth. They both filled her so completely. They both were miracles, and she knew that Jack felt the same way, too. But he was every bit as protective of their young boy as he was of Ruth.

Little Jackie careened into the kitchen.

"Cake!" he cheered. He looked up at Ruth, whom he idolized. "Cake for you and me!"

Ruth ruffled his hair and smiled. "Hey, squirt."

Jackie laughed hysterically. "Squirt! Squirt!"

Grace wrapped Jackie in her arms, burying her face in his still-soft baby's neck. Jackie squealed happily to get away, reaching for the three-layer chocolate butter-cream cake Grace had just iced.

Indeed, there was cake. Lots of cakes, though Grace had finally turned over the task of cake-making for FluffCakes.com to a production-sized kitchen. The success of the dot.com business had put her on the covers of an assortment of business and women's magazines. Mark now ran the company, while Grace took a lesser role, her days filled with parent-teacher associations and play-groups, and all the white-picket-fence activities she thought she'd never experience.

"Mom, please, can you talk to Dad?" Ruth begged, dipping her finger into chocolate and popping it in her mouth.

Grace tilted her head. "How about a compromise?"

"Like what?" Ruth asked skeptically.

"What if both Dad and I take you down to the Piers? I'm sure Jackie would love it down there."

"Mom! That isn't a compromise."

"Okay, what if Uncle Hugh goes with him, then he won't be hovering over you every second."

"Oh, wow! Uncle Hugh is so cool. Okay. I'll call Miranda."

"Hold on, I've got to ask first."

Grace walked out into the stairwell, down the steps to the ground-floor apartment, where Jack had set up his practice. Pediatrics neurosurgery.

"Hello, Grace," Suzie the receptionist called out to her when she entered.

They had bought the space from Mrs. Neimark six months after they were married. Now they owned the entire building, turning the top four floors into a family home, and the bottom floor into Jack's doctor's office. The setup was perfect, and while Grace knew there were days when Jack actually missed the ER, he had found a sense of peace and rightness in his new practice.

"Dr. Jack was just asking about you," Suzie said gaily.

"Was he now?"

Grace walked back to his office, and as soon as she

entered, she felt the flutters of a schoolgirl in her heart. Even after all this time she couldn't imagine loving any man more.

"Hello, Dr. Berenger."

Jack looked up from a file he was reading. At the sight of his wife, he leaned back and smiled, a slow burn of heat igniting in his eyes.

"Hello, Mrs. Berenger. What brings you here?" He stood and came toward her.

Grace smiled, relishing the feel of her husband's strong arms closing around her.

"Mmmm, you feel good," he said, nuzzling her cheek. "Perhaps I should cancel the rest of my appointments."

"Ha, that would be the day."

"True. But we have all weekend."

"Well, maybe a little less of the weekend."

Jack stood back and looked at her, one dark brow raised in question.

"I was thinking that you haven't seen Hugh often enough recently."

"I saw him on Sunday. Remember, he had dinner with us and with your family. Which reminds me, your dad and I are going to a medical conference together in April. We were thinking you and your mother would like to join us."

Grace shook her head. "It's still hard to imagine that my parents have gotten back together."

"I don't think they ever got over each other."

"Maybe, or else he just got tired of her stalking him." She smiled fondly as she thought of her parents acting like adults half their age. "But I'm glad. I've never seen either of them so happy. But that's beside the point."

"Which is?"

"You and Hugh. You haven't had any guys' time together. You know, just you and Hugh, hanging out at, let's say, Chelsea Piers, hitting golf balls."

Jack's eyes narrowed. "This *guys' time* wouldn't perhaps include taking my daughter along, would it?"

"With her friends. Jack, please."

He returned to his seat.

She came up behind him and leaned over, wrapping her arms around his neck, placing her cheek on the top on his head. "You can't smother her, Jack."

"I can keep her safe."

"You will. You always will, as best as anyone can. But you can't watch over her every minute. She's a good girl, Jack. Give her some room to grow."

He grumbled, but she knew he would come around. It was always a balance for him, one she helped with every day.

After a long second, he placed his hand on her forearm, rubbing gently back and forth. "Yeah, she is a good kid. As is Jackie."

Grace could feel the smile pull at her husband's lips.

"They take after their old man," he added with that brand of arrogance and assurance that made Grace feel alternately bemused and safe.

Safe.

All she had ever wanted was to find her place, a place where she felt secure. With this strong, vulnerable man who loved her, she had. With two children. Like mismatched pieces coming together to make a whole.

"All right, I'll call Hugh," he conceded, then added softly, "but only because I love you."

Then he surprised her when he swiveled his chair and pulled her in one fell swoop down into his lap. Grace went willingly, her laughter bubbling up inside her as she held on tight, relishing the feel of his lips on hers, knowing at last that in all ways that mattered, she had found her way home.

Read on for a sneak peek
at the next wonderful contemporary romance
from Linda Francis Lee,
LOOKING FOR LACEY,
coming in Spring 2003 ...

When bad-boy quarterback Bobby Mac McIntyre returns to his hometown, he is anything but happy to learn that his sister has hired Lacey Wright, a prim little do-gooder, to run his sports bar.

Lacey Wright stood behind the massive desk and tried not to gawk at the equally massive man staring back at her. She felt hot beneath the primness of her clothes as she clasped her hands together to keep from wringing them. For one startling second she could only stare at him.

He was tall, much taller than she, with wide shoulders that tapered into a slim waist. He had the brooding good looks of a movie star, and dark hair just long enough to sweep back from his forehead and brush against his collar. He wore a crisp white button-down, long-sleeve shirt tucked into hard-pressed Wrangler jeans, and the round-toed roper boots she had noticed were popular with the strong Texas men. His eyes were blue, his lips full, and not a broken nose or playing field scar to spoil his strong, square jaw. Just the kind of man who could make the average woman go weak at the knees.

He was beautiful in a ruggedly sensual way, making her feel hot and cold, her skin tingling at the thought of reaching out and touching him—just the sort of thought he must make most women feel.

The realization brought her up short and she bristled.

She was not like most women. In recent years, she had worked hard to rise above foolish infatuations with the kind of man who turned sensual prowling into an art form. And this chiseled athlete wasn't going to undo all her efforts.

He looked at her, his eyes narrowing. "It's time we get a few things straight."

This didn't sound good.

"I might be stuck with you," he stated, "but this is *my* office. This is my desk." He rummaged around in the bottom drawer and found his Sweet Thang mug, clomped it down like a dog marking his territory. He smiled, then he pointed to the corner of the room. "You can use that."

That consisted of a small wooden desk, just this side of the stash of weights and exercise machines, its top loaded with an assortment of Bobby Mac paraphernalia, and a hardwood ladder-back chair that looked like it belonged to a schoolteacher in a 1950s classroom. Lacey was on the verge of telling him just what he could do with his desk and his grinning likeness, when the image of her daughter came to mind. Smiling, happy.

She nearly hung her head. No matter how far he pushed her, she would not let this man run her off.

The things a mother will do for her child.

So she smiled, or she hoped she smiled, and headed for her new desk. "Perfect," she replied with sunny brightness.

"Just stay on your side of the office," he said with a pained expression. "And at night, keep it down."

Then silence. "Excuse me?"

"Didn't Beth tell you?" Full-fledged amusement resurfaced. "You're not the only person who lives upstairs, darlin'."

"What? You mean— You live—"

"Yep, my apartment is right across from yours."

"But you have a house! Your very own house. I heard all about it. Some gigantic mansion you built on the cliff above Rim Road."

He dismissed the comment with a wave of his hand. "It's not that big."

"Big. Little. What does it matter?"

He looked at her with a sleepy-eyed sensuality that made her knees feel weak. "That depends on what you're talking about."

It took her a second to absorb his meaning. "Your house!" She felt the panic start to take over. It would be hard enough to deal with this man in the office, but across the hall, too? "Why would you live over a bar when you have a perfectly good home on a hill, no doubt replete with some gaudily shaped bed set high on a rotating pedestal and a life-sized blow-up doll to keep you company?"

He crooked a brow. "You stay awake all night coming up with that one?"

"I'm serious!"

"So was I. Your little rotating pedestal speech was a good one."

She started to preen. "Thank you." Then she gasped. "Wait a minute, stop trying to avoid the subject."

"There's nothing to avoid, Miz Wright. When I'm in town, I stay here much of the time, so stay out of my way."

The telephone rang again, and Bobby snatched up the receiver. "McIntyre here," he barked.

Lacey turned toward the window, her mind doing double time to rein in the very real desire to launch herself across his massive desk and strangle him. Her day had gone from bad to worse. Was there no justice in the world? she wondered miserably. She'd never have a moment of peace with him so close twenty-four hours a day. She could just imagine the sort of late-night parties he would give with loud music blaring from a complicated stereo system.

She spun around to say exactly that, but he was still on the phone. She watched as a visible easing settled on his face. After a second of listening intently, a reluctant though genuine smile hinted at one corner of his mouth, and he sat back down in the desk chair. Just the sight of that smile did something strange to her insides, and she had the startling thought that this was the look that made women melt.

Instantly she cursed herself and must have glared, because by then Bobby had shifted his gaze to her and raised a dark brow.

"Yeah, she's still here," he said into the phone, looking Lacey up and down, his blue eyes filling with a sensual burn. "No, I haven't killed her. Though just about now, I'd guess she'd like to kill me, probably in some way that involves extreme pain and mutilation. No one bothered to tell her about my apartment upstairs," he added, his mouth curving at one corner. "From the looks of her, I'd say she's afraid of things that go bump in the night. But I'll be there to protect her."

The image of Bobby coming across the hallway leaped into Lacey's mind. She saw him opening the door of her bedroom, those eyes locking with hers as he drew closer. Then leaning over her as she lay in a tumble of comforter and sheets. His mouth. His touch.

A rush of heat made her skin go damp at the thought, and she whirled away, embarrassed, mortified and confused by her body's reaction.